DEBT OF
HONOR

Professionally Published Books by Christopher G. Nuttall

Angel in the Whirlwind

The Oncoming Storm
Falconez Strike
Cursed Command
Desperate Fire

The Hyperspace Trap

ELSEWHEN PRESS

The Royal Sorceress

The Royal Sorceress (Book I)
The Great Game (Book II)
Necropolis (Book III)
Sons of Liberty (Book IV)

Bookworm

Bookworm
Bookworm II: The Very Ugly Duckling
Bookworm III: The Best Laid Plans
Bookworm IV: Full Circle

Inverse Shadows

Sufficiently Advanced Technology

Stand-Alone

A Life Less Ordinary
The Mind's Eye

TWILIGHT TIMES BOOKS

Schooled in Magic

The Decline and Fall of the Galactic Empire

HENCHMEN PRESS

First Strike

DEBT OF HONOR

CHRISTOPHER G. NUTTALL

Published by 47North, Seattle

www.apub.com

Amazon, the Amazon logo, and 47North are trademarks of Amazon.com, Inc., or its affiliates.

ISBN-13: 9781542019569
ISBN-10: 1542019567

Cover design by Mike Heath | Magnus Creative

Printed in the United States of America

DEBT OF
HONOR

PROLOGUE

"That's all you could find?"

The two officers winced in unison, as if they expected to be marched to the airlock and unceremoniously thrown into space for failing to accomplish the impossible. Once, Admiral Zaskar acknowledged ruefully, they might have been right. Failure was a sign of God's displeasure, a proof that the failure—the failed—deserved to be punished. But if that was true, and he no longer believed it was so, what did that say about the Theocracy?

He studied the manifest on the datapad for a long moment, trying to hold back a tidal wave of depression. A few crates of starship components, some so old they probably dated all the way back to the early days of spaceflight; boxes of ration bars that were older than most of the men who were going to eat them . . . It was a far cry from the supplies they *needed* to keep the fleet alive. The fleet—the squadron, really—was on the verge of breaking down completely. In truth, he'd started to lose faith in his ability to keep his ships and men together long enough for the enemy to give up the pursuit.

"And the asteroid base?" He looked up at the officers. "Were there any people who might be interested in joining us?"

"No, Admiral," the older officer said. "They refused our offers."

And we can't make them a little more compulsory, Zaskar told himself. *We'd be betrayed within the week.*

He cursed his former masters under his breath. His crew was composed of the ignorant and the fanatics, neither of whom could do maintenance work worth a damn. The only thing they could do was remove a broken component and slot in a replacement, which had worked fine until their supply lines were destroyed once and for all. Even the finest engineers in the fleet couldn't repair *everything*, let alone build new components from scratch. He'd had to cannibalize and abandon a dozen ships just to keep the rest of the squadron going. And he was all too aware that their time was running out.

"Go see the cleric for ritual cleansing," he ordered shortly. "And then return to your duties."

The two officers bowed, then retreated. Zaskar watched them go and tapped a command into his terminal. A holographic image snapped into existence, flickering slightly. Zaskar's eyes narrowed as he studied his fleet. The flicker was tiny, but it shouldn't have been there at all. A grim reminder of their predicament. The onboard datanet was glitched, and no one, not even their sole computer expert, had been able to fix it. His entire ship was breaking down.

He wanted to believe that the handful of light codes in the display represented a powerful force. Four superdreadnoughts, nine cruisers, twelve destroyers, and a pair of courier boats . . . On paper, it *was* a powerful force. But one superdreadnought could neither fire missiles nor energize a beam, and ammunition was in short supply in any case, and five of the smaller ships were on their last legs. Each failure, small in itself, led to a cascading series of failures that simply could not be fixed. Zaskar rather suspected that the Commonwealth wouldn't need an entire superdreadnought squadron to wipe out his fleet in a stand-up battle. A single superdreadnought would be more than enough.

Which is why we are here, he thought, switching to the near-space display. *They won't come looking for us here, not until we are betrayed.*

He gritted his teeth in bitter rage. The asteroid settlement was the sort of place he would have destroyed, if he'd stumbled across it before the war. Smugglers weren't allowed to operate within the Theocracy, which hadn't stopped a number of high-ranking personnel from trading safety and political cover for items that they simply couldn't obtain anywhere else. And now . . . He swore, angrily. The smugglers might be their only hope, if they could find something to trade. But the squadron had very little to offer the scum of the galaxy.

Except ships, he reminded himself. *And we're not that desperate, are we?*

Zaskar tapped the console, shutting off the display. He didn't want to admit it, even to himself, but perhaps they *were* that desperate. His fleet was dying. And its crew was dying too. Discipline was steadily breaking down—internal security had logged everything from fights to a handful of unpopular officers being murdered in their bunks—and he didn't dare try to crack down. His crewmen were too ignorant for now to realize just how bad things really were, but he knew it was only a matter of time. The squadron was well on its way to collapsing into irrelevance. The Commonwealth wouldn't have to lift a finger to destroy them. They'd do that for themselves.

He took a breath, tasting something faintly unpleasant in the air. The air circulation system was starting to break down too. He'd had men cleaning the vents and checking—and rechecking—the recycling plants, but if their air suddenly turned poisonous . . . that would be the end. It wouldn't even have to be *that* poisonous. An atmospheric imbalance, perhaps an excess of oxygen, would be just as bad. A spark would cause an explosion. Hell, merely breathing in excess oxygen would cause problems too.

The hatch hissed open. Zaskar looked up, already knowing who he'd see. There was only one person who would come into his ready room without ringing the buzzer and waiting for permission to enter. Lord Cleric Moses stood there, his beard as unkempt as ever. Zaskar couldn't help thinking there were more flecks of gray in his hair than

3

there'd been yesterday. Moses was nearly two decades older than Zaskar himself and hadn't had the benefit of a military career.

And he isn't even the Lord Cleric, Zaskar reminded himself, dryly. *He just took the title on the assumption that he was the senior surviving cleric.*

The thought brought another wave of depression. Ahura Mazda had fallen. The Tabernacle had been destroyed, and the planet had been occupied . . . if the wretched smugglers were to be believed. Zaskar wanted to believe that the smugglers had lied, but . . . he'd been there, during the final battle. He was all too aware that the Royal Tyre Navy had won. And his fleet, the one that should have fought to the bitter end, had been all that remained of the Theocratic Navy. He sometimes wondered, in the dead of night, if it would have been better to stay and die in defense of his homeworld and his religion. At least he wouldn't have lived to see his fleet slowly starting to die.

"They found nothing, it seems," Moses said, taking a seat. "They didn't even find any worthy women."

Zaskar snorted. Some of his officers had suggested, quite seriously, that they leave Theocratic Space entirely and set out to find a new home somewhere far from explored space. But his fleet's crew consisted solely of men. Kidnapping women was about the only real solution to their problem, but where could they hope to find nearly a hundred thousand women? Raiding a midsized planet might work—and he'd seriously considered it—yet he doubted they could withdraw before the occupiers responded. Come to think of it, he wasn't even sure he could punch through the planet's defenses. His fleet was in a *terrible* state.

"No," he said.

"And they heard more rumors," Moses added. "More worlds have slipped from our control."

"Yes," Zaskar said. "Are you surprised?"

The cleric gave him a sharp look. Zaskar looked back, evenly. The days when a cleric could have a captain, or even an admiral, hauled off his command deck and scourged were long gone. Moses had little real power, and they both knew it. Speaking truth to power was no longer a dangerous game. And the blunt truth was that the Theocracy had alienated so many locals on every world they'd occupied that the locals had revolted almost as soon as the orbital bombardment systems were destroyed.

Moses looked down. "God will provide."

Hah, Zaskar thought. God had turned His back. *We need a miracle.*

His console bleeped. "Admiral?"

Zaskar stabbed his finger at the button. "Yes?"

"Admiral, we just picked up a small scout ship dropping out of hyperspace," Captain Geris said. "They're broadcasting an old code, sir, and requesting permission to come aboard."

"An old code?" Zaskar leaned forward. "How old?"

"It's a priority-one code from four years ago," Captain Geris informed him. "I'm surprised it's still in our database."

Moses met Zaskar's eyes. "A trick?"

Zaskar shrugged. "Captain, are we picking up any other ships?"

"Negative, sir."

"Then invite the scout to dock at our forward airlock," Zaskar ordered. "And have its occupant brought to my ready room."

"Aye, Admiral."

Zaskar leaned back in his chair as the connection broke. A priority-one code from *four* years ago? It could be a trap, but outdated codes were generally rejected once everyone had been notified that they were outdated. The Theocracy had been so large that it had been incredibly difficult to keep everyone current. And yet, four years was *too* long. It made little sense. The code dated all the way back to the Battle of Cadiz.

"They wouldn't need to play games if they'd found us," he said, more to himself than to Moses. The scout could be crammed to the gunnels with antimatter, but the worst they could do was take out the *Righteous Revenge*. "They'd bring in a superdreadnought squadron and finish us off."

"Unless they want to be sure they've caught all of us," Moses said. "The Inquisition often watched heretics for weeks, just to be certain that *all* their friends and fellow unbelievers were identified."

Zaskar smiled. "We'll see."

He couldn't help feeling a flicker of shame as the guest—the sole person on the scout, according to the search party—was shown into his ready room. Once, it would have taken a mere five minutes to bring someone aboard; now, it had taken twenty. He dreaded to think of what would happen if they had to go into battle. A delay in raising their shields and activating their point defense would prove fatal.

Their guest didn't seem perturbed by the delay, or by the armed Janissaries following his every move, or even by the obvious fact that *Righteous Revenge* was on her last legs. He merely looked around with polite interest. Zaskar studied him back, noting the hawk-nosed face, tinted skin, and neatly trimmed beard. The man had gone to some lengths to present himself as a citizen of Ahura Mazda. Even his brown tunic suggested he'd grown up on Zaskar's homeworld.

And he has a dozen implants, Zaskar thought, studying the report from the security scan. The visitor was practically a cyborg. *And that means he's from . . . ?*

"Please, be seated," Zaskar said. He kept his voice polite. Advanced implants meant that their guest was from one of the major powers. The Commonwealth was right out, of course, but there were others. Some of them might even see advantage in backing his fleet. "I'm Admiral Zaskar, commander of this fleet."

"A pleasure," the man said. He inclined his head in a formal bow. "I'm Simon Askew."

"A pleasure," Zaskar echoed. The name meant nothing to him, but he rather suspected it wasn't the man's real name. "You seem to have come looking for us."

"Correct," Askew said. He leaned forward. "My . . . superiors would like to offer you a certain degree of support in your operations."

"Indeed?" Zaskar wasn't sure whether he believed it or not. Keeping his fleet going would require an immense investment. "And the price would be?"

"We want you to keep the Commonwealth busy," Askew said. "It is in our interests to see them get bogged down."

"Is it now?" Zaskar frowned. "And who would be interested in seeing them bogged down?"

"My superiors wish to remain unnamed," Askew informed him. He reached into his pocket and removed a datapad. "But they are prepared to be quite generous."

He held the datapad out. Zaskar took it and scanned the open document rapidly. It was a list of everything the fleet needed to keep functioning, everything from starship components to missiles and ration bars. It was . . . it was unbelievable. It had to be a trap. And yet . . . and yet, he *wanted* to believe. If the offer was genuine, they could keep wearing away at the Commonwealth until it withdrew from Theocratic Space. They could *win*!

Moses reached out his hand for the datapad. Zaskar barely noticed.

"You want us to keep the Commonwealth busy," he said. It was suddenly very hard to speak clearly. "It seems a reasonable price."

His mind raced. No smuggler could transship so much material into a war zone, not without running unacceptable risks. And no smuggler would have access to cyborg technology. Only a great power could supply the weapons and equipment . . . and only a great power would benefit from keeping the Commonwealth tied down. The list of suspects was relatively short.

And it doesn't matter, he told himself. They'd have to be alert for the prospect of betrayal, but that was a given anyway. The Theocracy had been the least popular galactic government for decades, even before the war. *We could win!*

"Very well," he said. "Let's talk."

CHAPTER ONE

AHURA MAZDA

The sound of a distant explosion, muffled by the forcefield surrounding Commonwealth House, woke Kat Falcone as she lay in her bed. Others followed, flickers of multicolored light dancing through the window as homemade rockets or mortar shells crashed into the forcefield and exploded harmlessly. She rolled over and sat upright, blinking as the lights automatically brightened. Her bedside terminal was flashing green. Pointless attacks had been so common over the last year that hardly anyone bothered to sound the alert any longer. The insurgents had yet to realize that no amount of makeshift rocketry would pose a threat to the Commonwealth HQ. Even without the forcefield, Commonwealth House could take the blow and shrug it off. The blasts wouldn't even scratch the paint.

Not that we're going to turn off the forcefield to let them try, she thought morbidly as she crossed her arms. *That would be pushing fate too far.*

She snorted at the thought as she forced herself to key her terminal to bring up the latest set of reports. There was no change, she noted wryly: an endless liturgy of shootings, bombings, gang rapes, robberies, and other horrors undreamed of on Tyre. But Ahura Mazda's population had been kept under tight control for decades, centuries even.

The sudden collapse of everything they'd once taken for granted had unleashed *years* of pent-up frustrations. She sometimes thought that the insurgency was really a civil war, with Commonwealth troops being engaged only when they got in the way. Ahura Mazda seemed to have gone completely mad.

Damn them, she thought. A final spread of makeshift rockets struck the forcefield outside, then faded away. *And damn their dead leaders too.*

She looked down at her hands, feeling as if she simply wanted to stay in bed. She'd had plans for the future, once. She was going to get married and see the universe, perhaps by purchasing a freighter and traveling from system to system, doing a little trading along the way. Instead, her fiancé was dead, and she was still in the navy, technically. She hadn't stood on a command deck for nearly a year. Instead, she was chained to a desk on an occupied world, trying to govern a sector of forty inhabited star systems that had just been liberated from one of the worst tyrannies humanity had the misfortune to invent. The chaos was beyond belief. Ahura Mazda wasn't the only world going through a nervous breakdown. She'd read reports of everything from mass slaughter to forced deportation of everyone who'd converted to the True Faith.

Years of pent-up frustrations, she reminded herself. She'd been lucky. She hadn't grown up in a world where saying the wrong thing could get her beheaded. And they have all been released at once.

There was a sharp knock at the door. Kat glared at it, resisting the urge to order the visitor to go away. There was only one person who could come through that door. It opened a moment later, allowing Lucy Yangtze to step into the bedroom. The middle-aged woman studied Kat with a surprisingly maternal eye as she carried the breakfast tray over to the bedside table. Kat had to fight to keep from snapping at her to get out. Lucy was a steward. Looking after Kat was her job.

"Good morning, Admiral," Lucy said. She managed to sound disapproving without making it obvious. "How are you today?"

Kat swallowed a number of remarks she knew would be petty and childish. "I didn't sleep well," she said as Lucy uncovered the tray. "And then they woke me up."

"You need to go to bed earlier," Lucy said, dryly.

"Hah," Kat muttered. She forced herself to stand, heedless of her nakedness. "There are too many things to do here."

"Then delegate some of them," Lucy suggested gently. "You have an entire staff under you, do you not?"

Pat would have cracked a rude joke, Kat thought. It felt like a stab to the heart. *And I would have elbowed him . . .*

She pushed the thought aside with an effort. "We'll see," she said, vaguely. In truth, she didn't want to delegate anything. Too much was riding on the occupation's success for her to casually push authority down the chain. And yet, Lucy was right. Ahura Mazda wasn't a starship. A single mind couldn't hope to keep abreast of all the details, let alone make sure the planet ran smoothly. If that was her goal, she'd already failed. "I'll talk to you later."

"I'll have lunch ready for 1300," Lucy said. "You can make it a working lunch if you like."

Kat had to smile, although she knew it wasn't really funny. *All* her lunches were working lunches these days. She rarely got to eat in private with anyone. Even cramming a ration bar into her mouth between meetings wasn't an option. She couldn't help feeling, as she tucked into her scrambled eggs, that she was merely spinning her wheels in mud. She went to countless meetings, she made decisions, again and again and again, and yet . . . was she actually doing *anything*? She kicked herself, again, for allowing them to promote her off the command deck. The Admiralty probably would have let her take command of a heavy cruiser on deep-space patrol if she'd made enough of a fuss.

It has to be done, she thought as she keyed her console to bring up the latest news reports from home. *And I'm the one the king tapped for the post.*

"Naval spokespeople today confirmed that the search for MV *Supreme* has been finally called off," the talking head said. He was a man so grave that Kat rather suspected he was nothing more than a computer-generated image. "The cruise liner, which went missing in hyperspace six months ago, has been declared lost with all hands. Duke Cavendish issued a statement reassuring investors that the Cavendish Corporation will meet its commitments, but independent analysts are questioning their finances . . ."

Kat sighed. Trust the media to put a lost cruise liner ahead of anything important. "Next."

"Infighting among refugees on Tarsus has led to a declaration of martial law," the talking head told her. "President Theca has taken personal control of the situation and informed the refugees that any further misbehavior, regardless of the cause, will result in immediate arrest and deportation. The Commonwealth Refugee Commission has blamed the disorder on poor supply lines and has called on Tarsus to make more supplies available to the refugees. However, local protests against refugees have grown . . ."

"And it could be worse, like it is here," Kat muttered. "Next!"

"Sharon Mackintosh has become the latest starlet to join the Aaron Group Marriage," the talking head said. "She will join fifty-seven other starlets in matrimonial bliss . . ."

"Off," Kat snapped.

She shook her head in annoyance. The occupied zone was turning into a nightmare, no matter how many meetings she attended, and the news back home was largely trivial. The end of war had brought confusion in its wake—she knew that better than anyone—but there were times when she thought that the king was the only one trying to hold everything together. The Commonwealth hadn't been designed for a war, and everyone knew it. And now all the tensions that had been put on the back burner while the Commonwealth fought for its very survival were starting to tear it apart.

Standing, she walked over to the window and peered out. Tabernacle City had been a ramshackle mess even before the occupation, but now it was a nightmare. Smoke was rising from a dozen places, marking the latest bombings; below, she could see marines and soldiers heading out on patrol. The civilians seemed to trust the occupiers more than they trusted the warring factions, but they were scared to come into the open and say so. They were afraid, deep inside, that the occupation wouldn't last. Her eyes picked out Government House, standing a short distance from Commonwealth House. Admiral Junayd and his people were trying to put together a provisional government, but it was a slow job. Their authority was weaker than most of the insurgent factions. She didn't envy them.

Her wristcom bleeped from the table. She stalked back to the bed and picked it up. "Go ahead."

"Admiral," Lieutenant Kitty Patterson's voice said. "You have a meeting in thirty minutes."

"Understood," Kat said. She allowed herself a moment of gratitude. Thirty minutes was more than long enough to shower and get dressed. "I'll be there."

She turned and walked into the shower, silently grateful that Commonwealth House had its own water supply. The local water distribution network had been on the verge of failing even before the occupation; now, with pipes smashed by the insurgents and entire pumping stations looted and destroyed, there were overpopulated districts that barely had enough water to keep the population from dying of thirst. Kat didn't understand how anyone could live in such an environment. She thought she would sooner have risked her life in revolt than waste away and die.

But it was never that easy, she thought. *This is how too many people here believe it should be.*

She washed and dressed quickly, inspecting her appearance in the reflector field before she left the suite. Her white uniform was neatly

13

pressed, her medals and her golden hair shone in the light . . . but there was a *tired* look in her eyes she knew she should lose. She was depressed and she knew it, and she really should talk to the shrinks, but training and experience told her that the psychologists were not to be trusted. None of them had commanded ships in battle, or made life-or-death decisions, or done *anything* that might qualify them to pass judgment on a spacer's life.

She took a long breath, gathering herself as she strapped a pistol to her belt, then walked through the door and down the corridor. The two marine guards at the far end of the corridor saluted her. She returned the gesture as the hatch opened in front of her.

They built the place to resemble a starship, she thought dourly. It had been amusing, once, to contemplate the mind-set of whoever had thought it was a good idea. Were they trying to remind everyone that, one day, the Commonwealth would leave Ahura Mazda? Or did they just want to pretend, for a few hours, that they were designing starships? *But they forgot to include a command deck.*

She drew herself up as she stepped through the next hatch, into the meeting room. It was large and ornate, although she'd managed to clear out the worst of the luxury. She didn't want people to get *too* comfortable in meeting rooms. Thankfully, most of her senior staff had genuine experience, either in combat or repairing and rejuvenating shattered planetary infrastructures. The war had created far too many opportunities to practice.

And I don't have many chairwarmers, she reminded herself as her staff stood to welcome her. *It could be worse.*

"Thank you for coming," she said once she'd taken her chair. "Be seated."

She cast her eye around the table as her staffers sat down. General Timothy Winters, Commonwealth Marines; Colonel Christopher Whitehall, Royal Engineering Corps; Major Shawna Callable, Commonwealth Refugee Commission; Captain Janice Wilson, Office of Naval Intelligence; Lieutenant Kitty Patterson, Kat's personal aide. It was a diverse group, she told herself firmly. And the absence of wallflowers, from junior staffers to senior staffers, allowed everyone to talk freely.

"I was woken this morning by a rocket attack," she said as a server poured tea and coffee. "I assume there was no reason to be alarmed?"

"No, Admiral," Winters said. He was a big, beefy man with a bald head and scarred cheekbones. "It was merely another random attack. The people behind it scarpered before we could catch them."

Because we can't fire shells back into the city, Kat reminded herself sharply. *The insurgents would claim we'd killed civilians, even if we hadn't.*

She felt a flash of hatred deeper than anything she'd ever felt for enemy spacers. She'd never seen her opponents in space, not face-to-face. It had been easy to believe that they weren't that different from her, that they weren't monsters. But here, on the ground, she couldn't avoid the simple fact that the insurgents *were* monsters. They killed anyone who supported the provisional government, raped and mutilated women they caught out of doors, sited heavy weapons emplacements in inhabited homes, used children to carry bombs towards the enemy . . . Kat wanted them all dead. Ahura Mazda would have no hope of becoming a decent place to live as long as those monsters stalked the streets. But tracking them all down was a long and difficult task.

"At least no one was killed," Major Shawna Callable said. "Admiral, we need more resources for the women's shelters. We're running short of just about everything."

"And they also need more guards," Winters told her. "The last attack nearly broke the perimeter before it was beaten back."

"Draw them from the reserves," Kat ordered. She didn't like deploying her reserves, not when she was all too aware of how badly her forces were overstretched, but she had no choice. The women in the shelters would be assaulted and murdered if one of their compounds was overrun. "And see what we can find in the way of additional supplies."

If we can find anything, her thoughts added. Ahura Mazda produced nothing these days, as far as she could tell. The infrastructure had been literally torn to shreds. Putting the farms back into production was turning into a long, hard slog. Shawna had been right. *We're running short on just about everything.*

She looked at Winters. "Is there anything we can do to make it harder for the insurgents to get to them?"

"Only moving the refugees a long way away," Winters said. "Personally, I'd recommend one of the islands. We could set up a proper security net there and vaporize anything heading in without the right security codes."

"We barely have the resources to keep the cities alive," Colonel Christopher Whitehall said, curtly. He was short, with black skin and penetrating eyes. His record stated that he'd been a marine before he'd been wounded and transferred to the Royal Engineers. "Right now, Admiral, I'm honestly expecting a disaster at any moment."

"So train up some locals and put them to work," Winters snapped. He thumped the table to underline the suggestion. "It's their bloody city. And their people who will die of thirst if we lose the pumping stations completely."

"The training programs are going slowly," Whitehall snapped back. The frustration in his voice was all too clear. "Half the idiots on this wretched ball of mud think that trying to fix a broken piece of machinery is sinful, while the other half can't count to twenty-one without taking off their trousers. We've got a few women who *might* be good at it, if they were given a chance, but we can't send them out on repair jobs."

"It's their schooling," Shawna told them. "They weren't encouraged to actually learn."

Kat nodded in grim understanding. The Theocracy's educational system had been a joke. No, that wasn't entirely true. It had done its job, after all. It had churned out millions of young men who knew nothing, least of all how to *think*. But rote recitals were useless when it came to repairing even a relatively simple machine. It was a mystery to her how the Theocratic Navy had managed to keep its fleet going long enough to actually start the war. Their shortage of trained engineers had to have been an utter nightmare.

They never picked on anyone their own size, she told herself. The Theocracy's first targets had all been stage-one or stage-two worlds. Very few of them had any space-based defenses, let alone the ability to take the fight to the enemy. *And the Theocrats certainly weren't prepared for a long war.*

Whitehall met her eyes. "We need more engineers, Admiral, and more protective troops. If we lose a couple more pumping stations . . ."

"I know," Kat said. They'd come to the same conclusion time and time again, in pointless meeting after pointless meeting. "Right now, Tyre doesn't seem to be interested in sending either."

"We could try to hire civilian engineers," Kitty suggested. She was the lowest-ranking person at the table, but that didn't stop her from offering her opinions. "They could take up some of the slack."

Whitehall snorted. "I doubt it," he said. "There's work in the Commonwealth for engineers, Lieutenant, and safer too. They won't be in any danger on Tarsus or . . . well, anywhere. I don't think we could get them out here."

Kitty reddened. "I . . . sorry, Admiral."

"Don't worry about it," Kat said, briskly. She looked around the table. "Are there any other solutions?"

"Not in the short run," Whitehall said. "We have water and power, Admiral. It's getting both to their destination that is the *real* problem. We've tried setting up purification centers near the sewers and . . ."

The building shook, gently. Kat tensed, one hand dropping to the pistol at her belt. *That* hadn't been a homemade rocket. A nuke? The Theocracy had supposedly thrown its entire nuclear arsenal at the navy, but she'd never been entirely sure they'd used all their nukes. Hell, the Theocrats themselves hadn't been sure. Their record keeping had been appalling. A nuke wouldn't break the forcefield but would do immense damage to the city.

Winters checked his wristcom, then swore. "Admiral," he said, "there's been an explosion."

"Where?" Kat stood. The blast had been very close. If the insurgents had managed to open a pathway into Commonwealth House, the defenders might be in some trouble. "And what happened?"

"Government House." Winters sounded stunned. "The building is in ruins. Admiral, Admiral Junayd is dead."

". . . Shit," Kat said.

CHAPTER TWO

TYRE

Peter Falcone—*Duke* Peter Falcone, he reminded himself savagely—stared at the heavy wooden doors and tried not to let his impatience show on his face. He was no callow youth, although he'd grown up in the shadows of Duke Lucas Falcone; he was one of the single most wealthy and powerful people on Tyre. It hadn't been easy to convince enough of the family to back him, even though he was Lucas's oldest child, but he'd made it. The Falcone family was in his hands now. He had no intention of failing in his duty to his people.

Assuming I ever get through my investiture, he thought as he looked at the doors. They were firmly closed, awaiting the king's pleasure. *Who thought it was a good idea to come up with such . . . such pageantry?*

He snorted at the thought. The planet's founders, including his great-grandfather, had created a corporate state. There had been fourteen corporations, at the time, and they'd divided the world up between them. It had been simple enough, he'd thought, but, to give the whole enterprise a veneer of legitimacy, they'd turned the planet into a monarchy, with the most powerful CEO declared king. And it had grown from there into a tangled system that worked . . . mostly. But the founders had never imagined the Breakdown, or the Commonwealth, or, worst of all, the recently concluded war.

And they didn't imagine one of the corporations collapsing either, Peter told himself. The Ducal Fourteen had always seemed too big to fail. But the Cavendish Corporation was on the verge of total collapse, and Peter had a nasty feeling that others might follow. His own corporation was barely treading water. *We never imagined having to splash out so much money on everything from weapons development to force projection.*

It was a sour point, one that had stuck in his craw ever since he'd discovered just how much money had been expended—and just how much remained unaccounted for. The government had raised taxes, as well as asked for voluntary contributions from the big corporations, but its accounting had been poor. The desperate rush to put as many warships into space as possible had done nothing for financial discipline. Peter was uneasily aware that nearly 30 percent of the budget for the last four years had vanished into black projects, projects he wasn't supposed to know about. It was a staggering amount of money, truly unimaginable, and it was one of the bones the House of Lords wanted to pick with the king. And yet, it wasn't the worst of them.

Trumpets blared. The doors were thrown open, revealing a pair of uniformed flunkies and, beyond them, the House of Lords. Peter pasted a neutral expression on his face as he began to walk forward, wondering just how many people were watching him make a fool of himself through the datanet. The entire ceremony was being broadcast live. His father had made the ceremony look solemn and dignified, but Peter suspected he looked like an idiot. The fancy robes and stylized hair came from a bygone era.

And true power lies in money, warships, and troops, he thought as he walked into the chamber. *I could wear rags and Eau de Skunk, and I'd still be one of the most powerful men in the known universe.*

He allowed his eyes to sweep the chamber as the doors were closed behind him. Seven hundred and ninety lords and ladies, crammed into a room that had been designed for only five hundred. For years people had been talking about expanding the House of Lords or rewriting the rules about who could and who couldn't attend via hologram or proxy, but nothing had come of it. The lords who could trace their bloodlines all the way back to the founders had been joined by newer noblemen, some who'd more than earned their right to a title and others who'd been rewarded for services rendered. A cluster of lords, sitting in the upper benches, wore robes to signify that they were colonials. And hadn't there been a thoroughly nasty fight over *their* right to sit in the chamber?

Peter sighed, inwardly, as he picked out a handful of names and faces. Prime Minister Arthur Hampshire, technically a commoner; Israel Harrison, Leader of the Opposition; Duke Jackson Cavendish, trying hard to look confident even though everyone knew he no longer had a pot to piss in . . . names and faces, some of whom were friends, some allies, and some deadly enemies. Peter wondered, careful not to show even a trace of doubt on his face, if he was *really* up to the task. There were men and women in the chamber who'd been playing politics long before he had been born.

There's no one else, he told himself firmly. *And I dare not fail.*

He sucked in his breath. He wasn't inexperienced. His father had made him work in the family corporation for years, pushing him out of his comfort zone time and time again. And chewing him out, royally, when he'd screwed up. Peter wasn't sure how he felt about that either. His father had been a good man, but he'd also been a *hard* man. The family could not afford weakness in the ranks. Peter, at least, had been given a chance to learn from his mistakes. Not everyone had been so lucky.

And others never had to take up the role, he thought, feeling a flicker of resentment, once again, towards his youngest sister. Kat had never had to study business, never had to take up a position within the family corporation. Instead, she'd gone to war and carved out a life for herself. *Some people have all the luck.*

Peter stopped in the exact center of the chamber and looked up. King Hadrian, first of that name, looked back at him. He was a tall man, with short dark hair and a face that was strikingly calculating. The king, Peter knew from experience, was a man who could move from affability to threat with terrifying speed. He was young too, younger than Peter himself. It was something Peter knew had worried his father. Peter, and the other corporate heirs, could learn their trade without risking everything, but the *king's* heir could not become king until his father had passed away. King Hadrian had been learning his trade on the job. And it was hard to tell, Peter had to admit, just how much was cold calculation versus sheer luck. And inexperience.

A shame the rumors about the king and Kat were groundless, Peter thought as he knelt in front of his monarch. *She would have made a good partner for him . . .*

He dismissed the thought, ruthlessly. There was no point in crying over the impossible. An affair was one thing, but marriage? The other dukes would have blocked the match without a second thought. And besides, Kat had been in love with a commoner. Peter couldn't help feeling another stab of envy. *His* marriage had been arranged, of course; his parents had organized the match, one of the prices he paid for his position. But Kat was free to fall in love as she pleased. He wasn't sure it was really a good thing. Kat had been devastated by her lover's death.

King Hadrian rose, one hand holding his scepter. He wore a full military dress uniform, although it was black rather than white. Peter thought, rather sourly, that the king had no right to wear so much gold braid, let alone the medals jangling at his breast. But then, the king *was* a hereditary member of a dozen military fraternities. He probably needed to wear the medals his ancestors had won. Some of his supporters would otherwise be alienated.

"It has been a year and a day since Duke Falcone was treacherously killed," King Hadrian said. His words were a grim reminder that nowhere, not even Tyre itself, was safe from attack. The Theocracy's strike teams had done a great deal of damage before they'd been wiped out, but the security measures introduced to combat them had been almost worse. "And now, with the period of mourning officially over, we gather to invest his son with the title and powers that once were his father's."

There was a brief, chilling pause. Peter felt his heart beginning to race, even though he was *sure* there was nothing to worry about. He *was* the Duke, confirmed by the family council; no one, not even the king, could take it from him. And yet, if the House of Lords refused to seat him, it could cause all manner of trouble back home. The family council might vote to impeach him on the grounds he couldn't work with the rest of the nobility and elect someone else in his place. Peter doubted he'd be permitted to return to the corporation after that! More likely he'd be sent into comfortable exile somewhere.

"But we must decide if he is worthy to join our ranks," the king said calmly. "Honorable members, cast your votes."

Peter tensed, telling himself again that he was perfectly safe. No one would risk alienating him over something so petty, not now. But the vote was anonymous . . . His family's enemies would vote against him, of course, but what about the others? There were people who might take the opportunity to put him on notice that he couldn't inherit the extensive patronage network his father had built up over the years. And others who would want to renegotiate the terms, now that his father was dead.

He wanted to look around to see the voting totals, but he knew it would be taken as a sign of weakness. He didn't dare look unsure, not now. Weakness invited attack. Instead, all he could do was wait. He silently counted to a hundred under his breath, wishing he didn't feel so exposed. The eyes of the world were upon him.

"The voting has finished," King Hadrian said. "In favor, seven hundred and twelve; against, forty-two."

23

And a number of abstentions, Peter thought. *Did they refuse to cast a vote because they don't want to take sides, even on something as pointless as this, or because they recognize the whole ceremony for the farce it is?*

"I welcome you to the House of Lords, *Duke* Falcone," King Hadrian said. He reached out and tapped Peter on the shoulder with his scepter. "You may rise."

Peter rose, feeling suddenly stiff. "Thank you, Your Majesty."

"Take your place among us," King Hadrian said. "I'm sure you will find it a very edifying discussion."

A low rustle ran through the chamber as Peter sat down on the bench. It was comfortable, but not too comfortable. Behind him, he heard a handful of lords and ladies leaving now that the *important* business was done. They were too highly ranked not to attend the investment, but neither wealthy nor powerful enough to make themselves heard during a debate. And besides, Peter reflected, they probably knew that half the business conducted in the chamber was meaningless. The real deals would be negotiated in private chambers. By the time they were presented to the Houses of Parliament, various initiatives would already have been revised thoroughly enough to make them broadly acceptable to everyone. The public debates would be largely meaningless.

The speaker came forward, bowed to the king, and took the stand. He was an elderly man, old enough to remember the king's grandfather. Peter felt a little sorry for him, even though he was sure that anyone who'd held such a position for so long had to know where the bodies were buried. The speaker had to wait at the back of the chamber while the king had played his role. But then, that too was part of the ceremony.

"Thank you, Your Majesty," the speaker said. He cleared his throat. "The issue before us . . ."

Peter glanced down at his datapad as the voice droned on. He'd received more than fifty private messages in the last five minutes, each one requesting a private meeting. Some were just feelers from friends and enemies alike, but others were quite serious. He hadn't expected a PM from Israel Harrison. Technically, Peter was on the Privy Council; practically, he'd been . . . discouraged . . . from claiming his father's seat. There'd been too much else to do over the last year for him to let that bother him.

"On a point of order, Mr. Speaker," Israel Harrison said. His voice cut through the hubbub, drawing everyone's eyes to him. "Is the government *seriously* proposing to expand the foreign aid budget?"

He went on before the prime minister could respond. "The emergency taxation and spending program was meant to be terminated with the end of the war. We were *assured*, when we gave our consent, that that would be the case. And yet, here we are, still paying the tax . . . and hampering our economy in the process. We need to cut back on government spending and resume economic growth."

The prime minister stood. "The fact remains that a vast number of worlds, inside and outside the Commonwealth, have been devastated by the war. Millions upon millions of people have been displaced, cities have been destroyed, food supplies have been sharply reduced or cut off entirely . . . uncountable numbers of people have had their lives destroyed. Our reconstruction program may be the only thing standing between those people and utter destitution."

"I fully understand why my honorable friend feels that way," Harrison countered. "But I fail to understand why *we* should risk economic collapse, and our own utter destitution, to save those worlds. Many of them were formerly enemy states. Others have been, if I may make so bold, ungrateful."

Peter gritted his teeth as the debate raged backwards and forwards, with government supporters exchanging harsh words with the opposition. It wasn't about the displaced people, he knew, and it wasn't about foreign aid in and of itself. It was the age-old question of just who got to control the budget. The government wanted to keep the emergency taxation program because it gave them more money to spend, while the opposition wanted to get rid of the program because it gave the government a great deal of clout to buy votes. And the hell of it, he knew all too well, was that the opposition, if elected into power, would want to keep the program too.

"The military budget is already too high," Harrison said. "Do we face *any* real threat from an outside power?"

Grand Admiral Tobias Vaughn rose. Peter thought he looked tired. Vaughn had been the navy's senior uniformed officer, which made him *de facto* senior officer for all branches of the military, for the last five years, a term that covered the entirety of the war. Rumor had it that Vaughn wanted to retire, but so far the king had convinced him to stay. Now that the war was over, Peter couldn't help wondering just how long that would last.

"There are two aspects to your question," Vaughn said. He *sounded* tired too. "First, we do not face a peer threat at the moment. However, our neighbors have been building up their own military forces over the last few years. We have reason to believe that they have been pouring resources into duplicating our advanced weapons and technology— unsurprisingly so, as they may regard *us* as a potential threat. It is possible that we may face an alliance of two or more Great Powers in the near future.

"Second, we have a responsibility to provide security for our territory, both within the Commonwealth and the occupied zone. There is, quite simply, no one else who will provide any form of interstellar security. We must deploy starships to protect planets and shipping lanes, and we must deploy troops to protect refugee populations and provide support to various provisional governments. The Jorlem Sector became increasingly lawless as a result of the war, honorable members. Do we really want the Theocratic Sector to go the same way?"

Harrison stood. "Is it going to be a threat to us?"

Vaughn looked back at him, evenly. "We have confiscated the remaining enemy industrial production nodes," he said. "In the short term, chaos in the Theocratic Sector will be very bad for the locals and largely irrelevant to us. However, in the long term, there will be pirates, raiders, and revanchists taking root within the sector. I submit to you, sir, that those forces will eventually become a threat."

"But the Theocracy is dead." Harrison tapped his foot on the ground. "How long do you want to continue to fight the war?"

"Until we win," Vaughn said. "Right now, sir, the sector is unstable, and we're the only thing keeping it under control."

"We have a debt of honor," King Hadrian said.

"A debt of honor we cannot afford to meet," Harrison said curtly. He didn't *quite* glare at the king. "And a debt of honor that was entered into without Parliament's consent."

Peter groaned, inwardly, as the debate grew louder. Harrison was right, of course. The king had promised much and, so far, delivered little. But the king had made promises he'd had no right to make, certainly not without Parliament's approval. No *wonder* his government wanted to keep emergency taxation powers. It was the only way to keep his promises to the Commonwealth.

And yet, we simply cannot afford to rebuild all the Theocracy's infrastructure, he thought. The expenditure would be unimaginably huge. *Even trying would be disastrous.*

He groaned again. It was going to be a very long day.

CHAPTER THREE

TYRE

"Observers on Ahura Mazda confirm that Admiral Junayd, the head of the provisional government, was killed in an explosion," the talking head said. "Admiral Junayd was the Theocracy's best naval officer prior to his defection, after which . . ."

Commodore Sir William McElney snorted rudely in the direction of the display screen, then returned his attention to his beer. The bar was a spacers' bar, with hundreds of men and women coming in, ordering drinks, and chatting to their mates in hopes of finding work on a starship before they ran out of money and had to go down to the planetary surface. It wasn't easy. William had discovered, upon his return to Tyre, that vast numbers of spacers had been released from the navy, and now that the drawdown was in full effect, there were ten spacers for every posting, perhaps more. The freighter captains could pick and choose as they wished.

He took a sip of his beer, wondering just how long it would be before a fight broke out. Raw desperation hung in the air like a physical force. Spacers *hated* going down to the ground, even for short periods, yet most of them knew it was just a matter of time before they were marched to the shuttles and unceremoniously sent down. Orbit Station Beta was immense, easily large enough to swallow a number of superdreadnoughts in its hull, but it didn't have room for thousands of spacers. A fight might kill the hopes of anyone involved when they were caught by the guards. These days, the shore patrol was extremely intolerant of anyone who caused trouble.

His lips twitched, sourly. It had been his fault, as much as anything. He could have stayed in the navy if he'd wished. But the refugees from Hebrides had needed his help . . . he'd thought. They were a hardy people but weren't used to the Commonwealth . . . or what life was like outside their dead homeworld. The refugee community hadn't precisely collapsed, not completely, but the youngsters had started to embrace the ways of their new homeworld and the older folk had been unable to stop them. William wasn't sure he blamed the youth either. He'd kept some of his homeworld's practices, after he'd joined the navy, but not all. A whole new world was opening up in front of the youngsters, a world where they could do more with their lives. And no one could stand in their way.

He glanced at his wristcom as the talking head started to babble about sports results. She was late. He wasn't even sure why she'd chosen a bar to meet . . . unless it was an elaborate joke of some kind. Perhaps it *had* been a joke. Like it or not, he was no common spacer. How many captains would want to hire a man who technically outranked them, someone who might not be aware that the *captain* was the ultimate authority on his ship? That was a matter of law—a captain could give orders to an admiral—but rank sometimes did odd things to brains. An admiral might forget that his rank didn't put him above the law.

A rustle ran through the room as someone stepped through the door. William looked up and lifted his eyebrows. The woman was no spacer. *That* much was clear, just by looking at her. She wore a white suit that hinted at curves without revealing them, her blonde hair in a long plait that reached down to her hips, and a faint professional smile. William nodded to himself, then raised a hand in greeting. She nodded back as she walked over to the table and sat down.

"Commodore William McElney?" Her lightly accented voice suggested she already knew the answer. "A pleasure to meet you in person."

"Likewise," William said. He didn't recognize her accent, although he was fairly sure that she'd spent years on Tyre. "Although it's just *William*, now. I'm retired."

"I read your file," the woman said. She held out a hand. "Tanya Barrington, Asher Dales."

William studied her for a long moment as he shook her hand. She had a strong grip; indeed, she was stronger than she looked. He wondered, absently, what she made of him. He'd always been short and stubby, despite endless rejuvenation treatments; his hair, slowly starting to turn gray, was grim proof that he hadn't been born on Tyre. And the long coat he wore over a basic shipsuit was proof he was hurting for money. He was too stubborn to look up some of his old friends for a loan.

And she looked at my file, William thought. That meant . . . what? A government? Or a corporation? Or merely someone with access to an information broker? It wouldn't be hard to get a copy of his naval record, if someone had the money. *Who is this woman?*

Tanya reached into her pocket and produced a privacy generator. "I assume you don't mind me using this . . . ?"

"Not at all," William said. He hadn't planned to record the conversation. "But we can go into a private room, if you wish."

"That might be preferable," Tanya said. "But we're still going to have to use the generator."

William nodded, signaling the bartender to make the arrangements. Tanya was young, then—young and a little naive. He found himself looking at her with new eyes as the bartender escorted them to a private meeting room. It was hard to be sure with people who'd had the standard genetic enhancements and suchlike, but he'd bet half his pension that Tanya wasn't long out of her teens. She walked like a professional, which probably meant she had some qualifications, yet little actual experience. In hindsight, perhaps she hadn't realized what a spacers' bar was like before making arrangements to meet in one.

"Here we are," he said, once the door was closed. The meeting room was very basic, but at least it was clean. He'd been in worse places. "What can I do for you?"

"To cut a long story short, we'd like to hire you," Tanya said. "You come highly recommended."

William narrowed his eyes. "Really?"

"Yes," Tanya said. She reddened, slightly. "Perhaps I should explain."

She took a breath, then began. "I was born on Asher Dales, a star system on the other side of the Gap," she said. "It was a very simple world, really; my father, a spacer captain, only used it as a homeport because my mother had fallen in love with it. Anyway, as you can probably imagine, I was five when the Theocracy arrived. Asher Dales had nothing more than a handful of outdated orbital defense platforms, so the battle began and ended very quickly."

"Ouch," William said.

"My father managed to sneak a bunch of refugees off the planet, including myself," Tanya continued. "We ran through the Gap and, eventually, made it to Tyre. There was"—she made a face—"some sort of deal between my father and ONI, which allowed my mother and me to gain permanent residency in exchange for service. I went into the local school system and, eventually, went into law."

"And then your planet was liberated," William said.

"Yes," Tanya agreed. "My father played a major role in the liberation, landing with enough troops to prevent the Theocrats from tearing the world apart before it was too late. He was rewarded by being elected president."

"I'm glad the story has a happy ending," William said, sincerely. The cynic in him thought that the refugees would discover that their homeworld was nothing like the idealized one they remembered. "But what does this have to do with me?"

"We want . . . we *need* . . . to build a space defense force," Tanya said. "And we need someone to command it."

William lifted his eyebrows. "And you don't have someone who can do it for you?"

Tanya shook her head. "No," she said. "A handful of refugees *did* go into the navy, but the ones I contacted were unwilling to return home. Most of them have permanent residency rights on Tyre and aren't willing to give them up. The others . . . don't have the sort of experience we require. Our database search, when we widened it, turned up you."

"I see," William said. He was tempted. No, he was *very* tempted. He could have stayed on a command deck if he'd stayed in the navy. Leaving had been a mistake. And now there was a chance to start again. "What exactly do you want?"

Tanya looked back at him evenly. "In the short term, you will have considerable power to purchase starships, hire crews, and build a dedicated force," she said. "In the long term, we will expect you to train crewmen from Asher Dales to serve on the ships."

William nodded, slowly. "How much have you done already?"

"Nothing beyond arranging a handful of meetings with shipyard owners," Tanya said. She held out a datapad. "We do have all the licenses we need."

"I hope so," William said. He'd dealt with a handful of shipyard owners. The decent ones tended to be anal about paperwork, while the crooked ones expected massive bribes in exchange for keeping their mouths shut. He scanned the datapad and nodded. "Have you applied to the Commonwealth for a grant?"

"Yes," Tanya said. "But we've been advised, purely off the record, that the odds of getting a grant are very low."

"I see," William said. He scanned the datapad, again. The licenses were indeed all in order, as were the credit notes from two different banks. For a planet that had only recently been liberated, Asher Dales had put together a quite impressive sum. "Well, we'll have to discuss terms, of course . . ."

Tanya smiled. He smiled back. She knew he was hooked. The chance to build a small fighting force from scratch, even if it was tiny compared to the fleets that had waged titanic war for the last four years, was not one he could miss. And who knew? Given time, Asher Dales might grow into an economic powerhouse, one that could afford a bigger fleet . . . and he'd be in at the ground floor.

And I'll be in space again, he told himself. *That alone would make it worthwhile.*

◆ ◆ ◆

"I can sell you this heavy cruiser," the dealer said, two days later. "She's outdated, but . . ."

William glanced at the datapad, then shook his head. "Not a chance," he said. He'd served on one of those starships, years ago. They weren't bad designs, but they were high maintenance. "We need to focus on destroyers and corvettes."

Tanya caught William's arm as the dealer turned away. "I thought the bigger, the better."

"Size isn't everything," William muttered back. "And that ship is really too large for our purpose. We won't have the maintenance facilities to keep her going."

He'd done a little research during the brief period between signing contracts and taking a shuttle to the scrapyard. Asher Dales didn't have *any* space-based maintenance facilities. Anything larger than a light cruiser would be in real trouble if she suffered a catastrophic systems failure. And there was no guarantee of getting help from the Commonwealth either. William disliked politics intensely, but he'd studied it enough to be sure that the Commonwealth would not be accepting new members anytime soon.

And besides, we need numbers, not firepower, he thought. *Our foes are not going to be flying in battleships and superdreadnoughts, but destroyers and frigates.*

"I have four destroyers here," the dealer said, reluctantly. "But they're quite old."

"They look suitable," William said. They weren't modern ships—the navy wouldn't be selling modern ships outside the Commonwealth—but they were suitable. Besides, they were also relatively easy to keep running. He'd seen similar ships survive and prosper despite the best efforts of their pirate crews. "We will, of course, have to go over them in cynical detail."

"Sir!" The dealer sounded offended. "They have CAB certificates."

"So they do," William agreed, lightly. He took the proffered data-pad without looking at it. "But we have to go over them anyway."

"I'll arrange a shuttle," the dealer said. "Is there anything else you need?"

"Weapons and a sizable number of spare parts," William said. "And at least one bulk freighter, armed."

The dealer's face fell. "Sir, they've been tightening up laws on armed freighters," he said slowly. "The government doesn't want . . ."

"Then a freighter with weapons mounts," William said. *That* wasn't good news. Despite the navy's best efforts, far too many freighters traveled without escort . . . and too many of them never came home. Piracy had been on the upswing even before the end of the war. Too many escort ships had had to be reassigned to the battle line. "Someone isn't thinking clearly."

"No, sir," the dealer said. "I'll see what I can do."

William grinned at Tanya. "I'll have to check out the ships," he said as the dealer hurried off. "Do you want to come with me or stay here?"

"I'll come," Tanya said. "It might be interesting."

The dealer returned. "This way," he called. "The shuttle's at the docks."

William took his chair and scanned the datapad as the shuttle undocked. The dealer had been telling the truth, unsurprisingly. All four destroyers had been checked before they'd been placed in long-term storage. William was mildly surprised they hadn't been broken down for recycling or simply sold for scrap; they *were* intact ships. They were worth more intact, if they could find a buyer. Besides, the navy had probably considered purchasing them for live-fire targets.

Tanya nudged his arm. "Did you manage to recruit crew?"

"A handful," William said. He'd reached out to a couple of old friends specifically, but the others had been contacted through recruitment agencies. "I'll have to interview them over the next few days."

He frowned as the shuttle docked with the first destroyer. That wasn't going to be easy, at least until he had a few trustworthy assistants to help with the hiring. He knew what to look for in naval crew, that wouldn't be a problem, but engineering and support staff were going to be a headache. Anyone who hadn't been snapped up by one of the bigger corporations was likely to have serious problems. An alcoholic, perhaps. William had no interest in hiring someone who might be more dangerous to his friends than his enemies.

The gravity shimmered slightly as the hatch opened. William felt his frown deepen. A mismatched gravity field or a sign of something far worse? He'd have to find out before they authorized the purchase . . .

"Let's go," he said. "Come on."

The dealer remained in the shuttle, to William's private relief, as they entered and inspected the destroyer. She was a small thing, only five decks; her energy weapons and missile tubes were active but outdated. William checked the computers, looking for obvious problems, then worked his way through the engineering section. Everything appeared to be outdated, but serviceable. There didn't seem to be any reason to reject the destroyer out of hand, but he'd have to make sure the life support, drives, and shields were checked and rechecked before money changed hands. Too much could go wrong too quickly for him to be willing to take chances with vital systems.

"It seems serviceable," he said finally, triggering the privacy generator. The dealer could easily use the destroyer's datanet to spy on his customers. "We will have to get a complete inspection team out here, but otherwise it looks good."

"And you have to check out the others," Tanya said ruefully. "I should have stayed behind, shouldn't I?"

William shrugged. "You need to know what you're buying," he said. "And you could easily get conned if you didn't know what to look for."

"I'll leave it in your capable hands," Tanya said. "If the four destroyers and the freighter are what you think we need, we'll buy them."

"As you wish," William said. "We'll also need to purchase a vast number of spare parts. A shortage at the worst possible time could doom us."

"I understand," Tanya said. Her lips thinned. "We do have to hurry, though. Have you seen the news reports?"

"Yeah," William sighed. He'd seen the reports and heard the rumors. "The navy could be withdrawn from Theocratic Space."

"And then Asher Dales will be unprotected," Tanya said. Her voice was very quiet, as if she didn't fully trust the privacy generator. "We need to get the ships in place before it's too late."

"We will," William assured her. "We'll make sure of it."

He took one last look around the destroyer as they made their way to the airlock. The dealer might be a sleazebag, but he knew his ships. It wouldn't take long to get the destroyer ready for space, once money had changed hands and she had a crew. They could reach Asher Dales in three weeks, if they pushed the drives hard . . .

"We might even be able to start sharing information with other worlds," he added thoughtfully. "The more pirates we can kill, the better."

"More will come," Tanya said.

William shook his head. "Pirates are basically cowards," he said. "They don't want to risk their ships and crew when it can be avoided. You just have to take out a few of them to make the others look elsewhere."

And if someone had made it clear to the Theocracy that they couldn't win the war, he added privately, *the entire war might never have been fought.*

CHAPTER FOUR

AHURA MAZDA

Kat had seen devastation before. She'd watched, helplessly, as enemy starships bombarded entire planets; she'd stared in horror as Hebrides had been turned into a radioactive wasteland. And yet, the crater in the ground where Government House had been was somehow worse. The hopes and dreams of an entire planet had died with Admiral Junayd.

She looked at General Winters, trying to keep her feelings under control. "There was a forcefield."

Winters looked grim. "The blast went off *inside* the forcefield," he said. "The post-battle assessment teams are already looking at the evidence, but it seems to me as though the forcefield actually trapped the blast and made matters worse."

"Fuck," Kat said. She could *smell* death on the air. "How did they even get a bomb past the security sensors?"

"I don't know," Winters said. "But I can guess."

Kat could guess too. Treason. Admiral Junayd had insisted on building up his own security forces as quickly as possible, pointing out that they'd work better with the local population than the Commonwealth Marines. Kat had reluctantly backed him, knowing that there would come a time, sooner rather than later, when the Commonwealth would have to hand the planet over to the provisional government. But all it took was a single traitor in a position of power to set the effort back years. It wouldn't even have to be a high-ranking traitor. A lone man in command of the sensors could let a bomb into the compound with minimal effort.

And he probably died in the blast, Kat thought. *Did he even know what he was smuggling in?*

She gritted her teeth as the wind blew stronger. The recruits had been tested—repeatedly—under lie detectors, and none of them had been working for the insurgents . . . not directly. But they hadn't been angels either. Admiral Junayd had been willing to accept a certain level of moral flexibility in exchange for loyalty. The troops hadn't committed atrocities on a regular basis, thankfully, but they'd had no qualms about smuggling or shaking prisoners down for funds. One of the smugglers had probably thought he was slipping drugs into Government House. This time, he'd been wrong.

Her heart clenched, just for a second. She'd never liked Admiral Junayd, and she hadn't wanted to trust him, but she'd come to believe that he meant well . . . that he *had* meant well for his people. There had been a certain amount of personal enrichment in there too. ONI had kept careful track of how Admiral Junayd had been rigging the provisional government to support his primacy, but by and large, he'd done a decent job. *And* he hadn't joined the factions that blamed the Commonwealth for the chaos.

He would be missed.

She allowed her eyes to sweep the blast zone as the recovery crews went to work, pulling out bodies and stacking them like cordwood by the side of the road. Marines followed, their eyes sweeping the streets for signs of trouble. The entire area had gone into lockdown, with the civilian population warned to stay inside and off the streets, but Kat was grimly aware that they could still be attacked at any moment. Captain Akbar Rosslyn, the commander of her close-protection detail, had made that very clear to her. If there was *anyone* on the planet more hated than

Admiral Junayd, it was Kat. The insurgents would spend their men like water if there was a chance of killing her.

Perhaps we should use me as bait, Kat thought morbidly.

She snorted at the thought, then turned her attention to the bodies. There were fewer than she'd expected, unsurprisingly. The blast would have destroyed the forcefield generator, of course, but there would have been a microsecond delay between the generator's destruction and the forcefield actually failing. Winters had been right. The blast would have been trapped, with nowhere to go. It was a minor miracle that so many bodies had survived intact. Admiral Junayd's corpse might never be recovered.

Winters checked his datapad. "Intelligence states that no less than seventeen groups have already claimed responsibility for the blast," he said. "So far, no actual confirmation."

Kat wasn't surprised. "Perhaps they'll go to war over it," she said. The insurgent factions hated each other almost as much as they hated the occupiers. She sometimes thought that the only thing keeping them from actually *winning* was that they spent half their time trying to take out their rivals instead of the common foe. "Do we have any solid leads?"

"Not yet," Winters said. "Perhaps not ever."

Kat nodded, sourly. In one sense, it simply didn't matter. The damage had been done. Government House was gone, the heart of the provisional government had been wiped out . . . and the occupiers had been made to look like weak fools, unable even to protect their collaborators. She didn't have to wonder how many others would start to edge away from the provisional government. She knew. *Everyone* would be reassessing their position, and some . . . some would start developing ties to the insurgents. It was hard to blame them too. They could hardly be expected to commit suicide for a government that couldn't even protect them.

"Have the families of the dead put through screening, then marked down for transport off-world," she ordered. In the distance, she heard the sound of guns. "They can set up somewhere else."

"If we can find somewhere willing to take them," Winters said.

Kat bit down a sharp reply. Winters was right. So many refugees were washing around what had once been the Theocracy that a few hundred more would *not* be warmly embraced. And these refugees would be coming directly from Ahura Mazda. They might be women and children, but they would still be about as welcome as a punch in the face.

"We will," she said, although she wasn't sure that was true. "Have your men . . ."

Another round of gunfire echoed over the city. A pair of helicopters, followed by a marine skimmer, flew overhead, heading for the sound of the guns. Kat tensed, expecting to see an HVM stabbing up to take out one of the helicopters, but there was nothing. Most of those weapons had been expended during the original invasion, although her intelligence staff kept picking up rumors of secret stockpiles that had only just been rediscovered by the insurgents. There was no way to be sure, but Kat suspected that all such stockpiles had been uncovered long ago. The insurgency desperately needed heavy weapons.

Captain Akbar Rosslyn hurried over to her side. "Admiral, there are reports of shootings closer, much closer," he said. "You really should head back to Commonwealth House."

Kat took a moment to compose herself. Rosslyn was a good man. It wasn't his fault that he wasn't Pat. But it still felt odd to be working next to a stranger. She hadn't made any attempt to get to know him . . . not, she acknowledged, that she should have done so. Pat had been her equal, or close to it, when they'd met. Rosslyn was so far beneath her that they might as well be on different planets. And yet, as her chief protector, he was very close to her.

41

And I sound like Candy, Kat thought ruefully. Her older sister was notorious for having affairs, including one with her bodyguard. *Rosslyn is doing his job.*

"Keep me informed," she ordered Winters. "I'll be in Commonwealth House."

Winters nodded. "I suggest we put all the local workers through another round of screenings," he said. "We have to be sure they're not under enemy control."

Kat sucked in her breath. There was one sure way to make someone untrustworthy . . . and that was to treat him as though he was untrustworthy. It was true on Tyre—her father had admitted, once, that he'd turned a loyal subordinate against him—and even more true on Ahura Mazda. Odd—before the invasion, a man could be arrested at the command of his superiors at will—but true. Interrogating the workers might simply create more enemies.

"Do it," she said reluctantly.

She turned and followed Rosslyn back to the armored car. The streets between Commonwealth House and Government House—what *remained* of Government House—were supposed to be safe, but there was no point in taking chances. She shouldn't have come here at all, as Rosslyn had pointed out. But Kat had known she needed to see the blast zone with her own eyes. It was the only way to grasp the scale of their failure. Admiral Junayd was only one man, had only *been* one man, but too many dreams had died with him.

The vehicle hummed into life as soon as the door was closed, outriders moving into position to provide covering fire if they came under attack. Kat took a moment to center herself, then reached for the datapad to check the reports. Her staff did their best to filter things that could be better handled at a lower level, but there were still hundreds of messages coming in every hour on the hour. The planet never slept.

She forced herself to work until the vehicle turned into Commonwealth House and drove straight into the secure garage. The marines saluted her as she exited, although Rosslyn and his men looked as if they wouldn't be happy until she was in her office. Kat returned the salutes, then took the lift straight to the upper levels. Perhaps there was a chance to grab a mug of coffee before the next meeting.

I really need to get back on a command deck, she thought. *It would be so much simpler.*

"Admiral," Kitty said, as Kat stepped into the antechamber. "Commodore Higgins requested a holoconference at your earliest convenience."

"Ah," Kat said. Commodore Fran Higgins wasn't known for jumping at shadows. "Set up the call in my office, then bring me some coffee."

"Aye, Admiral," Kitty said. "You're also scheduled for meetings with . . ."

Kat held up a hand. "I'll deal with them later," she said, tiredly. Her afternoon schedule was full. Of *course* it was full. Meeting after meeting after meeting . . . was she actually doing *any* good at all? Or was she simply wasting away? "Have some lunch sent up as well, please. I think I'm going to need it."

"Aye, Admiral."

Kat rubbed her forehead as she stepped into her office, feeling a headache starting to form behind her temples. The office was immense, bigger even than a flag officer's quarters on a superdreadnought . . . She couldn't help wondering, sourly, if she'd made a mistake in accepting it. She didn't have to show off her status, either as a fleet admiral or privy councilor. Everyone who was anyone already knew who she was.

And some of them see me as their meal ticket, she thought crossly. She'd met a handful of sycophants in the navy, yet there were entire departments in the civilian sphere that seemed to be composed of nothing *but* sycophants. *They think they can ride me to heights of power they couldn't reach by doing their damn jobs.*

Commodore Fran Higgins's image appeared in front of her. "Admiral," she said. "Thank you for seeing me."

"You're welcome," Kat said, sitting down at her desk. "I trust things are well with the squadron?"

Fran frowned. "Unfortunately, Admiral, that was what I intended to raise with you."

Kat looked up, studying the older woman. Fran's career had nearly been destroyed by her former commander, one of Admiral Morrison's sycophants. She might have lost everything if the Theocracy hadn't attacked Cadiz, giving her a chance to save her ship and crew from enemy fire. The commendations she'd earned for preserving her super-dreadnought, and the desperate need for experienced officers, had ensured that her career continued to prosper.

"I see," Kat said. The last set of reports had insisted there weren't any problems, beyond a shortage of suitable shore leave facilities. "Is there an issue?"

"I received instructions to prepare to transfer two destroyer squadrons back to the Commonwealth," Fran said. "Apparently they're not going to be replaced."

Kat winced. "I haven't heard anything about it," she said. "Let me see . . ."

She reached for her datapad. Had she missed an update? Or hadn't it been sent to her in the first place? Technically, *she* was the senior officer in the sector, but Fran was in command of the task force. Fran should have been bumped up to admiral when the responsibilities had fallen on her . . . Kat wasn't sure why she hadn't been. Politics, probably. Anyone who reached high rank in the navy was either extremely well connected or the client of someone who was. But Fran wasn't anyone's client.

Unless she's mine, Kat thought, flicking through the message headers. There didn't seem to be anything relating to fleet deployment. *And that would link her to my entire family.*

She shook her head. "Nothing," she said. "What's the deadline?"

"Two months," Fran said. "They want me to send out the recall orders now."

"Hold them for a day," Kat ordered after a moment's thought. "I'll contact the Admiralty and ask for . . . *clarification*."

"Please do," Fran said. "Admiral, if we have to strip eighteen destroyers out of our line of battle . . ."

Kat nodded, irritated. She knew the dangers. The two squadrons of superdreadnoughts orbiting Ahura Mazda were not designed to escort freighters, hunt pirates, or even patrol the fringes of explored space. The navy might as well swat flies with sledgehammers. No, escorting and patrol duties required a large number of destroyers, frigates, and cruisers, not superdreadnoughts. Cutting eighteen destroyers out of the task force and sending them home would put a severe crimp in the task force's ability to operate. Even recalling them to Ahura Mazda, prior to sending them home, would be inconvenient.

"Don't recall them immediately," she said. She wasn't going to order escorts to simply abandon the ships they were supposed to be accompanying. "I want them to complete their current missions first."

"Aye, Admiral," Fran said.

"But cut orders for them to return here once their missions are completed," Kat added after a moment. She could stall for a few days, perhaps even a couple of weeks, but after that she would have no choice. She'd have to send the ships home. "Orders are orders . . ."

She cleared her throat. "I take it there's been no sudden upswing in pirate activity?"

"No, Admiral," Fran said. "There were a handful of raids along the fringe, but nothing too serious. The *real* problem, right now, is providing security for refugee transports, keeping in mind we need to *provide* the refugee transports. And we have no idea where to put half of them."

Kat made a face. "I wish I knew," she said. "This world seems intent on tearing itself apart."

Fran met her eyes. "Did you read Captain Bartholomew's report? From Judd?"

"Yes," Kat said. "He didn't paint a pretty picture."

"It won't be long before the lid blows off," Fran said. "And then there will be bloodshed."

Kat nodded. The Theocracy hadn't just left behind troops and administrative staff. It had left behind collaborators, true believers . . . and their families. Some people had genuinely believed in the True Faith, others had merely pretended to accept it as the price for survival . . . and now that the war was over, there was no place for either type. None of the liberated worlds wanted to keep their collaborators. Kat had no sympathy for men who'd gloried in the opportunity to lord it over their fellows, but . . . what about their families? Or the ones who'd had no choice? Did they all deserve to die?

And yet, we don't have anywhere to put them, she thought. *No world wants to take them . . .*

"We may wind up having to expand settlements here," she said. "At least the occupiers know about keeping a planet running."

"Don't count on it," Fran said. "Judd was a very fertile world before the Theocrats arrived. Now they're struggling to feed themselves. A decade of mismanagement led to a near-complete collapse in production."

Which helped to keep the population under control, Kat thought sourly. The Theocrats had had no compunction about brutalizing Ahura Mazda's population. Why should they have hesitated to brutalize infidels? *No wonder their occupations were so horrific. Their troops knew no better.*

She looked up as Kitty entered the room, carrying a tray of coffee and biscuits. "I'll speak to you later," she told Fran. "And inform me at once if you receive any further directives."

Fran's image vanished. Kat glared down at her hands. The Admiralty should *not* be sending instructions to her subordinates without copying her, even if Fran was the task force's commander. Kat was in charge of the sector . . . what would have happened, she asked herself silently, if she'd started making plans that depended on those destroyers? The sector's economy was a mess in any case. Taking away eighteen destroyers would only make it worse.

She nodded to Kitty. "Contact Tyre," she said. "Inform them that I require an urgent conference with the king."

"Aye, Admiral," Kitty said. "Do you want to cancel your afternoon meetings?"

Kat tapped the datapad, bringing up the schedule. "Yes," she said. She had a feeling that the conference would go on for some time. Besides, none of the meetings were particularly important. Everyone involved could get some work done for a change. "Cancel the first two and place the third on the back burner."

"Aye, Admiral."

CHAPTER FIVE

Uncharted Star System

There was nothing to recommend the star system to anyone, save for a handful of orbiting asteroids and a couple of comets that had gone unremarked during the first and last official visit by a survey ship. A dull red star marked the system as practically useless, as far as the Theocracy was concerned. There was certainly no large population of unbelievers to enslave for the greater glory of God. The only people who might be interested in the system were pirates, smugglers, and colonists who wanted to remain undiscovered. It didn't even have a *name*!

We'll have to fix that, Admiral Zaskar thought, as *Righteous Revenge* made her slow way towards the asteroids. *Perhaps something with the proper tone.*

He kept a wary eye on the display, expecting enemy icons to pop into existence at any moment. The long-range passive sensors were picking up nothing that might suggest there was any technological presence in the system, but he knew better than to take that for granted. Commonwealth cloaking technology had been dangerously advanced even before his remaining sensor nodes had begun to decay. It was quite possible, as some of his officers had pointed out, that they might be flying directly into a trap. But he'd chosen to take the risk. They didn't have much choice.

"Hold position on the edge of the asteroid cluster," Askew said. The mystery agent had shown no signs of discomfort on the superdreadnought, even though the ship's slow collapse had to be obvious. "We'll take a shuttle into the base."

Admiral Zaskar gave him a sharp look. "Did your . . . *backers* . . . build this for us?"

"I'm afraid not," Askew said. "The settlement originally belonged to a bunch of colonists who launched themselves into space to find paradise. They hollowed out one of the asteroids and established a colony, only to discover that they were short on practically everything they needed to live. The last of them passed away twenty years ago. My backers made a careful note of the colony's location for future use."

"And no one else knows about it," Admiral Zaskar said.

"As far as we know," Askew assured him. "There weren't many records left behind."

Admiral Zaskar scowled. He wasn't sure he believed the story, not completely. There were thousands of colonies, mainly asteroid settlements, which existed off the books, but they were alarmingly close to the Theocracy. He found it hard to imagine an isolationist group that wanted to remain unnoticed setting up shop here. And yet, he had to admit they might have been right. The unnamed system had attracted no interest, even during the height of the war.

A pirate base would be more believable, he thought. *But too many people would know where to find it.*

"Hold position," he ordered the helmsman. "And have my private shuttle prepared."

Askew looked impatient, the first genuine emotion Admiral Zaskar had seen on his face, but he waited quietly while the shuttle was prepared. Zaskar was mildly surprised. Any experienced spacer would have known that prep could have been done more quickly if the crews had started work before they reached their destination. But then, he'd been determined to sweep as much of the dull system as possible before risking exposure. An enemy force lurking under cloak might just give itself away . . .

"We'll go," he said to Moses. "Are you coming?"

"Of course," Moses said.

Admiral Zaskar tried to keep the tension off his face as they made their way to the shuttle and cast off, heading straight for the asteroid. Askew took the controls, handling the craft with a grace and precision that suggested he'd flown such a vessel before; Admiral Zaskar resisted, barely, the temptation to ask Askew *where* he'd flown before. It didn't have to be in the Theocracy, he had to admit. The shuttle design had been stolen from New Washington and put into mass production. Askew could have flown such shuttles anywhere.

"There are actually four habitable asteroids," Askew commented, steering a course towards the nearest. "One was designed for constant rotation, but we canceled the spin when we took control. It would have been far too revealing. The other three were mined for raw materials and later converted into living space. They never had gravity in the first place."

"That may be an advantage," Admiral Zaskar commented. "We're going to have to refit the ships anyway."

"And reload with newer weapons," Askew told him. The asteroid came closer, a bulky shadow looming against the darkness. "Give me a moment . . ."

His fingers worked the console, sending an IFF code. There was a pause, just long enough for Admiral Zaskar to wonder if something had gone wrong, then a chink of light appeared on the side of the asteroid. He leaned forward, trying to see as much as possible, as the light rapidly expanded into a giant hatch. Inside, he could see a handful of crude machines predating the Theocracy, he thought, and a number of crates lashed to the rocky wall. A giant hangar bay . . .

"Here we go," Askew said. He steered the shuttle inside and gently landed it on the deck. Low vibrations ran through the craft as the hatch slid closed. "We'll have to wait a few moments for the chamber to pressurize."

Admiral Zaskar glanced at him. "No forcefield?"

"No," Askew said. "I believe the original founders didn't have forcefields."

"It doesn't matter," Moses said. "As long as the supplies you've promised us are here . . ."

"They are," Askew said. The hatch popped open. "As you can see, we've been ready for quite some time."

But you needed to find us, Admiral Zaskar thought, as he followed Askew through the hatch and took a deep breath. The air smelled fresh. *That must have taken longer than you hoped.*

He took another breath as the shuttle's gravity field faded away. It had been years since he'd exercised in zero-g, but the body never forgot. He found himself smiling as Askew took hold of the nearest handhold and led the way towards a distant hatch. It felt good to relax, just for a moment, and smell the clean air. The asteroid base might be old, but it wasn't on the verge of breaking apart. His superdreadnought might never smell so well again.

"In here," Askew said, opening the hatch. "I think you'll like what you see."

Lights came on, so bright that Admiral Zaskar winced. Inside, the chamber was *crammed* with supplies . . . *Theocratic* supplies. He stared in disbelief, trying to understand what it meant. Someone had raided a supply dump . . . or was *this* a supply dump? The asteroid settlement might easily have been raided by the Theocracy, once upon a time. Or . . . his mind spun as he tried to understand what he was seeing. The supplies in front of him were familiar.

He pulled himself after Askew. "Where the hell did you get these?"

"It's a long story," Askew said. "Suffice it to say that they fell into our hands."

Admiral Zaskar glared, but Askew refused to be drawn any further. Instead, he led them on a brief tour of the asteroid, pointing out supply rooms, refreshment chambers, and everything else they needed to repair and operate the fleet. Admiral Zaskar doubted his forces would be able to keep the fleet going indefinitely—there was a distinct shortage of machine tools and anything else that might make them self-sufficient—but the supplies would definitely give them a new lease on life. They might even be able to survive long enough for the Commonwealth to withdraw.

"Well?" Askew smiled at them. "What do you think?"

"A gift from God," Moses said.

Admiral Zaskar wasn't so impressed. "But at what price?"

"I told you," Askew said, patiently. "Keep the Commonwealth tied down."

"We have no choice," Moses said. "We accept your offer."

"But first, we have to repair and rearm our ships," Admiral Zaskar said before Moses could promise an immediate attack on Ahura Mazda. The last report had stated there were four enemy superdreadnought squadrons based there. His ships wouldn't stand a chance if they risked an engagement. "And then we can begin our campaign."

"Yes, Admiral," Moses said. "But at least we have hope!"

His words echoed in Admiral Zaskar's thoughts as his crews sprang to work, some reopening the older asteroids while others transferred the spare parts and weapons to the fleet. He felt *good* being able to throw out old components once again, even though Admiral Zaskar was ruefully aware they could probably be repaired with the right tools.

Slowly, day after day, his fleet started to heal. Once his missile tubes were reloaded, he even became a little more confident in his ability to win an engagement against a numerically equal force.

And yet, the question of just who Askew actually worked for hung in his mind, taunting him while he tried to sleep. Askew couldn't be a Theocrat, no matter how he looked; he simply didn't have the attitude of someone who'd grown up in the Theocracy. And yet, he'd either liberated an old supply dump or transferred the supplies to the base from somewhere else. But where? Admiral Zaskar had assumed that they'd be given spare parts with no fixed origin, but instead they'd been given Theocratic spare parts. The more he thought about it, the more he wondered: Could Askew be working for someone in the Commonwealth?

It made no sense, yet . . . the thought refused to go away. The Theocracy hadn't been able to sell spare parts on the galactic market before the war, hadn't even been able to *give* them away. So where had the spare parts come from? If the Commonwealth had overrun a supply depot, the supplies could have been sold onwards . . . but who would buy them? Even the missiles weren't worth that much on the market. Pirates were about the only people who'd want them. Anyone else could buy more advanced weapons on the open market.

If someone in the Commonwealth is backing us, he thought, *why?*

He tried not to think about it as he inspected his fleet, stalking the decks and listening to the commanding officers as they assured him that their ships were ready for battle. He'd tried hard to impress upon his subordinates that he preferred honesty to worthless promises, but he didn't know just how well the lesson had taken. Too many commanders had grown up knowing that they could be executed for failing to accomplish the impossible. Even Admiral Zaskar himself once had problems. But they could no longer afford to force men to choose between lying or losing their heads. They were at war, in dire straits.

"Well," he said a week later, "we seem to have made a *reasonable* start."

He allowed his eyes to survey the compartment. He'd invited his commanding officers to attend, either in person or via hologram. He was oddly gratified to see how many had chosen to attend in person, despite the claims on their time.

"Our ships are generally in better condition now," he added. It would be a long time before they were back to peak form, if indeed they ever were, but at least they were on the way. The cynic in him noted that they might last *five* minutes, instead of one, if they encountered a numerically equal force. "And our crews are well fed for the first time in weeks."

"They've certainly started attending services again," Moses commented. He was about the only person who would dare interrupt the fleet's commanding officer. "God has truly blessed us."

"Indeed he has," Admiral Zaskar agreed, concealing his annoyance. He was the fleet's commanding officer, but who knew which way his subordinates would jump if he moved against the cleric? "However, the question now is simple. Where do we strike first?"

Captain Yam hit the table with his fist. "We recover the home-world," he snarled. "Let us kick the unbelievers off our land and . . ."

"That would be suicide," Captain Abraham said. "The enemy is too strong."

"God is with us," Captain Yam snapped. One hand dropped to the dagger at his belt. "Or are you afraid to place your faith in Him?"

"That's the kind of thinking that cost us the war," Captain Abraham snapped. "Do you want to throw away everything we've done, for nothing?"

Admiral Zaskar tapped the table before an actual fight could break out. Captain Yam was a brave man and a terror to his crew, but he rarely bothered to think; Captain Abraham genuinely *did* think, which had earned him some attention from the inquisitors before the war had come to a sudden and catastrophic end. They went together like fire and gunpowder.

"I have no intention of wasting this opportunity," Zaskar said firmly. "And we do not have the firepower to win a stand-up fight against four enemy superdreadnought squadrons."

He met Captain Yam's eyes, daring him to disagree. It wasn't just the raw numbers, although thirty-six superdreadnoughts could pump out enough missiles in a single broadside to utterly obliterate his fleet.

The enemy's technology, everything from sensors to point defense and missile targeting, was generally *better*.

And if I retreat, my crews will grow discontented and my subordinates will plot my overthrow, he thought. Their sheer ignorance was a terrifying problem. *The captains have to understand that we have to play our cards carefully.*

He keyed the console, bringing up an image. "Judd," he said. "If the latest intelligence reports are to be believed, Judd still plays host to a considerable population of loyalists. They are held down, of course, by the new government, but they yearn to be free. I think we should give them that opportunity."

"It is our duty," Moses agreed.

"We will leave here in two days, taking every ship that can make the journey," Admiral Zaskar continued. "We will, of course, attempt to escape detection while we're in hyperspace, particularly when we cross the shipping lanes. We don't want to accidentally lead the searchers back to our base. Once we arrive at our destination, we will carefully recon the system to make sure the enemy hasn't assigned a large covering force, then move in and engage the enemy. We will not, of course, take prisoners."

He smiled, coldly. The last report insisted that the enemy had only stationed a trio of light cruisers in the system. That might have changed, of course, but he doubted it. Judd was practically friendly territory, as far as the unbelievers were concerned. The vast majority of the locals were unbelievers themselves, while the believers had been rounded up and placed in concentration camps. There was no need to assign a large garrison to police the planet's surface. The locals could do that for themselves.

But not for long, he told himself. Three light cruisers would be no match for his fleet, unless they had some utterly insane weapons system that he'd never imagined. It was possible, he supposed, but unlikely. The Commonwealth had produced a great many new weapons systems during the war, yet most of them had really been nothing more than improvements and upgrades of previous designs. *Once we get into firing range, those cruisers are doomed.*

"We will land troops, briefly," he added. "Our goal will be to free the prisoners and cause havoc, *not* to occupy the planet. We will fall back as soon as that goal is achieved. By the time enemy reinforcements arrive, we will be long gone."

He looked around the table, silently picking out the men he *knew* were going to cause problems. The fanatics, the power hungry, the ones who thought they could do better than him . . . they'd always been a problem, but now it was far worse. There just wasn't any way to keep them under control. Half the internal security systems were still offline.

"We will depart in two days," he reminded them. "If there are any problems, I want to know about it. This is war, not an opportunity for personal glory. I expect you, each and every one of you, to remember that. Our goal is nothing less than the restoration of the Theocracy and the reinstatement of the True Faith. Dying gloriously will not serve our goal. Dismissed."

He sat back and watched them leave, wondering again which ones were going to disobey him. It was easy to think that glory was the way to power. Here, they might be right. The Theocracy no longer existed, save in the hearts and minds of his crew. There was no force capable of preventing them from putting someone more energetic into the command chair . . .

"You seem confident," Askew observed. He hadn't moved from his chair. "Are you sure you can hit Judd?"

"It's a convenient target," Admiral Zaskar told him. The Commonwealth had raided Theocratic space repeatedly during the war. Now the boot was going to be on the other foot. Let *them* run around trying to smash raiding parties for a change. "Some distance from us, of course, but barely defended."

"Unless that's changed," Askew said.

"We'll see any reinforcements before they see us," Admiral Zaskar assured him. "And if they have sent a squadron of superdreadnoughts to protect the planet, we'll back off."

"Good thinking," Askew said. He lowered his voice. "Will you survive?"

Admiral Zaskar smirked, understanding the real question. "Survive my own people? We will see."

CHAPTER SIX

TYRE

"Well," William said, "we have ships, and we have crews."

Tanya studied the manifest he held out to her. He'd moved himself and his possessions, one carryall of clothes and datachips, to HMS *Dandelion* as soon as the sale had been concluded and the destroyer handed over to her new crew. The captain's quarters, which doubled as the ready room, were tiny, but at least they were *his*. Besides, he hadn't had much time to make use of his bunk. When he hadn't been recruiting crewmen, he'd been supervising the engineers as they checked and rechecked every last component. Tanya looked a little out of place on the ship but never complained. William was tempted to ask why she'd never joined the navy herself.

She looked up. "Are they *good* crews?"

"I believe so," William said. He knew some of the officers and crewers he'd recruited personally. The others had taken a little more care. He'd read their files carefully—evidently, Asher Dales had an agreement with the Commonwealth allowing a certain level of access—and contacted their former commanding officers for references. They were all good crewers. "They certainly know their jobs."

And they're experienced, he added to himself. *The crew may drink, or set up illicit stills, but they won't let things get out of hand.*

He allowed himself a tight smile, even though he knew there was still a great deal of work to do. He hadn't felt so happy since . . . since he'd stood on the bridge of his first command, back before the mission to Jorlem. *Unlucky—Uncanny*, he reminded himself sharply—had been in poor condition, but she'd been his. The four destroyers and one freighter he'd purchased for Asher Dales were in a better state, while their crews had practically been handpicked. He might no longer have access to the vast supply network that had kept the Royal Navy functioning, but having sole command more than made up for it. He'd taken care to purchase all the supplies he'd need to keep the squadron running for three to five years.

"As long as you trust them," Tanya said. She looked around the tiny compartment. "I don't know anything about naval affairs."

"Which makes you smarter than far too many lawyers I've had to deal with," William said truthfully. Tanya would probably have made a pretty fair lawyer if she hadn't been called back to her homeworld, a homeworld she'd admitted she barely remembered. "Suffice it to say that we should have enough firepower to deal with plausible threats."

Tanya lifted her eyebrows. "*Plausible* threats?"

"Well, we won't be able to do much if the sector is invaded by aliens," William said dryly. "Or if one of the other Great Powers goes fishing in troubled waters."

He looked at the holographic starchart for a long moment. It was hard to be sure, as he'd never been able to follow politics on Tyre, not when he hadn't been raised on the corporate world, but it looked as though a number of politicians wanted to withdraw the navy from the Theocratic Sector. Not a reassuring thought. William knew his destroyers could handle pirates, if any of them came knocking, but not a larger threat. The remnants of the Theocratic Navy were out there somewhere. William liked to think that their poor maintenance habits had finally caught up with them and their ships had broken down in interstellar space, but he couldn't allow himself to believe it. And while the Commonwealth had no interest in a little expansion, whatever the locals thought, there *were* other interstellar powers out there. One or more of them might see advantage in snapping up the liberated worlds before they developed space-based defenses and industries of their own.

"Then it's better to depart now," Tanya said. "We're not going to get there in a hurry, are we?"

"*Dandelion* and *Primrose* will reach Asher Dales in three weeks, unless something goes wrong with the drives," William told her simply. "*Lily*, *Petunia*, and *Macdonald* will take longer."

He concealed his annoyance with an effort. The *Flower*-class destroyers were good ships, even if they were slightly outdated. They'd been the fastest things in space in their day. But now, two of them had to be detached to escort the freighter. *Macdonald* was armed, but William had no illusions. She wouldn't be any match for a pirate ship with a brave or desperate crew.

And if they knew what the freighter was carrying, they'd take whatever risks they had to take to get their paws on her, William reminded himself. *They'll be desperate for top-of-the-line spare parts.*

"I'll be traveling with you, of course," Tanya said. "Or would you rather I stayed on the freighter?"

"You won't see much difference," William told her wryly. "The freighter cabins are even smaller than *our* cabins."

Tanya's lips curved into a smile. "Impossible."

"Believe it," William said. He'd earmarked a cabin for her, the second-largest on the ship. It still didn't have enough room to swing a cat. She was lucky she wasn't a midshipwoman. The midshipman quarters were so tiny that only one person could move about at any one time. Everyone else had to stay in their bunks and pray they weren't late to their duty stations. "Bring your kit and anything else you want onto the ship by 1700."

He made a show of checking his wristcom. "We'll be leaving at 1900. If you're not aboard, we'll go without you."

"That would be embarrassing," Tanya said, deadpan.

William snorted. It would be more than *merely* embarrassing. An officer or crewman who missed the deadline for returning, who was left behind when his ship departed, would be in deep shit.

"I don't have much to bring," Tanya assured him, standing. "And I have it all at Orbit Station."

"Just remember we do have mass limits," William said. The last transport he'd traveled on had been crammed with civilians bitching about the mass limit. They hadn't realized that the starship had only limited space. Thankfully, experienced spacers generally knew better. "And don't try to evade customs."

Tanya laughed and left the compartment. William watched her go, then turned his attention back to the datapad. The final set of checks had been completed, some under his personal supervision; there were no problems, as far as his crews could tell, with the destroyers. But it would only be a matter of time before *something* developed. William had been a spacer long enough to know that a component would wear out or someone would make a mistake in the listings or . . . *something* . . . that would cause problems. And then . . . he'd just have to pray it was a problem they could fix. Being without the supply line was going to be a major headache.

Which means I've probably forgotten something, he thought sourly. He looked down at the manifests, tiredly. They'd need something they hadn't thought to bring. Years of experience convinced him of it. And yet, what? There was no way to know. *We'll just have to wait and see.*

His terminal chimed, loudly. "Captain?" Commander Patti Ludwig sounded as tired as William felt. "Captain Young requests a holoconference."

"Put him through," William said. "And then contact System Command and inform them that we wish to confirm our departure time."

"Aye, sir."

William leaned forward as the starchart blinked out of existence, to be replaced by Captain Gary Young's head. He was a strikingly handsome young man, at least in appearance; his navy file made it clear that he was only five years younger than William himself. William wasn't sure what to make of Young's vanity—he seemed to spend half his salary on cosmetic rejuvenation—but there was no denying his competence. His red hair and too-perfect face masked a very sharp mind. William would never have hired him if he'd had the slightest doubt of Young's skills.

"Commodore," Young said.

"Captain," William said. He was both *Dandelion*'s commanding officer and the squadron commander. It wasn't something he could maintain forever, particularly if Asher Dales started to grow a bigger navy, but for the moment he was happy to wear both hats. "What can I do for you?"

"Well, I'd *like* a battlecruiser and perhaps a few more freighters filled with supplies," Young said, "but I'm really calling to confirm that we will be ready to depart as planned."

"Good," William said curtly. He'd like a battlecruiser too. "Did you manage to link up with a convoy?"

"Yes, sir," Young said. "We'll be traveling to Cadiz with Convoy Golf-Echo-Nine, then proceeding through the Gap to Maxwell's Haven with Convoy Sierra-Alpha-Three. After that, we're on our own. They pulled too many ships off the front lines to search for *Supreme*."

William winced. A cruise liner, even one the size of a superdreadnought, was tiny on an interstellar scale. The odds of finding her were so low that . . . that William had greater odds of being declared King of Tyre and Emperor of the Galaxy. If pirates had taken *Supreme*, the ransom demands would have started to come in by now. Far more likely the ship had suffered a catastrophic failure in hyperspace and either been destroyed or made a crash-transition back into realspace. And if she'd lost her vortex generators, she wouldn't have a hope of reaching the nearest inhabited planet before life support failed.

But the navy can't say that to the rich and powerful aristocrats who had family on the liner, he reminded himself. *They have to make a show of hunting for her, even though they know it's useless.*

"There's no immediate hurry," he said. He would have preferred to use all four destroyers to escort the freighter, but he didn't like the way things were going in Parliament. Better to have two destroyers on station before it was too late. "That freighter has got to be protected."

"I understand, sir," Young said. "I shall guard her with my life."

"Very good," William said. "And I expect you to avoid engagement, if possible. No heroics."

"Yes, sir," Young said.

He didn't sound disappointed, William noted wryly. But then, any *sensible* naval officer would know better than to go *looking* for trouble when they were on escort duty. The convoys tended to attract trouble. Pirates knew better than to engage escorted freighters, but the Theocracy had managed to take out a number of supply convoys during the early days of the war. Their efforts hadn't been wasted, William conceded. They'd probably prolonged the war by several months.

"There is another point," Young said. "I heard . . . I heard that the dealers were facing new regulations on what they can and can't sell to foreign governments."

"So far, nothing seems to have firmed up," William said slowly. Asher Dales was, technically, an ally, but Tyre seemed to be having second thoughts about selling modern technology to anyone. Parliament was starting to think of the Commonwealth and the liberated worlds as potential rivals rather than allies. It didn't bode well. "Still, we need to secure as much as possible before it's too late."

"Yes, sir," Young said. "But are *we* foreigners?"

William hesitated. *He* might be a colonial, but Young wasn't. He'd been born and raised on Tyre. And yet . . . he'd taken service with a foreign government. William didn't think there was any prospect of Asher Dales going to war against Tyre, but technically . . . He shook his head, dismissing the thought. The little squadron had obtained the proper clearances to go to Asher Dales and join the fledgling navy. That was all that mattered.

"They don't want to sell their most advanced technology to anyone," he said curtly, using his annoyance to hide his own misgivings. They weren't doing anything wrong, or illegal, but they weren't in the navy any longer either. "But we don't need it to swat pirates."

"It still feels odd," Young complained.

William smiled, humorlessly. "Welcome to life on the poverty level," he said. Tyre was a rich world. The aristocrats could purchase a squadron of superdreadnoughts out of pocket change. Asher Dales was lucky to be able to scrape up enough cash to buy and equip four destroyers and a freighter. "You were on half pay when I snapped you up. Do you want to go back to it?"

"No," Young said quickly. "But it just feels *off.*"

"I know," William said. "But you will have to cope with it."

He smiled, rather thinly, as Young's image vanished. Young had never lived anywhere but Tyre. He probably didn't understand, at an emotional level, the realities of life on a rougher world. Or, for that matter, how people in distant offices could make decisions that wreaked havoc on defenseless planets. William doubted the restrictions on tech transfers would cause any immediate problems, not for him and his little squadron, but they might cause all sorts of issues in the future. Such limitations would hamper Asher Dales and the other liberated worlds as they sought to take control of their destinies.

But they have a long way to go before that becomes a problem, he told himself. *First, they have to survive.*

He spent the next few hours reading through the final reports from the four destroyers and the freighter, then downloading news bulletins from the planetary datanet and reading them too. It looked as though no one could make up their minds about *anything*, although there was no shortage of talking heads ready to expound on The Meaning of It All. William read through one explanation, noted that the writer clearly knew nothing about the realities of naval life, and dismissed the rest of the bulletin unread. Whoever was running the news service wasn't interested in *facts*. There was no shortage of officers on half pay who'd be happy to supplement their income by writing articles for the media companies.

Tanya returned to the ship on time, to his private amusement. He checked on her as she settled into her cabin, reminding her to spend time in VR simulations or something else that might distract her from the bulkheads pressing in, then hurried to the bridge. It was tiny, compared to *Uncanny*'s, but still the nerve center of the ship. He sat down in the command chair and surveyed his kingdom. The weight of command responsibility fell around him like a shroud.

I never thought I'd command a ship again, William thought. Losing two ships in quick succession and suffering the first mutiny on a naval starship had blotted his record beyond repair. The mutiny hadn't been his fault, and the inquest had made that clear, but he'd been lucky beyond words to get a second command. *And I won't lose this one.*

He sucked in his breath. "Engineering, power up the drives."

"Aye, sir."

William smiled as he felt a low rumble echo through the ship. They'd powered up the drives before, just to make sure they were in working order, but this was *real*. He watched the power curves form on his display, the drive fields readying themselves to push the ship out of orbit, and felt his smile widen. He'd been deluding himself, when he'd gone to live with his people. A starship command deck was where he belonged.

"XO, signal System Command," he ordered. "Inform them that we are ready to depart."

"Aye, sir," Patti said.

William tapped his console, bringing up the near-space display. Tyre was surrounded by green and blue icons: hundreds of orbiting asteroids, thousands of military and civilian starships coming and going. It was hard to be sure, but he thought there were fewer civilian starships than he'd expected. The economy was having problems transitioning back to a peacetime footing. He grimaced. No wonder the politicians were considering cutting their military commitments. The end of the war had brought a severe drop in tax revenue.

And they can't rely on the Commonwealth to soak up much of their production, he thought. He didn't pretend to understand how the interstellar economy worked. Every explanation he'd heard sounded like a junior officer's attempt to explain just what he'd been thinking to an annoyed superior after his bright idea had gone spectacularly wrong. *No wonder so many spacers are out of work.*

"System Command has cleared us to depart, sir," Patti reported.

"Very good," William said. "Helm, take us out of orbit. When we reach the gateway point, take us into hyperspace."

"Aye, sir."

"And then set course for Asher Dales," William added.

"Aye, sir."

William settled back in his command chair as *Dandelion* moved out of orbit, *Primrose* following at her heels. The destroyer wasn't a heavy cruiser, but she was *his*. He was the last of the absolute monarchs, as long as he sat on her command deck. Tanya wanted him to train up local officers and crew to take his place, but it would be a long time before he stepped down. He felt a flicker of pity for Kat. She should never have let them promote her to flag rank. How could she command a starship now?

A shame she can't join us, he thought sincerely. *But her family will never let her go.*

CHAPTER SEVEN

TYRE

Peter Falcone had never liked his father's business office. It was immense, yet empty: a single desk, a large window overlooking Tyre City, and a handful of expensive paintings on the walls. There was none of the charm and elegance of his father's private office, or even the homeliness of Peter's original office. Its only role was to impress guests and, perhaps, host people Lucas Falcone hadn't wanted to take into his private office. Peter rather suspected that the two men facing him fell into that category.

He kept his face carefully blank as he studied the two men. His father had hired them personally, buying out their firm, Masterly and Masterly, to ensure that he had sole call on their services. Peter wasn't sure how he felt about that. Alexander and Clive Masterly were good and experienced men, according to his father's private files, but he'd never been able to escape the sense that they were always keeping their eyes open for ways to exploit matters to their own advantage. Peter's own people hadn't been able to dig up any evidence, one way or the other, yet that was meaningless. The network of financial transactions that made up the heart of the Falcone Corporation was so complex that anyone with the right access could hide a money transfer, or something more subtle, and be reasonably sure it wouldn't be noticed.

And anyone with that sort of access would know if we carried out an audit, he thought. *By the time we had proof, they'd be halfway to Marseilles.*

"Very well," he said, stiffly. "Please, explain it to me."

Alexander Masterly leaned forward. He was a dapper man in a neat business suit, with a rather large nose. Alexander was established enough not to have to care what he looked like.

"We have been carrying out a prolonged financial assessment of the corporation and its subunits over the last two months," Alexander said. He had an aristocratic burr to his voice, although it was strong enough for Peter to be reasonably sure it was an affectation. The two men had been born commoners. "Our conclusions have been extensively detailed . . ."

"Summarize them," Peter snapped. "What is the problem?"

Alexander tapped a switch. A giant holographic chart shimmered into existence. It looked like a galaxy, featuring hundreds of planets orbiting countless stars, but it was in fact far more detailed. Peter sucked in a breath as he studied the image, feeling a flicker of the old awe. The hologram in front of him *was* the Falcone Corporation, from the industries owned directly by the family to the sidelines, from people who worked for the family to a network of clients who didn't know where their patronage chains actually ended. It was hard, even for someone who'd grown up surrounded by wealth and power, to trace the tangled threads from one end of the display to the other. Peter didn't know how his father had endured his role for so long.

He liked the idea of being a spider at the center of the web, Peter thought. *And he knew which threads he needed to pull if he wanted something.*

"We have two main problems, at the moment," Alexander said. He centered the display on a profit-loss statement. "First, in the short run, our military contracts are going to come to an end within the next twelve months. I've heard that the military is already trying to figure out ways to get out of the contracts early, as they don't need the ships, weapons, and components any longer. We may be able to rationalize some of the contracts down to a more reasonable level without losing them altogether, but it seems unlikely that we will have many military contracts by the end of the year. There simply isn't any need for them."

"I see," Peter said.

"What makes this worse," Alexander added, "is that the bulk of the military production line cannot be converted for other markets. A third of the technology we produce is thoroughly embargoed for civilian use, at least not without extensive licensing, while the remainder doesn't have much *use* for civilians. They don't need military-grade sensor suites, particularly when the mil-grade equipment is five or six times as expensive as the civilian models."

Peter tensed. "I was under the impression that military gear was highly sought after."

"It is," Alexander said. "But smaller companies and independent freighter captains also have limited funds. We've been looking at ways to reduce prices, in hopes of picking up extra sales, but we're already running on the margins as it is. The military contracts were relatively steady, sir. They weren't going to make us rich."

"We did cream a profit, didn't we?" Peter studied the charts for a long moment. "I believe the money was reinvested."

"It was," Alexander confirmed. "But the vast war machine we built to fight the war is no longer required."

And so we have to scale back our operations, Peter thought. *Which is going to be very bad.*

Clive cleared his throat. "The second problem is that we, and most of the other corporations, are going to have to cut costs sharply. This will necessitate getting rid of a great many subdivisions, and people. A considerable number of employees will have to be downsized and . . ."

"You mean *sacked*," Peter said sharply.

"Yes, sir," Clive said. "We may have to lay off up to 30 percent of our workforce."

Peter swallowed, hard. The age-old contract between employers and employees was about to be broken. They'd promised the workers that they'd take care of them, hadn't they? A job with a big corporation was a job for life. Peter's father had aggressively encouraged his subordinates to seek out new talent and promote it, encouraging ambitious youngsters to rise to the limits of their competence. A man could start on the ground floor and climb to the very top. Peter's former office had contained a whole string of success stories that had boosted the corporation's profits and given hope to the workers that competence would be rewarded.

But not now, he thought. No one was fired without due cause. God knew the corporation worked hard to put square pegs in square holes. *What will happen when we tell 30 percent of our people that they have to go?*

"It may get worse," Clive added, slowly. "If the rumors about Cavendish are true . . ."

Peter gritted his teeth. There was a yawning financial black hole at the very heart of the Cavendish Corporation. Duke Cavendish was doing everything in his power to patch together the cracks in the edifice, but he might as well be putting a tiny plaster on a broken arm. It wouldn't be long before people, *important* people, started jumping ship. And once *that* happened, the Cavendish Corporation was doomed. Millions of people would be out of work.

"There will be a planetary economic downturn," Clive said. "If vast numbers of people lose their jobs, they'll stop buying things; if people stop buying things, more and more sub-businesses will go bust. And then, chaos."

"And there's no way we can save even *part* of Cavendish," Peter said. Cavendish was technically a rival, but if one ducal corporation went under, the others would tremble. "We can't afford it."

"No, sir," Alexander said. "We could snap up a few of their subdivisions, at bargain- basement prices, but the cost of saving even a small percentage of their operations would bankrupt us."

Clive nodded. "What makes matters worse, sir, are the subsidies. And the military tax."

Peter winced. "How do you imagine they'll play out?"

"It depends on the politics." Alexander looked acutely uncomfortable. "The military tax has not—yet—been repealed. If it isn't repealed, for whatever reason, it will be yet another expenditure we will be hard-pressed to meet. Even if it *is* repealed, we will still have difficulty meeting our usual obligations. The king needs to be made aware of the dangers of excessive taxation.

"The subsidies, both to the Commonwealth and the former Theocratic worlds, are a different kettle of fish. In the short run, canceling them would save money; in the long run, they would cause economic trouble for our allies, which would lead to resentment. I'd honestly advise doing a full audit on the subsidies before we consider canceling them, but . . ."

He shrugged, expressively. Peter understood. The king considered the subsidies to be a necessary payment, one of his flagship projects to build the Commonwealth into a genuine interstellar power. Peter agreed with his reasoning, but he was concerned about the *cost* of the project. When times were good, people didn't care where the money went; when times were hard, people got angry when payments, even minor ones, were made to those who didn't work. People who paid taxes felt they should get something in return and woe betide any government official who tried to tell them otherwise.

"Right," he said. "I assume you have proposals for . . . downsizing?"

"Yes, sir," Alexander said. He altered the display. "As you can see, sir . . ."

Peter's terminal bleeped. He held up a hand to stem the tide of words as he keyed the switch. "Yes?"

"Sir," Yasmeena Delacroix said. His terrifyingly efficient secretary sounded perturbed. "His Excellency Israel Harrison, Leader of the Opposition, has just landed on the pad. He's requesting an immediate meeting."

Peter blinked in surprise. He'd heard that Israel Harrison was supposed to be a little eccentric, but *this*? He couldn't just drop in for a meeting with a duke, certainly not on his home territory. Normally, his people would speak to Peter's people, and a time and place would be organized. There were plenty of places they could talk in reasonable privacy without one of them looking like a supplicant. Dropping in for a chat simply wasn't done.

He forced himself to think. Agreeing to the meeting would have implications, particularly in the minds of anyone watching from a distance, but so would refusing it. He was a duke, not a member of the House of Commons. There was nothing *wrong* with meeting the Leader of the Opposition. And yet . . .

"Have him shown up," Peter said, finally. "And then bring us some tea."

He closed the connection, then looked at the two men. "I'll speak to you both later, after I've had a chance to assess your work," he said. He had no doubt it would be comprehensively detailed, but he wanted to make sure he understood the data before coming to any final decisions. He'd learned to watch for people trying to snowball him into making a fatal mistake. "Until then, please keep your findings to yourself."

"Of course, sir," Alexander said. He deactivated the holographic projector. "Our files are already in your terminal."

The two men rose, bowed, and made their way out of the giant office. Peter barely noticed them go as he pulled up the files on Israel Harrison and skimmed them, quickly. His father hadn't had much to say about the Leader of the Opposition, beyond the simple fact that he'd started amassing power from a very young age. Not a nobleman, oddly enough. Peter wasn't sure what to make of that. Putting himself on the list of people in line to receive a Patent of Nobility wouldn't be hard. Perhaps the king, or the previous king, had quietly refused to ennoble the man. It wouldn't be the first time someone had been denied a title they deserved.

"Israel Harrison, Your Grace," Yasmeena said.

Peter rose. "Mr. Harrison," he said as they shook hands. "I must say this meeting is a surprise."

"I have often found that being unpredictable has its advantages," Harrison said. He sounded distinctly plebeian in private conversation. "Is this room secure?"

Peter sat back at his desk, motioning the older man to a seat. "It has the finest security money can buy," he said truthfully. The corporation's security division swept the entire building daily. Industrial espionage had been alive and well on Tyre since the Ducal Fourteen had turned the world into their base. "You can talk freely."

"Let us hope so," Harrison said. He cocked his head. "I trust you are settling into your new role?"

Peter snorted as Yasmeena brought them both tea, then retired. He'd been the Duke from the moment the family council had elected him to succeed his father. The Duke was dead, long live the Duke. There was no way he could afford to wait a year before taking the reins. The family council would have impeached him on the spot.

"It could be better," he said tightly. He met Harrison's eyes. "Mr. Harrison, I am a very busy man, and you have forced your way into my schedule. Can I ask you to get to the point?"

Harrison smiled, as if Peter had cracked a joke. "Here's a question for you," he said. "Do you believe the king has the best interests of his planet at heart?"

Peter blinked. "Do you believe otherwise?"

"I have reason to believe that the king does not intend to ask for the military tax to be repealed," Harrison said. "Worse, I believe that he has yet to realize that his spending—*our* spending—is dangerously out of control. My people have been trying to trace the money, Your Grace, and there are considerable sums that remain unaccounted for. We don't know where the money went."

"They were throwing money into hundreds of research programs," Peter pointed out. "And a *lot* of black ops stuff."

"Billions of crowns," Harrison said. "A small fraction of our war-time budget, to be fair, but not an insignificant amount. Our desperate rush to gird our loins and defend our worlds made it impossible to exercise any financial discipline."

"When you're in trouble," Peter quoted one of his father's speeches, "don't count the pennies getting legal representation."

"Wise words," Harrison agreed. "I was there when that speech was delivered, Your Grace."

"I know," Peter said.

"Right now, we have commitments we cannot hope to meet," Harrison said. "We have committed ourselves to the Commonwealth, the king has committed us to the Theocratic Sector, we have a looming economic crisis . . . and the king wants to up our expenditures. I have reason to believe that he intends to ask for extra subsidies when Parliament reopens at the end of the summer. And he might just be able to drum up enough support from the Commons to get them into the Lords."

Peter sucked in his breath. Once the bill was in the House of Lords, it would be harder to engage in backroom dealing to rewrite the law to something more satisfactory. "Are you sure?"

"Yes, Your Grace," Harrison said. "I have an . . . operative . . . in the prime minister's office."

The report could be deliberately designed to mislead you, Peter thought. He'd never liked the cloak-and-dagger shenanigans that his father had so loved, but he knew enough to be careful. A person slipping information to someone else might have their own motives, even if they were telling the truth. *The prime minister could be trying to lead you into a trap.*

"There are other issues," Harrison added. "The king has also been pushing his patronage rights about as far as they will go. A number of naval officers who happen to be corporate clients have been sidelined, while others, who happen to be the *king's* clients, have been pushed forward. He's been replacing naval officers with loyalists."

Peter felt cold. "Are you sure?"

"I imagine your clients have had the same problem," Harrison said. "We were at war for four years, Your Grace. That's more than long enough for the king to put his people in the right places to take full control of the navy."

"And then what?" Peter looked down at his hands. "We still control the orbital defenses, don't we?"

"Yes," Harrison said. "But even *they* are under threat." He took a long breath. "The king may simply be building up his power base," he said. "Or he might have something more sinister in mind. Either way, it poses a threat."

"Perhaps," Peter said. "It may also be nothing more than paranoia. How many of *us* would put people who weren't our clients in positions of power?"

"We understand where the lines are drawn," Harrison countered. "Does the king?" He glanced at his wristcom. "They'll have noticed I came here," he said shortly. "If you want to . . . ah . . . discuss matters further, I suggest we do it over a secure communications line."

Peter's eyes narrowed. "Do you think the king will intercept our communications?"

"I think the king has a black ops division of his own," Harrison said. His tone was light, but his words betrayed just how seriously he took his concerns. "And I also think he's too young to understand the dangers of playing with fire. His father understood the rules of the game."

"I see your point," Peter said. The king had always been the most powerful of the noblemen, yet there were limits on his power. Or there were supposed to be limits. War had given the king an opportunity to expand his power in ways his father could never have considered, even for a moment. "But I hope you're wrong."

"So do I," Harrison said. "So do I."

CHAPTER EIGHT

—

JUDD

Captain Amy Layman was deeply immersed in a Regency VR sim when the attack began.

It wasn't something she would have allowed herself during the war. HMS *Gibraltar* had seen action in nearly a hundred engagements, from raids into enemy territory to convoy escort missions and, finally, the first and second Battles of Ahura Mazda. Amy knew, deep within her bones, that the alert could come at any time. And yet, as days had turned into weeks and months of boredom, she'd allowed herself to slip. She'd never really considered that anyone would attack Judd.

She tore off the VR jack as the alarm howled through the light cruiser, swallowing hard to keep from throwing up as the world spun around her. It couldn't be a drill, she told herself sharply. God knew she'd slacked off on combat drills as well as everything else. Nausea assailed her as she jumped up from the bed, one hand grabbing her jacket while the other found the emergency hypospray. She blessed her forethought, what little of it she'd had, as she pressed the device to her arm and pulled the trigger. The drugs would make her sweat buckets later, but they'd clear her head. She breathed out a sigh of relief as the nausea started to fade, then headed for the hatch. The sound of her crew running to battlestations echoed through the hull as she hurried to the bridge.

"Report," she snapped.

"Captain," Commander Isobel said. "We have multiple enemy contacts on attack vector!"

"Bring up the drives and weapons," Amy snapped as she threw herself into her command chair. "And prepare to leave orbit."

"Aye, Captain!"

She studied the display, cursing her own stupidity as her starship powered up. The display was practically glowing with red icons, row upon row of superdreadnoughts . . . *Theocratic* superdreadnoughts. Panic yammered at the back of her mind, threatening to overwhelm her before she told herself, firmly, that the contacts couldn't be real. If the Theocracy had so many superdreadnoughts, more than a hundred, according to her sensors, the war would have gone the other way. No, most of those starships had to be nothing more than fake sensor images, with no more substance than a soap bubble. But her sensors couldn't tell the real starships from the fakes. They'd need to get a great deal closer . . .

"Launch a probe," she ordered. If even *one* of those superdreadnoughts was real, she didn't dare risk taking her ship any closer. The massed volleys of a single superdreadnought would be more than enough to reduce *Gibraltar* to atoms. "And alert the planetary authorities."

A low hum echoed through her ship as the drives were brought online. Amy silently kicked herself for allowing matters to get so far out of hand. She could have kept the drives powered up without putting significant wear and tear on the engines, couldn't she? But she'd heard too many stories of supply officers snatching back their authority, now that the war was effectively over. They'd give her hell if they knew she'd burned out her drive components for no good reason.

I fucked up, she thought, stiffly. It had been sheer luck the enemy had come out of hyperspace so far from the planet. If they'd risked opening a gateway closer to Judd, they would have been on top of her before she'd had a chance to respond. *And everyone is going to pay for it.*

"*Edinburgh* and *Aberdeen* are standing by," the communications officer reported. "They're ready to engage the enemy."

Amy fought to keep her face expressionless. Three light cruisers were no match for the immense firepower bearing down on them. She was morbidly certain that at least one of the superdreadnoughts had to be real, perhaps more than one. But she wouldn't know until the probe started to pick out the real ships from the fakes, or the real ships opened fire. The sensor ghosts wouldn't be able to fire missiles . . .

Her mind raced, searching for options. There weren't many. She could open gateways and run, but that would mean abandoning Judd to its fate. If those *were* Theocratic ships . . . she wouldn't give two crowns for Judd's continued survival. The Theocrats would probably smash the planet flat from orbit, then piss on the rubble. There was no one around to stop them either. It would take at least four days for reinforcements to reach the doomed world, assuming they were dispatched at once. And no one knew reinforcements were needed.

We should have extended the StarCom network out here, she told herself savagely. *Perhaps if I'd argued for it . . .*

"Communications, contact *Aberdeen*," Amy ordered. "They are to disengage and fly directly to Ahura Mazda. Once there, they are to inform Admiral Falcone of the situation and request immediate reinforcements."

"Aye, Captain," the communications officer said. There was a pause as he worked his console. "Captain, *Aberdeen*'s skipper is protesting . . ."

"Tell him that that is an order, which he may have in writing if he wishes," Amy said. She didn't quite recognize her voice. It was so cold. She understood the man's desire to stay, even though doing so was certain death, but she couldn't allow it. *Someone* had to warn Admiral Falcone that the war wasn't quite over. "He is to leave, now."

She turned back to the display. Her ship didn't have a superdreadnought-sized tactical deck, but her crew was doing the best they could. A handful of enemy superdreadnoughts had already been flagged as prospective sensor ghosts, while a dozen more had been marked as potentially suspect. A couple had even been positively identified as *real* . . . not, she supposed, that it mattered much. A single superdreadnought had more missile tubes than two entire squadrons of light cruisers.

Their ECM is good, she thought. *Better than it should be.*

"Deploy ECM drones, then stealth platforms," she ordered, dismissing the thought. There would be time to worry over who was supplying the enemy later. If there was a later. "And then angle five of the probes to record what happens here. I want to leave a message . . ."

The display sparkled with red lights. "The enemy have opened fire," the tactical officer said, sharply. "Captain, their missiles are roughly comparable to our Mark-XVs!"

Someone's been giving them help, Amy reminded herself. She'd thought she had more time before the enemy opened fire. *What sort of idiot sells them advanced missiles?*

"Stand by point defense," she ordered, although she knew the gesture would be futile. "And engage as soon as they enter weapons range."

She glanced at the planet on the display, feeling a stab of guilt. The enemy superdreadnoughts—and only three of them were real, judging by which ships had opened fire—were going to take the high orbitals. There was nothing she could do to stop them. They'd blow her two remaining ships out of space and wreak devastation on the world below. And there was nothing the planet's inhabitants could do to stop them either.

They don't deserve this, she thought as the enemy missiles roared into engagement range. *They were free.*

But she knew, as her ship started to fight for her life, that what the planet deserved didn't matter.

◆ ◆ ◆

"You fired off a great many missiles," Askew commented as the second enemy cruiser vanished from the display. "Overkill, hey?"

Admiral Zaskar ignored him. Firing the missiles had been immensely satisfying, even though he knew he'd be cursing himself later. Askew was right. It *was* overkill. But he'd wanted to eliminate all chances of enemy resistance, and he'd succeeded. Watching the two enemy cruisers die had merely been the icing on the cake.

"Launch probes," he ordered instead. "Tactical, isolate potential targets on the planet's surface."

"Aye, sir!"

"And find those camps," he added. "I want the troops ready to deploy at a moment's notice."

"Aye, sir!"

Askew coughed. "Our intelligence suggests that there are no enemy ships within a day of Judd."

"We can't take that for granted," Zaskar pointed out as the first set of targets appeared on the main display. "If an enemy superdreadnought shows up at the worst possible time . . ."

"God is with us," Moses assured him. "He will not let us die so easily."

God helps those who help themselves, Admiral Zaskar thought. It had once been the Theocracy's motto. Somewhere along the way, it had become verboten. *And if we neglect basic precautions, we're finished.*

"Admiral," the tactical officer said, "I have a list of targets."

Zaskar studied them for a long moment. The enemy had been building rapidly over the last year. Judd no longer had any space-based industry, beyond a cloudscoop he intended to destroy on his way out of the system, but they'd repaired and expanded their cities and ground-based industrial estates. A handful of military bases and spaceports were clearly visible, along with several fusion plants. One of them, judging from the electronic signature, had been taken directly from a midsized starship. The engineer in him wondered how they'd managed to get the ship down without crashing it into the surface.

No matter, he told himself.

"Open fire," he commanded. "And then order the troops to hit the camps."

A rumble echoed through the mighty ship as it launched the first volley of KEWs. There was a limitless supply of kinetic energy projectiles—really nothing more than rocks dropped from high orbit—and while their targeting left something to be desired, he had no compunctions about dropping several more projectiles if the first missed. He had no particular qualms about destroying large chunks of the city too. The locals had sworn to follow the True Faith, but they'd lied. They'd ended their devotion as soon as their world had been liberated.

Of course they stopped, he thought, darkly. *How could they follow a religion imposed upon them at gunpoint?*

He shied away from that thought as enemy targets started to vanish. It was hard to remember, as whoops of joy and shouted prayers echoed around the compartment, that the lights on the display represented real people. People—unbelievers, to be sure, but people—were under those flashing lights, people who were dying as the KEWs hit their targets and destroyed them. He wondered just how many would perish in the months and years to come. The targeting matrix included just about every government building that had been in use during the occupation.

And many of the survivors headed into the hills, he thought. Judd was a heavily populated world, but the hills had never really been developed. The files had stated that the mountain people had never embraced the True Faith. *Even now, we cannot find many of their hiding places.*

He shook his head. Zaskar wanted to lay claim to Judd once again, to land in force and punish the unbelievers with whip and flail, but he knew better. He and his forces couldn't allow themselves to be pinned down. It wouldn't be long before the Commonwealth responded in strength to their move. If they were still at Judd when the enemy fleet arrived, they'd be wiped out within hours. He couldn't take the risk.

"The troops are on the way," the tactical officer reported. "They'll hit the camps in twenty minutes."

"Remind their commanders that they don't have much time," Admiral Zaskar said. He'd refrained from softening up the defenses around the camps, insofar as there *were* any fixed defenses. He didn't want to kill his own people. "We have to be back in hyperspace as quickly as possible."

"Aye, sir."

◆ ◆ ◆

"Run," a voice shouted. "Get up and run!"

Millicent Barbara grabbed her coat and ran for her life, unsure of where she was going. The Commonwealth Refugee Commission HQ was supposed to be safe, certainly when compared to the bases on Ahura Mazda or a couple of other worlds that had been under Theocratic control long enough for the True Faith to sink deep roots into the population's minds. She'd been reluctant to work on Judd, at first, but she'd come to believe that the locals were genuinely decent people, although they wanted to be rid of anyone who followed the True Faith or collaborated with the occupation. It wasn't something Millicent particularly understood.

She ran out into the cold morning air, just in time to hear explosions echoing over the distant city. There hadn't been any real trouble since the Theocrats had been rounded up, something Millicent found deplorable even though her superiors had told her not to make a fuss. The locals had endured a decade of oppression—a decade of watching their men be brainwashed, women brutalized, and children raised in the True Faith. She supposed she should be grateful that the vast majority of the converted hadn't been killed out of hand. The blood had flowed for weeks on a dozen worlds.

An aircraft flew overhead, heading north. She looked up to follow it and saw a streak of light dropping down from low orbit to strike a target in the distance. There was a blinding flash when it touched the ground, followed by a billowing fireball and a rumble of thunder. She stopped and stared, her mind finally realizing what she was seeing. Judd was under attack, heavy attack. More projectiles followed, some falling within the city. She turned just in time to see a distant skyscraper topple and fall. She thought she heard people screaming as the remains hit the ground.

"Millie," a voice called. She turned to see one of the military liaison officers. Dave or Charlie or . . . she couldn't remember his name. They were all interchangeable, all in firm agreement that the refugees had to be relocated somewhere else as quickly as possible. "We have to move!"

Millicent found her voice. "What's happening?"

"The planet is under attack," Dave said. She was *almost* sure he was Dave. "The high orbitals have fallen, and the enemy is bombarding the surface."

Another projectile landed within the city. Millicent looked away as she saw a towering fireball rising up and over the land. It was . . . Judd City wasn't the largest city in the explored universe, not by a long chalk, but there were hundreds of thousands of people living in the skyscrapers or occupying the slums on the riverbank. They were being slaughtered, brutally slaughtered. She couldn't imagine what sort of mind-set would do such a thing. The attackers weren't firing at military targets. One of the projectiles looked to have come down in the slums.

Dave caught her arm. "We have to move!"

Millicent stared at him. "And go where?"

"We can't stay here," Dave said. "You know how close we are to the spaceport?"

Millicent nodded curtly. The spaceport had been taken over by the provisional government almost as soon as the planet had been liberated, then made over to the Commonwealth as a base of operations. Her superiors had insisted on placing the HQ right next to the spaceport, so refugees could be moved through the scanners once transport was actually arranged and then shipped straight to orbit. Now . . . now, she had the nasty feeling their location might have turned into a liability.

"The spaceport will either be turned into a bridgehead or bombed," Dave said. He pulled her away from the HQ. "Come on!"

Millicent hesitated, then followed him. Military or not, he was the only friendly face in the area. The spaceport was largely isolated from the nearby city, but it wouldn't be long before people started flocking to the compound. She'd studied refugee flows enough to know that *some* people would try to take the shortest route to the spaceport, convinced that it would somehow magically allow them to escape the entire planet. Others, meanwhile, would head to the hills. They'd very rapidly turn desperate, then feral. Offworlders, and both of them were offworlders, would be attacked on sight.

"What do we do?" Panic yammered at the back of her mind. She'd never envisaged being caught in the middle of a war. "Where do we go?"

"There're a few places we can hide until the navy shows up," Dave said. Another round of explosions underlined his words. "I don't think there'll be much of a provisional government by this time tomorrow."

Millicent didn't want to agree with him, but there was no way to avoid conceding that he might be right. Judd's provisional government had been held together by spit, baling wire, and a great deal of luck. *And* subsidies from the Commonwealth, she admitted in the privacy of her own mind. There was a good chance the planetary president was dead, along with the leaders of most of the factions. The remainder would probably start blaming each other for the disaster or simply go their own way. Civil war was a very real possibility.

"I thought there were marines by the embassy," she called. Thunder echoed in the sky. "Why can't we go there?"

"I'll be surprised if the embassy still exists," Dave said. "And even if it does, I don't fancy our chances of getting there. All hell is breaking out on the streets, and I've only got a pistol. Do you have a gun?"

"No," Millicent said. She'd done the basic firearms certification course, as it was a requirement for her position, but she'd never bothered to keep up with the training. "I don't need one."

"You need one now," Dave told her. "This world is collapsing into chaos."

Millicent had a nasty feeling that he was right.

CHAPTER NINE
JUDD

"Dig that fucking hole," Sergeant Lewis shouted. "Dig, dig, dig!"

Private Alicia Callahan felt sweat dripping from her brow as she struggled to dig the trench in the unyielding soil. Guard duty was supposed to be easy, damn it. A company of provisional government militia, assigned to guarding the wretched refugee camps . . . she'd thought it would make a pleasant break from sniping at the occupiers before the sudden liberation. It had been positively cathartic to watch the Theocrats be on the wrong side of history for a change. The bastards had squirmed whenever they'd seen her jacket, just a little tighter than it needed to be, and the gun in her hands. A woman with a gun was their worst nightmare.

She shivered at the thought, despite the heat. She'd been captured, once. She knew she was lucky to be alive, but . . . part of her wished she'd had the time to commit suicide before they'd started in on her. The piece of battered meat the resistance had rescued had needed years to recover, years she hadn't had. Going back to the war, going back to killing the bastards, had been better therapy than anything else, but . . . she'd been looking forward to the peace, damn it. Once their homeworld was cleansed of the infection, once the devotees of the True Faith had been banished, she could finally feel safe.

It isn't fair, she told herself. They'd won, or rather they'd been liberated. Judd had been looking forward to a time of peace and prosperity. Instead, they'd been attacked. Enemy shuttles were inbound, and Alicia knew all too well that the only reason the camp hadn't been bombed from orbit was that the Theocrats wanted to rescue their allies. *It just isn't fair!*

"They'll be here in five minutes," Lewis bellowed as streaks of light fell from the sky. "Get your weapons ready!"

Alicia gritted her teeth, cursing the loud thunder echoing over the hills. Not *real* thunder. The KEWs were landing in the nearby city, she thought. Garston had been a hive of resistance, back during the war; the Theocrats had done their best, but they hadn't been able to keep the city under tight control. Now, they were simply flattening the locale from orbit, slaughtering the population before they could flee. She muttered a silent prayer for her friends and relatives in the region, then ducked into a trench as shuttles flew overhead. A single HVM rose up to blast a shuttle out of the air, the wreckage falling to the ground, but the remainder kept flying on. They seemed determined to land just outside engagement range.

At least they're not dropping in on us, Alicia thought grimly. She checked her ammunition pouch, wishing she'd thought to carry more. During the war, she'd loaded her belt and pockets with so much ammunition that she'd practically clinked when she'd walked. Now, she'd picked up bad habits. *If we survive the day, we must never become complacent again.*

A low rumble echoed through the air. She leaned forward, spotting the first tank as it advanced up the road, turrets swinging from side to side as it searched for targets. The Theocrats might not be able to build a decent sensor suite or vortex generator without help, but she knew from grim experience that their assault weapons and support vehicles were first-rate. They'd built them to be as simple as possible, she'd heard.

She'd certainly never had any trouble using captured weapons against their makers.

"Stay low," Lewis shouted as a second tank came into view. "Wait for my signal!"

Alicia nodded. The Theocratic tanks weren't heavily armored—they'd found *that* out during the war—but the defenders didn't have many antitank weapons. It was sheer luck they had *any*. The POW camp wasn't meant to be heavily defended. The guards had been more concerned about prisoners breaking out than defending the camp against an outside enemy. Most of them would probably have looked the other way if a lynch mob had arrived to slaughter the prisoners.

Her eyes narrowed as she saw the enemy soldiers, using the tanks for cover as they advanced with the squeamish determination of untried men. Whoever was in command over there had a working brain, she decided. That wasn't good news. The Theocrats had often turned victories into defeats through overplaying their hands, or launching human wave attacks, but *this* CO seemed to be smart enough to avoid heavy losses. But then the Theocrats had presumably lost a once-infinite source of manpower. They had to conserve their forces or risk losing everything.

"Fire," Lewis snapped.

Two antitank rockets flared towards their targets, punching through the thin armor and detonating inside the tanks. Alicia felt no sympathy for the tankers, cooked before they had a chance to realize they were under attack; instead, she aimed at the nearest enemy soldier and shot him down. The other enemy troops dropped to the ground, but kept advancing forward with grim resolution. Clearly, the Theocracy *hadn't* learned *too* many lessons from the war. They would have been better advised to fall back and call in an airstrike.

She cursed as a volley of machine-gun fire cracked over her head. A third tank had come into view, firing with gay abandon towards the trenches. Alicia ducked as low as she could, swearing out loud as she saw the bullets digging into the ground and tearing the trench into a muddy nightmare. She saw a man stand up to hurl a grenade, only to be disintegrated by the enemy machine guns. Sweat ran down her back as she tried to spot a target without exposing herself. It was only a matter of time. The defense wasn't strong enough to stand up to a sustained assault. They had no time to dig proper trenches, establish pillboxes, or do anything that might do something more than slow the enemy down for a few moments.

"Fall back," Lewis shouted. "Fall . . ."

Alicia saw him fall, half of his head missing. She swallowed, hard, as she crawled back towards the camp. Lewis had led a charmed life, until now. He'd never even been scratched by enemy fire . . . now he was dead. She found a vantage point and fired a handful of shots towards the advancing troops, seeing two of them fall before the remainder ducked for cover and returned fire. There was no hope of getting out alive. Perhaps they should have abandoned the POW camp as soon as the enemy starships had entered orbit. Or killed the prisoners. She didn't want to *think* about what they'd do to the local population.

The tank kept inching forward, crushing the remainder of the trenches beneath its treads. Alicia reached for a grenade, took careful aim, and hurled it towards the tank, trying to get it underneath the vehicle before it exploded. The resistance had learned, the hard way, that the tanks weren't as solidly protected underneath. A minefield would probably have stopped the invasion force in its tracks.

Until they started using prisoners to clear the minefield, she thought as the grenade exploded. The tank shuddered to a halt. *I think . . .*

Something struck her, hard. She was on her back, her thoughts blurring in and out of existence, before she quite knew what had hit her. Someone had shot her. And she could hear someone running towards her. She tried to reach for her other grenade, but her fingers felt as if they were no longer listening to her. A man was looking down at her, a gun pointed directly at her face . . .

It barked, once. Silence fell.

◆ ◆ ◆

"The camps have been liberated, sir," the tactical officer reported. "We're sorting out the prisoners now."

Admiral Zaskar barely looked away from the display. "Casualties?"

"Forty-seven men dead in total, along with five tanks," the tactical officer said after a moment. "Nineteen others injured."

"Have the wounded men returned to the shuttles," Admiral Zaskar ordered. They could no longer afford to spend men like water. Besides, being seen to care for his men would do wonders for morale. He could no longer hammer men for dissent either. "And execute any surviving enemy personnel."

"Aye, sir."

There was a pause. "I'm picking up a radio transmitter, five miles from the capital," another officer said. "Should I send them a bomb?"

"Yes," Admiral Zaskar said. The enemy needed radios to coordinate military operations, now that their ground-based telecommunications system had been destroyed. He had no intention of allowing them to muster resistance. It didn't *look* as though there was anything they could do that would pose a threat to his ships, but he didn't want to discover that he was wrong the hard way. "Take them out."

He leaned back in his chair, studying the display. They'd rained death on the planet, hitting every military and governmental facility . . . and then striking everything that even *looked* as though it might help the planet rebuild. Hundreds of thousands of unbelievers would have died already, he was sure, and hundreds of thousands more would die in the next few weeks and months. Judd simply didn't have the food to feed its population, nor the vehicles or transport network it needed to move what food it did have from the warehouses to where it was needed. The Commonwealth could fill the gap, if the infidels were prepared to make a major commitment, but they would have too many other things to worry about. He'd see to that personally.

As long as we withdraw without being caught by enemy ships, he thought. It had been nearly two hours since they'd dropped out of hyperspace and engaged the enemy ships. He wanted to be gone in less than five hours. They didn't dare risk being intercepted so quickly. *We really don't want to lose our second chance before we make a* real *impression on the enemy.*

"Admiral, we've finished assessing the prisoners," the tactical officer reported. "Fifty-seven of them may be useful, for the fleet; ninety-two are women. The remainder are of little use."

"Have the useful ones, and the women, loaded onto the transports," Admiral Zaskar said. "The remainder are to be given weapons and told to give the enemy a hard time."

He smiled, rather grimly. There was no way the remainder of the prisoners would be able to recapture the planet, not with the handful of weapons he could give them, but they'd give the planetary defenders a headache or two. They'd have to waste time tracking down the escaped prisoners instead of repairing the damage to their infrastructure. Who knew? Enough armed prisoners might be able to spearhead an insurgency of their own. Judd had been a Theocratic world long enough for the True Faith to grow roots. And a long, drawn-out insurgency might lead to a political solution . . .

It isn't likely to happen, he told himself. *But God may have other ideas.*

He dismissed the thought. "Are our long-range sensors still clear?"

"Yes, sir," the sensor officer said. "The system is empty."

Or anyone within sensor range has shut down their drives and active sensors, Admiral Zaskar reminded himself. Judd had once had a small space-based industry of its own that had been destroyed during the invasion, but the provisional government would have every reason to want to restart it as soon as possible. *We could be being watched by unseen eyes.*

He looked at Askew. "I trust this is suitable?"

"It is more than suitable," Askew said. The man hadn't shown any reaction whatsoever to the carnage the fleet had unleashed on Judd. He seemed to view the attack as perfectly normal. "The Commonwealth will be kept very busy indeed."

"And they'll have to waste their resources rebuilding the system," Admiral Zaskar added. He had no idea if the Commonwealth would make a major commitment to Judd or not, but they'd pay a price no matter what they chose. "It will be very difficult for them."

He turned to his subordinates. "Order the transports to expedite the loading," he added. "We need to be moving soon."

◆ ◆ ◆

"Damn those bastards," Rupert Flinty swore. "Damn them to hell!"

"Watch your mouth," Simon Laager snapped. "We don't want to be seen up here."

He kept his own feelings to himself as they lay on the ledge, peering down at the POW camp in the valley below. It had been sheer dumb luck that they hadn't been with the rest of the company when their comrades had made their last stand. They'd been sent out to hunt for deer, and they'd been too far away from the camp to rejoin the company during the attack. Now all they could do was watch.

It wasn't a pleasant sight. The defenders, all too aware of the fate that awaited anyone who surrendered, had fought to the death. A handful of soldiers who'd been too wounded to fight had simply been shot down like wild animals. Now the invaders were going through the prisoners, dispatching half of them to the shuttles and pointing the other half towards the road leading down to civilization. It looked as if the

Theocrats were having everything their own way. A couple of prisoners who objected, from what little they could see, had simply been shot, their bodies left to rot where they'd fallen.

"They're taking all the women with them," Flinty commented. "Good."

"Not for them," Simon said. He had no sympathy for the male prisoners, be they faithful or simple collaborators, but the women had been treated like dirt. It was hard to understand why *any* of them had refused the offer of a better life somewhere else. "They're going straight to hell."

He ducked down as the first shuttle started to rise into the air. If they'd had an HVM . . . He shook his head. It wasn't as if they'd needed antiaircraft missiles to go hunting. In hindsight, the camp should have expected an attack from the air, or space, but no one had considered the possibility. They'd believed the Theocracy was dead. The shuttles, two more rising even now, proved that they were wrong. He didn't want to think what the plumes of smoke, rising from the direction of the nearest city, meant. The Theocrats might have flattened every building they could see.

And they certainly tried to destroy the caves, he thought, remembering the nightmarish days when the Theocrats had realized that the resistance was using the caves to hide. They'd bombed the entire region from orbit, crushing hundreds of fighters below fallen rock. *They'll probably try to do it again.*

He scrambled to his feet as the fourth and last shuttle clawed for space. The pilot didn't seem inclined to go looking for trouble—his human cargo was presumably vital—but there was no point in staying anywhere near the camp. If Simon was any judge, the Theocrats would probably destroy it from orbit once the former prisoners had scattered. Even if they didn't, he didn't want to stick around anyway. The former prisoners would be hunting for any survivors from the garrison.

Flinty caught his eyes as they scrambled down the ravine. "So . . . where do we go?"

Simon had to think. "Allenstown," he said finally. The locale had been a resistance stronghold, once upon a time. And it was only a few short hours away. "It'll do for starters."

And if we can't make contact there, we'll have to find somewhere else to go, he added privately. *That won't be easy.*

But he couldn't think of anything else to do.

◆　◆　◆

"The shuttles have returned to the ships, Admiral."

Admiral Zaskar nodded. "Is local space still clear?"

"Yes, Admiral."

"Then take us out of orbit," he ordered. "Detach a cruiser to take out the cloudscoop, then rejoin us at the first waypoint. We'll head straight back to base from there."

"Yes, Admiral."

Moses nudged him. "The women will have to be purified."

"And treated well," Admiral Zaskar added. He knew exactly how his all-male crew would react once they heard women were aboard. Riots and mutinies would be on the horizon if he wasn't careful. "Make sure they are well protected."

He settled back in his command chair as the superdreadnought slowly rose out of orbit and headed away from the planet. It was a tiny victory, compared to some of the titanic clashes between starships during the war, but a victory nonetheless. The enemy would hear about it soon, of course, yet . . . what would they do? They couldn't afford to cover *every* possible target, unless they wanted to spread their forces so thin he could score a series of easy victories . . . and they couldn't find his base, unless they stumbled across it by sheer luck.

They did it to us, he thought wryly. Admiral Junayd, one of the most able commanders the Theocracy had produced, had been unable to prevent the Commonwealth from raiding behind the lines. It had cost him everything. His successors hadn't been able to do any better. *And now we will do it to them.*

He smiled, rather coldly. Perhaps he couldn't win, in the long run. Perhaps his forces couldn't reestablish the Theocracy, not in any shape they'd recognize. But they'd make the enemy pay a high price, in blood and treasure, for its victory. And, when he was done, the victory would turn to ashes in their mouth.

"Admiral, the fleet is ready to enter hyperspace," the communications officer reported.

"Then open a gateway," Admiral Zaskar ordered. The enemy was going to be raging when they discovered he'd entered the system, smashed it flat, and retreated without taking any damage. "It's time to take our leave."

CHAPTER TEN

AHURA MAZDA

"So, as you can see, we need more supplies," Director Fiona Ferguson said. "We're quite short on everything we need."

Kat nodded as she surveyed the refugee compound. It was nearly fifty miles from the nearest population center but was still heavily defended. The refugees were almost all women, fleeing abusive husbands or fathers or even sons. She found it hard to believe that so *few* women had fled to the center, even though she'd pledged that none of them would ever have to go home, but the reports clearly indicated that most of the refugees were suffering from deeply embedded trauma. They found it difficult, perhaps impossible, to stand up for themselves.

They think I'm an alien, she thought grimly. Princess Drusilla had been able to face her as an equal, of sorts, but the remainder of the Theocracy, male and female alike, seemed to think she was a man in a woman's body. They simply couldn't wrap their heads around a woman who was something other than a daughter, a wife, or a mother. *And they don't see that they too can reach for the stars.*

"I'll do my best," she promised quietly. "But is there any hope of them becoming . . ."

Her voice trailed off. She simply didn't know how to put it into words. Ahura Mazda had been an intensely stratified society, with women right on the bottom. A man might be dumped on by his boss, then go home and take it out on his wife or daughters. And far too many women believed that it was perfectly normal. Some of them had even argued that men who didn't hit them didn't *love* them. It was an attitude that Kat found utterly incomprehensible. A man wouldn't have to break his wife's bones to go to jail on Tyre. But then, women weren't property on Tyre.

Fiona sighed. "Perhaps not *here*, Admiral," she said. "But we are teaching them new skills and . . . and showing their sons a better way to live. It is a gradual process, but it will eventually succeed."

"Let us hope so," Kat said. Ahura Mazda had been a pressure cooker too. No *wonder* there had been an explosion of violence when the Theocracy had finally been destroyed. Too many people had been repressed for too long. "And . . ."

Her wristcom bleeped. "Admiral, this is Winters," a voice said. "Can you please return to Commonwealth House?"

Kat's eyes narrowed. She'd been scheduled to visit two more refugee camps, then a training center for policemen . . . although the latter might have been canceled anyway. The police cadets were being vetted, again, after the last shooting in a police station. Captain Rosslyn had practically threatened to sit on her if she wanted to go before the vetting was completed, pointing out that *she* was the number one terrorist target. Even the king came a distant second to the woman who'd ripped the Theocracy apart.

"Understood," she said. If Winters was reluctant to discuss the matter over a secure commlink, it had to be important. Important enough to override whatever Kat was doing. "I'll be on my way in a moment."

She signaled Captain Rosslyn, then turned to Fiona. "I have to go," she said. "But I will do what I can."

"Please," Fiona said. She walked Kat out of the building and down to where the armored aircar was waiting. A pair of attack helicopters sat next to it, bristling with weapons. Their crews seemed to regard escort duty as a chance for target practice. "And thank you for coming."

Kat nodded and clambered into the aircar, leaning back into the comfortable seat as the craft hummed to life. She was wasting her time on Ahura Mazda. There was nothing that she could do that couldn't be handled by dedicated staff. All she was really doing was making it look as though the government had the situation under control while they systematically starved the occupation forces of the resources they desperately needed. She hadn't forgotten the attempt to draw down her destroyer squadrons, or how much political capital she'd had to spend to get the Admiralty to reverse its decision.

"We'll be back at Commonwealth House in ten minutes," the pilot said. "Our flight path is already being cleared."

Kat sat upright and peered out of the window as the aircar picked up speed, heading directly towards the city. It was illuminated by bright sunlight, but the glowing buildings that had been featured in enemy propaganda were long gone. They'd been replaced by tawdry constructions that fell down if someone coughed, barracks put together from prefabricated components, and layer after layer of makeshift slums. She didn't envy the marines who had to patrol the district. Their technological advantages shrank rapidly in such an environment. Nor did she envy the people who had to live there. She'd been on stage-one planets with better accommodations for the poor and dispossessed.

But most stage-one planets have no trouble finding work for their people, she reminded herself, as the aircar banked over the city and settled down on the landing pad. *Here, there's no work for anyone.*

Kat shook her head, despondently. The facts and figures she'd seen simply couldn't convey the sheer level of hopelessness gripping Ahura Mazda. The vast majority of the population had no work and no prospect of getting any work, save perhaps for the lowliest of jobs. She'd seriously considered forcing people to work or starve—street cleaning and rubbish collection was terminally undermanned—but the Refugee

Commission had convinced her superiors to overrule her. It didn't look as though most of the locals *wanted* to go back to work. The few who did were often attacked by their former fellows . . .

She stood as the aircar landed neatly, clambered out, and made her way to the briefing room. A handful of armed marines were on guard, suggesting the situation was serious. Kat wouldn't have expected any enemy attack to make it so far inside Commonwealth House, but she understood the importance of being ready for anything. An attacking force would probably bring a bomb along and blow themselves and the building to hell rather than try to capture hostages. They knew better, these days, than to think they'd be allowed to take the hostages out of the building.

And none of us would want to be their hostages anyway, she thought as she strode into the briefing room. General Winters, Commodore Fran Higgins, and Captain Janice Wilson rose to greet her. *We'd sooner die.*

"Be seated," she said tersely. There was no time for formal protocol. "What's happened?"

"*Aberdeen* just dropped out of hyperspace," Fran said. The commodore looked deeply worried. "She's reporting a major enemy attack on Judd."

Kat felt the bottom drop out of her stomach. "The missing enemy ships?"

"We haven't completed the analysis of the records yet," Fran said, "but we believe so. The enemy fleet was definitely operating Theocratic superdreadnoughts."

"Most of them have to be sensor ghosts," Winters said. "They are *not* flying hundreds of superdreadnoughts."

"Show me the records," Kat ordered.

She forced herself to calm down as the recording started to play. Hundreds of enemy ships . . . Winters was right. Most of them *had* to be sensor ghosts. She wasn't quite sure what to make of it. ONI had never been entirely sure how many enemy starships had escaped destruction, as the Theocracy had managed to destroy far too many of its records before the hammer came down. But she was fairly sure there couldn't be more than ten superdreadnoughts unaccounted for. A hundred? No, they couldn't exist. The war would have been lost within the first year if the Theocracy had an extra hundred superdreadnoughts.

Curious, she thought as the recording started to repeat itself. *They showed us enough ships to make sure we knew most of them were fakes.*

She looked up at Fran. "What about the other cruisers?"

"We're unsure as yet," Fran said. "Captain Layman *should* have been able to disengage."

"She had her drives and weapons stepped down," Winters growled. "Admiral, that was fucking careless handling. *Aberdeen* had to flash-wake her vortex generator to get out."

Kat winced, inwardly. A general, even a *marine* general, criticizing a commanding officer from another service was a severe breach of etiquette. Captain Layman would have to be judged by a board of her peers, not by someone who wasn't versed in the finer points of starship operations. But she couldn't disagree. Captain Layman had kept her drives and weapons offline and paid a steep price for it. Perhaps she had managed to disengage in time to escape. Or . . . perhaps she was already dead.

We'll find out, she promised herself.

She looked at Janice. "Does ONI have anything to add?"

Janice looked uncomfortable, but held her ground. "My office hasn't had a chance to *really* come to grips with the recordings," she said. "However, our preliminary assessment is that only three or four of those superdreadnoughts are actually real. Furthermore, they clearly have access to some advanced technology. I'd go so far as to suggest they might have opened up communications with another interstellar power."

"That would mean war," Fran said. "They'd have to be insane."

"They'd just have to be very careful to ensure they had plausible deniability," Janice corrected. "They won't have given anything that can be traced straight back to them, just stuff that could be purchased on the black market. There'll be a line of cutouts between them and the actual source of supplies."

She shrugged. "That said, they may be using some advanced tech from the war that we never knew existed. There's a lot we don't know about enemy R&D."

Because they didn't know it themselves, Kat thought, remembering the battleship they'd faced in the Jorlem Sector. *They might have designed something game-changing and never realized it.*

She cleared her throat. "Best case, Captain Layman managed to land a couple of hits before being blown away," she said. "Does anyone dispute it?"

Her eyes swept the room. No one answered. Kat nodded to herself. Even one enemy superdreadnought would be more than enough to take the high orbitals and lay waste to the planet below. A handful of antimatter bombs would exterminate the entire population . . . She shuddered. If the remnants of the Theocracy had embraced the nihilism that had been part of their faith from the beginning, they were likely to inflict horrendous damage before they were wiped out. She dreaded to think just how many worlds might be condemned to eternal winter if they weren't rendered completely uninhabitable. A nightmare.

"Very well," Kat said. She came to a grim resolution. "Commodore, prepare Beta Squadron for departure within one hour. I'll be taking command personally."

"Admiral," Fran said. "I . . ."

"Your place is here," Winters said at the same time. "Admiral . . ."

"It's not up for dispute," Kat said firmly. "I *have* to see it for myself."

She kept her feelings hidden behind an expressionless mask. Winters was right, technically. Her place *was* on Ahura Mazda. But there was nothing she could do on the Theocratic homeworld that Winters and her staff couldn't do without her. Taking the superdreadnought squadron and rushing to Judd might be a little unprofessional, perhaps even reckless, but the mission would break her out of her funk. Besides, she hadn't lied. She *needed* to see what the enemy had done, if only so she'd be able to grasp it.

"Admiral," Janice said carefully, "it's highly unlikely the enemy ships will have remained at Judd."

Kat nodded shortly. "I know," she said. "But we have to make a show of responding to the threat."

She tapped the terminal, bringing up the starchart. The vast majority of the liberated worlds were completely defenseless, save for the handful who'd managed to capture Theocratic starships or buy, beg, or borrow starships from the Commonwealth. And there was no way she could afford to position ships at each and every potential target. She simply didn't have the numbers. The only good news, as far as she could tell, was that the enemy probably weren't strong enough to run the Gap. They'd have to punch through the fleet covering Cadiz before they could slide into the Commonwealth itself.

"As long as they are careful, they can avoid contact with superior forces indefinitely," she said slowly. She'd done it herself, although she had to admit that the enemy had baited a trap for her. It was a shame Admiral Junayd was dead. He might have had some useful insights. "But we're going to have to find a way to track them back to their base."

"Unless they've set up a fleet train in deep space," Janice said.

"I doubt it," Fran said. "Even *we* had problems transshipping supplies and making repairs in interstellar space. I wouldn't bet a single rusty crown on the Theocrats being able to do it without risking a major disaster. No, they'll have a base somewhere in unexplored space."

Kat nodded stiffly. Fran was right. But finding the base was going to be an absolute nightmare. Even something as large as the giant fleet bases that had supported the Royal Navy was little more than a speck of dust against the immensity of interstellar space. There was no way she could search all the prospective star systems thoroughly enough to be certain there was no base there. Trying to do so would force her to pull ships off guard duty and convoy escort, leaving her weak elsewhere.

"I want to detach destroyers and place one or two in each possible system," she said after a moment. "Their orders are not to engage, but to attempt to shadow the enemy fleet as it returns to its base. Once they get a solid lock on its position, they can report back here, and we'll send a squadron of superdreadnoughts to smash the base into atoms."

"It really needs to be taken intact," Janice said. "We have to find out who's supplying them."

"If, indeed, someone *is* supplying them," Fran pointed out. "You could be wrong."

Kat rose. "I'll discuss the matter with the king," she added. She'd been due for a holoconference with King Hadrian anyway. It would just have to be brought forward. "And then I'll move my flag to the Beta Squadron."

She looked at Winters. "You'll assume command here, upon my departure. Dismissed."

"Aye, Admiral."

Kat strode out of the conference room and down to her office. Kitty must have heard that Kat had returned early, because there was a mug of steaming coffee and a plate of sandwiches sitting on the desk. Kat sat down, keyed the terminal to open a StarCom link to Tyre, and started to eat. Nearly twenty minutes passed before the communications link solidified and the king's face materialized in front of her. Kat allowed herself a tired smile as she pushed the remains of her snack to one side. She liked the king. He'd always struck her as someone willing to go the extra mile for his people.

"Your Majesty," she said. Technically, as a privy councilor, she could call the king by his first name, but she'd always felt weird doing so. They weren't social equals and never would be. "Thank you for taking my call."

"You said it was urgent," the king said. His voice was calm. "And it got me out of a boring meeting."

Kat frowned. "I'm afraid things are about to become a great deal less boring," she said, and outlined what had happened at Judd. "The Theocracy may not be dead after all."

The king's eyes narrowed. "I warned them," he snapped. "Just because we won the battles doesn't mean we'd won the war."

"No, Your Majesty," Kat said. "We need more ships out here, as quickly as possible."

"Parliament isn't going to like that," the king told her. He sounded bitterly amused. "They're already talking about drawing the military down still further."

"Then millions of people are going to die," Kat said. She made a mental note to write a letter to her brother, although she suspected it would be useless. Peter had been a stiff-necked, colorless man practically from birth, if the nurses were to be believed. He'd certainly never had time to play with the young Kat. But then, Peter had practically been an adult when Kat had been a little girl. "You have to make that clear to them."

"I will," the king said. "But politics . . ."

Father would never have allowed matters to get so far out of hand, Kat thought. Her father had been a great man, even if he too hadn't had much time for her as a child. *But Peter doesn't have the experience to lead the family.*

She told herself, firmly, that she was being unfair. There was no way to get such experience, save by doing it. And Peter couldn't have taken over a family leadership role until their father's death. Any plans for a smooth transition of power had been wrecked when Duke Falcone had been assassinated. The Theocracy had probably never known it, but they'd done a great deal of damage to the Commonwealth. She dreaded to think where it might end.

"I'll push the matter as hard as I can," the king said. "I take the issue seriously."

"I'll make sure you have plenty of footage from Judd," Kat said. She allowed herself a moment of warmth towards him. The king was trying to do something, which was more than could be said for the bottom-warmers in Parliament. "And from the next attacks."

"Please," the king said. He raised one hand in salute. "Take care of yourself, Kat."

"And you, Your Majesty," she told him. The king was young, barely two years older than Kat, but he was carrying the weight of an entire sector on his shoulders. "Take care of yourself too."

CHAPTER ELEVEN

ASHER DALES

"That was a boring flight," Patti complained crossly as *Dandelion* entered the Asher Dales system. "We didn't encounter a single pirate."

"They probably saw us coming and ran the other way," William said dryly. It would be a rare pirate who decided to pick a fight with two destroyers, particularly when they weren't escorting any freighters. They might decide that the destroyers had to be transporting something small yet valuable, like datachips, but the odds were against it. "There'll be plenty of pirates in our future."

He raised his voice. "Helm, take us out of hyperspace near the planet."

"Aye, Captain," Lieutenant Tim Arthur said. "Vortex opening in twenty seconds."

William smiled to himself, doing his best to project calm across the bridge. Asher Dales hadn't been surveyed very thoroughly, neither by the original settlers nor the Theocracy, and there was always a chance, a very slight chance, of running into a gravity shear and being blown out of hyperspace. Thankfully, despite its proximity to the Gap, Asher Dales didn't seem to attract many energy storms. He still wanted to survey the system himself as quickly as possible.

He tensed as the vortex opened, allowing the two destroyers to slip back into realspace. There was no way to be *sure* what they would encounter at their destination, despite Tanya's assurances. The latest news from the Theocratic Sector had not been encouraging. Too many provisional governments were proving unstable, now that the common foe had been removed. Tanya's father and his government might already have been kicked out of power.

"Local space is clear, sir," the sensor officer reported. "I'm picking up one artificial construction in orbit. Warbook calls it a Class-III Orbit Station."

"Transmit our IFFs," William ordered. The orbiting station had once belonged to the Theocracy, but the resistance had captured it when the Commonwealth had liberated the system. An impressive feat, even though the locals hadn't said much about how it had actually been done. "And then take us into high orbit."

He settled back in his command chair as the holographic display began to fill with icons. Asher Dales had almost no spacefaring presence, save for the orbiting station, but that didn't mean that the system was useless. Four gas giants, two rocky worlds, and a giant asteroid field . . . Asher Dales was poised to become an industrial powerhouse, if it ever had the chance to develop properly. William rather suspected that it would take decades. The Theocracy hadn't even bothered to set up a cloudscoop!

But the inhabitants do have a chance, he thought. *Assuming, of course, they manage to lure more outside investment.*

"Captain," the communications officer said. "We've been formally welcomed to their system, sir, and you have an invitation to dinner."

He paused. "They also want to speak directly to Miss Barrington."

"Then patch a link through to her cabin," William ordered. It had been easy to tell that Tanya hadn't enjoyed the trip, but she hadn't complained. "And then inform them that I will be happy to accept the invitation."

He kept a wary eye on the sensors as they approached the planet and entered orbit, but nothing materialized to trouble him. They'd have to inspect the orbiting station with a fine-toothed comb, he told himself firmly; the design was relatively common, dating all the way back to the UN, but the Theocracy had been the ones to turn the design into reality. It didn't look as though they'd made a mess of it . . . He shook his head. He'd seen enough of what passed for engineering in the Theocracy to not take anything for granted.

"Prepare a shuttle," he ordered once they were safely in orbit. "Miss Barrington and I will head down to the surface."

Tanya met him outside her cabin, looking more cheerful than she'd seemed for the last two weeks. William understood how she felt, even though it wasn't something he shared. There was never any shortage of tasks on a starship, from the lowliest midshipman to the commanding officer himself. Boredom was rarely a problem. Tanya, on the other hand, had been confined to a tiny cabin. She hadn't even been able to see the stars outside.

"We made it," she said as they entered the shuttle. "Thank you."

William lifted his eyebrows. "Did you doubt it?"

Tanya said nothing. William smiled as he motioned for her to strap herself in, then took the pilot's chair for himself. It had been a long time since he'd flown such a shuttle, but he'd managed to keep up with his flying certifications over the last year. Besides, it wasn't easy to *forget* how to fly a shuttle.

He disengaged from the destroyer then steered the craft down towards the planet below. Asher Dales looked like any other blue-and-green world, although he thought there was more green than blue. A glance at the shuttle computers told him that there was definitely more land surface relative to water than the average human-compatible world. It was unlikely that Asher Dales would have a problem with living space anytime soon.

"I've locked onto the beacon," he said, as the shuttle flew into the atmosphere and headed north. "Is that the capital city?"

"Yep," Tanya said. "We don't have a particularly big spaceport. The original one was smashed during the occupation, and the bastards weren't interested in repairing or replacing it."

"We'll manage," William assured her.

He had to smile as Landing came into view. The city was relatively small for its importance; it was centered around a single colony ship and a handful of orbital dumpsters that had been dropped to the surface. The spaceport itself was nothing more than a large field covered in concrete. William thought he would have missed it if there hadn't been a couple of other shuttles sitting in the open. There was only one hangar, which didn't look to be large enough to take more than one full-sized shuttle.

"Most of the population lives outside of Landing," Tanya commented as William carefully landed the shuttle on the concrete pad. "That made resistance easier, apparently. The Theocrats couldn't pen most of the inhabitants into the cities."

William glanced at her. "How many people live on Asher Dales?"

Tanya bit her lip. "The last census claimed three million," she said. "But that was before the war."

And it might have dropped since then, William thought. Barely a tenth of Hebrides's population remained alive, thanks to the war. Asher Dales had been luckier, in some respects, but unluckier in others. *It will be a long time before any of the inhabitants will trust the skies again.*

He shut down the shuttle, then stood. The local gravity felt a little stronger than the gravity on Tyre—he made a mental note to adjust the gravity on the destroyers to match—but wasn't enough to slow him down. Tanya seemed to be having more trouble, for all that she'd been born on Asher Dales . . . William puzzled over that for a moment, then reminded himself that she'd left her homeworld when she'd been a child. She probably remembered almost nothing. He wondered, as he opened the hatch and stepped outside, if that was a good thing or not. He'd take the memories of Hebrides, as it had been before the war, to his grave.

A small welcoming committee was waiting at the edge of the field. Three men, two of them carrying rifles slung over their shoulders. William waited for Tanya to step out of the shuttle, then allowed her to lead the way towards the committee. Up close, he could see that their clothes were homemade, perhaps on Asher Dales itself.

"Captain McElney," the first man said. He held out a hand. "Richard Barrington, Planetary President."

William studied him for a long moment. Richard Barrington reminded William of his brother, something that wasn't entirely a good thing. They had the same roguish scoundrel look, the same devil-may-care attitude towards life, the same smile . . . He reminded himself, sharply, that Richard Barrington had done a lot more for his home-world than Scott McElney had ever done for his. Richard Barrington had worked tirelessly to free Asher Dales from foreign occupation. He deserved credit for that, if nothing else.

"Pleased to meet you," he said, shaking Barrington's hand. "And your friends?"

"Andrew Gellman and Jackson Ford, both members of my cabinet," Barrington said, with a hint of a smile. "Their roles keep changing, for better or worse. Things are still a little unsettled here."

"I see," William said.

"If you'll come with us, we have a meal prepared," Barrington said after a moment. "And we have much to discuss."

William wasn't sure if he should be charmed by what he saw as he walked through the streets, such as they were, or deeply worried. Asher Dales looked more like a new colony than one with a population of three million people, although he had to admit that spreading three million people over an entire planet would leave them pretty scattered. Barrington and his subordinates kept up a constant running chatter, telling William about their small industrial base and their long-term plans for the future. They had big plans.

"We always intended to move into space," Barrington told him as they reached a small cottage. It took William a moment to realize that the building was Barrington's home. "The Theocracy got there first."

William smiled. "And now you plan to make sure you can never be conquered again?"

"Essentially," Barrington said. "As I believe Tanya told you, our long-term goal is to develop our own space-based industry."

"That will take some time," William said.

"There *are* shortcuts," Barrington said. He jabbed a finger upwards. "The real problem is getting to orbit. Once we're there, we're halfway to anywhere."

That wasn't particularly accurate, William thought as they sat down at the table, but he understood the man's point. Getting heavy payloads out of a planet's atmosphere had been a problem that had bedeviled mankind until antigravity drive fields had been invented. Asher Dales could put together the technology to build a lunar base without many problems and, once they solved the problem of getting the base to the moon, they'd have no trouble turning it into a mining center. William had no idea if they really *could* build something to rival Tyre, one day, but he admired them for trying.

"You'll notice that much of our food is very simple," Barrington told him. "But feel free to eat as much as you like."

William felt an odd burst of nostalgia. He'd taken part in enough barn raisings as a young man to remember how the men would do the outdoor work while the women would lay out a fantastic spread. The meal in front of him was very similar. There was bread and cheese, cold meats and eggs and salad . . . The men tucked in without hesitation. Tanya seemed a little more reluctant to eat. William rather suspected she'd forgotten what people *ate* on Asher Dales.

"So far, things have been relatively safe out here," Barrington said, once he'd satisfied his hunger. "But we're expecting that to change. The Commonwealth is doing what it can, but there simply aren't enough ships on patrol to make a difference. We've already heard of a couple of worlds that were forced to supply food and drink"—he nodded at the jugs of water and juice—"to pirate ships. It won't be long before more pirates start making their way into the sector."

"Assuming you have anything they want to take," William pointed out.

"Our industrial base is small, but quite flexible," Barrington told him. "We could supply a pirate with quite a few components, if he demanded our compliance at gunpoint."

William lifted his eyebrows. "And the Theocracy didn't?"

Gellman smirked. "Most of our engineers went underground as soon as we realized what was coming our way," he said. "And they took quite a few things with them."

Barrington dabbed his mouth with a handkerchief. "Your role, Captain, as Tanya told you, is threefold. First, we want you to protect this system against pirates and . . . die-hard fanatics. Second, to eventually link up with other worlds in the sector and provide protection for convoys and suchlike. And third, to create a training school for our young men and women. Do you foresee any difficulties?"

William took a moment to consider his answer. "A great deal, Mr. President, depends on factors beyond our control . . ."

"Please, call me Richard," Barrington said. "I've been assured that my head is already too swollen for my own good."

"Yes . . . *Richard*," William said. He couldn't recall ever having such an informal dinner with a planetary president. He'd joined Kat and her late father for dinner, once, but even that had been absurdly formal. "There are several issues that need to be addressed. The first, put simply, is that we only have four destroyers. We can be reasonably sure of handling any pirate ship, should it decide to press the issue, but diehards might be harder to handle. And if we lose one of the destroyers, our ability to meet our commitments will be greatly reduced."

"We understand the limitations," Barrington said.

He used to be a smuggler, William reminded himself. *He probably understands the limitations of our technology better than the groundpounders.*

"Second, we cannot send away a destroyer, even for a short period of time, without being unable to recall her if there are . . . developments back here," he added. "We don't have a StarCom node here, let alone access to the interstellar communications network. A destroyer on escort duties will be out of reach until she returns. Nor will we know what happened to her if she just . . . vanishes.

"Third, training crewmen to operate the destroyers will take time. We did purchase simulators and suchlike, and they're on their way, but there are things that can only be learned by doing. The newbie crew may take years to learn their role, particularly if you want them to be more than . . . well, more than Theocratic crewmen. Training them to repair damaged components in the machine shop is *not* something that can be done quickly."

"But it can be done," Gellman said quietly.

"Yes," William said. "However, there's also a problem with employing the trainees once they have gained their certifications. There may be no positions for them to use their newfound skills."

"I plan to bring my remaining freighters here," Barrington said. "Given time, we may be able to turn this system into an interstellar shipping hub. There will be no shortage of work for the graduates."

William frowned. "What do you intend to ship?"

"There's quite a growing market for all sorts of mass-produced items," Barrington assured him. "And we can get in on the ground floor."

"I have a different question," Ford said suddenly. "We were promised that the Commonwealth would provide support to rebuild our economy, but the funds have . . . *unaccountably* failed to materialize. Do you believe the Commonwealth will *keep* their promise?"

William hesitated. "I am not in a position to speak for anyone on Tyre," he said after a moment. "But my impression is that the king overpromised. The Commonwealth was having problems even before the war, problems it was ill-equipped to handle. I think that Parliament put the brakes on the first payments before they could be made."

"Bah," Ford said. "And so we are on our own."

"You are not badly off, compared to some of the other planets in this sector," William pointed out.

"What do you think of him?" Gellman leaned forward. "The king, I mean?"

"I only met him once," William temporized. He would have shared his opinions with someone he knew well, but not a man he'd only just met. "I wasn't privy to any of his innermost thoughts."

Barrington cleared his throat. "We'd be happy to give you accommodation on the surface for the night," he said. "Or you can go back to your ship . . . ?"

"I'll go back," William said, glancing at his wristcom. "I have a lot of work to do."

"Your crews are more than welcome to visit the surface," Barrington said. "I'll catch up with you later."

"I'll show you back to the shuttle," Tanya said.

She didn't say anything else until they were back on the streets. "It feels strange to be back," she said quietly. "This is my home, yet I barely remember it."

"That will change," William told her. "I was a grown adult when I left my homeworld."

He looked up at the darkening sky. "You won't ever feel like you fit in here," he added, recalling his one visit to Hebrides during the war. "But you may carve out a role for yourself anyway."

"Part of me wants to go back home," Tanya said. She let out an odd little chuckle. "Tyre *feels* like home."

"Choose, but choose wisely," William said. "You can't live in two places at once."

"Are you talking about me," Tanya asked, "or yourself?"

William said nothing. He could see her point. Tanya was a trained and certified lawyer, but her degree was worthless on Asher Dales. Her father might find a role for her, or he might not. It would look bad to put his daughter in a position of undeserved power, even if she *was* the best-qualified person he had. Perhaps Tanya would be happier going back to Tyre.

"I don't know," he said finally. He'd come to realize, long ago, that there was nothing to be gained by living in the past. "I used to tell myself that I would go home, one day. And I kept telling myself that until I *couldn't* go home. But living here doesn't look *too* bad."

"Maybe not for you," Tanya said. "But for me . . ."

CHAPTER TWELVE

JUDD

"We will enter realspace in five minutes, Admiral," Commander Chanson Barrie reported, grimly. "We have not yet picked up any traces of enemy vessels."

Kat nodded, unsurprised. HMS *Violence* and her sisters had pushed their drives to the limits, cutting down the transit time between Ahura Mazda and Judd to three days, but she was fairly certain the enemy would have departed long ago. She'd had plenty of time to second-guess herself as she'd sat in her cabin, reading and rereading the tactical staff's assessments of the recordings from Judd. She had to see what had happened but, at the same time, she'd arguably abandoned her post.

"Bring the squadron to battlestations," she ordered. The superdreadnought commanders had allowed their training to slip. A mere year after the war and they'd have a very hard time coping with a Theocratic squadron. She silently kicked herself for not keeping their noses to the grindstone. "And prepare to engage the enemy."

She settled back in her command chair as the timer counted down the last few seconds. She'd be astonished if they actually *did* encounter the enemy—anyone with half a brain would have fled the system before reinforcements could arrive—but it was well to be careful. Whoever was in command of the remnants of the Theocracy's fleet could have decided to stake everything on one roll of the dice . . . or been replaced by someone with more fanaticism than common sense. ONI's estimates for how long the Theocrats could keep their fleet operating had been badly wrong. Kat wondered, sourly, if they'd missed a major enemy base somewhere. The Theocracy's record keeping had been poor even *before* they'd started to deliberately destroy their files. It was easy to imagine an enemy fleet base just vanishing from the paperwork.

They wouldn't have been able to afford it, Kat thought. The more she looked at the figures, the more she wondered how the Theocracy had managed to survive for so long. But then, they'd never faced a peer before. The single greatest challenge they'd faced before Cadiz had been a lone system with a tiny defensive fleet. They'd smashed them flat in an afternoon. *They simply weren't prepared for modern war.*

The superdreadnought shuddered as she sliced her way back into realspace. Kat leaned forward, bracing herself. The odds of being ambushed were very low, but that didn't mean she could afford to ignore them. War was a democracy, after all. The enemy got a vote. Her lips twitched at the thought—the Theocrats had forgotten that when they'd started the war—then thinned as the display began to fill with data. There were no enemy starships within sensor range, while the planet itself was as cold and silent as the grave.

They didn't drop an antimatter bomb, she told herself. Judd's population had been dispersed, first by the settlement planners and then by the war. The Theocrats would have to render the entire planet uninhabitable if they wanted to slaughter everyone. *There's that, at least.*

"Raise the planet," she ordered, trying to suppress her doubts. The Theocrats could have nuked everything bigger than a village and her ships wouldn't know about it until they got much closer. "Inform them . . . inform them that we are entering orbit."

Her eyes narrowed as she studied the display. There was no sign of HMS *Gibraltar* or *Edinburgh*, not even cooling wreckage slowly falling into the planet's atmosphere. Kat wasn't entirely surprised, although she was *pissed*. Captain Layman had clearly been asleep at the switch. Kat promised herself that she'd make damn sure that everyone knew that they had to remain on alert, at least until the enemy force was hunted down and destroyed. She suspected she knew what Captain Layman had been thinking, but she didn't care. Layman should have been in a position to break contact and escape.

"Admiral, I have been unable to establish contact with the planet," the communications officer said. "However, I *am* picking up a stealthed recon drone. It responded to our sweep."

"Download its memory core," Kat ordered as an icon flickered into existence on the display. Hopefully, the drone had recorded enough of the battle to be useful. "And put the recordings on the main display."

"Aye, Admiral."

"And keep trying to raise the planet," Kat added. She wasn't sure *what* she'd do if they couldn't contact anyone on the surface. Land shuttles at random in hopes of finding someone in authority? *Was* there even any authority left on the surface? The Theocrats had clearly bombarded the planet heavily. Judd's unity might have been shattered beyond repair. "Let me know the moment you make contact."

Her console bleeped. The data download was ready to view. Kat keyed the display and watched the whole engagement from beginning to end. Captain Layman had *definitely* been caught with her pants down—her mind provided a whole string of cruder metaphors—and two cruisers had been blown out of existence without even managing to scratch the enemy's paint! Kat felt a sinking feeling as she reran the record, watching the engagement for a second time. The enemy missiles seemed to have extended range, more than she would have thought possible. Captain Layman might well have been caught by surprise . . . No, she *had* been caught by surprise. There had been no reason to think that the missiles might have been improved until it was too late.

Someone definitely helped them, Kat thought. The Theocrats could barely keep their starships running. Anyone competent enough to modify missiles on the fly wouldn't have been assigned to the fleet. They'd have stayed in the Ahura Mazda shipyards and probably been killed when the Commonwealth invaded. *But who?*

She keyed her console. "Tactical, I want a full analysis of the engagement by the end of the day," she said. "And I *particularly* want to know how many of those superdreadnoughts are real."

"Aye, Admiral."

Kat forced herself to think as she replayed the recording, once again. Only *three* enemy superdreadnoughts had opened fire, which suggested they were the only *real* ships in the phantom fleet. Three superdreadnoughts were nothing to laugh at, and they could wreak havoc until the Commonwealth finally hunted the ships down and destroyed them, but they weren't an unmanageable threat. And yet . . . she knew that there was no way she could be sure. There might have been five superdreadnoughts, with two of them holding their fire. It wasn't as if they'd needed more than one superdreadnought to take out two cruisers.

They're lucky they didn't hit the planet, Kat thought. She didn't like the implications of the Theocrats firing off so many missiles in a single engagement, not against a vastly inferior force. They clearly thought there was no chance of running out of missiles. *Who's helping them?*

"Admiral," the communications officer said, "I've managed to establish a link with a General Fox. He claims to be the current chief executive, as everyone above him in the line of succession is either dead or out of communication."

Kat tapped her console, bringing up the files on Judd. There was no reference to a General Fox . . . or anyone, really, below the planetary president and his cabinet. The Commonwealth hadn't bothered to collect any information on the planet . . . *In hindsight*, she told herself, *that might have been a mistake.* On one hand, Judd was independent; the locals could sort out their problems for themselves. But, on the other, she had no way of knowing who was the legitimate head of state. General Fox apparently didn't know either.

They didn't have time to set up a proper government since they were liberated, she reminded herself numbly. *And now they've been bombed back into the stone age again.*

"Put him through," she ordered.

"Admiral Falcone," a voice said. There was no image. It took Kat a moment to realize that General Fox, wherever he was, didn't have access to a camera. She couldn't believe it. Just how badly had the planet been hit? "I'd like to welcome you to Judd, but as you can see, we're in no state to receive visitors."

"I understand," Kat said quickly. The general's accent was thick. She thought she heard resentment underlying his words, but it was hard to be sure. "Can you give me a sitrep?"

General Fox laughed humorlessly. "They hammered us," he said. "Every governmental building and military base has been destroyed, along with dozens of bridges, warehouses, and buildings I think were targeted at random. Oh, and they landed at the POW camps and armed the prisoners. The bastards are now causing havoc wherever they go."

Kat frowned. There was something about the attack pattern that didn't quite make sense. The Theocrats hadn't nuked Judd, but they'd hit the planet hard enough to destroy the government and trigger a refugee crisis. It wouldn't be as bad as they'd probably hoped, she thought, yet . . . they could have simply nuked the planet. Or dropped bigger KEWs. Had they *wanted* to set off a crisis?

Perhaps they did, she thought. *We'd have to help the locals, which means draining our resources still further.*

She glanced at the out-system display. The cloudscoop was gone. She guessed that the HE3 stockpiles on the planet's surface had also been destroyed. Judd was going to have a power shortage along with everything else, although . . . She shook her head. There was no point in looking for small mercies. Thousands of people were going to die in the next few weeks, and there was nothing she could do about it. Even if she put in an immediate request for assistance, it would take too long for it to arrive.

"I see," she said, racking her brain. There had to be *something* they could do. "How may we assist you?"

General Fox laughed again. "If you have shuttles or aircraft, it might be useful," he said. "But unless you have your ships crammed with ration bars, I'm not sure what else you *can* do."

"We'll do our best," Kat promised. Her marines had plenty of experience working with desperate refugees. Here, thankfully, there was little chance of being caught up in an insurgent attack. "I'll start shipping supplies down to you at once."

"Thank you," General Fox said. "Admiral . . . how long can your ships remain in orbit?"

Kat grimaced. "I don't know," she said slowly. She'd have to dispatch the courier boats to alert the other systems within the sector, but . . . but it wasn't as if there was anything most of the liberated worlds could do to defend themselves. "We'll stay as long as we can."

"Which won't be long enough," General Fox told her. "What happens when they come back?"

They won't, Kat wanted to say. But she knew there was no way she could guarantee that. The Theocrats might return, sooner rather than later, and smash Judd flat once again. And she couldn't keep her fleet on guard permanently. She'd have to go haring off to the *next* enemy target. *There's no way we can stay here.*

"I don't know," she said honestly. "But, for the moment, you're safe."

"Hah," General Fox said.

He closed the channel. Kat took a long breath. She didn't blame General Fox for being angry, both at the Theocrats and the Commonwealth. He and his former superiors had believed that the navy would protect them. But no one had anticipated a massive enemy force dropping out of hyperspace and blowing two cruisers to atoms. She considered, briefly, splitting up her superdreadnought squadrons and dispatching one or two of them to every threatened world. It was workable, in theory, but it ran the risk of a lone ship being attacked by superior force.

We'd take a bite out of them, she thought. She was fairly sure that one of her superdreadnoughts could take on two enemy ships at once. *But we might well lose our superdreadnought in the engagement.*

She dismissed the thought with an angry grunt as she keyed her console. "Major Harris, you are authorized to land," she said. "Coordinate your relief efforts with the planetary government"—*such as it is*—"and . . . and do everything you can for them."

"Aye, Admiral," Major Harris said. "Do you have a timescale?"

"Not as yet," Kat admitted. She gritted her teeth in annoyance. There was no way she could give the marines a *definite* leaving time. "But we'll be here for at least two days."

"Aye, Admiral."

Kat sighed as she closed the connection. It wasn't enough to help the planet. It wasn't anything *like* enough. They'd barely scratch the surface of what needed to be done. But they *had* to try.

Unless we pull the marines out in a couple of days, because we have to go elsewhere, Kat thought as she brought up a starchart. *The enemy could be hitting another world right now.*

She considered the problem for a long moment, silently reflecting on the irony. It was what *she'd* done, three years ago. And now she was on the receiving end.

Too many possible targets, she told herself. *And yet, too many of them are effectively worthless.*

Her thoughts ran in circles. But the conclusion was inescapable. There was no way she'd be able to catch the enemy, save by sheer luck. Trying to shadow them back to their base might work, given time, but she knew that idea was a long shot. Unless, of course, she managed to bait a trap. A couple of ideas had already occurred to her.

"Detail one of the courier boats to take a copy of the engagement records back to Ahura Mazda," she ordered. "And then detail three of the remaining boats to alert everyone within fifty light-years. I want every liberated world to be taking precautions."

"Aye, Admiral," the communications officer said.

Kat sighed. It wasn't enough, and she knew it. But it was all she could do until she got reinforcements.

And if the last report from home is any indication, she thought, *I'll be lucky if I don't get half my ships taken away.*

◆ ◆ ◆

Millicent Barbara had always admired the sheer resilience of the planet's population. Judd hadn't been an easy world to tame, back when the colony ship had first landed, and then they'd spent a decade under the Theocracy's iron heel. They'd bounced back after the liberation; they'd repaired their cities, settled new farms, and even started a long-term plan to develop the remainder of their star system. She'd thought nothing could keep them down.

But now, looking at the men and women in the makeshift refugee camp, she wondered if the Theocracy had finally broken the planet's population. A handful of refugees had volunteered to assist the militia and aid workers, but the remainder were just sitting there as if they expected to be fed and watered like animals. They didn't even have the *entitlement* she'd come to hate on Ahura Mazda, the belief that they had a right to be given food and drink without payment. She shuddered as she saw the listless eyes and unmoving bodies. They didn't even have the drive to pick up the pieces and start again.

She shook her head, morbidly, as she saw a pair of shuttles come in to land. The Royal Marines had been helpful, but there was little they could do. There just weren't enough supplies to feed the refugees. And even if they had enough, now, soon they would run out completely. She had no idea what would happen then, but she didn't think it would be pretty. The local farmers were already grumbling about supplying food to the refugee camps. It wouldn't be long before they either ran out or refused to supply any more.

And it's only been seven days, she thought. *What will happen when winter comes?*

"Millie," Dave called. "There's someone here you need to see."

Millicent followed his gaze . . . and froze. The young woman walking towards her, surrounded by a trio of marines, was one of the most famous people in the Commonwealth. Kat Falcone looked even younger than Millicent had realized, going by the newscasts; she would have taken the woman for someone in her early twenties if she hadn't known that Kat Falcone was a decade older. Blonde hair, cropped closer to her scalp; a dazzling white uniform . . . she looked good, but there was something haunted in her eyes.

Millicent understood, better than she cared to admit. The Commonwealth had failed Judd.

"Admiral Falcone," she said, suddenly unsure how to address their visitor. "I'm Millicent Barbara. Welcome to the camp."

"Thank you," Kat Falcone said. "What's the situation?"

"Grim," Millicent said as they walked around the edge of the camp. "Most of the refugees have lost the will to do anything, even to live. They're just sitting around and waiting to die."

Kat shot her a sharp look. "You can't find them work? Something to *do* with their time?"

Millicent snorted. "There's no shortage of work," she assured her. "But the will to actually *do* it is lacking."

She waved a hand towards the nearest tent. "Everyone here went to the city to build new lives for themselves, lives that were just snatched away a week ago. They've lost partners and children, friends and coworkers . . . they've simply given up. They might go back to work if they were starved, which is what may happen in the next week or so, or they might simply lie down and die. They've been broken."

"Shit," Kat Falcone said.

"This world needs help, Admiral," Millicent told her. She waved towards the marines, who were digging a well. "We need help, not . . . not penny-pinching."

"That may be difficult," Kat Falcone told her. Her voice was flat, emotionless. "This may just be the beginning."

CHAPTER THIRTEEN

ASHER DALES

"The station *isn't* on the verge of falling apart," Commander Patti Ludwig commented after the engineering crews had spent two days inspecting every last inch of the orbiting station. "I don't believe it."

William nodded in agreement. The station was clearly marked by signs of slapdash construction and maintenance—there was no point in trying to pretend that someone other than the Theocracy had built it—but was surprisingly intact. Whoever had been in command must have been smarter, or simply more knowledgeable, than the average Theocratic commander. Maybe they'd been exiled for daring to know more than they should about engineering, he speculated silently. Or perhaps they'd simply forced themselves to learn when they realized that their life *depended* on everything working right.

"I checked the computer core," Lieutenant Jennifer Flowers said. "It's primitive, by our standards, but it can handle everything. We probably don't even have to replace it."

"Not at once anyway," William said. "But we will have to replace it eventually."

"Agreed," Patti said. "Who knows *what* they might have done to it."

William winced. There were literally billions of lines of code inside a modern computer core. The Theocrats could easily put a backdoor into the system that would allow them to take over, or simply turn off the life support, at a moment's notice. He doubted that any of the crewmen would be able to remove it, even if they'd realized that the backdoor was there. The Theocrats probably believed computers to be magic. And even if there *wasn't* a backdoor or hidden virus planted within the system, there was a good chance the system would fail anyway, sooner or later. He didn't think they'd have bothered to keep up with the latest system patches.

He scowled as he surveyed the command center. The station was large, but most of it consisted of storage compartments and a lone fusion core that was nearly thirty years out of date. There wasn't much room left for everything else. He was used to living on starships and space stations, but he couldn't help thinking that the crew would have been on the verge of going insane before they'd been killed. Tiny compartments were one thing; a complete lack of entertainment was quite another. They'd worked, prayed, and slept . . . without even a hint of anything else. It made him wonder precisely how the locals had managed to take the station. Getting up to orbit alone should be impossible without clearance.

Maybe the enemy sensor network failed at a crucial moment, he thought. *Or maybe they were distracted.*

"We can proceed, I believe," he said. "We'll leave a small crew on the station, for the moment, but we can't go any further until the freighter arrives."

He nodded to his subordinates, then strode off the command deck and down the corridor to the airlock. The station was easily large enough to allow the destroyers to dock comfortably—it had been designed to handle much larger freighters—but he hadn't been inclined to take the risk until the station had been checked thoroughly. Even though it was safe, or as a safe as a piece of Theocratic technology ever got, he wasn't keen on docking his ships. The station was a sitting duck. A single nuclear missile would take it out, along with any vessels that happened to be docked at the time. Losing a sizeable chunk of his squadron like *that* would be extremely embarrassing.

Tanya was waiting for him when he returned to *Dandelion*, looking edgy. She'd been in charge of giving his crewmen a couple of days of shore leave, something he thought she'd embrace, but she didn't seem to be enjoying her homecoming. It made William wonder if she'd try to book a flight back to Tyre the next time a freighter passed through the system. It would take months—there were no regular services flying through the Gap yet—but she could do it. Hell, she could probably trade free legal advice for passage. Freighter captains were permanently fretting about winding up on the wrong side of the law.

"William," she said, "is the station usable?"

"For the moment," William told her. "*That* was a bit of a surprise."

Tanya had to smile as they headed down the corridor to his office. "They told me that the station was in good condition," she said. "And besides, beggars can't be choosers."

"True," William agreed. Richard Barrington was a rich man, richer than William had appreciated at first, but there were limits. He wasn't nearly as rich as Kat's family. "I'm sure the station will survive long enough for us to replace it with a modern installation."

"Or even one that works perfectly," Tanya said. The hatch hissed open as they approached, allowing them to walk into the office. "Father wanted to know when you'd be ready to start exercises."

"Today, I think," William said as he sat down. He keyed his console, bringing up the in-system display. The system looked empty, although he knew that could be completely meaningless. The entire Royal Navy could be hidden within the system and he'd be none the wiser, as long as the starships kept their drives and sensors stepped down. "I've sent *Primrose* to survey the outer edge of the system, but she should be back today."

Tanya lifted her eyebrows. "You think it needs to be done?"

"Our navigation charts are badly out of date," William said. "And if we fly into a gravitational eddy we didn't know was there, we'll be lucky if we *only* get kicked back into realspace."

He shrugged. An encounter with an eddy wasn't too likely to happen, but an ounce of prevention was better than a pound of cure. Besides, Barrington presumably *didn't* want to make life difficult for anyone visiting his system. An independent freighter captain might think twice about flying to Asher Dales if there was even the slightest prospect of running into trouble. It was dangerous enough flying through the liberated sector without making it worse.

"We'll start once *Primrose* returns," he added. "And once the rest of the ships arrive, we can . . ."

He stopped as the alert bleeped. "Captain," Lieutenant Yang said, "a courier boat has just dropped out of hyperspace. She's transmitting a priority-one signal to us and the planet."

William sucked in his breath. A priority-*one* signal meant . . . what? An imminent threat to the planet? They'd only just *gotten* to Asher Dales! He forced himself to think, fast. Who'd be attacking them? There was nothing that might draw an interstellar power to attack Asher Dales . . . was there?

"Have the signal copied to my terminal," he said. "And then request the courier boat to hold position."

"Aye, sir," Yang said.

Tanya cleared her throat. "What is it?"

"Bad news," William guessed. The message blinked up on his terminal. "You may have to call your father."

He read the message with a growing sense of disbelief. An enemy force, a *Theocratic* force, had attacked Judd, leaving the planet in ruins. The recording made disturbing viewing, even though the analysts had noted that most of the enemy superdreadnoughts were no more than sensor ghosts. A lone superdreadnought would have no difficulty turning his squadron into atoms, then trashing the orbiting space station and the planet below. Three, or four, or five were overkill. But the enemy had already shown a disturbing fondness for overkill.

". . . Shit," he said slowly. He swung the terminal round so Tanya could see the message. "You *definitely* have to call your father."

"I will," she said. "But it may take some time for everyone on the surface to stop panicking."

They'll have a point, William thought. He had no idea how Barrington had financed the purchase of four destroyers, but he had to have pushed his resources to the limit. Losing them would be utterly disastrous. *Asher Dales is practically defenseless against anything larger than a light cruiser.*

He forced himself to think as Tanya watched the message again and again. The enemy ships would have reached Asher Dales by now if they'd flown directly from Judd. Looking at the time stamps on the reports, he could see that the attack had actually taken place seven days before the alert had been dispatched. There was no reason to assume, he told himself firmly, that Asher Dales was about to be attacked. But that might change. Anyone intent on causing problems, both for the Commonwealth and the liberated worlds, would want to destroy Barrington's investment in nuclear fire.

And smash the planet-side industries too, William thought. He'd been brought up to think that industrial nodes should be in space, where there was limitless energy and no need to worry about pollution, but he could see why Asher Dales didn't have any choice. *They could bomb Asher Dales back to bedrock in an afternoon.*

"I have to call my father," Tanya said. "Do you mind if I use your terminal?"

"Not at all," William said. "Do you want me to stay?"

"He'll probably want to speak to you," Tanya said. She smiled weakly. "I'll call him now."

William brought up the starchart and studied it quickly. The worst-case assumption, according to ONI, was that the enemy had five superdreadnoughts. William privately doubted that figure—he doubted the rogue Theocrats could keep five superdreadnoughts operational without shipyards and supplies—but the scenario still had to be taken seriously. The enemy could ravage the sector and . . . there was very little the Commonwealth could do to stop them.

Too few potential targets too, William thought. Ahura Mazda and Maxwell's Haven were probably the bigger ones, the targets the enemy would *love* to hit, but they were both heavily defended. The Theocrats would be blown to atoms if they faced the Royal Navy in open battle. *We might be quite high up their list of realistic targets.*

"That's the long and short of it, Father," Tanya said. She raised her voice, drawing William's attention. "We may be attacked at any moment."

"I see," Barrington said. "William? Do you concur with this assessment?"

"I don't see any reason to panic," William said after a moment. "The situation is grim, let us not think otherwise, but it's not a complete disaster. There *is* a good chance we will be targeted . . ."

"As I said," Tanya commented.

". . . But we have no way to know when, or even *if*, we will be hit," William finished. "I don't think anyone knows that you've assembled a small fleet, at least not yet. They might not consider Asher Dales to be a particularly important target."

"And if you're wrong?" Barrington's voice was very cold. "What happens then?"

"We lose," William said flatly. "There is no way that four destroyers can stand off five superdreadnoughts. But there *are* ways we can make them pay . . ."

Or possibly even deter them from attacking, he thought. It wouldn't be *that* hard to rig up a pair of drones to pose as superdreadnoughts. The illusion wouldn't last for long, but it might just convince the enemy that Asher Dales was too big a target to be hit safely. They wouldn't want to tangle with superdreadnoughts even if they had numerical superiority. *As long as we don't have to open fire, we should be able to fool them.*

"There's no way they can be made to pay *enough*," Barrington said savagely. "What are they thinking?"

William shrugged. It was possible the rogue ships were reaching the end of their lifespan. It wouldn't surprise him. A superdreadnought needed one day in a shipyard for every ten days on active duty, and the Theocrats had lost *all* their shipyards. Their commanders might have decided to go out in a blaze of glory, or, perhaps worse, think they could wear the defenders down with atrocity after atrocity until the Commonwealth withdrew from the sector, leaving them to pick up the pieces and rebuild the Theocracy. They might manage it too. They had more firepower than most of the liberated worlds put together.

We need support from the Royal Navy, he thought grimly. *But the navy can't hope to cover* every *potential target.*

"Right," Barrington said. "Captain, you are to do everything within your power to prepare to defend our world. And . . . if they do attack in force, I expect you to make them pay as high a price as possible before you withdraw."

Tanya gasped. "Withdraw?"

"A pair of light cruisers were destroyed at Judd," Barrington said sharply. "And what do we have? Two *destroyers*."

William scowled. He didn't like the thought of abandoning Asher Dales to the Theocrats, not when it was all too clear that everything Barrington and his people had built would be destroyed from orbit. Asher Dales didn't have a refugee problem, thankfully. There were no POW camps for the enemy to raid. But Barrington was right. The two destroyers, four if the remainder of the squadron arrived before the enemy, wouldn't stand a chance if the Theocracy attacked. The vessels of Asher Dales *might* be able to land a blow or two—William was already starting to turn his vague ideas into something *usable*—but the outcome was inevitable.

"We will do what we can," he promised. "And I already have a couple of ideas."

"Good luck," Barrington said. "I'll be dispersing the population down here. Hopefully, they'll blast empty cities rather than crowded farms."

William winced. Hebrides had followed a similar strategy, back when the pirate attacks had begun. It had worked, to some extent, but hadn't kept the pirates from extorting food, drink, and women from the planetary population. And Asher Dales was facing the Theocracy. A pirate ship might give up and go away. The Theocracy wouldn't leave unless they encountered superior force.

They'd be fools to allow themselves to be pinned down so easily, he told himself. *They might just make one pass through the system, blast anything that looks important, then retreat at once.*

"Perhaps we should set up decoys on the surface," he said. "A handful of ECM pods, perhaps. If we configure them to look like they're industrial nodes, they might bomb them and miss the *real* targets."

Barrington smiled, wanly. "And rig explosives underneath them to make it look like they went up with a bang," he added. "Let them *think* they hurt us."

William's lips twitched humorlessly as he recalled an old joke. One side of a war had set up a dummy airfield, complete with dummy hangars and dummy aircraft. The enemy had promptly bombed it, with dummy bombs. It might work, he told himself. If the explosions were spectacular enough, the Theocrats wouldn't want to look any closer. They wouldn't want to think that they'd been tricked.

Except this lot seem alarmingly smart, he thought. *They might be more careful.*

"It should work," he said. They had nothing to lose by trying. "If nothing else, we might just manage to give them a bloody nose."

"Then get right on it," Barrington ordered. "I'll talk to you two later."

His image vanished. William looked at Tanya. "He's taking it remarkably well."

"Father has always been . . . somewhat phlegmatic," Tanya said. "The slings and arrows of outrageous fortune are a part of his life, he says."

William nodded in wry approval. "*Primrose* will be back soon," he said. "Once she's in position, we can start our planning."

Tanya met his eyes. "Can you *really* hurt them?"

"We will try," William said. The firepower disparity was going to hurt his little squadron. "Like I said, we should be able to give them a bloody nose. A little deception, and they might not even push us to the wall."

And if someone proposed this as a solution to a naval problem, he added in the privacy of his own thoughts, *they'd be lucky not to be hauled in front of a court-martial and charged with gross stupidity.*

She rose. "I'll leave you to get on with it," she said. "Dinner tonight, at the usual time?"

"Perhaps not," William said. "I'll have to meet Captain Descartes for dinner. We need to do some advanced planning."

He looked down at the desk. "Perhaps we should have escorted the freighter directly here after all."

"We'd still be in transit," Tanya said. "Wouldn't we?"

She walked through the hatch, which hissed closed behind her. William smiled ruefully, then keyed his terminal. They'd crammed the destroyers with supplies, but the shortage of internal volume had really limited what they could bring. The local industry could make up some of the shortfall, but other items would need to wait until the other ships arrived. Unless, of course, he requested help from the Royal Navy. Kat would understand the need, he was sure.

But not everyone will, he thought. There had always been a pervasive anti-colonial sentiment in the upper ranks, something that had only been made worse by the mutiny on *Uncanny*. It was funny how colonial officers and men seemed to be the first selected for involuntary discharges. *Some of them will decide we can look after ourselves.*

He shook his head as he keyed his terminal. "Communications, ask the courier boat to wait for five more minutes," he said. It wasn't something he could order, not anymore. "I have a message I need them to take to Ahura Mazda."

"Aye, sir."

CHAPTER FOURTEEN

AHURA MAZDA

"Your shuttle is ready, Admiral," Captain Rosslyn said. "We are cleared to depart."

Kat barely moved from her chair. The flight back to Ahura Mazda had been uneventful, although she'd hoped in vain that they'd stumble across the enemy fleet. She'd detached two of her superdreadnoughts to cover Judd, all too aware that she was taking a serious risk by breaking up the squadron. It had been easy, during the five days she'd spent in transit, to second-guess herself time and time again. The Theocrats weren't going to return to Judd . . . were they?

They might, just to make us look like fools, she thought. *And if they do, we'll be ready for them.*

She stood, slowly. She'd spent the voyage trying to find a way they could handle the situation without reinforcements, but nothing had come to mind. She just didn't have enough ships . . . the refrain had echoed through her head, time and time again. There was no way she could cover *all* the possible targets without spreading her forces too thin. Cold logic told her she should abandon a number of worlds, but the thought was unbearable. The Commonwealth had sworn to protect the liberated planets.

And the horrors the bastards unleashed on Judd will be repeated a millionfold, she told herself glumly. The Theocrats hadn't aimed at occupation, not this time. They'd set out to make the planet's inhabitants miserable, and they'd succeeded. *How long will it be until another world is hit?*

Her mind was elsewhere as she followed her close-protection detail to the nearest airlock. She'd downloaded a tactical update as soon as they'd dropped out of hyperspace, but all it had been able to tell her was that the Theocrats hadn't shown themselves . . . not in the last few days anyway. The bastards could attack a world on the other side of the sector and she wouldn't know about it for weeks, if she was lucky. Next time, they might manage to ensure that *no* word got out until it was far too late.

She kept mulling the situation over and over in her mind, paying no heed to the shuttle's brief flight through the atmosphere. The pilot was good enough to bring the craft in for a smooth landing, somewhat to her relief. She'd never minded flying through turbulence when *she* was in command of the shuttle, but being a passenger worried her. She wasn't in control when someone else was flying the craft. Logic told her there was nothing to fear—the shuttle's automatics could handle almost anything—but her emotions told her something different. She *liked* to be in control.

I really shouldn't have let them promote me off the command deck, she thought again. She shook her head in annoyance. *Maybe I can trade my admiral's rank stars for a post on a starship . . .*

It was a nice thought, but she knew it wasn't going to happen. She would never command a starship again, not really. A squadron or a fleet . . . but not a starship. Unless she bought the ship herself. There was enough money in her trust fund to buy a midsized freighter, if she wanted it, but . . . She sighed as she rose and headed for the hatch. She and Pat had planned a future together, after the war. That future was now as dead as Pat himself. And, somehow, she had to go on.

You have your duty, she reminded herself severely. *Both as an admiral in the navy and as a privy councilor.*

Lieutenant Kitty Patterson met her outside the shuttle. "Admiral," she said, saluting. "The remainder of your officers are waiting in the conference room."

"Good," Kat said, striding past her. She didn't relish the thought of going straight into a meeting, but there was no choice. "Have food and drink sent in, if you please. It's going to be a long day."

She felt a flicker of grim concern as she walked into the conference room. A giant holographic starchart hung over the table, bright spheres showing the ever-growing volume of space hiding the enemy ships. Civilians might think that the sphere could be searched, but military officers knew better. The sphere was so unimaginably vast that a *billion* superdreadnoughts would go unnoticed. Kat had no doubt the Theocrats had taken every precaution to escape detection.

And they won't have attacked the closest world to their base anyway, she thought. *They'll have done everything in their power to escape being detected.*

"Be seated," she ordered stiffly. The stewards rolled in a trolley of food, then withdrew as silently as they came. "I assume you've seen the reports from Judd?"

"Yes, Admiral," General Winters said. "It doesn't look good."

"There is no way we can provide the level of support they require," Major Shawna Callable said. Her voice was very cold. "They're going to be thrown back on their own resources."

"They need help," Kat said.

"We don't have the equipment or manpower," Shawna informed her. "The vast majority of our supplies are already earmarked for one world or another. Even if we switched them all to Judd, just *getting* them there would be a problem. We'd have to gather the transport and then provide an escort . . ."

"And we might simply be giving the enemy more targets to shoot at," Winters added. "They will be watching for any chance to weaken us."

"Or to make us look like idiots," Kat snapped. She glowered at Janice. "What's ONI's take on the recordings?"

"Five enemy superdreadnoughts, at most," Captain Janice Wilson said. "Long-range scans were disrupted by their ECM, which appears to have been significantly upgraded, but I think we can be fairly sure there were no more than five superdreadnoughts present at the engagement. The vast majority of enemy contacts simply didn't produce any drive turbulence or rogue energy signatures. A handful of analysts actually believe there were no more than *three*, but not everyone finds their case convincing."

It's what we'd want to believe, Kat told herself.

She took a breath. "And the smaller ships?"

"About half of them were real, if the scans were accurate," Janice said. "But they were bunched up."

"They're also immaterial," Commodore Fran Higgins said. "They won't pose a threat without the superdreadnoughts."

"Someone is supplying them," Winters rumbled. "Who?"

"We don't know," Janice admitted. She leaned back in her chair, looking tired. "On one hand, they seem to have indigenous weapons and sensors . . . simply heavily modified. The handful of nonindigenous systems are devices they could probably buy on the black market. We were never as effective as we might have wished in cutting off supplies from outside the Theocracy."

Because the other Great Powers wanted to test their weapons on the battlefield, Kat thought cynically. If the war had done anything, apart from killing millions of people, it had taught the spacefaring powers that their imaginations had been somewhat inadequate. *And they didn't want to ship the weapons to us, because we'd simply copy them.*

"Then we have to find their purchasing agent," Winters said. "Assuming they actually *have* one."

"That's something to follow up on later," Kat said. She tapped the table. "I will, of course, be requesting reinforcements from home. However, until they arrive, we need to handle the situation with what we have on hand. That will not be easy."

"No," Winters agreed. "They can pick and choose their targets at will."

Kat nodded. "Maxwell's Haven can look after itself," she said. The planet had practically been annexed after the war, although the inhabitants hadn't offered a word of protest. "The fixed defenses can handle the enemy fleet, if it risks an attack so close to the Gap. We will withdraw the superdreadnoughts covering the planet and add them to our deployable forces, along with one of the two superdreadnought squadrons here. That gives us four squadrons to deploy."

"Minus the two superdreadnoughts you left at Judd," Fran said quietly.

"Yes," Kat said. She wondered, sourly, if there was anything to gain by trying to protect Ahura Mazda. The whole planet was a mess. There were times when she'd simply considered advising the king to cut his losses and abandon the wretched planet. Anyone who wanted to come with the departing fleet would be welcome. "That can't be helped."

She nodded to the starchart. "We will parcel out the superdreadnoughts in squadrons of four and five ships, positioning them in places where they will be able to speed to the rescue of any attacked world. Ideally, they will be able to intercept and destroy the enemy fleet. Even if they don't, they'll make the enemy think twice about attacking if they think there's a reasonable chance of being caught."

"Risky," Fran observed. "It will be tricky to reconcentrate our forces if there is an emergency."

"No one is going to invade the Theocratic Sector," Janice said.

"No one would *want* to invade the Theocratic Sector," Shawna commented. "Is there anything here anyone actually *wants*?"

Kat shrugged. The Commonwealth was the closest interstellar power, and Tyre had no stomach for further expansion. It was difficult

---

enough absorbing the worlds that had joined the Commonwealth before the war. Anyone else . . . She supposed that Marseilles or a couple of others might be interested in setting up trading posts, just to give themselves some influence, but they'd hardly want to annex the sector. The locals, on the other hand, might want to be annexed.

"We'll be setting up an emergency StarCom network," she said. "We have the prefabricated units in storage. It's time we put them to use."

She smiled coldly. The bean counters were going to be screaming for her head when they figured out what she'd done, but she found it hard to care. She hadn't been promoted to admiral just so she could look calm and resolute as the sector fell into anarchy. There was a crisis now. They could set up the network and to hell with the cost.

Winters grinned. "Yes, Admiral."

"There will be outrage back home," Colonel Christopher Whitehall warned. "And you may be forced to pay."

That would wipe out the old trust fund, Kat thought, with a flicker of amusement. Her plan wasn't much—she was all too aware it wasn't much—but it might just give them an edge. The Theocracy had built the first portable StarCom, an innovation no one had expected, yet the Commonwealth had improved upon the design. They were still hideously expensive, but at least they didn't explode when someone looked at them the wrong way. *And if I have to pay for them . . .*

She shook her head. The StarComs had been produced for emergencies . . . and this, she was sure, was an emergency. She would sooner endure the wrath of the wretched bureaucrats who'd moan and whine about her spending billions of crowns than watch another world die under enemy fire. The only downside was that the portable units wouldn't last long. They simply lacked the shielding to keep them operational indefinitely. Hopefully, the situation would be resolved quickly. And if it wasn't . . .

Parliament will need to vote on an emergency spending bill, she thought. *That's not going to go down well.*

"I'll deal with the consequences," she said firmly. "We will also be distributing courier boats throughout the sector, which will allow us to react faster when there isn't a StarCom in the system. It isn't a perfect solution, but it will have to do."

Her eyes swept the room. "If any of you have better ideas," she added wryly, "please feel free to offer them."

"Finding their base is a great idea in principle," Winters said. "But in practice . . ."

"We'll step up our survey efforts," Kat said. The Theocracy had never bothered to survey the farther reaches of their sector. It was an oversight that puzzled her, although she supposed that they'd probably been bent on conquest ever since they'd realized that Earth was nothing more than radioactive rubble. There was nothing to conquer in that direction, save perhaps for a handful of isolated colonies. "We *might* get lucky."

"And we'll focus on isolating their supply lines." Janice grimaced. "Too much war material got onto the black market after the war."

"Work on it," Kat ordered. She remembered William's brother and scowled. "If worse comes to worst, I expect we can hand out a few pardons if they lead to bigger fish."

It might be worth trying to get in touch with him, she thought. She hadn't *exactly* lost touch with William, but . . . messages had become more and more infrequent as time had gone by. The last she'd heard, he'd gone to his new homeworld. She'd have to check with her family, then send a priority message. William was, technically, a family client. *Someone* would be keeping an eye on his movements. *And his brother might be able to help us.*

"They might be glad to get a chance to go legit," Winters said. "But most smugglers already *have* that option."

"We will see," Kat said. "Commodore, have your staff draw up a plan to deploy StarComs and disperse the fleet. I'll take command of one of the task forces personally."

"Aye, Admiral," Fran said. "Do you want me to remain here?"

"Yes," Kat said. "They *might* come calling."

"I doubt it," Janice said. "What would be the point?"

"An attack here would make us look weak," Whitehall pointed out. "And everything we'd done on the surface would be lost."

Kat couldn't disagree. The enemy could not be allowed to recapture their former homeworld or even hold the high orbitals for an hour or so. An hour would be more than long enough to smash the Commonwealth garrisons and give the insurgents a chance to reclaim the surface and kill the collaborators. By the time her fleet returned, Ahura Mazda would be in ruins. Again.

And we wouldn't even be able to evacuate the people who worked with us, she thought. *The people who placed their lives in our hands.*

"We will keep a superdreadnought squadron here, under cloak," she said. "They *might* take the bait."

She rubbed her forehead, feeling a headache starting to blossom beneath her skin. She wanted—she needed—to take *action* . . . but all she could do was wait. The enemy would determine their next target and then . . .

If we're lucky, we'll have a task force close enough to intercept, she told herself. *And even if we are not, we might be able to trace them back to their base.*

"We'll meet again this evening," she said. "And then we'll start dispersing the fleet. Dismissed."

She watched them go, then sat back in her chair. She'd taken a gamble—a big one. There were too many things that could go wrong, too many places the enemy might attack . . . The Theocrats, like it or not, would dictate the pace of the conflict. She might get lucky—she certainly *hoped* she'd get lucky—but the odds weren't on her side. The Commonwealth could do everything right and still lose.

Which happens, sometimes, she thought, recalling a piece of advice from one of her instructors. The Royal Navy had been preparing for war and the cadets, regardless of their family background, had deliberately been put into a no-win scenario. *You do everything in your power, you do everything you can . . . and you lose anyway.*

She tapped her terminal, writing out a brief message for the family manager back home. He'd check the records, locate William, and reply. She'd have to contact her older brother, sooner rather than later, but she couldn't face him right now. Peter hadn't been happy when she'd accepted a seat on the Privy Council, even though it gave her a voice at the king's table. He'd pointed out that it conflicted with her duties to the family.

Not that he cared before, she thought. *I was just his annoying kid sister.*

She shook her head as she stood, brushing the crumbs off her uniform. She wasn't a little girl any longer, or a teenager who was slowly starting to realize that there was no place for her within the family; she was a grown woman, with a career and a life of her own. And Peter wasn't the stuffy big brother either.

I suppose we never really grow out of our childhood until our parents are gone, she told herself ruefully. The people who'd killed her father had never been caught. That worried her, more than she cared to admit. *And now . . . we have to be adults.*

Kitty stepped into the room. "Admiral?"

"I'll be in my quarters," Kat said. "Were there any *urgent* developments on the planet while I was gone?"

"No, Admiral," Kitty said. "A handful of minor problems, but nothing that demands your attention."

"Good," Kat said.

She walked back to her quarters, feeling tired. If she took a nap . . .

A message was blinking on her display when she walked into the room. She frowned, then sat down in front of the terminal and placed her hand against the sensor. The message decrypted itself a moment later.

"Lady Falcone," the family manager said. "Commodore Sir William McElney returned to Tyre two months ago, where he was hired as a naval officer by Asher Dales. I'm afraid that we have been unable to obtain direct contact details . . ."

Kat froze the message and checked the starchart. Asher Dales? She'd heard that name before . . . Margaret Falcone had mentioned it as a suitable long-term investment, if she recalled correctly. Kat knew very little about Asher Dales, but she trusted her sister's judgment. If Margaret said it was a good investment, it was a good investment.

"Ah," she said. She keyed her wristcom. "Fran? I want my task force to escort the StarCom ship to Asher Dales."

"Aye, Admiral," Fran said. "May I ask why?"

Kat hesitated. "I have an idea," she said. It wasn't a social call. Not a *completely* social call, at any rate. "But I'll discuss it with you later."

CHAPTER FIFTEEN

TYRE

At least we don't have to wear the absurd robes this time, Peter Falcone thought as he found his place on the ducal bench. The other dukes nodded to him. There would be no open discussions in the Houses of Parliament. *We'd be hot and sweaty by the time the session was over.*

He leaned back in his seat and surveyed the giant hall. The aristocracy occupied the upper seats, while their commoner counterparts and the colonial representatives were at the bottom. A neat bit of symbolism, he felt, that was lost on absolutely no one. The king and his supporters might want to make the colonial representatives feel welcome, but hardly anyone else shared their view. The Commonwealth was a money sink, as far as they were concerned. Any hopes they'd had for upgrading the member worlds to full equality had been destroyed in the fires of war.

Shaking his head, he keyed his datapad and scanned the latest set of updates from his staffers while waiting for the session to begin. There had been a small surge in the planetary stock market, although it didn't seem focused enough for him or his staff to suspect insider trading. He studied the boosted stocks, then dismissed the thought. It didn't *look* as though anyone was positioning themselves to take advantage of ill-gained knowledge. The stockbrokers probably assumed that everyone else would be distracted with the parliamentary session.

Peter's lips twitched. *As if we didn't have staff to keep an eye on the markets for us.*

A low rustle ran through the hall as the prime minister and the Leader of the Opposition entered together, another bit of symbolism that irritated Peter more than he cared to admit. No one expected Prime Minister Arthur Hampshire and Israel Harrison to be *friends*, although they were supposed to understand that their real job was keeping the government running. Disagreement was one thing, and there were plenty of legal ways to challenge or reverse government policy, but outright opposition could never be tolerated. Such a stance was practically treason.

Not practically, Peter told himself. *Identical.*

He studied the prime minister for a long moment, frowning. Arthur Hampshire was the king's man, through and through. He was simply too much of a nonentity to hold *any* position without a powerful patron. And he'd do whatever it took to make sure he *kept* his position. Politics was a drug, and Arthur Hampshire, like so many others, was addicted. Peter had read his father's files very carefully. Hampshire had proved a loyal client to his master.

A trumpet blared as the king himself strode into the hall, wearing a black naval uniform covered in gold braid. Peter had to admit that it made the younger man look devilishly handsome, although he rather doubted the king had any moral right to wear it. Technically, the king was commander-in-chief of the navy; practically . . . Peter scowled. The king had swapped enough personnel around in the last couple of years to ensure that *his* clients were in control of most of the navy. It was fairly normal for a patron to do everything in his power to promote his clients—their success was *his* success—but the latest moves worried Peter. Israel Harrison had been right. The king was starting to challenge the structures set up to limit his power.

He stood, along with everyone else, as the king walked to his chair. It wasn't *precisely* a throne, but the chair was large enough to signify he was in charge symbolically at least. Peter eyed the king thoughtfully, wondering if that really was frustrated ambition in his eyes. He'd had to see off a handful of challenges from family members who thought *they* should be in charge. The king was already so powerful that *any* restraints had to seem intolerable. It wasn't a pleasant thought.

The king stood in front of his throne, clasping his hands behind his back in parade rest. He had never been in the armed forces, yet his posture was perfect. Peter kept his face impassive as the room waited, wondering what the pose meant. The king had never been in the military, but neither had Peter himself. And while the files insisted that his lack of military service grated on the king, Peter wasn't so sure. *He'd* never had any ambitions to command starships or wage war on distant worlds. The thought of wading through a muddy swamp or crawling across a bloody battlefield was enough to make him feel queasy. And yet, he'd never really had a choice in life. He'd been the firstborn. He'd been trained to succeed his father from birth. He dreaded to think what his father would have said if Peter had asked for a naval commission.

Kat managed to join the navy, he reminded himself. *But Kat was never required to serve the family.*

He felt an odd flicker of envy, which he ruthlessly suppressed. The king was beginning his speech.

"We won the war," he said. "Four years ago, we feared we would lose; now, with the enemy crushed and our forces occupying their worlds, we know that we have won. But victory on the battlefield does not always translate to victory on the political field. The cost of war has been high, in both blood and treasure. Millions of lives have been lost; millions more, alas, have become refugees, fleeing in hopes of finding a safety that does not exist. The liberated worlds face many problems in adapting to an existence without the Theocracy . . .

"And now, we discover that a sizable number of enemy starships survived long enough to resume the offensive. We have all seen the reports from Judd."

Peter kept his face impassive. He'd seen the official reports, of course, but his clients in the MOD had also slipped him copies of the reports that *hadn't* been made part of the public record. They'd confirmed that the enemy starships were receiving help from someone, although they didn't know who. There was a list of potential suspects attached to one of the reports, but Peter suspected that it would be difficult to find actual proof. Whoever was helping the Theocrats wouldn't want to be identified.

"We must secure our victory," the king told them. "We made commitments, both to the Commonwealth and to the liberated worlds; we promised the former that we'd help them rebuild and the latter that we'd provide protection long enough for them to stand on their own two feet. And now, with a resurgent enemy threat, it is more imperative than ever that we *meet* our commitments. Failure now will be disastrous. On one hand, our standing as an interstellar power is at risk; on the other, perhaps more importantly, millions of *lives* are at risk. Judd was the first world to be attacked. It will not be the last.

"There are those who say that we should back off, that we should withdraw our ships and troops and leave the Theocratic Sector to its own devices. But I say that to do so would be a betrayal of everyone who died in the war. We bought our victory with their lives. We owe it to them to press on until our victory is secured."

But we already won the war, Peter thought. *Didn't we?*

"And even if that wasn't true, let us consider the misery heaped on Judd. The Theocrats killed hundreds of thousands and condemned hundreds of thousands more to starvation and death. Do you think it will stop there? If we withdraw our forces, if we allow the enemy to run rampant, millions—*billions*—of people will die. They will die because we abandoned them! And if the Theocrats manage to reestablish the

Theocracy, what then? Will we be forced to refight the war in fifty years? Or a hundred? Let us settle the matter now!

"This is not a time for petty party politics. This is not a time for bickering over tiny issues or for putting personal disputes ahead of serious issues. This is a time to reach forth and claim the fruits of victory! Lives—countless innocent lives—depend upon us! Will we refuse the challenge? Or will we continue the good fight until it is truly won?"

He sat, firmly. The rest of the chamber sat too. Peter frowned inwardly, silently replaying the speech in his head. The king had made a good case, he had to admit, but it was long on emotional calls to action and short on hard detail. There were a great many issues that would have to be addressed, starting with the balance of power within the Commonwealth, that he hadn't even mentioned. Peter suspected that boded ill for the future. If the king had chosen not to mention these details . . .

Or if he didn't know he had to mention them, Peter thought. Tyre had been able to build a mighty navy, but only because it had a substantial economic and financial base. *That might be more worrying.*

Arthur Hampshire rose, his eyes scanning the chamber. The prime minister looked distinctly nervous, although he was trying to hide it. Peter felt a flicker of unwilling sympathy. Client or not, Hampshire probably had a better appreciation of the political realities than his royal master. *And*, perhaps, an understanding that he would be the scapegoat if the king's political gambit went disastrously wrong. Peter couldn't help wondering just how much input Hampshire had been allowed into the budget. The king might not have taken his opinions seriously.

It wasn't a pleasant thought. Peter's father had warned him, time and time again, that he had to let his people talk freely, even when they disagreed with him. Indeed, Lucas Falcone had made it clear that disagreement—constructive disagreement—was often more valuable than fawning praise. But staffers, people who could be fired at any moment, were often reluctant to speak frankly to their bosses. It was safer to be a yes-man than risk openly contradicting your supervisor. A man who was dismissed for speaking his mind too bluntly would have trouble finding employment elsewhere.

And Dad went out of his way to teach me the dangers of getting too full of myself, Peter thought ruefully. He hadn't *enjoyed* learning that the only reason vast numbers of girls and boys had thrown themselves at him had been because of his family wealth, but he had to admit that he'd needed the lesson. He'd definitely been getting too full of himself. *I wonder if the king learned the same lesson?*

Hampshire cleared his throat. "It is vitally important that we pass the budget as quickly as possible," he said flatly. "His Majesty is not looking for a debate. There is simply too much to be done."

An angry rustle echoed around the chamber. Peter resisted the urge to smirk or roll his eyes. *That* had been a misstep, all right. Parliament might or might not be inclined to pass the budget without significant changes, but the MPs wouldn't be pleased with the suggestion that they shouldn't debate the issues. No one *wanted* to write the king—or anyone—a blank check. Too much money had been wasted or expended on classified projects during the war. Peter had been assured that new technology would be entering the civilian sphere soon, but he wasn't sure he believed it. The military presumably wanted to maintain its edge as much as possible. Besides, with the financial downturn, the likelihood that *anything* new would save Tyre from a recession was minimal.

Hampshire droned on, outlining a budget that Peter knew wouldn't pass without substantial modification. Subsidies to the outer worlds and the liberated worlds were to be increased, the naval budget was to be expanded . . . item after item, each one a serious issue in its own right. The whole budget was an indigestible bulk. Peter studied Hampshire thoughtfully, wondering just how the prime minister had managed to drop the ball. He should have warned the king that there was no way the budget would pass.

And there are to be no reductions in tax either, Peter thought as Hampshire finally came to an end. The details of the bill popped up on his datapad. *That alone will doom it.*

He skimmed through it quickly, wondering if there was any way to modify the bill. The government would need to keep the wartime taxes in order to fund its projects, which wouldn't please the House of Lords; the government would be spending money in the Commonwealth or the Theocratic Sector rather than Tyre, which wouldn't please the House of Commons. They'd be united by shared dislike of the bill. Peter shook his head in disbelief. The king *had* to know the budget would never go through. Only a complete idiot would think otherwise.

The king might be trying to manipulate events so we have to bargain him down, Peter considered. It was the only explanation that made *any* kind of sense. *But it's politically risky.*

Israel Harrison rose. "If it pleases my honorable friend," he said, "there are a number of points that need to be made before we get to the meat of the matter."

He paused, just long enough to allow his words to echo around the chamber. "We in Opposition were reluctant to grant any excess taxes at all, and, as I must remind you, we only conceded high taxes over the last four years because of the war. It was better to spend money than have our heads removed by a victorious Theocracy. But the war is now over, and it is our belief that taxes should return to their peacetime level.

"Second, I fail to see why we should make an open-ended, perhaps even permanent, commitment to the Theocratic Sector. The commitments to which His Majesty refers were made by him, unilaterally, without the approval of either the Houses of Parliament or His Majesty's own Privy Council. I believe a number of his older councilors resigned in protest. I do not consider the Kingdom of Tyre, or the Commonwealth as a whole, to be bound by such commitments. The king had no legal right to make them on his own authority.

153

"But those points pale next to the final two issues. We are facing a financial crisis of unparalleled magnitude. Whether we care to admit it or not, the strain of founding and funding the Commonwealth, and then the war, put immense pressure on our economy. We need time to breathe, not massive financial commitments that will not provide any relief for our people. And while His Majesty has chosen to present the issue in terms of dealing with a later threat, it is the considered opinion of a number of analysts that there is no danger of a Theocratic revival. Their remaining ships simply *cannot* remain operational for long. They may cause havoc, they may ravage the sector, but they pose no threat to us. Indeed, honorable members, the expense of waging war against the hold-outs may do more damage than the hold-outs themselves."

He paused again. "Let us be brutally honest. This bill is not a rational response to the problems facing our world. We simply cannot *afford* to keep spending at our current levels. I doubt, if I may make so bold, that the trustees of the Royal Corporation will disagree with me."

Peter had to smile as a faint ripple of amusement ran through the chamber. The king looked, just for a second, extremely displeased. Peter understood his irritation more than he cared to admit. Technically, the king ruled the Royal Corporation; practically, the trustees would put a brake on uncontrolled spending. And the Royal Corporation faced the same dangers as the others. The king might face opposition from within his own family.

"The war is over," Harrison concluded. "It is time for us to recognize that we have won and move back to a peacetime footing. We no longer need to maintain huge fleets or sizable garrisons. Let us, instead, concentrate on repairing the damage and building for the future instead of wasting our resources on pipe dreams."

He sat down. Peter watched him for a moment, feeling reluctantly impressed. Israel Harrison could *not* have known what was coming, or he would have made sure to galvanize resistance to the bill before it was ever entered on the parliamentary record. A united front would have successfully blocked the king and his servants from putting the budget in front of Parliament, let alone putting it to a vote. Instead, Harrison had to make his speech up as he went along. Thankfully, judging by the number of MPs who were even now demanding the right to speak, it didn't look as if matters would proceed to a vote by the end of the day.

Unless the king uses his authority to demand an immediate vote, Peter thought. *But would he win?*

He studied the king thoughtfully, grimly certain that King Hadrian was asking himself the same question. Could he win if he pushed for an immediate vote? Peter rather doubted it, but the king had already gambled. Why *not* raise the stakes? But, as MP after MP rose to praise or denounce the bill, he slowly discerned that passions were running high. Too many people would vote against the bill, merely to make clear that they wouldn't be manipulated. The king might not have lost the first round, but he certainly hadn't won either.

And so we will find out, sooner or later, just how far the king is prepared to compromise, Peter thought. Somehow he doubted the king would be willing to do anything of the sort. He'd staked too much of his personal prestige on the bill. He wouldn't give up easily. *And just how far we might have to go to stop him?*

CHAPTER SIXTEEN

TYRE

"I trust this room is secure?"

"My staff swept it personally," Peter said. "And so did the others."

He accepted a glass of brandy from one of the servitors and sat back in his chair, sipping it gratefully. His body had been extensively modified while he'd been in the exowomb, with dozens of genetic improvements spliced into his DNA, but he still had a pounding headache after spending hours in the Houses of Parliament. He'd wondered, when he was younger, why his father preferred backroom deals to open politics; now he thought he understood all too well. The matter might have been settled in an afternoon if *everyone* hadn't wanted to have their say. The less formal power they wielded, the more verbose they seemed to be.

But that isn't too surprising, Peter thought wryly. *They cannot force us to do as they wish, so they have to convince us.*

He wasn't too surprised that Israel Harrison had called for a meeting after Parliament had recessed for the day, or that a simple one-on-one meeting had mushroomed into a larger gathering. Three dukes, a handful of Opposition MPs, and a couple of political researchers . . . it was more of a planning session than anything else, but a planning session for what? He couldn't help feeling like a member of a revolutionary cabal plotting an uprising. The combination of political and economic power was enough to make even the king sit up and take notice, although he might be able to put together a coalition that would be strong enough to counter the Opposition. And yet, that would mean abandoning his spending plans, probably throwing Arthur Hampshire under the aircar, and committing himself to supporting his new allies. Peter doubted that would sit well with the king.

"I think we're all eager to get home to bed," he said after taking another sip of his expensive brandy. His body was engineered for alcohol tolerance, even though there were days when he wished he could get good and drunk. There were other ways to forget the world for a while, if he wished. But then he'd seen people who used electric stimulation to pleasure themselves. They eventually gave up on the real world. "Shall we move right to the point?"

"The king's spending bill is unacceptable," Harrison said. "And it is *quite* beyond any suitable modification."

"He's bursting out of his britches," Duke Rudbek snapped. "That bill is . . . outrageous."

"His father would certainly never have tried to force us to lend our assent to . . . to something that would ruin us," Duchess Zangaria agreed. "How many of us can *really* afford to keep paying wartime taxes?"

"We would certainly be better off *not* paying them," Peter said. "Falcone has been pushed to the limits over the last five years."

He looked from one to the other, trying not to feel inferior. Duke Rudbek might be rude and crude, but there was a sharp mind behind his flabby face, while Duchess Zangaria had always made him nervous. She was old enough to be his grandmother, yet she ruled her corporation with a rod of iron. She'd certainly never shown any signs of losing her grip, even as her heirs grew increasingly impatient for real power. Peter knew, all too well, that he didn't enjoy anywhere near as much support from *his* family. Too many of his relatives wanted to build their own power bases now that their former leader was dead.

157

At least they're not plotting to knife me in the back, he thought. *Not yet anyway.*

"He's a young man," Duchess Zangaria said. "Young and foolish and determined to make his mark on the galaxy."

"Then let him fund his plans from the Royal Corporation," Duke Rudbek sneered.

Janet Brisket leaned forward. "Can he *hope* to fund his plans from the Royal Corporation?"

"Not unless he's found a whole new way of making money," Peter said. The Royal Corporation was large, and it had guaranteed contracts from the government, but it wasn't *that* large. There was no way the king could fund *everything* he wanted from the corporation's revenues, even if he funneled all the profits into the budget. "The trustees would lynch him if he tried."

"Sounds like a reasonable solution," Duke Rudbek muttered.

Harrison cleared his throat. "What are the odds of the bill being passed?"

A brown-haired young woman, sitting at the far end of the table, looked up nervously. Peter felt a flicker of droll understanding, and sympathy. The poor girl would be highly qualified in her field, of course, but nothing could have prepared her for attending a meeting with so many high-ranking people. She simply lacked the power to make her voice heard easily.

Except she's one of the best political analysts in the world, he thought, pulling up her file on his datapad. The woman, Pamela Collins, had a distinguished record of making accurate political predictions. He couldn't help wondering why she'd signed up with Israel Harrison and the Opposition. A record like that could have led her to far greater heights. *Maybe she believes in their cause.*

Pamela coughed. "On the face of it, the bill has very little chance of being accepted *in toto*," she said. "The taxation issue alone will not find favor with anyone, save perhaps for MPs who believe that the big corporations will be the ones paying the tax. They will argue, and they will have a point, that the general public will *not* be paying anything directly. However, the *indirect* effects—corporations cutting back, job losses, and suchlike—will have a major impact on their constituents. The smarter MPs will not want to be in a position where they can be blamed for a sudden increase in unemployment."

"Except unemployed people can't vote," Duke Rudbek said.

Pamela colored and looked down. "That is not wholly accurate, Your Grace," she said quietly. "It is true that the franchise is purchased by the Voting Tax, but there is a fixed amount that unemployed people can pay if they wish to retain their vote. Even if they do not, they will still have the vote until they fail to pay the tax at the start of the *next* tax year. There will be a period, around six to nine months, when a considerable number of newly unemployed people will have the vote. And yes, they may retain it during the *next* tax year."

"And they will be demanding recall elections if their MPs let them down," Harrison said. "What will *that* do to our politics?"

"It will make them more poisonous," Pamela said. "The unemployed, and desperate, will demand concessions the MPs will be quite unable to grant."

She took a breath, then went on. "That said, the king *may* be able to make deals with a number of people in both Houses of Parliament. There *are* people who will benefit from the bill, and he can count on their support—or trade horses with them until they agree to support it. At that point . . . we'll be in uncharted waters."

"And we have to decide how far we're prepared to go to resist," Duchess Zangaria commented. "Can he tax us without our consent?"

"He can certainly find ways to pressure us," Peter pointed out. "The orbital towers are controlled by the government, for example, along with the StarComs. He can use them as leverage to make us submit."

"Which would spark off a *real* crisis," Janet Brisket said. "Do we have *any* reason to believe he's prepared to go so far?"

Harrison looked at Pamela, who winced. "His opening speech did not admit of much, if any, maneuvering room," she said. "He effectively backed himself into a corner. There are few concessions he could offer without looking as though he's climbing down. It would have been better to keep the speech purposefully vague and handle the negotiations in private."

Brilliant, Peter thought sarcastically. *The king can't back down.*

"Either he's a political imbecile or a lunatic who thinks he can push the matter as far as necessary," Harrison stated. "Or he could easily be both."

"Very well," Duchess Zangaria said. "What do we do about it? How many of us will support the bill?"

Janet made a face. "About a third of the commons will support the king, even after the reality of the situation dawns on them." Her voice was very cold. "They are linked to the king's patronage network. Another third could probably be talked into providing support, in exchange for later concessions. At worst . . . the king might be able to muster enough votes to get it through the House of Commons."

"And yet, they'd have to get it through the House of Lords," Duke Rudbek pointed out. "We could invoke the Ducal Veto."

"We'd have to get all thirteen dukes to agree," Peter pointed out.

"They all stand to lose," Duchess Zangaria said. "They have no reason to support the bill."

Peter frowned. The king knew that . . . surely. He'd probably be getting chapter and verse from the Royal Trustees about the political and financial realities soon enough, if he hadn't heard them out already. He had to know the House of Lords would kill his bill. It made no sense.

Unless he wants to blame us for his failure, Peter thought. *But . . . what would it get him?*

A nasty thought struck him. "Does anyone know which way Cavendish will jump?"

Harrison sucked in his breath. "Shit!"

"The king could offer the Cavendish Corporation a loan to keep the corporation afloat long enough for them to restructure," Pamela said slowly. "They'd have great difficulty in meeting their obligations, even if the best-case scenario is true, but they'd survive. The king could make sure they get enough contracts to stave off a complete collapse. And . . . if that is the case, Duke Cavendish will not join the Ducal Veto."

"Which will ensure that we can't veto the bill," Peter finished. He glanced at Rudbek. "If we can't veto, can we still kill the bill?"

"Perhaps," Rudbek said. "But the king does have his supporters in the House of Lords too."

Peter gritted his teeth in frustration. The king would have problems getting the bill through the House of Lords, but it wasn't impossible. Peter could easily imagine the king horse trading like mad, making deal after deal until even *he* couldn't remember just how many promises he'd actually made. It would all catch up with him very quickly—patrons who forgot to reward their clients tended to have their clients looking for support from more generous patrons—but Peter suspected the king was past caring. If he was determined to force the bill through, he'd make whatever deals he had to make and worry about keeping them later.

"Perhaps it is time to consider the nuclear option," Duchess Zangaria said. "We impeach him."

"That would be tricky," Harrison said. "We could challenge him openly and demand a vote of confidence, but . . . we might well lose. Not everyone in the Lords would be comfortable with demanding impeachment because of a bill that hasn't even been passed!"

That, Peter admitted sourly, was true. The House of Lords included a number of people who'd won a peerage through sheer merit, but the vast majority of Lords were hereditary aristocrats. They might not like the king, and they might not grant him their automatic support . . . yet they'd be opposed to anything that challenged their power. An opposition that brought down the single most powerful man on Tyre would have no difficulties in dealing with a mere earl or knight. The aristocracy wouldn't want such a precedent to be set without *very* solid cause. Someone who didn't run a vast corporation might not agree that such cause existed.

"So," Duke Rudbek said, "what do we do?"

"Perhaps we could find a compromise," Janet said. "If we agreed to fund some of his programs—the naval patrols in the occupied territories perhaps—he might agree to drop the others."

"Except the commitment is likely to keep draining our resources," Harrison growled. "We should cut it completely."

Duke Rudbek eyed Peter. "What does your sister say about all this? Does she even know?"

"She hasn't expressed an opinion to me," Peter said crossly. "I intend to discuss the matter with her once we have decided on a response."

He scowled at the table. It was hard to hide just how irritated he was. Kat was going to find herself in an invidious position. If she'd thought to ask him, as her superior, before she'd accepted the seat on the Privy Council . . . He sighed. Their father had neglected her political training. She should have realized that the seat would trap her between two masters. Technically, he should order her to choose between the Privy Council and the family; practically, he rather feared he knew how she'd respond. Kat had never allowed her older brother to dictate to her when she'd been a child.

And she might not even know what's happened, he thought. *Did the king tell her?*

It wasn't a pleasant thought. The king's Privy Council included quite a few people who *should* have known just how many people would resist the wretched taxation and spending bill. Kat was no political authority, but . . . Peter wondered, sourly, if the king had thought to ask for advice from *anyone*. It would be interesting to see how many privy councilors resigned over the matter. He wasn't precisely obliged to consult his councilors, but it was generally accepted that he should.

"We need to build up a solid resistance to the bill," Harrison said. "If nothing else, we merely need to mobilize one-third of the MPs and Lords against it."

"And we should at least try to find a compromise," Janet said.

Harrison's voice hardened. "And if one boy steals a bag of sweets from another, would you advocate that they compromise by sharing the sweets?"

He ground on before she could answer. "We agreed to the wartime taxation because it was better than the alternative. Everything we loved would have been destroyed if the Theocrats had won the damned war. We preferred to spend millions of crowns on defense instead of offering one teeny tiny crown for tribute. But now the war is over. The king has no damn right to claim so much from us, nor does he have any right to dictate to us. He has shown he has no interest in anything *we* might recognize as a compromise. His actions indicate either stupidity or malice. And the more we agree to . . . *humor* him, the more he will demand."

His eyes swept the room. "His demands will ruin us. You all know that to be true. We *cannot* allow him to force them on us. We must resist him now, doing everything in our power to curb his ambitions, or, when we finally try to resist him, we will find the task far harder."

"Fight now or fight later, when he is stronger and we are weaker," Duke Rudbek said.

"A political fight could disrupt the government," Janet pointed out. "Or worse."

Peter kept his thoughts to himself as the argument raged back and forth. In truth, he wasn't sure which way to jump. The budget had to be resisted—on that, he agreed with Harrison—but how far were they prepared to go? He keyed his datapad, sending a series of messages to his staff. By now, news of the proposed taxation and spending bill would have already hit the datanet. Masterly and Masterly would have a write-up for him by the time he returned home.

"We need to find ways to bring pressure to bear on him," Harrison said. "Whatever it takes, we must do it."

Or try to find ways to talk him down, Peter thought. It was a shame the king's father hadn't lived longer. Peter's father wouldn't have let him make such a public mistake. *There's no way he can back down easily.*

He sighed, understanding, once again, why his father had preferred backroom dealing to public politics. The former allowed the participants more room to maneuver or back away without making utter asses of themselves. If the king had been someone else, a political rival perhaps, Peter would have enjoyed watching him make an unforced mistake that would haunt him for years. But now, the stakes were too high for such indulgences. He . . . they . . . needed to find a way to help the king save face. He just didn't know how.

"We also need to consider the worst-case scenario," Duke Rudbek said. "What happens if he refuses to go quietly?"

"Or tries to use the military against us," Duchess Zangaria agreed. "He's been putting his own people in command slots."

Peter shuddered. Technically, the military was under the king's direct command; practically, the military council issued the orders. But too many things had changed over the last four years. It was astonishing how much could be done during a state of emergency. He had a nasty feeling that his intelligence agents hadn't ferreted out anything like the whole story.

He suddenly had difficulty speaking. "You don't think he'd . . . he'd turn on us?"

"Let us hope not," Rudbek said. "His father would never even have considered it."

"Then we tighten our grip on the planetary defenses," Peter said. That, at least, was under Parliament's direct control. "And . . . and we start resisting his attempts to gain control of the military."

"Which may make matters worse," Janet pointed out.

"He's gone too far to back down easily," Rudbek snapped. "I think we must start making plans for the worst."

And hope that we never need to implement them, Peter thought. *Because if we do start shooting at each other, where will it stop?*

CHAPTER SEVENTEEN

UNCHARTED STAR SYSTEM

It had been dangerous—it was *still* dangerous—to show one's inner-most feelings in the Theocracy. A hint of fear or resentment or hatred was often enough to have one reported to the clerics for unbelief, which resulted in a cleansing session that supposedly purified one's soul. Admiral Zaskar could never have risen in the ranks without being skilled at hiding his true thoughts and feelings, even now. Showing doubt or weakness could easily get him killed.

He hid his disgust behind a mask as he studied the men in the cage. They were naked, weak, and helpless; their backs were covered with bleeding lacerations from where they'd been flogged. They'd been chained so heavily that they could barely move. The stench of piss and shit and blood hung in the air, revolting him. Clerics moved from man to man, whispering words of comfort in exchange for gasped confessions. The fallen would be redeemed soon enough, Admiral Zaskar knew, or they would be cast into the fire. He hoped it would be the former. His fleet *needed* those men.

"Admiral," Moses said. The cleric looked pleased, even though blood stained his red robes of office. "These men have been redeemed."

"Good," Admiral Zaskar said, biting down a number of sarcastic answers. A man would say anything under torture as long as the words made the pain stop. The inquisitors had been experts at keeping a man in agony without inflicting permanent harm. He rather suspected the enthusiastic amateurs Moses had recruited wouldn't have quite so much self-control. "How long until they can take up their duties?"

Moses seemed surprised. "They are ready now, Admiral."

Admiral Zaskar looked at the nearest man. He was almost as still as a corpse. If he hadn't been breathing, his chest rising and falling, Admiral Zaskar would have believed him dead. Blood trickled from his wounds and pooled on the deck beneath his bare feet. The whips had been designed to ensure that the scars didn't heal quickly.

"That man requires medical attention," he said curtly. "And so do the others."

He turned away, allowing Moses to follow him. "Did they know anything useful?"

"They were seduced from the path of righteousness," Moses informed him. "They thought they could find acceptance among the infidels . . ."

"Anything *useful?*" Admiral Zaskar cut him off, sharply. "Anything we might be able to use?"

"No," Moses admitted. "But their stories do make wonderful cautionary tales."

"Quite," Admiral Zaskar said. They walked slowly down the corridor. "Make sure they have all the medical attention they need before going on duty. I don't want them keeling over and dying while they're on my ships."

"Yes, Admiral." Moses didn't sound happy.

Admiral Zaskar kept his face impassive. Askew had brought them a great deal of medical supplies, as well as everything else. And yet the cleric would be reluctant to "waste" them on his victims. The Theocracy had had a shortage of both doctors and medical supplies, the latter caused by unreasonable production demands. It wasn't uncommon for even serious wounds to go untreated because there were no supplies. Now . . .

We can't have our engineers dying on the job, he thought coldly. *And we don't want them to think that they have no hope.*

He rubbed his forehead in frustration. If only they had more engineers! It wouldn't have been hard to train more, surely. Or . . . what had the Tabernacle been thinking?

"The remainder of the male recruits joined us eagerly," Moses said. He sounded as though he was determined to change the subject. "It is a promising sign for the future, is it not?"

Admiral Zaskar shrugged. It was nice to think there were millions of Theocrats, held down by the occupiers, who would join them the moment the fleet captured the high orbitals. But he had his doubts. He was prepared to admit, in private, that the Theocracy hadn't been the most . . . *decent* of occupying powers. Genuine recruits had been relatively rare. And, if there truly were millions of Theocrats on the liberated worlds, how long would it be before they were liquidated? The Commonwealth seemed to be oddly squeamish about such things— they had never retaliated in kind, even after Hebrides had been depopulated—but the local resistance forces had no such qualms. Admiral Zaskar doubted the Commonwealth would pretend to care if the refugees were simply slaughtered.

"Let us hope so," he said finally. Moses might have become more and more certain that they were *bound* to win, but he had to keep a level head. The odds of ultimate victory were very low. "And the women?"

Moses coughed. "A quarter were the wives and daughters of our new recruits," he said. "I've given orders to keep them isolated from everyone else. The remainder . . . they should be parceled out to the men."

With one for you, no doubt, Admiral Zaskar thought coldly. *But that will just make matters worse, won't it?*

"Award them as prizes for good work," he said. "And make sure it stays honest."

"As you command," Moses said. "Do you wish one yourself?"

Admiral Zaskar shook his head, concealing his disquiet. His wife was somewhere on Ahura Mazda . . . if, of course, she was still alive. She'd been staying at her father-in-law's compound. He hoped she was still alive, but he had no way to tell. If the unbelievers knew who she was, they'd have taken her by now. Or she might have simply been killed in the fighting. The battles for Ahura Mazda had been savage.

They stepped into an intership car, which whisked them back to the CIC. Admiral Zaskar glanced at the main display as soon as they left the car, just to make sure there was nothing hostile within the system. It looked empty, as always, but that was meaningless. If an enemy scout ship had found them, it would creep out as carefully as possible and whistle up a couple of superdreadnought squadrons. They'd have to spend the rest of their lives watching over their shoulders until the Commonwealth either withdrew or blew them out of space.

It has to be endured, he told himself firmly. *There are no other choices.*

Askew was sitting inside his office, drinking something that smelled like strong coffee. Admiral Zaskar felt a flicker of irritation, which he rapidly suppressed. It was annoying to have the younger man make himself at home without asking permission to enter, let alone sit down, but . . . they were dependent on Askew and his mysterious backers. Admiral Zaskar had pried as tactfully as possible, yet no matter what he said, Askew refused to name names. It was *galling* to depend on the kindness of strangers . . .

"I just got back," Askew said, sitting up. He'd left the ship almost as soon as they'd reached their base. "I trust you had a pleasant few days."

"There was work to be done," Admiral Zaskar said dryly. Shore leave was an impossible dream. The asteroids simply didn't have the facilities to give his crew a break. "And yourself?"

"I reported to my superiors," Askew said. "They were quite pleased with your operation."

"I'm glad to hear it," Admiral Zaskar said. "Did they have anything else to say?"

"Merely a suggestion that you should move to the next target as quickly as possible," Askew said. "They would very much prefer you to keep the pressure on."

"Duly noted," Admiral Zaskar said.

He thought, fast. Askew hadn't been gone for long. Four days . . . Assuming he'd spent less than two days in transit, each way, he couldn't have gone very far. His tiny ship might be as fast as a courier boat, but still . . . there were only a limited number of possible destinations. And that meant . . . He sighed and gave up. There was no realistic hope of working out who was behind Askew with such limited data.

"That is our intention too," Moses said. "God has smiled on us."

"Quite," Askew said. "Where do you intend to hit?"

Admiral Zaskar brought up a starchart, reminding himself, once again, that the tactical data was badly out of date. He no longer had access to the StarCom network or the small fleet of courier boats that had once carried data from one end of the Theocracy to the other. The enemy would have reshuffled their deployments as soon as they heard about Judd. It was nice to think they might not have yet heard about the attack, but he doubted it. One of their wretched ships had escaped, after all.

"Falladine, I think," he said. "It has been trying to position itself as a sector leader, among other things. And that cannot be tolerated."

Askew lifted his eyebrows. "It is hardly an undefended target."

"No," Admiral Zaskar agreed. "But that is precisely why we should target it."

He took a long breath. "We will depart in a day and head for a point near the target system, which will give us a chance to scout out the defenses before committing ourselves," he added. "By that point, we'll have a worthwhile plan to hit the system . . . unless, of course, the enemy is too firmly entrenched."

"God will be with us," Moses said.

"We dare not challenge superior enemy firepower," Admiral Zaskar reminded him, once again. God wouldn't help someone who made a fool of himself. "If the place is heavily defended, to the point where we cannot prevail without taking substantial losses, we will leave it alone . . . for the moment. I will try to find other ways to hit the target."

He looked at Askew. "Do your backers want us to be daring? Or merely *noisy?*"

"They want you to keep the Commonwealth off-balance," Askew said. "What do you have in mind?"

"There are two other worlds near Falladine," Admiral Zaskar said. He nodded to the starchart. "Neither particularly important. One of them is really nothing more than a quasi-habitable wasteland"—his lips twitched as he remembered how the locals had practically welcomed the Theocrats as saviors—"while the other has long-term potential. I believe we should attempt to hit both worlds with smaller units. It will not alter the balance of power in any real manner, but it will irritate the Commonwealth."

Particularly if they have to pick up refugees from the wrecked world, he thought. *That would put another strain on their shipping resources, would it not?*

"An excellent idea, if you believe you can pull it off," Askew said. "And what if you're wrong?"

"There is always an element of risk in war," Admiral Zaskar reminded him. "But the alternative is merely sitting here until our life support fails and we die."

"God will not forgive us for abandoning the cause," Moses said.

Admiral Zaskar wasn't so sure. They had women now. A small number of women, to be sure, but women nonetheless. They could set sail into unexplored territory and find a world to settle, using the remains of their starships for raw materials. A few hundred years later . . . who knew *what* would happen? Something of the Theocracy would survive, wouldn't it?

He sighed inwardly. The clerics would never let him get away with it. They wanted to continue the war, whatever the cost. Who knew? They might even be right. The Commonwealth might indeed retreat from the sector, allowing them to reclaim their homeworld and start rebuilding. It wasn't as if any of the other worlds had any real hope of taking their place.

"I like it," Askew said. He made a show of clapping his hands. "I'll be accompanying you, of course."

"Of course," Admiral Zaskar echoed. Whatever else could be said about the mystery man, he was no coward. Merely being on a Theocratic ship would be enough to unnerve anyone who lacked nerves of steel. Askew had nothing to fear from the ship's commanders, but their subordinates might react badly to the infidel's presence. "I look forward to having you on my bridge."

He smiled as best as he could. "Do you have any news from the outside universe?"

Askew lifted his eyebrow, challengingly. It was a rare Theocratic officer who'd take an interest in such matters, not when even a hint of such leanings could blight or destroy a man's career. Why, it was alarmingly close to suggesting there was *value* in such matters. But Admiral Zaskar stared back, daring the younger man to make an issue of it. The Theocracy could no longer afford to ignore the outside universe.

"I have a news breakdown," Askew said finally. "And a considerable number of updates from all over the Commonwealth. I'm afraid they *do* know about Judd."

Admiral Zaskar nodded, tightly. It wasn't a surprise.

"We'll review them together," he said to Moses. The enemy wouldn't put their battle plans on the datanet, let alone broadcast them all over the galaxy, but the news might give him some insight into what the enemy were thinking. Were they gearing up to find his fleet and grind it into powder? Were they seriously considering abandoning the sector? Or something in-between? "We need to determine what they might be planning."

"Of course," Moses said.

Admiral Zaskar stood. "I'll see you both later," he said. "For the moment, I have a ship to inspect."

"And plans to draw up, I imagine," Askew said. "I'll be in my cabin." He walked out of the hatch, which hissed closed behind him.

Admiral Zaskar considered the younger man for a long moment, wondering again just who was behind him. He'd taken the precaution of having the man's cabin searched while he'd been absent, but the searchers had turned up nothing of interest. Askew didn't have anything that pointed to his homeworld, save perhaps for a datapad and a small collection of unmarked datachips. Admiral Zaskar hadn't dared risk trying to read them. He suspected they'd be heavily encrypted.

And reading captured enemy datachips was impossible, he thought. *They tended to erase themselves when we tried.*

"I'll be at my prayers," Moses said. "I will pray for success."

"Please," Admiral Zaskar said. "The crew will appreciate it."

He walked through the hatch and into the CIC. The crew were running a drill, supervised by the tactical officer. They'd shown a remarkable degree of improvement over the past couple of months, thanks to the combination of new equipment and better treatment. Admiral Zaskar promised himself that, if they ever did return to Ahura Mazda, they would treat people better. The endless oppression had probably cost the Theocracy the war. He understood the importance of keeping unbelievers firmly under control, but abusing their own people was dangerous and stupid.

And they hate us, he thought. He didn't want to think about what had happened to a particularly unpopular cleric after they'd fled the homeworld. The ship's doctor hadn't been able to find all the bastard's body parts. *And eventually they turn on us.*

He found himself mulling it over as he toured his ship from bow to stern, silently noting how efficient his crew had become over the last two months. He'd done everything in his power to encourage his people to talk and question, but . . . it hadn't been easy. Too many questions were still a bad thing, according to the clerics. And yet . . . he'd heard the Commonwealth *allowed* its officers to question. And the Commonwealth had won the war.

If only we'd had more time, he thought, although he suspected that disaster had been inevitable from the start. Rumor claimed that the Commonwealth was growing stronger while the Theocracy had peaked out. Admiral Zaskar supposed the Tabernacle had decided it might be better to fight now, rather than risk war against a vastly superior foe at a later date. *But they didn't need to fight at all!*

It wasn't true, he admitted, if only to himself. The Theocracy had imposed itself on every world it had conquered, crushing their pre-war institutions and grinding any resistance out of existence. Men had been forced to attend religious instruction, women had been stripped of all rights and forced to stay in their homes . . . children had been raised to be good little Theocrats, to the point where they believed they'd go to hell if they didn't betray their parents. No one would want the Theocracy to occupy their world. Given a choice, the locals would have gone for the Commonwealth. The two systems simply could not coexist.

The galaxy wasn't big enough for both of us, he thought as he gave orders for the fleet to set out before returning to his cabin. *And one of us had to lose.*

He sighed as he pulled up the planetary data for Falladine, Dorland, and Asher Dales. The data was out of date, of course, but he doubted things had changed *that* much. Asher Dales and Dorland couldn't hope to muster resistance, even against a lone destroyer. He'd make them pay for betraying the Theocracy.

But tell me, a voice whispered at the back of his head, *can you blame them?*

No, Admiral Zaskar admitted. *But does it matter?*

He ran his hand through his hair. No, it didn't matter. Moses might believe they could win, that they could reclaim their homeworld, but Admiral Zaskar knew too much to believe it. The odds of victory were very low. All that mattered was revenge. They would hurt the enemy until their luck finally ran out and they died.

The Commonwealth will not have an easy time here, he thought. *That, at least, I promise them.*

CHAPTER EIGHTEEN

ASHER DALES

"Captain," Commander Patti Ludwig said. "We may have visitors."

William looked up from his display. "Show me."

Patti keyed her console. "Long-range sensors picked up an energy spike here," she said, indicating a location two AU from Asher Dales. "It might have been a vortex."

"Signal the planetary government, then order the remainder of the squadron to go into full stealth," William ordered. An energy spike there suggested that someone was trying to sneak up on the planet. There was no reason for a friendly visitor to come out of hyperspace so far from Asher Dales. It would be grossly inefficient. "Launch two stealth probes and then take us into stealth too."

"Aye, sir," Patti said. The lights dimmed slightly, warning the crew that they were now in stealth mode. "Stealth engaged, sir."

William sucked in his breath as he studied the sensor readings. They could be overreacting. It could be nothing more than a false alarm. But the survey of the system, in both realspace and hyperspace, hadn't given him any reason to think there would be many random energy flickers so close to the star. Asher Dales was surprisingly quiet for a populated star system.

His lips twitched. There was a scientist who'd claimed, apparently seriously, that opening vortexes into hyperspace actually weakened the fabric of the universe itself. His fellows had scoffed—of *course* vortexes tore holes in the universe—but the scientist had insisted that the human race would pay a price for its deeds. One day, hyperspace might start flowing into realspace and then . . . well, no one actually knew. But the scientist insisted that the phenomena might bring civilization crashing down in ruins.

And no one really believes him, he thought as he watched the display. *No one wants to consider that he might be right.*

He dismissed the thought in irritation. He'd never liked waiting— he'd refrained from sounding battlestations to keep his crew from wearing themselves out before battle was actually joined—but there was no choice. There was no point in dispatching his other ships to hunt down the intruder. Someone who'd come out of hyperspace so far from the planet would probably be able to see Orbit Station, but it was unlikely that they'd observed the ships before he'd ordered them into stealth. And so . . .

His mind considered a list of possible options. The intruder, if there actually *was* an intruder, might just sweep through the system, then depart as stealthily as he'd arrived. That would be, in many ways, the worst possible case. William would never *know* the intruder had departed. And if someone had come out of hyperspace far too early, either through a navigational mishap or systems failure, they'd have started screaming for help by now. No, the intruder was definitely hostile. The unknown ship might already be crawling towards the planet, preparing to attack.

And they'll see a defenseless globe, William thought. The handful of satellites orbiting Asher Dales were commercial models, not automated defense platforms. They wouldn't pose any threat to a freighter armed with popguns, let alone a proper warship. *They'll come in for the kill.*

He worked his way through the vectors, one by one. A pirate would probably take the time to be *sure* the system was defenseless, although he'd have to light up his active sensors if he wanted to do a proper sensor sweep. A Theocratic warship, on the other hand, would probably come charging in, bombard the planet, and vanish into hyperspace before reinforcements could be dispatched from Ahura Mazda. Or maybe the CO would take the time to work Asher Dales over thoroughly. He probably assumed there was no way the locals could signal for help.

And he'd be right, William conceded. *It isn't as if we have a StarCom in the system.*

"Captain," Patti said, "the planetary government is requesting an update."

At least they're using laser links, William told himself as he checked his console. A radio transmission might have warned the intruder that there was more in the system than his passive sensors could detect. *Better to let them come in fat and happy.*

"Inform them that we are preparing an ambush," William said. It was true enough, although incomplete. He needed to know more about the intruder before he risked finalizing any plans. "And remind them to keep radio transmissions as limited as possible."

"Aye, sir."

William leaned back in his chair, forcing himself to relax. He had to show a calm face to the crew, even though his emotions were churning inside. They'd conducted drill after drill, during and after the transit, but they'd never faced a real enemy. There would always be *something* when the shit hit the fan, something the simulations had left out. His lips twitched, again. The emergency, of course. A simulation, no matter how detailed, wasn't real. The crew *knew* it wasn't real too.

The enemy has to come here, he reminded himself again. *There's nowhere else to go.*

It felt like hours before the alert pinged. "Captain," Patti said, "the probes picked up an energy signature, heading towards the planet."

"Not an advanced cloaking device, then," William mused. He studied the sensor readings for a long moment, stroking his chin thoughtfully. The data didn't *prove* that the intruder was a Theocratic warship, but the primitive cloaking device was a definite hint. Pirates rarely had cloaking devices. "Can you match the signature to anything in the warbook?"

"Not at this range, sir," Patti said. "Do you want me to steer the probe closer?"

William shook his head. "Just keep a lock on their position," he ordered. "And inform me the minute they alter course."

His lips thinned as he eyed the sensor display. The enemy ship was real, at least. He felt relieved, even though he knew he shouldn't be too happy. A false alarm would have been embarrassing, but no one would have been injured or killed. The sensor readings suggested that there was only one ship, although he knew better than to take that for granted. A vortex could admit multiple ships into realspace. If there was a second ship, it might have sneaked off in a different direction . . .

Or it might be too close to the first ship for us to differentiate them, William thought. *That would be irritating.*

He wished, suddenly, for a proper analysis deck. A team of analysts could take a look at the data, sparse as it was, and come up with some proper results. They'd be able to tell if there was more than one ship there; they'd probably even be able to determine precisely what sort of ships were heading towards the planet. But he had to rely on a combination of automatic programs, which he knew had their limits, and his own experience. It looked as though they were facing nothing larger than a destroyer, but he couldn't be sure. A skillfully handled light cruiser could masquerade as a destroyer until it was far too late for her enemies to avoid contact.

"They'll be within bombardment range in twenty minutes," he said, more to himself than anyone else. The enemy ship was picking up speed. It was time. He tapped the alert switch, sounding battlestations throughout the ship, then sat upright. "Communications?"

"Yes, sir?"

"Signal the squadron," William ordered. "We'll intercept the intruder here"—he tapped his console, designating a location—"and challenge. *Dandelion* will take the lead; the remainder of the squadron will remain in stealth until we have confirmation that the intruder is definitely hostile. Our objective will be to capture the intruder, but . . . if we have to destroy her, I'll understand."

He looked at the helmsman. "Move us into position."

"Aye, sir."

William felt his heart start to race as *Dandelion* moved to slip into attack position. The plan was not ideal, for all sorts of reasons, but it would have to do. He'd strongly prefer to ambush the enemy ship without warning—his crew had never taken their new ships into combat—yet he couldn't be entirely sure the ship was unfriendly. A Royal Navy vessel might come sneaking around without permission, perhaps in hopes of ambushing genuine raiders. Hell, a Royal Navy CO might mistake William's squadron for pirates. The ships had been purchased at Tyre, with all the proper permits, but it wouldn't be the first time the Navy's right hand had forgotten to tell the left hand what it was doing. Whoever was sneaking into the system might not know that Asher Dales had purchased the ships.

Particularly when so many ships have been taken out of service, William thought. *And when so few liberated systems can afford to buy any ships.*

"They'll enter engagement range in five minutes," Patti said. "The remainder of the squadron is in position."

"On my mark, take us out of stealth and broadcast a challenge," William ordered. "And be ready to raise shields and return fire."

He tried to put himself in the enemy commander's shoes. What would *he* do if he was challenged? He wouldn't have any IFF codes he could use to bluster his way out of the situation, so . . . opening fire might be the simplest and safest course, particularly if he didn't know there were actually four destroyers within attack range. Launching everything he had at William might just give him a chance for victory, or escape. He could simply reverse course and beat feet out of the system, on the assumption that Asher Dales wouldn't want to start a fight, but that would let William have a chance to land the first blow. And besides, William couldn't let the intruder go. The last thing he wanted was for the Theocracy to return with more ships. He knew, all too well, that the planetary defenses were flimsy.

Perhaps we should have bought that battlecruiser after all, he thought wryly. *We'd only have to hire thousands of extra crewmen and spend vast sums on her upkeep.*

"The intruder will enter engagement range in one minute," Patti said. "Sir?"

William frowned. It was definitely starting to look as though the intruder was alone, unless there were two ships flying in tandem. He hadn't seen anyone try that outside the war, and even then they'd been pretty desperate to consider it. Normally, the risks of one ship colliding with another were minimal, but flying in tandem magnified them. He couldn't imagine the Theocracy taking the chance. They wouldn't be getting any replacements if they accidentally destroyed their own ships.

He reassessed the situation rapidly. "Take us out of stealth when they enter engagement range," he said reluctantly. There was something to be said for waiting until the enemy got closer, when they'd have less time to bring their point defense online before his missiles struck home. But that worked both ways. His ship needed time to prepare too. "And send the challenge."

"Aye, Captain," Patti said. There was a long pause. "Leaving stealth . . . now!"

"Active sensors coming online," the sensor officer added. He let out a gasp. "Captain, she's a Class-XI destroyer!"

Theocrats, William thought. The Theocracy might have lost a destroyer to pirates, but it wasn't too likely. There had never been many pirates within the Theocratic Sector. The Theocrats had paid pirates to take themselves, their ships, and their depredations into the Commonwealth. It had proved quite effective in the early days of the war. *They have to be Theocrats.*

"No response to our challenge," Patti said. "They're dropping their cloak . . ."

The display sparkled with red icons. "They're opening fire!"

"Return fire," William snapped. The enemy CO had external racks. He cursed under his breath. If he'd known the system was going to be attacked, he would have made sure to fit external racks to his ships too. As it was, the enemy had an advantage in the opening round. "And bring point defense online *now!*"

Dandelion lurched as she emptied her missile tubes. The other ships dropped out of stealth a moment later, adding their firepower to the engagement. William watched the enemy ship alter course, trying desperately to get out of the combat zone before it was too late. The enemy CO had reacted quickly, but clearly he'd been caught by surprise. He needed time to get his shields and point defense online . . . time he no longer had.

A pity we didn't dare fire until we were sure of our target, William thought. *We could have blown the enemy to atoms without risking ourselves.*

He forced himself to watch as the enemy missiles closed in on his ship. They were dumb, too dumb to be easily decoyed; he wondered, absently, if that was a deliberate precaution or simple bad luck. Probably the latter, he decided. The enemy missiles weren't trying to evade his point defense either. His defense was racking up kills as the missiles entered attack range. If there hadn't been so *many* of them, he would have regarded the engagement with complete satisfaction.

A missile slipped through the defense grid and slammed into his shields. *Dandelion* rocked. William checked the display a moment before a *second* missile struck home. The shields held, thankfully. *Dandelion* had been shaken badly, but there was no real damage.

Everything will have to be checked, of course, William reminded himself. Something important could easily have been shaken loose by the impacts. The shield generators might even need to be replaced. *Someone might even have been injured.*

"The enemy ship has been seriously damaged," Patti reported. "She's losing power."

"Streaming atmosphere too," William commented. He doubted the Theocrats could repair the damage in time to matter. Their maintenance standards were so poor he was surprised they'd managed to build an interstellar empire. "Keep us back. See if they . . ."

The enemy ship went dark. "She's lost power completely," Patti said. "Sir?"

William hesitated. If he'd had a marine contingent, he wouldn't have hesitated to try to board the powerless hulk. Taking the ship intact, or as close to intact as possible, would give him a chance to recover priceless intelligence, including perhaps the location of the enemy base. But a boarding party consisting of spacers might walk straight into an ambush . . . or die, when the enemy hit the self-destruct. They might no longer be able to blow the fusion cores, but there were plenty of other ways to destroy a ship *and* an enemy boarding party.

"Request volunteers for a boarding party," he said finally. Did they have time to go back to the planet and pick up some militiamen? The idea was tempting. His crew knew how to handle themselves on a ship, but none had fought on the ground before. "And monitor the enemy ship closely."

"They might be dead," Lieutenant Tim Arthur pointed out.

"They might be," William agreed, although he doubted it. A *competent* CO would have made sure his personnel were in shipsuits, ready to put on their masks if the hull was breached. But the Theocracy rarely used shipsuits. They regarded most of their crewmen as expendable.

"We won't take chances. Someone could have managed to don a proper spacesuit before it was too late."

"Yes, sir."

He sat back and waited as the boarding party was assembled, then dispatched towards the enemy hulk. He'd seriously considered leading the boarding party himself, although cold logic and duty told him such a move was impossible. His place was on the bridge, not risking his life on away missions. Instead, he quietly wrote an updated report for the planet and another for the Royal Navy. Kat Falcone would have to know what had happened at Asher Dales.

"They've landed safely," Patti reported. "The ship's an airless wreck."

"Tell them to be careful," William said stiffly. Airless didn't mean harmless. Besides, any modern-day starship was designed to close airlocks and hatches at the merest hint of a hull breach. There might be pockets of air deeper into the hull. "And watch where they go."

Nearly an hour passed before the boarding party confirmed that there were no enemy survivors. William frowned—a survivor might have known something useful—and then ordered the away team to try to access the ship's computer. Normally, the datacores would self-destruct if the ship lost power, but it was just possible that one of them might have survived. The enemy ship had been hit hard enough to dislodge a great many things.

"The datacores appear to be badly damaged," Patti said. "The engineers aren't sure if they can be powered up safely."

"Then we'll just have to be very careful," William said. He studied the remains of the enemy ship for a long moment. "Do they believe the ship can be repaired?"

"The engineers will have to take a proper look at her," Patti said. "But sir . . . I doubt it. We'd probably find it cheaper to buy a new ship."

"Probably," William agreed. A fifth destroyer would have been very helpful. The wreck might *still* be helpful. If nothing else, she was an excellent demonstration of the importance of keeping one's shipsuit on at all times. He hoped his future trainees would take careful note. "Have them prep the datacores for transfer to Orbit Station. We can decide what to do with them then."

"Aye, sir."

"And send a signal to all ships," William added. He allowed himself a smile. "Today, we fought our first engagement and won. Well done."

He sobered as he sat back in his chair. Yes, they'd won the first engagement . . . against an enemy they'd caught by surprise and out-numbered four-to-one. The next engagement would be harder. When, *if,* the Theocracy came looking to find out what had happened to their missing ship . . .

Let them have their moment, he told himself. *We can resume our preparations to meet a greater threat later.*

CHAPTER NINETEEN

FALLADINE

"Got a freighter just coming out of hyperspace," Lieutenant Randy Elkin reported. "She's the *Testing Time*, a free trader out of Jorlem."

Commander Elizabeth Robinson lifted her eyebrows. "She's a long way from home," she said. There were nearly a hundred light-years between Jorlem and Falladine; it was actually a great deal farther, as a starship either had to pass through the Gap or go the long way around. "Does her ID check out?"

"It appears to be genuine, Commander," Randy said. "She's registered with the Free Traders Association. And she's also requesting permission to dock."

Elizabeth shrugged. It wasn't as if anyone would *thank* her for turning a freighter away, particularly not when the provisional government on the planet below was doing everything in its power to turn Falladine into a shipping hub for the new era. The Theocracy had failed to destroy most of the orbital infrastructure before the surrender, giving Falladine an excellent chance of prospering . . . if it managed to interest enough freighters in passing through the system. The situation was unstable enough that very few independents wanted to take the risk unless they had armed escorts and guaranteed profits, neither of which were likely to materialize.

And yet . . . Jorlem *was* a long way away.

They could be testing the waters, so to speak, she thought. The Commonwealth wasn't always friendly to independent shippers, not when the big corporations formed semilegal cartels to drive the little ones into less lucrative sectors. *There might be a great deal of profit here for someone who managed to get in on the ground floor.*

"Invite them to dock," she said reluctantly. "And ask them for a copy of their manifest."

There was no choice, even though something was nagging at the back of her mind. She had no grounds to refuse, or to order the freighter searched. Independent shippers tended to find forced searches objectionable, and the FTA would register protests with both the local government and the Commonwealth. She suspected she'd wind up being turned into the scapegoat if things got out of hand. They could blame everything on her and send her right back to the navy.

"They've uploaded the manifest," Randy said. "It's nothing more than trade goods."

Elizabeth scanned it, rapidly. Someone clearly hadn't known what to bring, so he'd brought some of everything. Farming tools rubbed shoulders with asteroid mining gear and even small power cores. It was a neat collection, she thought; Falladine would be able to use some of the supplies, while others could be passed on to stage-one and stage-two colony worlds. And it was cheap enough for people to actually *buy*. Who knew? This freighter might merely be the first of many.

She turned to the giant portholes and looked out over her domain. The orbiting station was surrounded by industrial nodes in various states of disrepair, as well as chunks of debris and the remains of an enemy battle fleet. The locals had been slowly taking them apart for spare parts, cannibalizing the ruined ships to rebuild their infrastructure. Elizabeth had to admire their determination, even though she feared the worst. Falladine was big enough to make a tempting target, but too small to justify a larger naval presence. The handful of ships on guard duty were nowhere near enough to stand off a squadron of superdreadnoughts.

And we might be losing some of them, she thought as she turned back to the display. *If rumors from home are true, half the fleet is going to be recalled.*

"The freighter is approaching the docking strut now," Randy reported. "They're handling themselves well."

"I suppose," Elizabeth said. The freighter was maneuvering like a wallowing pig. She'd seen *superdreadnoughts* handled with more grace and elegance. She couldn't tell if the crew were unsure of themselves or unsure of the station itself. Anything built by the Theocracy couldn't be wholly trusted. "I should ask her captain to dinner this evening."

"I'm sure he'd appreciate a change from shipboard rations," Randy agreed. "Even *station*-board rations would be an improvement."

Elizabeth nodded. Her crew had been eating ration bars for the first two months of their deployment, although, as the planet managed to repair the damage to its farms, their diet had been supplemented with meat and veg. It was a shame they couldn't spend more time on the surface, she'd often thought, but she was short-staffed as it was. The Royal Navy had refused to assign more than a handful of officers and crew to the station. Falladine simply wasn't as important as a dozen other worlds.

The freighter docked, gingerly. Elizabeth glanced at the manifest again, wondering if the ship was also carrying fine china. But anything truly fragile would be in a stasis field . . . wouldn't it? Perhaps the freighter couldn't *afford* stasis pods. It was possible, but she doubted that they'd risk carrying anything fragile and expensive without them.

"They're opening the hatches," Randy said. He tapped a switch, putting the live feed from the security monitors on the display. A pair of customs inspectors were already waiting by the inner airlock. They'd check the crew's certificates before allowing them farther into the station. "I . . ."

He broke off as the inner airlock exploded into a hail of flying debris. Elizabeth stared in horror as a team of black-clad men stormed out of the freighter, weapons at the ready. The two inspectors, already injured, were stunned before they could react. Dozens of men flowed into her station, spreading out in all directions.

The ship had been a Trojan horse, and she'd let it dock!

"Seal the hatches," she snapped, shaking off her paralysis. The intruders would presumably have more shaped charges or even cutting tools with them, but they would need some time to cut through *every* hatch. "And get everyone on alert . . ."

Her mind raced. There were no marines on her station. Her staff weren't even *armed*; they didn't need to be armed to do their jobs. And they were probably already badly outnumbered as well as scattered. She couldn't imagine her team delaying the intruders for long, let alone long enough for the marines on the naval ships to get over to the station. The display was insisting that the intruders were already cutting their way through the next set of hatches.

She had a feeling she was going to lose her station before help could arrive.

"Tell everyone in the lower sections to make their way to the escape pods," she ordered grimly. "They're to blast free as soon as they're aboard . . ."

New alerts sounded. The near-space display filled with red icons. Elizabeth stared in horror as three superdreadnoughts materialized from cloak, launching missiles with terrifying abandon. The naval patrol— four cruisers and a destroyer—had gone to battlestations as soon as she'd sounded the alert, but there was no way they could stop so many missiles from tearing their ships to atoms. She hoped . . . she prayed . . . that one or more of them would have the sense to open vortexes and run, even with missiles heading directly towards the planet itself. There was no way they could stand against such firepower.

"The planetary defenses are coming online," Randy reported.

Elizabeth snorted. The planetary defenses *might* frighten a pirate, but not a trio of superdreadnoughts. They were already smashing every orbital installation within range, save for her station; they didn't seem to know, or care, if they were hitting genuine targets or merely smashing installations that had been defunct for years. The cruisers were picking up speed, attempting to get away from the planet, but it was too late. Elizabeth watched as, one by one, they died.

"The escape pods are launching now," Randy said.

"Tell them to go dark," Elizabeth ordered. Escape pods were designed to start screaming for help the moment they were launched, but in a warzone . . . there was a good chance they'd draw fire. It might not even be deliberate. An automated system might mistake an escape pod for a mine and blow it out of space without ever realizing the error. "And . . ."

The deck shuddered beneath her feet. "They're in the lower shaft," Randy said. "They'll be here in a moment."

"Purge the datacores," Elizabeth ordered. She'd lost the station. The only thing she could do was minimize the damage as much as possible. "And then we have to . . ."

She swore as the hatch exploded inwards. A team of men advanced into the room, their weapons sweeping for targets. One of them pointed a stunner at her . . .

. . . and the world went black.

◆ ◆ ◆

"The boarding party was a success, sir," the communications officer reported. "They never had a chance to resist."

"God was truly with us," Moses agreed.

Admiral Zaskar kept his thoughts to himself. He'd never admit it out loud, but he'd deliberately sent some of the most fanatical of his people on the boarding party. If they'd been killed . . . it would have been annoying, yet it would have worked in his favor too. His fleet didn't need people who were more interested in dying gloriously than in making the enemy die gloriously.

"They've taken twelve prisoners," the communications officer added. "Five of them are women."

Poor souls, Admiral Zaskar thought.

He pushed the uncomfortable thought out of his mind. "Order them to transfer the prisoners to the ship, then start looting the station," he said. "I want everything that can be of use transferred to the freighter as quickly as possible. The enemy reinforcements will already be on their way."

"Aye, sir."

Admiral Zaskar turned to the main display. Falladine was surrounded by a small halo of debris, hundreds of pieces already falling out of orbit and burning up in the planet's atmosphere. A handful of larger chunks would probably survive the fall and strike the surface; he wondered, absently, if they'd do any real damage. The remainder of the debris, in relatively stable orbits, would have to be cleared before the planet could start to rebuild its space-based industries. It was yet another problem the Commonwealth would have to solve if it wanted to keep the sector.

Not that it'll take them that long, he thought. *A lone destroyer could sweep up most of the debris in a few weeks.*

"Take us into high orbit," he said. "Have you locked KEWs on our targets?"

The weapons officer hesitated. "Admiral . . . some of our targets do not appear to exist."

"Impossible," Moses snapped.

"They may have been moved," Askew pointed out smoothly. "Or they may never have existed at all."

Admiral Zaskar ignored the byplay. "Target the ones we can see from orbit," he said. "And if you locate any other possible targets, take aim at them too."

He watched as the targeting list was rapidly updated. Falladine, unlike Judd, had *known* there was a prospect of being attacked. They hadn't had enough time to upgrade their defenses to the point where they could scratch his paint, but they'd certainly had the time and opportunity to relocate facilities, disperse their planet-side industry, and scatter their population. He would be very surprised if the bombardment killed even *one* member of the planetary government. In his experience, unbeliever governments did everything in their power to guarantee their safety. They feared to meet God after they died.

"I've located a handful of additional targets," the weapons officer reported. "But sir . . . some of the energy signatures look too good to be true."

Decoys, then, Admiral Zaskar thought. *But we have no way to find out for sure.*

"Target them anyway," he ordered, curtly. KEWs were cheap; it was easy to mine asteroids for rock, and it was easier than explaining to the cleric why he hadn't bombed an obvious target. "And then you may open fire."

"Aye, sir," the weapons officer said.

Admiral Zaskar nodded and watched as, one by one, the targets blinked out of existence. It was hard to be sure that some of the targets truly *were* targets, but there were enough real targets included in the list that Falladine would need years to recover. By then . . . either the Theocracy would be reborn, or his fleet would have been wiped out. His eyes narrowed as he saw a freighter dropping back into realspace a few light-seconds from the planet, only to reverse course as soon as her commander saw what was going on. He tapped his console, detailing a pair of destroyers to try to run the freighter down. She'd run straight to the nearest enemy base and scream for help.

"The bombardment is complete, sir," the weapons officer reported. "All targets were hit twice."

"Very good," Admiral Zaskar told him. Falladine would *definitely* need years to recover. "And the station?"

"They're sorting through the manifests now," the communications officer said. "But everything appears to be a little out of place."

"Tell them to grab everything they can," Admiral Zaskar ordered. Even farming equipment would be useful, if there came a time when they had to set out for unexplored regions of the galaxy. "But they have to hurry."

He ran through the vectors in his head, once again. There hadn't been a strong enemy presence at Falladine, which meant . . . there might well be one close by. How close? He had no way to know. An hour away? A day away? A week away? The countdown had already started. He just didn't know how long he had until it reached zero. They'd just have to grab everything they could and head out for the RV point. By then, the ships he'd sent to Dorland and Asher Dales would probably be back too.

"They have six hours," he said, finally. "After that, we're leaving."

And we'll make sure to blow up what remains of the orbital station as we go, he added to himself. *They won't find it easy to rebuild.*

◆ ◆ ◆

Elizabeth awoke slowly, her body fighting her every inch of the way. She honestly wasn't sure what had happened. She hadn't felt so vile since her friends had taken her out for a night on the town when she'd won her place at Piker's Peak, when they'd drunk so much that they'd nearly been arrested by the police. Her head was pounding, her throat was hellishly dry, her arms were stiff and uncomfortable and immobile . . . She started as she remembered what had happened.

The station had been attacked.

I was stunned, she remembered through a haze of pain. Stunners sometimes caused short-term memory loss, or worse. *They boarded the station and stunned me and . . .*

She forced herself to concentrate. She was lying facedown on a hard metal surface, her hands firmly bound behind her back. It was dark, too dark. She'd been blindfolded. Her hands felt numb; her uniform felt as if someone had searched her roughly, just to make sure she wasn't carrying any weapons. Elizabeth needed a long moment, in her confused state, to realize that someone had *also* removed her rank badges. She couldn't help thinking that was surprisingly petty.

Her blood ran cold as reality hit her. She was a prisoner of the Theocracy. She'd heard all the horror stories, all the tales of atrocities perpetrated on prisoners . . . particularly female prisoners. A handful of women had escaped over the years, particularly Princess Drusilla and her sister, and the stories they'd brought with them had horrified the galaxy. Elizabeth had wondered, privately, if the stories were exaggerated. How could *anyone* keep such a system going indefinitely? She had a nasty feeling she was about to find out.

I am a naval officer, she told herself as she heard footsteps crossing the deck. *It is my duty to survive and escape if I can.*

A strong hand grabbed her arm and hauled her to her feet. Elizabeth winced in pain. She knew she should look weak and harmless, at least until the day she could turn her captor's complacency against him. Her head was pounding like a drum. It wasn't an act. She just hoped they wouldn't expect her to get better.

She allowed her captor to half drag her along the corridor, wishing he'd take the blindfold off. She wanted, she *needed*, to see where she was going. She wasn't sure where she was now. Was she on the station, or had she been transferred to a starship? She hoped it was the former, even though she was a prisoner. She knew where the weapons and other supplies were kept. A starship, on the other hand, would be unfamiliar territory.

The deck hummed beneath her feet as she passed over a step . . . an airlock, perhaps. She was on a starship. They'd moved her onto the freighter. And that meant . . . She shivered as she heard voices speaking unfamiliar tongues. The language was beyond her comprehension, but the tone was all too clear. They'd rape her if they could. She was sure of it. A hatch opened, followed by another and another. She was being taken farther into their ship.

I need to find a way to kill myself, she thought, but nothing came to mind. *What will I do if they . . .*

Survive, her own thoughts answered. *Survive and find a way to fight back.*

The sound of the drives grew louder as she was shoved through a hatch and pushed to the floor. A strong hand removed the blindfold, revealing a tiny cell. She twisted, just in time to see a pale-faced man retreating out the hatch. His eyes met hers, just for a second; the hatch closed before she could force herself to talk. But what could she have said to him? She was a helpless prisoner and . . .

As long as they see me as helpless, they won't take me seriously, she told herself. The drives were growing louder. *And I will find a way to strike back.*

CHAPTER TWENTY

DORLAND / IN TRANSIT

Become a farmer, they said, Daniel Greenhorn thought, sardonically. *Be your own boss, they said.*

He turned in a slow circle, surveying his farm. Everyone *said* it was a farm, at least. He held title to it and everything. But it was really nothing more than a square mile of unbroken ground, which needed to be smashed up and turned into soil before anything would grow. He really should have read his contract more carefully, he told himself sourly. The vast benefits awarded to him and anyone else willing to break hardened ground into soil came with a steep price. He couldn't walk away from his farm unless he found someone willing to take over.

And no one will, he thought, as he wiped sweat from his brow. Dorland was a poor world, with much of the population struggling to draw sustenance from a land that hated them. The original settlers had chosen to leave technology behind when they'd left Earth in search of a new idyll, and *this* was the price. Backbreaking labor for men and women, with a government that constantly promised everything and delivered nothing. *This farm won't be viable for years.*

He looked south, towards the colony. The original set of colony elders had done a good job of wiping out records from the outside universe, but the Theocracy had blown the gates open wide and the new government knew better than to try to return the population to a state of ignorance. Daniel knew, as did many of the other farmers, that modern-day terraforming equipment would solve Dorland's problems in a decade or two. They wouldn't have hesitated to overthrow the government if there had been a reasonable prospect of obtaining such technology, but no one seemed to want to sell it to them. The Theocracy hadn't cared about Dorland, and the Commonwealth . . . the Commonwealth didn't seem to be any better.

And I have to get on with it, he thought as he picked up his shovel. The inspectors would be calling in a week or so, and they'd expect him to have made considerable progress. If they deemed his progress insufficient, they'd cut off his rations or simply send him to the penal camps. It was funny how no one had discussed *that* with him until after he'd signed the contracts. *Anyone would think they wanted me to trap myself . . .*

The sky turned white, just for a second. Instinctively, Daniel threw himself to the hard ground, cursing out loud as he landed badly. The thunder hit a second later, a dull rolling sound that echoed off the distant mountains and shook the unbroken ground beneath his chest. He looked up a second later, just in time to see a streak of fire fall from high above and plummet towards the distant town. There was a flash of light when it struck the ground, followed by a colossal fireball and another round of thunder. More followed, the sound shaking the entire colony. He heard a crashing sound from his shack, positioned at the far edge of the field. It hadn't been designed for earthquakes. Dorland was geologically inert.

That's not an earthquake, he told himself as yet another rumble of thunder echoed through the sky. *The planet is under attack!*

He rolled over and peered up at the bright blue sky. Dorland was right on the edge of the habitable zone, close enough to the primary star to be dangerously hot even though, thankfully, there was no greenhouse effect. He couldn't see anything up there, but streaks of fire were still tumbling towards the ground. Was one of them aimed at him? He couldn't imagine an unseen man deciding to kill him, but . . . he couldn't imagine anyone attacking Dorland either. There was literally nothing on the planet worth taking, except perhaps the population itself. And any interstellar slavers would surely not want to kill the people they intended to enslave . . . right?

The thunder slowly died away. Daniel forced himself to stand and make his way towards the shack. As he'd expected, the roof had collapsed. His meager possessions and the room he'd hoped to one day share with a wife had been crushed. He recovered a handful of items, then walked towards the tractor. There was barely enough fuel in its tank to get to town, but it would have to do. If there was one rule on Dorland that everyone followed, it was that people who needed help had to be helped. No one could be a loner on a world where everyone had to fight to survive. A person who helped another on Monday might wind up needing help himself on Tuesday.

It took him longer than he'd expected to steer his way down the dusty track and set course for town. The attackers, whoever they were, had dropped a bomb right in the middle of the road, smashing it beyond repair. Daniel couldn't imagine what had been going through their minds. There was literally nothing to be gained by making life harder for rescuers. And besides, all he'd had to do to get around the crater was steer the tractor off the road. The move would burn up more of his fuel, which he doubted he'd be able to reclaim from the government, but it didn't matter. People needed help.

He saw the plume of smoke rising in the distance long before the town itself came into view at the end of the road. It had been built within a valley, the better to hide from the sun, but he knew, the moment he laid eyes on it, that the town was doomed. The bombs, whatever they were, had smashed the valley walls. It wouldn't be long before the townspeople had to move elsewhere. But where could they go?

Parking the tractor at one end of the valley, he jumped off and hurried down towards the collapsing buildings. A number had already turned into piles of rubble, even though they'd been designed to stand up to the elements. Adults were working desperately to get the kids out of the valley, then dig through the wreckage to recover trapped or dead townspeople. It was so bad that Daniel honestly wasn't sure where to begin.

They didn't have to do this to us, he thought as he ran towards the nearest building. *We were harmless.*

He shuddered as the full implications struck him. Dorland was doomed. He hated the government, but he also understood that the government *had* to force its people to turn the land into a place humans could live and grow. The planet had always been on the margins; he *knew* that to be true, as much as he might resent it. Survival trumped everything else. But now . . . if the attackers had ruined a small town, what had they done to the rest of the planet?

And there's no way to leave, he realized. *We're all going to die.*

◆ ◆ ◆

"Those lousy murdering fucking . . ."

"That will do," Captain Ian Hales said. "Concentrate on your duties."

The helmsman subsided. Ian sighed, inwardly. He didn't blame the younger man for wanting to throw their cover to the winds and attack the Theocratic ship, but they had a mission to carry out. It had been sheer luck that HMS *Peacock* arrived on station in time to see the enemy cruiser enter the system and begin its murderous attack. He had no intention of wasting the opportunity to deal a decisive blow to the enemy fleet, even if it meant letting a crew of murderers get away. They'd get theirs, he promised himself. He'd see to it personally.

"Keep us near their position," he added. "And *don't* let them see us."

"Aye, sir."

Ian scowled as the enemy ship completed its bombardment. She was a modified light cruiser, according to the warbook; *Peacock* couldn't have taken her unless she'd already been worked over by something nastier than a destroyer. He'd seriously considered ramming the enemy ship, taking her out at the price of losing his own vessel, but he had his orders. The navy *had* to trace the enemy ships back to their base.

"She's moving away from the planet," the tactical officer said. Her voice was grim. She'd served in the navy for four years, but most of it had been spent on the border. She hadn't seen much of the war. "I think she's preparing to leave."

"Get ready to take us into hyperspace immediately after her," Ian ordered. The enemy cruiser could *not* be allowed to detect their presence. She'd either turn on her shadow or lead her on a merry dance. She might even fly too close to an energy storm to keep *Peacock* from keeping a solid lock on her hull. "Stand by weapons and shields."

He felt a pang of guilt. The people on the planet below weren't citizens, not of the Commonwealth, but it didn't matter. They'd done nothing to deserve having their planet bombarded, certainly not in a manner that would render their civilization unsustainable.

And any survivors will become refugees, he thought. *As if there weren't already millions of people looking for a safe place to live.*

"The enemy ship is opening a vortex," the sensor officer said.

"Take us into hyperspace," Ian snapped. For a handful of seconds, the enemy sensors would be blinded by their own vortex. Even the most advanced systems would have trouble picking up *Peacock*'s presence. "Now!"

He braced himself as his starship opened a vortex and slipped into hyperspace. If they were wrong, if they'd made a mistake, they were about to be attacked. He had no doubt of it. The Theocrats would have to be utterly insane to let him get so close to one of their ships. But, as the seconds slowly ticked away, he allowed himself to relax. Their target was already setting course away from the system she'd devastated.

"Shadow her," he ordered. "But hold the range open as much as possible."

"Aye, Captain," the helmsman said.

The sensor officer looked worried. "Captain," she said, "if we hold the range open, we may lose her in a sensor distortion."

Ian nodded. Tracking starships through hyperspace was an art, not a science . . . and one that was frighteningly easy to get wrong. Hyperspace had been playing tricks on sensors ever since humanity had first figured out how to open vortexes and use the dimension to circumvent the light barrier. It wasn't uncommon for starships to pick up sensor ghosts, or for hyperspace distortions to make it look as though a ship hundreds of light-years away was actually right on top of the sensor. He'd been on enough deployments to know that *nothing* could be taken for granted in hyperspace.

But they didn't want to be detected either.

"Do your best, Betty," he said as reassuringly as he could. "We need to know where they're going."

"Aye, sir."

He settled back into his command chair, trying not to think about the dead and dying they were leaving behind. Dorland had never attracted much attention—the locals seemed to be happier that way—but his ship had received copies of files captured on Ahura Mazda. The planet was permanently close to the edge. He honestly didn't understand why the locals hadn't abandoned their arid homeworld long ago.

They don't have a choice now, he thought. *And if we don't manage to get them some help, they won't survive the year.*

♦ ♦ ♦

Elizabeth felt . . . unwell.

She wasn't sure how long it had been since the attack, or since she'd even had something to eat or drink. Her throat was parched, while her stomach kept rumbling ominously. She'd looked around the tiny cell, but there was nothing to eat even if her hands *hadn't* remained bound behind her back.

The hatch clicked, then opened slowly. Elizabeth rolled over and looked up. A man stood in the hatchway, silhouetted by the light. He tapped his lips once as he stepped into the cell, warning her to be quiet. She wasn't sure if she should do as he wanted or make as much noise as she could. The guards would hear, wouldn't they?

She studied him for a moment, feeling an odd shiver of . . . something. The man *looked* like a Theocrat, right down to the hawk-nosed face, skin, and neatly trimmed beard, but there was something about him that caused her to doubt it. He looked more like an actor playing a part than anything else. She'd once met Cyril Worthington-Gore, star of seven *Space Marine Extraordinaire* productions, and there had been something false about him. He'd simply been *too* good to be true. His scriptwriter had probably helped.

"Keep your voice down," the man hissed. He spoke perfect Standard. There wasn't even a hint of an accent. That was odd, wasn't it? The Theocrats rarely spoke anything other than their own language. She'd heard that, once. It kept them from being corrupted by outside influences or something. "Here."

He pressed a glass to her lips. Elizabeth drank gladly, even though she knew the water might be drugged. But they hardly needed to resort to tricks to force her to drink. The water tasted faintly odd and left her tongue feeling numb. She opened her mouth to protest, but it was already too late. The sensation was spreading rapidly. She couldn't even move.

"This is the only mercy I can grant you," the man said quietly. She thought, as her vision started to blur, that he genuinely meant it. "If things were different, I would have tried to get you out. But the mission comes first."

Elizabeth wanted to ask him what he meant by that, but the words refused to form. Killing her was a mercy? A Theocrat being *merciful*. It struck her, in her last seconds of life, that her killer wasn't a Theocrat. Who was he?

But she knew, as the last of her awareness drifted away, that she'd never know.

◆ ◆ ◆

"The bitch is dead," Moses said.

Admiral Zaskar looked up. "What bitch?"

"The unnatural woman," Moses said. "The one who claimed to be in command."

"Oh," Admiral Zaskar said. The clerics might rant and rave about women who overstepped their bounds, but he found it hard to care. He doubted the poor woman's captors had bothered to feed or water her. Maybe she'd just starved to death. Or maybe she'd had a suicide implant. "Put the body out the airlock and forget about her."

Moses didn't look very happy—he'd been looking forward to teaching the woman the error of her ways—but Admiral Zaskar ignored him. He had a worse problem. The destroyer he'd sent to Asher Dales had not returned. And that meant . . . The files claimed that Asher Dales was defenseless, but the files were out of date. The Commonwealth could easily have stationed a ship or two in the system in the hopes of catching one of his ships by surprise. They might just have succeeded.

And if I send a ship back to find out what happened to the lost ship, he thought, *I might lose that ship too.*

He shook his head, then keyed his terminal. "Take us back to base," he ordered. "We'll sort through the captured supplies there."

"Aye, sir."

◆ ◆ ◆

Ian had taken *Peacock* out of hyperspace as soon as it became clear that the enemy ship was leaving hyperspace herself. He'd expected to encounter another ship, but instead the entire enemy fleet was spread out in front of him. Thankfully, they didn't appear to be very alert, yet the shock was enough to make him rethink his tactics. If they'd come out of hyperspace a little closer, they might have been detected and blown away before they realized what they'd found. As it was, they were dangerously close to the enemy fleet.

"Hold us here," he ordered. He had to fight to keep his voice under control. The urge to whisper was overwhelmingly powerful, even though he *knew* the enemy couldn't hear him. "And monitor the enemy position."

"They're preparing to return to hyperspace," the sensor officer said. "Their vortexes are opening . . . now."

"Take us back into hyperspace with them," Ian ordered. His heart sank. Tracking a fleet was harder than tracking a single ship. Hyperspace would make life interesting for the enemy fleet, but harder for him. "And don't let them slip away."

"Aye, sir."

Ian braced himself as the enemy fleet returned to hyperspace. "Keep us at a distance," he ordered, quietly. Hyperspace was already being churned up by the presence of so many starships in close formation. "And try to keep a solid lock on them."

"They're deploying energy mines," the sensor officer said. He worked his console for a long moment. "Captain, we're losing them!"

"Clever of them," Ian said as the last of the enemy ships vanished from the display. The energy mines would disrupt hyperspace long enough for the departing fleet to make a clean break. He wasn't sure if they'd spotted his ship or not, but it didn't matter. The energy storms would make it harder to get relief ships into the sector. "Helm, set course for the nearest StarCom."

"Aye, sir."

CHAPTER TWENTY-ONE

ASHER DALES

"Admiral, we're being pinged," the communications officer said as the squadron glided into the Asher Dales System. "They sound a little alarmed."

Kat lifted her eyebrows. If William was in command, over there, he'd recognize a squadron of Royal Navy superdreadnoughts when he saw one. A man like William McElney didn't lose his competence so quickly. And even if it wasn't William in command, their warbook should have identified the superdreadnoughts as soon as they arrived. She wasn't playing games with her squadron's drive signatures or IFF transmissions.

"And there's a Theocratic destroyer in orbit," the tactical officer added. "She's completely powered down."

"Resend our IFF, then transmit a standard greeting," Kat ordered. "And order the *Morse* to start preparations to deploy the StarCom."

"Aye, Admiral," the communications officer said. She paused. "We're being hailed."

"Put them through," Kat said.

She smiled, warmly, as William McElney's face appeared in the display. He looked older and scruffy in a manner that would have given Kat's mother fits, but she couldn't help thinking he looked *happier*. The files hadn't said much about what William was doing at Asher Dales, but she had no doubt it was something her former XO would find rewarding and challenging. The days when he was kept back by an accident of birth were long over.

"William," she said. "It's good to see you again."

"You too, Kat," William said. He rubbed his stubble mischievously. "We had a visitor, as you can see."

Kat nodded towards the display. "An enemy destroyer," she said. "Where did you get *that*?"

"We were attacked," William said. He sounded proud. "Luckily, we saw them coming in ample time to get ready."

"Ah," Kat said. A single destroyer was nothing compared to the forces that had waged titanic combat during the war, but Asher Dales had done very well. Given what they'd started out with a year ago, they'd done very well indeed. "I need to . . ."

"I would like to formally request your assistance in examining the hulk," William said, wryly. "We just want copies of everything you find."

Kat relaxed, slightly. They needed to examine the hulk . . . even though, technically, the vessel now belonged to Asher Dales. It would have been embarrassing if she'd had to *take* the captured ship. But William had understood the problem and opened the door for her. She hoped his new superiors wouldn't take his kindness amiss. The die-hard Theocrats were everyone's problem.

"I'll send you copies of the records," William added. "You may find them of interest."

"Thank you," Kat said. It was also the most *successful* engagement since the crisis had begun. If nothing else, losing a ship would make the enemy more careful about picking on supposedly undefended worlds. "We do need to talk. Your place or mine?"

William smiled. "I'd like to offer you *Dandelion*'s hospitality," he said. "And the planetary government would probably like to offer you theirs as well."

And you want a chance to show off, Kat thought wryly. She didn't blame him. William had always had something to prove. *And we have to talk in private.*

"I'd be happy to visit," she said. "And then I'd like to welcome you to *Violence.* We have much to talk about."

"I look forward to it," William said. He gave her a jaunty salute. "Over and out."

His image vanished from the display. Kat smiled, again. She'd missed him . . . but she hadn't realized how *much* she'd missed him until now. Perhaps she could convince him to come back to the Royal Navy. Or maybe . . . She shook her head, dismissing the thought. William wouldn't be happy if he had to abandon Asher Dales. He was a man of honor. And besides, the Royal Navy would never reward him as he deserved.

Particularly now, Kat thought. Too many colonial officers had been thanked for their services and mustered out since the end of the war. *And even with his connections, his career might not be safe.*

"Admiral, *Morse* reports that she is ready to deploy the StarCom," the communications officer said. "They can begin on your command."

"Consider it given," Kat said. A StarCom network wouldn't solve *all* their problems, but it would make it easier to coordinate her fleet. It would probably also lead to a great deal of micromanagement from home . . . She shrugged. She'd just have to put up with the hassle. "And make sure the locals have access to the network."

"Aye, Admiral."

Kat stood. "And inform the captain that I will be visiting *Dandelion,*" she added. "He's to take command of the squadron until I return."

◆ ◆ ◆

"I thought the navy handed out prize money for captured ships," Tanya said as they waited by the airlock. "Why are you just *giving* the ship to her?"

"I'm not giving the ship to anyone," William said patiently. Tanya hadn't been happy when she'd heard he'd invited Kat to send people to examine the captured ship. "And there's no way *anyone* will pay us any prize money for the ship."

He kept his face impassive. Kat had been in an unpleasant position from the moment she'd realized they'd captured an enemy ship. On one hand, she needed to examine the ship from top to bottom in the hopes of finding something useful; on the other, the ship was unquestionably someone else's property. Kat might have no choice but to seize the captured ship . . . riding roughshod over Asher Dales in the process. Her career might suffer if Asher Dales and the Commonwealth protested loudly enough, yet she *needed* to track down and destroy the raiders before it was too late. William had given her an easy way out of the dilemma. And besides, they *did* need to destroy the raiders.

The airlock opened. Kat stepped through, wearing a basic uniform. William relaxed, slightly. He'd half expected her to wear her dress uniform. That would have been embarrassing, if only because Asher Dales had *no* dress uniform. The planetary defense force hadn't grown large enough to allow inexperienced sadists to claim positions of power. And whoever had designed the Royal Navy's dress uniform was very definitely a sadist.

He studied Kat for a long moment as she saluted the flag. Dear God . . . what had *happened* to her? Her face looked the same, but there was a . . . *beaten* air around her that worried him more than he cared to admit. He knew that she'd taken Pat Davidson's death badly, yet . . . He winced, inwardly. Kat had lost her father and fiancé in the same month. No wonder she was depressed. And leaving the command deck probably hadn't helped. She'd been a great commanding officer.

"Welcome aboard," he said, saluting. "It's good to see you again."

"Likewise," Kat said. She sounded tired. "You didn't change the dedication plaque?"

William glanced at the plaque, which still read HMS DANDELION. "It didn't seem as important as getting the ships into space and into service," he said as he invited Kat to follow him to his office. Tanya fell in behind them. "Besides, Asher Dales hasn't agreed on a formal ship prefix, let alone anything else. I imagine the ships will be renamed at some point in the future."

"Probably," Kat agreed. "You did a good job."

"With the ships or with the battle?" William grinned at her. "We tried."

Kat smiled back, tiredly. "Both, I suppose," she said. "But the battle in particular."

"It would have gone the other way if they'd come in firing," William said. He'd done everything in his power to make that clear to the planetary government, although he wasn't sure they'd believed him. Victory was better than defeat, of course, but it had a nasty habit of going to one's head. "They might have been able to inflict serious damage on the planet even if we *had* destroyed them."

"They didn't, thankfully," Kat said. Her expression darkened. "Judd will need years to recover."

William said nothing as they stepped into his cabin. The reports had been vague and outdated, but the planet had clearly taken a beating. Years of work had been smashed back to bedrock. It was quite possible that the locals wouldn't have the grit and determination to rebuild, even after the enemy force was destroyed. He'd been on planets that had lost the will to live. They were not *pleasant* places to visit. He hated to imagine what it might be like to live there.

"Please, take a seat," he said, waving towards the sofa. It was yet another unessential item he hadn't bothered to have replaced. Kat, at least, wouldn't be upset that he hadn't covered the frame in gold and replaced the navy-issue cushions with silk. "Would you care for a glass of the local vintage?"

"Just a glass," Kat said. She sat on the sofa and crossed her legs. "What *did* you pull out of the wreckage?"

"Very little, so far," William said. He poured three glasses of wine and passed them around, then took a chair himself. Tanya remained standing, her face utterly impassive. "The datacores were quite badly damaged by the engagement. We haven't even started to untangle them, if indeed it's possible. Your experts might be able to do a better job."

And Asher Dales won't be blamed if they fail to pull anything from the datacores, he added silently. *Kat* would understand that, sometimes, it simply wasn't possible to recover data, but her political masters might not be *quite* so understanding. *Better to let someone else take the blame.*

He studied Kat, feeling oddly uneasy. She still looked young— if she'd been born on Hebrides, he would have said she was in her midtwenties—but the way she held herself suggested she was an old woman trapped in a young woman's form. And yet, she wasn't *that* old. Kat was in her late thirties. She still had years ahead of her. But she'd lost too much over the last year. She deserved much better.

"We did examine the bodies," he said, putting the thought aside for later consideration. "Of the fifty-one corpses pulled from the wreck, forty-five of them were almost certainly from Ahura Mazda. They had the usual lack of genetic enhancements, as far as anyone can tell; the remainder appear to have come from somewhere else. We just don't know where."

Kat's lips thinned. "Converts or traitors?"

"Or merely pirates out for a good time," William said. He didn't *think* that any pirates would willingly join the Theocrats, but he'd been wrong before. "It's also possible that they were conscripts. The Theocrats presumably need people to help keep their ships running."

"We know they took people from Judd," Kat agreed. "And they'd take people from here too, if they had the chance."

William nodded. "I've ordered my people to carry weapons at all times," he said. "But I don't know how it will work out."

"At least they'll have a chance to resist capture," Kat said.

Or kill themselves before they can be captured, William told himself grimly. *No one wants to fall into enemy hands.*

Kat cleared her throat. "Do you remember when we were sent out to raid enemy territory?"

"Yes," William said. The irony wasn't lost on him. "And now they're doing the same thing to you."

Kat looked pained. "You're not the first person to say that," she said. "The Commonwealth was able to deal with raiders, William, because most of the stage-two and upwards systems were defended. Here . . . Asher Dales is one of the few systems that managed to raise any kind of defense force. The others are effectively defenseless. I've parceled out most of my ships in hopes of catching the raiders in the act, but . . . the odds of actually succeeding are quite low."

"Then you need to expand the local defenses," William said. "The ships *we* purchased weren't the only ones being sold."

"Against pirates, you might have a point," Kat said. "I believe the king was pushing for subsidies for self-defense forces. But against a set of superdreadnoughts . . . there's no way we can afford to give *every* world the defenses they'd need to stand them off. The cost would be astronomical."

William frowned. "How long can they even keep those superdread-noughts *operational*?"

Kat sighed. "I don't know," she said. "Their maintenance routines are shitty. You *know* that. I believed the ships that escaped the final battle would rapidly degrade without access to shipyards or even spare parts. No pirate or smuggler ring could provide them with what they'd need to keep the ships running. *Someone* is helping them."

"But who actually benefits?" William considered the matter, carefully. "Have there been conflicts with the other Great Powers?"

"Nothing of great concern," Kat said. "There were a handful of minor disagreements. A few people were upset that Britannia refused to dispatch more than a couple of ships to search for *Supreme*, but nothing anyone would actually go to war over. And if we caught someone supplying the Theocrats, we probably *would* go to war. It would be an insane risk."

William had his doubts. Hebrides had been a rough world even *before* the Theocrats had turned his homeworld into a radioactive hellhole. Its population knew, on a very basic level, that the world around them and the universe outside the planet's atmosphere were red in tooth and claw. Might made right, in the crudest possible sense. His people couldn't hide from the realities of life.

But Tyre was different. Tyre had been a comfortable place to live ever since it had been settled. The population enjoyed considerable advantages, from excellent schools to a social network that had banished starvation and want. There might be a social stigma to accepting free food and lodging from the government instead of earning enough to pay one's own way, but people didn't starve. And they'd come to believe that that was how the universe worked, even after the war began. They were, in some sense, tired of war.

And very few of them care about the people out here, he thought. *The liberated worlds aren't part of the Commonwealth. And they were having problems with the Commonwealth even before the war made all problems worse.*

"I hope you're right," he said. "Do you think we missed a shipyard, somewhere?"

Kat shook her head. "Their record keeping was terrible, but I think we can be reasonably sure they didn't hide more than a handful of storage depots in deep space. They grabbed everything they could just to throw at us during the final battle."

"But you can't be sure," Tanya said, speaking for the first time. "There *could* be a working shipyard out there."

"Our analysts have tried hard to account for every last ebb and flow of their economy," Kat said. If she noticed the blatant challenge in Tanya's voice, she didn't show it. "Impossible to be entirely sure, as you say, but we believe that relatively little war material remains unaccounted for. Certainly not enough to build and maintain a secret fleet of starships."

She smiled, although it didn't touch her eyes. "They were lying to themselves. Their people were pressured into increasing their production, so they basically lied and said that yes, production was increasing. They kept wearing out their equipment because they were trying to meet impossible demands. Their economy was overheating even before we started shooting at each other. There's a good chance it would have collapsed completely in a few years anyway."

"And yet they went to war," William said. "They must have been desperate."

"It makes you wonder just how much else they didn't know," Kat said. "If everyone was . . . *massaging* the data to create favorable facts . . . did they believe that half the Royal Navy simply didn't exist? Or did they genuinely believe they could win the war in six months?"

"Their plan wasn't *that* bad," William reminded her. "If we hadn't been at Cadiz, Admiral Morrison's fleet would have been caught by surprise and wiped out. That would certainly have given them an opportunity to take the war farther into the Commonwealth."

"They still wouldn't have been able to take Tyre," Kat said. "And even challenging the defenses could have cost them the war." She leaned back. "We'll see what we can learn from the captured ship," she said. "And, under the circumstances, I feel justified in transferring a number of replacement missiles to you."

"That would be very welcome," William told her.

Kat smiled. "I thought so too."

She ran her hand through her hair. "We won the war, William," she said. "And yet, we seem to be losing the peace."

"They can't run rampant forever," William assured her. "Sooner or later, their luck will run out. And then you'll be there to meet them."

"I hope so," Kat said. "But right now . . . it feels like we're running around trying to put out fires with water pistols."

Her wristcom bleeped. "Excuse me."

"Admiral," a voice said. "We made contact with Ahura Mazda. I . . . I'm afraid there have been two more attacks."

William felt his heart clench. *Two* more attacks? No, there had been *three* attacks, if one counted the attempted raid on Asher Dales. The enemy was getting bolder.

"Understood," Kat said. She rose. "I'm on my way."

"I'll see you planet-side, if you have time to visit," William said, standing. "If not . . . I'll understand."

"I have to stay here anyway, at least until we pull everything we can from the wreck," Kat said. "If we find something that will lead us to the enemy base . . ."

William nodded in agreement. If they located the enemy base, Kat could take her superdreadnoughts there and smash the Theocratic fleet into rubble. The move wouldn't solve *all* their problems, but it would deal with the immediate crisis. And if the only thing they had to worry about, after that, was pirate raiders . . . well, he'd be relieved. He could handle pirates.

"I'll see you soon," he said. "And good luck."

"You too," Kat said. "You've done very well here."

CHAPTER TWENTY-TWO

TYRE

Father definitely had the right idea, Peter thought as he listened to yet another long-winded Member of Parliament droning on about his constituency's interests. *There's no reason I couldn't vote by proxy, or even have each debate summarized for me . . .*

He glanced at his datapad, wondering when, if ever, the MP for Hawking Park would get to the point. It felt like he'd been talking for hours, despite the speaker putting a strict time limit on speeches. The man definitely loved the sound of his own voice. Peter rather thought he'd said the same thing over and over again. By the time the MP sat, to a ripple of relieved applause, Peter was nursing a pounding headache.

The speaker stood. "The Honorable MP for Gridley wishes to propose a Private Member's Bill."

Peter sat upright, feeling a sudden flicker of excitement. Anyone could propose a PMB, but it wouldn't be put up for debate unless a handful of other MPs had already agreed to sponsor it. And then . . . the MP was gambling. If his bill didn't receive a certain level of support from the Houses of Parliament, according to the rules, he'd have to face a vote of confidence from his constituents. The MP for Gridley— an independent MP, according to the man's file—was taking a huge chance. His constituents might not thank him for failing to represent them properly.

Particularly as an independent will have problems getting the backing to get anything done, Peter thought. Party MPs had much more clout. *They may come to regret electing an independent.*

"Honorable Speaker, Honorable Members, I will be brief," the MP for Gridley said. "We have spent the last week dancing around the question of passing the budget bill and arguing—pointlessly, I daresay—over our duty to the liberated worlds. To me, the issue is not up for debate. The liberated worlds are not members of the Commonwealth, we have no treaties with them that we should honor . . . and, as many others have pointed out, what commitments were made were made without Parliament's consent."

Dangerous waters, Peter thought, amused. The MP hadn't mentioned the king, but *everyone* knew who'd made the commitments. *His career will either rise to terrifying heights or come crashing down in flames.*

"I say that we have *no* commitments," the MP for Gridley said, his voice rising. "And I say that we have no *interest* in trying to civilize the barbarians. The people of Ahura Mazda do not *want* to live in a civilized society, and all our efforts to impose a new order on them are doomed to failure. There is literally nothing to be gained by an expensive commitment to the liberated sector. The Royal Navy exists to protect our worlds and our shipping. It does not exist to play galactic policeman!"

He paused, significantly. "I propose the immediate withdrawal of our ships and our bases from the Theocratic Sector. Let the locals handle their own defense, if they are so inclined; let the barbarians wallow in their own barbarism. The Theocracy is gone. In time, they will evolve newer and better ways to live. We should not believe that we have a *duty* to assist them. Even if we did, they have shown us what they think of our . . . assistance.

"Honorable Speaker, I request that we move to an immediate vote," he concluded. "Let the matter be decided now, once and for all."

Peter sucked in his breath. Another gamble, on top of the first? The MP *had* to be confident of victory. But there was no *reason* to be confident. Peter's analysts believed that, at most, only a third of the MPs would support immediate withdrawal. The House of Lords was keeping their cards closer to their chests, as always, but Peter doubted that they'd be keen to support the bill. The corporations had made a number of loans to the liberated worlds.

Loans we couldn't expect to have repaid if the sector collapses into chaos, Peter thought. They weren't *big* loans, not compared to the amount of money that would be needed to rescue Cavendish, but collectively they were quite significant. *And chaos on the far side of the Gap might easily spread into our territories.*

His datapad bleeped, inviting him to cast a vote. Should the proposed bill be put to an immediate vote or not? He smiled, humorlessly. They were voting on whether or not they should be allowed to vote on the bill. No, he corrected himself. That wasn't quite accurate. They were trying to decide if the bill should be put to the vote now or later, the latter giving anyone who disagreed with the bill time to organize resistance. It made him wonder if there were ties between the bill's proposer and Israel Harrison. The Leader of the Opposition might have dreamed up the whole scheme to challenge the king without revealing his hand too openly.

Something to consider, he told himself as he voted *nay*. *No one takes such a gamble unless they're convinced of powerful support.*

He allowed himself a sigh of relief as the *nays* had it, two to one. Too many MPs hadn't liked the idea of being forced to vote on a bill without debating first, even if it meant *more* long-winded speeches. Peter checked his datapad once again, noting when the debate had been scheduled. There would be plenty of time to organize resistance . . . if, of course, he wanted to organize resistance. From a practical point of view, withdrawing from the occupied sector would save billions of crowns.

And it would put less pressure on the Royal Navy, Peter thought. *It's something else I'll have to discuss with Kat.*

He took a long breath as the speaker rose, again.

"Honorable Members," he said. "We have one final issue to discuss. The Royal Wedding Bill."

Peter sighed, inwardly, as the MPs started a mixture of cheers and boos. The Royal Wedding was a touchy subject, particularly when the kingdom was expected to help pay for it. A number of MPs and talking heads had asked, not too politely, why the king couldn't pay for it himself, as he was probably the richest landowner in the system. The Royal Corporation wouldn't begrudge him a few million crowns to throw the wedding of the century.

Except there's precedent for the kingdom to fund the ceremony, Peter thought. *And that gets awkward when half the kingdom dislikes the bride.*

He listened, carefully, as the prime minister stood and extolled the virtues of the match. Princess Drusilla—she wasn't really a princess, but the title had stuck—was not, in some ways, a bad choice. She had no ties to the local aristocracy, so the wedding wouldn't give any one family an unexpected prominence; she was a war hero, someone who'd risked her life to warn the Commonwealth of the oncoming storm . . . Yes, she did have her advantages. But she was also a foreign national, the child of someone who'd waged war on the Commonwealth and, perhaps, not to be trusted. The people who feared the effects of creating and widening the Commonwealth had no reason to like Drusilla. They would sooner the king married a talented commoner from Tyre.

And he chose his bride-to-be himself, Peter remembered. *That didn't go down well with the people who expected to help him choose.*

He couldn't help feeling a moment of genuine *respect* for the king. Peter's marriage to Alison had been arranged by both sets of parents, although he'd known his future bride for years before the match was arranged. It had been a fairly typical contract, with provisions for children, temporary and permanent separations, and a strict division of property. He didn't *dislike* his wife, but . . . he didn't really love her either. The only good thing about the arrangement, apart from their children, was that Alison understood the rules as well as he did. As long as she did nothing to embarrass him in public, or vice versa, he would turn a blind eye to her private affairs. Everyone had expected the king would have a similar arrangement with his future bride.

But, instead, he'd chosen a foreign-born woman.

The prime minister sat down. Israel Harrison stood.

"Mr. Speaker, Members of the House, I will be blunt," he said. "I acknowledge that Princess Drusilla did us a considerable service, five years ago. I also acknowledge that His Majesty has the right to choose his own bride. But I am not blind to either the political implications of the match, or the financial implications. We are suffering from financial embarrassment"—there were a handful of chuckles—"and we will have to make quite considerable cutbacks in the next few months. Or does anyone believe we can keep printing money *without* setting off a massive rise in inflation?"

He paused, dramatically. "This is not the time for displays of wealth and consumption," he added. "You may be thinking . . . hey, a few million crowns here, a few million crowns there . . . pretty soon, we'll be talking about *real* money. But, right across the kingdom, people are having to tighten their belts. They are scared, scared that they will be among the first to lose their jobs as the corporations rush to restructure themselves to save what they can. And you wish to taunt them with a Royal Wedding?

"I say no. I say that the public purse should *not* fund the wedding. And I say that the wedding should be as simple as possible."

He sat down. A number of MPs buzzed for attention. The speaker pointed to one at random.

"My honorable friend said he would be blunt," the MP said. Peter recognized him as Kevin Hastings, a close friend of the prime minister. "I will be equally so.

"This is not about money. This is not about public perception of His Majesty and his growing family. This is about xenophobia, plain and simple. The Opposition has opposed the Commonwealth for so long because it is driven by *xenophobia*!"

Another mixture of cheers and boos filled the air. The speaker gaveled for silence as Hastings went on.

"The Opposition has spearheaded the removal of colonial-born officers and crew from Royal Navy ships. The Opposition has demanded strict limits to the number of work permits issued for foreign-born workers on Tyre. The Opposition has reduced or canceled programs to improve the lives of people on stage-one and stage-two colony worlds; the Opposition has even stated its—hah—opposition to helping refugees find new homes. And now, for all their fine words about financial prudence, their opposition to the Royal Wedding is *really* about their refusal to accept a foreign-born woman as *queen*.

"We cannot demand service from the colonials, then refuse to treat them as equals; we cannot open up our world, then decline to share. We built the Commonwealth on the principle of founding a new interstellar order, not exploiting people who were helpless to defend themselves. The Royal Wedding would signify, once and for all, that there is a place in our world for people who were *not* lucky enough to be born on Tyre. And the Opposition wishes to deny it because it does not *believe* that such a place exists!"

Peter frowned as the shouting grew louder, despite the speaker's best efforts. There was a nasty grain of truth in Hastings's words, although the Opposition would deny them. Tyre had never been keen on accepting immigrants, particularly vast numbers of immigrants who refused to assimilate into society. There was no shortage of horror stories about worlds that had accepted incompatible settlers and wound up collapsing into civil war. And yes, there *was* a fear that immigrants would steal jobs. He wouldn't care to be an MP who voted for expanding the number of work permits. His constituents would see it as a betrayal.

And they're the ones with votes, Peter thought. An immigrant had to work hard before he was allowed to claim citizenship. *An MP who betrayed his people would be recalled to face a vote of confidence.*

He sighed, inwardly. It wasn't about xenophobia, he thought, although it did play a role. And it wasn't about financial prudence either, even though *that* too played a role. It was about punishing the king. The budget bill had gone nowhere, with both sides refusing to compromise even slightly for fear that such an act would be taken as a sign of weakness. Peter had tried to play mediator, but the king and his government hadn't offered any concessions . . .

The noise grew louder. MPs were on their feet, shouting insults at their enemies; Peter was mildly surprised they weren't throwing pieces of paper like children. The lords were slightly more restrained, but it was clear that feelings were running high. It looked as though the speaker was on the verge of ordering the chamber cleared, which would unite the MPs and Lords against him. Peter wasn't sure he'd have the nerve to take such a drastic step. A speaker could be removed by a simple voice vote.

Shaking his head, Peter stood and walked out of the rear door. A handful of Parliamentary Security officers stood outside, looking nervous. The last time the chamber had been cleared had been back during the Putney Debates and, while no one had suffered *officially* for their role in the affair, a number of promising careers had stalled immediately afterwards. Politicians could be quite vindictive when they felt affronted, even when it had been the speaker who'd given the orders. Peter didn't blame the officers for being worried about the consequences of laying hands on the wrong person.

He nodded to the officers and headed down the corridor. People would talk, once they noticed he'd left, but it didn't matter. The debate had been worthless. It didn't look as if there was going to be any actual voting for days, if not weeks, and he'd be alerted if someone managed to force a vote anyway. Neither side would really want a vote when tempers were on the brink of exploding into violence. More likely the grown-ups on both sides, if such people existed, would call a time-out, get everyone to calm down and then . . . what?

It doesn't matter, Peter thought as he reached his office and stepped inside. The room was blessedly quiet. *We're not making any progress at all on the real issues.*

He sat down on a comfortable chair and keyed the terminal. A string of reports appeared in front of him, ranging from an industrial dispute in an orbiting factory to another set of attacks in the Theocratic Sector. His heart sank as he realized the problem wasn't going away. The optimists who'd predicted that the Theocratic starships wouldn't last much longer had clearly underestimated them. He was surprised the prime minister hadn't used the reports in a bid to rush Parliament into passing the spending bill. But then, it probably would have blown up in his face.

Yasmeena entered, carrying a mug of coffee. "I thought you might need this, sir."

Peter gave her a smile filled with warm affection. "You're a miracle worker," he said. "Did anything come in while I was . . . occupied?"

"Nothing of great significance," Yasmeena assured him. "A couple of directors want to discuss additional cost-cutting measures with you; I think, reading between the lines, that they want to protest. They certainly saw fit to bypass the regular channels."

"They can wait, for the moment," Peter said. His lips twitched. "Do we have any updated political projections?"

"The Government and the Opposition are currently battling for the support of a relative handful of MPs and Lords," Yasmeena said. "However, there are suggestions that some MPs may be on the verge of breaking their pledges and jumping across the aisle. Both sides are throwing promises around like candy."

"Brilliant." Peter sighed. The MPs would pay a price for their betrayal during the next election cycle . . . assuming, of course, they made the wrong choice. Treason never prospered, as the bard had said, because no one dared *call* it treason if it did prosper. There was too much at stake for a handful of ambitious men to wreck it. "And who is going to keep those promises?"

"The reports don't say, sir," Yasmeena said. She looked downcast. "Do you need me for anything else?"

"No, thank you," Peter said. "I'll see you later."

He took a sip of his coffee as he skimmed through the rest of the reports, knowing that most of the issues had already been handled by his subordinates. He could never hope to micromanage something the size of the Falcone Corporation. He'd just have to pray the issues had been handled in a way that wouldn't cause problems elsewhere. Yet, his subordinates sometimes forgot they were working for him. They preferred to think of themselves as lords of their own petty baronies.

Yasmeena returned. Peter looked up, surprised. "Yasmeena?"

"The Royal Equerry just called me," she said. "The king would like a private meeting at your earliest convenience."

Peter tensed. "Just the king and I?"

"I believe so," Yasmeena said. "It's in His Majesty's private suite."

"I see," Peter said.

He forced himself to think. Was it *wise* to go? He wasn't sure. There was no way he could give his support to the king's proposed budget, but . . . perhaps, if they met face-to-face, he could convince the king to be reasonable. There had to be ways to make good on some of the king's promises without destroying the economy. And if the king refused to compromise, Peter could oppose him with a clear conscience.

At least he would have tried.

"Very well," he said finally. "Inform the Royal Equerry that I will see His Majesty within the hour."

CHAPTER TWENTY-THREE

ASHER DALES

"This is the Admiralty?" Kat stared at the small building in disbelief. "Really?"

"Yep," William confirmed. "What do you think?"

Kat found herself lost for words. The Admiralty on Tyre was a massive building at the center of the city, only a few minutes' walk from the Houses of Parliament. The Admiralty on Asher Dales was *tiny*, really no larger than the average family house on Tyre. She was surprised they hadn't used a prefabricated building or even set up the offices in one of the dumpsters that had brought the original colonists to the planet. And yet, there was a certain charm about the stone building that was undeniable. It certainly had less room for uniformed politicians who'd never seen, let alone commanded, a starship.

"It's . . . small," she said finally.

"It's big enough for us," William said. Kat sensed, more than heard, Tanya sniff in disapproval. "And it'll be a long time before we need more than a handful of administrative staff. Right now, I can do nearly everything in my head."

Kat looked at him as they stepped through the door. "What happens if you die?"

"The staff will take over," William said. "I'm planning to rotate officers between staff billets and starship postings, once we get properly organized. There won't be anyone here who hasn't had at least *some* real experience."

"I wish that was possible on Tyre," Kat said, honestly. "There are too many people back home who don't understand the practical realities."

William nodded in agreement, then led her on a tour of the small building. There were a handful of offices, a meeting room, and a pair of datacores, hidden below the building. Kat guessed there was a third datacore somewhere nearby, twinned with the original two and kept well out of sight. William wouldn't be fool enough to let a lucky hit put his entire organization out of business. There'd be someone who knew where to find it once the enemy retreated too, unless the entire planet was rendered uninhabitable. The planetary government seemed to take the threat very seriously.

"And this is the dining room," William finished. "It's very basic . . ."

"But efficient," Kat said. A wooden table, three chairs, and very little else. "I like it."

She smiled. She'd sat through Admiralty dinners that were more about making contacts and networking than plotting the latest offensive. They'd be even more tedious now that the war was over. Here, there was no room for networking.

"Food will be served in a moment," William said, motioning for her to take a seat. "Did your techs find anything useful?"

"Nothing directly useful," Kat admitted. "They swept the captured ship from top to bottom, then started to take the datacores apart, but they found very little. No navigational data, certainly. We still don't know where they're based. And yet, we did find some things. Their missiles were heavily modified by *someone*."

William leaned forward. "Who?"

"I don't know," Kat said. "It would take a full-fledged shipyard to do the work."

"Maybe they built a mobile shipyard," William said. "We know they built all sorts of boondoggles."

"Perhaps," Kat said. "But you know how hard it was for *us* to produce a workable mobile shipyard. They're still incredibly inefficient. I can't see them actually *succeeding*."

"True," William agreed. "So who helped them?"

"We may never know," Kat admitted. "The missiles might have been modified, but all the modifications were based on freely available technology. There's nothing that points to a single source."

"And the crewmen probably didn't even keep diaries," William said. "A shame none of them survived to be interrogated."

"Don't blame yourself for it," Kat said. She grinned at him. "Someone back home will be happy to do it for you."

"I know," William said.

He looked downcast, just for a second. Kat felt a pang of sympathy. William had escaped *official* censure for being the victim of the first mutiny on a naval starship, but his career had practically stalled anyway. He would have been sidelined completely if he hadn't had connections to the Falcone family. And yet . . . she was morbidly sure that someone back home would blame him for not taking prisoners. A half-wit who knew nothing of the realities of interstellar war would probably convince himself that William had deliberately killed everyone on the enemy ship.

"We didn't find any personal writings among the crew," Kat said. "They probably weren't allowed to write anything."

"It would be a security nightmare," William agreed quietly. "And they'd be able to enforce it too."

Kat nodded. There was no way to prevent naval officers from keeping private journals, if they wished. They'd been warned, time and time again, not to include anything the enemy might find useful, but it was hard to tell *what* the enemy might find useful. A note of transit times between two points might seem harmless, yet it might tell the enemy where the ship had been and what it had done. There were security officers who'd probably prefer to ban personal records altogether. Kat understood their thinking even though she disagreed with it.

She looked up as a uniformed server wheeled a tray into the room and started to unload the contents onto the table. Cold chicken, beef, and ham, served with bread, butter, and sliced vegetables. A strikingly simple meal compared to what she would have eaten on Tyre, but she didn't mind. William indicated that she should tuck in, and she did.

"I take it you never caught the attackers," Tanya said. There was a faint hint of hostility in the woman's tone. "Or anyone else?"

Kat concealed her amusement. Tanya had a crush on William, she was sure, just as she was sure William hadn't noticed. It was hard to be sure that *Tanya* had noticed her own feelings. She might see Kat as a rival without ever quite realizing *why*. Perhaps nothing would come of it, perhaps . . .

"No," she said, dismissing the thought. William's private life was no longer her concern. "I dispatched reinforcements at once, but . . . by the time they got there, the attackers were gone."

"And the planets were in dire straits," William said softly. "How bad is it?"

Kat winced. "Dorland is going to have to be evacuated," she said. "The planet was barely sustainable even before the Theocracy arrived. Now . . . there's no way they can rebuild before they run out of supplies. I've detailed a considerable number of transports to evacuate the population, but I have no idea where to put them. No one seems to be interested in providing homes for refugees."

"The nearby worlds had too many immigrants dumped on them during the occupation," William said. "It's easy to see them as nothing more than troublemakers."

"No one *here* wants them," Tanya confirmed. "How long would it be until the planet was no longer ours?"

Kat opened her mouth to point out that there was an empty continent on the far side of Asher Dales that could accommodate millions of refugees, but closed it again without saying a word. The UN had dumped hundreds of thousands of unwanted settlers on dozens of worlds, without bothering to check if the original settlers *wanted* them. It had been a major cause of the wars. Now, every world had the right to determine if it would or wouldn't take refugees. She couldn't ignore their wishes without sparking off yet another crisis.

I could just dump them on a stage-one colony, she thought. *But could they even be fed long enough to integrate?*

She shook her head in frustration. Modern technology could feed the refugees, but where could she put them? There was no easy answer. A handful of refugees with vital skills could be accommodated, she was sure, but what about the others? And, with the enemy fleet running around attacking randomly, it was quite possible the refugees would move from the frying pan into the fire. Perhaps she could find a way to bribe a world to take them. But it would have to be a very big bribe.

William changed the subject, quickly. "Have you been following events on Tyre?"

"Yeah," Kat said, silently relieved. "Having a StarCom isn't an unmixed blessing, is it?"

"A commander's authority can no longer be absolute," William agreed. "You can now be bossed around by someone on the other side of the galaxy." He leaned forward. "But what is *happening* on Tyre?"

Kat met his eyes. "The king is trying to deal with the situation here"—she waved a hand in the air—"and the politicians are trying to stop him."

William looked back at her. "Perhaps," he said. "But it's also true that the king is demanding too much."

"I would have thought you'd be on his side," Kat said. "He's the one supporting colonial officers. *And* colonial development."

"I can see his point," William agreed. "But Kat . . ." He looked down, just for a second. "I only met the king once," he reminded her. "I mean . . . I saw him a few times, but I only *met* him once. That was when I was knighted. And the impression I had, in that brief meeting, was that he was a junior officer who was in way over his head. It's not something uncommon."

Kat nodded. She'd made her fair share of mistakes and outright screw-ups when she'd been a junior officer herself. Having to explain to a cold-eyed superior that something absurd had, in fact, sounded perfectly reasonable at the time had *not* been the highlight of her life. The only good that had come out of the mistakes was learning not to let her enthusiasm get in the way of common sense.

"But the king isn't a junior officer," she pointed out. "He's . . . he's the *king*."

"And yet, the principle is the same," William countered. "Here he is, desperately demanding everything he *wants*, rather than trying to get everything he *needs*. It's a common mistake for young officers, just on a much larger scale. And I fancy *no one* could teach him what he needed to know before he took the throne. He doesn't have any actual experience, does he?"

"I don't think so," Kat said. She knew the king had never been in the military, but he could easily have been involved with his father's diplomacy. "He's trying to deal with a growing crisis."

"Which he made worse," William said. He corrected himself. "No, he's *making* worse." He ran his hand through his hair. "That's typical junior officer behavior," he added. "He makes a mistake, and then he makes another mistake in trying to cover it up, and then . . . well, before he knows it he's in quicksand and sinking fast. Here . . . the king is demanding everything from Parliament, and Parliament is dragging its heels."

Kat wasn't sure what to make of it. She trusted William. She respected his opinion. And yet, it was the king who was trying to solve the crisis. He was pushing for increased commitments to the occupied sector, commitments that might save millions of lives. Kat would be glad of any reinforcements—the threat of being summarily withdrawn from the sector had chilled her to the bone—but even something as small as a couple of superdreadnought squadrons would go a long way towards making further attacks impossible.

"We made commitments," she said, finally. Her father had taught her that she should always honor her commitments, even if they became inconvenient. A reputation for being unreliable, he'd said, could be far more dangerous in the long run. Besides, it wasn't as if they'd promised to defend the sector against an overwhelmingly superior foe. "And if we pick up our toys and go home, what then?"

"The king's enemies would say that the commitments should never have been made in the first place," William pointed out. "He certainly never ran them past anyone who might object."

"But they should have been made," Kat protested. "Have you *seen* that hellhole? Ahura Mazda?"

"I've heard the news," William said. "But *can* the planet be saved?" He shook his head. "I understand the urge to do everything in one's power to help people," he said. "But I also understand that there are times when you *can't* save everyone. You have to choose who to help and who to leave to die."

"Triage," Kat said.

"Exactly," William said. "Do you save one person who is on the verge of death? Or do you use the resources you would have used to save him to tend to three more people? Maybe those people will die without attention, maybe they won't . . ."

"I am not unfamiliar with the concept," Kat said stiffly. "But the first person is going to die."

"Yes," William said. "But three more will live."

He cleared his throat. "The king has shown consistent bad judgment," he said. "I don't deny he has good points, and I don't disagree

230

with his logic, but it seems to me that *paying* for everything he wants is impossible. And his reluctance to propose a more *meaningful* compromise means that Parliament is determined to block him completely. The catfight over the Royal Wedding, of all things, is merely a symptom of a more serious problem."

Kat smiled, humorlessly. "You've been studying."

"I studied politics for a long time," William said. "It's never been as . . . *poisonous* . . . as they have been now."

"You're lucky to be out of it," Tanya said.

"Am I out of it?" William snorted, expressively. "Whoever rules Tyre will have immense influence on the surrounding sectors. If the king comes out ahead in this political battle, the Royal Navy will deepen its commitment to the sector; if his opponents get to set the agenda, the navy will be withdrawn as quickly as possible. Either way, Asher Dales will be affected."

"I'm afraid so," Kat agreed, quietly.

"It could get worse," William added. "The Commonwealth was never *designed* to fight a war. King Travis couldn't turn it into a more federal structure, despite his best efforts. King Hadrian managed to make inroads during the war, but at the cost of making all the prewar tensions worse. And now the war is over, and we have to deal with the consequences of his actions."

"He did what he had to do to win the war," Kat said. "My father supported him."

William nodded. "Yes," he said. His voice was very quiet. "But now . . . I don't like what I'm hearing, Kat. People are choosing sides. All those tensions are coming into the open, and . . . and I don't know where they'll lead. The Commonwealth could be on the verge of civil war."

"Impossible," Kat said. "It's . . . unthinkable."

"Is it?" William looked down at his hands. "Suppose Tyre slaps new restrictions on colonial labor? Or puts limits on tech transfers? Or even starts ejecting planets from the Commonwealth completely? How long would it be until outright civil war broke out?"

"Not long," Kat said. "But even *trying* to eject planets would be dangerous."

"Yes," William said. "People are scared. And scared people do stupid things."

Kat sat back, unsure what to make of it. She didn't want to believe that civil war was possible, let alone probable. And yet, she also knew she'd been isolated. She'd heard worrying stories from back home, but she hadn't *seen* anything for herself. Perhaps she should be relieved at being so isolated. If people really were choosing sides, all hell might break out at any moment.

"I hope you're wrong," she said, finally. "Anyway, there's something else I came to ask you. Are you still in touch with your brother?"

William's face went very still. "I can send him a message, if you like," he said. "I have a StarCom code for him, although I have no idea how frequently he checks it. It's just a dead-drop message account, really. Why?"

"Someone is supplying the Theocrats," Kat reminded him. "If we can find that person, if we can shut them down, we might be able to put a lid on the crisis."

"It might work," William agreed. "But I doubt any *sane* smuggler would have anything to do with the Theocracy."

"Some people will do anything for money," Kat pointed out. "And smugglers are constantly on the brink of losing their ships."

"Yes, but they'd be aiding and abetting destruction and atrocities on a massive scale," William countered. "They'd have to account for their complicity in war crimes when they get caught. And the force they'd be supplying will *not* survive indefinitely. Even if it did, even if the Theocracy was resurrected . . . they'd be fools not to expect a knife in the back."

"True," Kat agreed. "Can you ask anyway? We're running out of options."

"Will do," William said. "What are you going to do in the meantime?"

Kat sighed. "I wish I knew."

"Put ECM drones in each of the threatened systems," William suggested. "They can pose as superdreadnoughts. They'll know that *some* of the ships are fakes, but which ones?"

"Good," Kat said. She grinned at him, remembering times when the universe had made more sense. Was it wrong of her to miss the comradeship of the war? "A splendid idea of mine that you thought of."

William saluted. "You're welcome."

CHAPTER TWENTY-FOUR

TYRE

"There is a crowd of protesters outside the palace," the driver said. "Traffic Control is redirecting us."

Peter frowned as he put his datapad away and peered out of the window. A mass of people was clearly visible outside the gates, shouting and screaming about . . . something. Large protests had been unknown on Tyre before the war; now, they were depressingly common. A number of protesters were clearly students, skipping classes in favor of shouting and screaming at the palace; others, more alarmingly, were middle-aged men and women, people who should be in professional jobs. He couldn't help wondering why they weren't at work.

They probably don't have any work any longer, he thought as the air-car banked to evade a handful of police and security floaters. *The really big layoffs have yet to begin, but too many people have already lost their jobs.*

His eyes scanned the palace warily. The palace had always been heavily protected, but the weapons emplacements that had been installed during the war were still clearly visible. He could see armed guards running around behind the walls, as if they feared the protesters would push through the forcefields and storm the palace. Everyone had beefed up their security during the war, but the king it seemed had never stopped. His forces looked to be constantly on high alert.

The aircar dropped down and landed neatly on a pad. A pair of security officers stepped forward, wearing the king's livery. Peter considered protesting as they scanned his body, then decided there was no point. He couldn't blame the king's protectors for feeling paranoid. The enemy agents who'd killed Peter's father had never been caught. And, judging by some of the chatter on the datanet, the king's life was in very real danger.

"Your Grace," a voice said. "His Majesty is expecting you."

Peter looked up and saw a pretty young woman wearing the red-and-gold uniform of a Royal Equerry. She looked young—too young; there was a hardness in her eyes, barely masked, that suggested she was considerably more dangerous than she appeared. Another protector, then: a protector hiding in plain sight. Peter was used to plainclothes security officers, but this was a new one. The king was *definitely* feeling paranoid.

"Thank you," he said.

The woman dropped a curtsy, then led him into the palace and up towards the king's private chambers. It wasn't the first time Peter had visited—the palace was a governmental complex, after all—but it was the first time he'd been honored with an invitation to the king's private chambers. He wasn't blind to the political implications or to what his enemies would make of it. Too many people would hear about the visit and draw the wrong, or at least inaccurate, conclusion.

Politics, Peter thought. The word was practically a curse. *We should just agree to govern rationally.*

His lips twitched. There was nothing *rational* about politics. He'd learned *that* lesson long ago. Self-interest ruled the more practical-minded politicians, while sentiment encouraged the others to try to *look* good rather than *be* good. The House of Lords had the advantage of not having to stand for election, which gave them a long-term view the House of Commons lacked, but the Lords needed to constantly defend their families and promote their clients. It was impossible to expect rationality from either House. The best he could hope for was that they would try to do the right thing.

And yet, we can't agree on what the right thing is, Peter thought as they stopped outside a large wooden door. *One man's right is another man's wrong.*

The door opened, revealing a large office. Peter looked around, interested. Everything was modern—everything. The style Peter had seen in a dozen offices—solid wooden desks, Regency armchairs, bookshelves, and paneled walls—was missing. Instead, a computer terminal sat on the desk, the chairs were comfortable rather than fashionable, and the walls were covered with smart panels. One of them was displaying the view from the palace's security monitors. The protest seemed to have grown larger in the last few minutes.

"Your Grace," the king said. He stood, revealing that he was wearing a simple business suit instead of his robes. "Thank you for coming."

"Thank you for inviting me," Peter said as they shook hands. "This is an . . . interesting room."

The king beamed. "Do you like it? I had to take out all the old furniture when I inherited the place."

"It's different," Peter said. "Less dignified, but more . . . modern."

"Please, take a seat," the king said, indicating one of the armchairs. "Would you care for a drink? Or something to eat?"

"Just coffee, please," Peter said.

He sat down, feeling the chair adjust itself under his weight until it was comfortable. It made him feel vaguely unsettled. He'd never really liked chairs that presumed to think for themselves, even though he had to admit that they had their uses. At least it wasn't trying to give him a massage. There was a subtle message, he was sure, in how the king had organized his chambers. The old had been removed, while the modern had been brought forward. He suspected it boded ill for the future.

"I trust that your mother is well," the king said as a steward poured them both coffee and withdrew as silently as he'd come. "She declined the invitation to the Betrothal Ball."

"My mother has yet to recover from my father's death," Peter said carefully. There was a great deal of truth in it, yet it was not the *whole* truth. Caroline Newport-Falcone had been horrified by the mere suggestion of the king marrying the runaway princess. "She keeps to herself these days. Even *I* don't see her as often as I should."

"It is the way of the world," the king agreed. "Those of us who have work to do"—he waved a hand at the smart panels—"have little time for everything else."

"Indeed," Peter said. He cocked an eyebrow. "And the princess? Is she well?"

"She has endured far worse than social scorn in her life," the king said. "She couldn't be happier."

Peter nodded in agreement. High Society could be a merciless place—there were people who were still shunned for events that had taken place long before Peter's birth—but it was nowhere near as cruel as the Theocracy. A woman could rise to the top, if she wished, or seek out a career of her own. She was not the property of her male relatives. And yet . . .

He shifted, uncomfortably. His marriage had been arranged. Neither he nor his wife had had any real choice. But they'd reached an accommodation, hadn't they? He hadn't locked her up in her room and forced her to bear child after child, or had her fixed so she couldn't talk or think for herself . . . no, there was no comparison. High Society was not the Theocracy. And anyone who suggested otherwise was an idiot.

"It must be quite different," he said. "To be here, a free society . . ."

"Indeed," the king said. "Do you realize that, for all her bravery, she had very real problems coping with our world? And *she* was perhaps the best-educated woman on Ahura Mazda. I daresay that many of her sisters would *not* cope with our world. They'd rush straight back into slavery rather than learn how to be free."

"Perhaps," Peter said. He wasn't sure how *he'd* cope if someone dumped him on a completely foreign planet. "She is to be commended for her success."

He took a sip of his coffee, wondering if he dared suggest that they got to the point. His time was money, a point his father had drilled into him from birth. Social chitchat to break the ice was important, he'd been told, but . . . not when he had too many things he needed to attend to personally. He couldn't fob *everything* off on his assistants.

The king seemed to sense his thoughts. "I'll come straight to the point," he said, sipping his own coffee. "I would like your support on the budget proposal."

Peter blinked. He'd wanted to get to the point, but like that . . . ?

He composed himself. "I'm afraid that won't be possible, Your Majesty," he said carefully. "Right now, the budget proposal is unacceptable."

"Unacceptable is a harsh word," the king said placidly.

"Yes," Peter agreed. "But it is also an *accurate* one. The kingdom cannot afford to meet the spending commitments you propose. Nor can we keep taxation at its current level without risking economic disaster. We have to staunch the bleeding before we bleed to death."

He had to struggle to keep his frustration out of his voice. The king *had* to know that his proposed budget was never going to pass. Everyone from the Royal Corporation's trustees to talking heads on the datanet had drawn the same conclusion. The king had to listen to the trustees, didn't he? Peter was sure the Royal Corporation was in the same boat as the rest of the corporations. Cavendish might merely be the first to fall. If the crash was bad enough, the rest of the corporations would quickly follow.

Uncharted territory, he thought.

"I appreciate that you are focused on financial affairs," the king said quietly. "However, as the monarch of the kingdom and the Commonwealth, I have to remain focused on the larger picture. In the short run, my analysts project there will indeed be *some* pain from implementing the budget; in the long run, they assure me that our economy, our interstellar economy, will be on a stronger footing. Furthermore . . ."

He took another sip of his coffee. "Furthermore, there are other issues involved than simple *money*. Peter . . . are you aware of the stresses and strains threatening to tear the Commonwealth apart? We do not want the member worlds to feel alienated from the Commonwealth, let alone Tyre itself. They made sacrifices to win the war too."

Peter looked back at him, as evenly as he could. "Would they be happier if we made the promises and then broke them, or if we simply never made the promises at all?"

"Commitments were made," the king said. "And not just the ones *I* made. My father was able to convince his parliaments to make and underwrite promises to the original set of member worlds. Those promises have to be kept."

"The Commonwealth Charter is not a suicide pact," Peter observed. "And the blunt fact remains that we are on the cusp of an economic recession. We *need* to cut back, now, before it's too late."

"And then what?" The king nodded to the protesters. "Will we dump uncounted millions of people onto the streets? Because we will, you know."

Peter scowled. "I suppose we could build a few hundred new superdreadnoughts," he said, dryly. "It would keep dockyard workers employed, would it not? But what would we *do* with them afterwards? Who is going to want to buy more superdreadnoughts? Even if the member worlds wanted to buy a superdreadnought or two, they wouldn't be able to run them without . . ."

The king cut him off. "That's why I'm suggesting a massive invest-ment in industrial nodes right across the Commonwealth," he said, sharply. "There will be work for everyone."

"I see your logic," Peter said. It made a certain kind of sense, if one failed to understand where tax actually *came* from. "But we simply don't have the cash to pay for it. And we've gone over this again and again and again!"

"My analysts say otherwise," the king said, sharply.

"I'd be very interested in seeing that analysis," Peter said, resisting the urge to snap back at him. "Because *my* analysts say that even *trying* to implement the budget will push us over the edge. And even if we're lucky enough to avoid immediate disaster, revenue will be down so significantly that we'll suffer another revenue shortfall *next* year."

The king looked at him for a long moment. "Are you saying no?"

Peter looked back at him. "I'm saying the budget will not pass through the Houses of Parliament," he said flatly. "And even if it does, your planned taxation will not raise enough funds to pay for your pet projects."

"And you'll resist me," the king said. "You . . . you will stop me from saving us from a far greater disaster."

Peter stiffened. "If I have to," he said. "Perhaps it would be bet-ter to come to some kind of compromise. If the budget was to be modified . . ."

"Rewritten, you mean," the king said.

"Yes," Peter said. "Right now, it *will not pass*."

"I have a duty to the kingdom," the king told him. "And I will do whatever I have to do to uphold that duty."

Peter felt ice running down his spine. Was that a threat? The big corporations wielded immense economic power, but . . . could the king threaten them? It was possible, he had to admit. Too many people in the navy owed their positions to the king. The orbital defense network was under Parliament's control, as per the original agreements, but the king might have been meddling there too. And . . .

He kept his face impassive with an effort. How had his father managed to handle the king?

"And we have duties to our corporations," he managed. His throat felt dry. They'd crossed a line. He'd have to do . . . do what? Push for immediate impeachment? Or something more drastic? They were entering uncharted waters. "Your Majesty . . . the corporations are the geese that lay the golden eggs. If you kill them, if you even weaken them, there will be no more golden eggs."

"And what happens," the king asked reasonably, "if the Commonwealth dies?"

"We have to save what we can," Peter countered. "Your Majesty . . . only a third of the member worlds are net gains to our economy. And even *they* are quite limited. The war cost us all."

"And the chaos in the Theocratic Sector?" The king tapped the table. "What happens when that spills back into our sector?"

"We will deal with it when it happens," Peter said. "But, right now, it is very much a minor problem."

"We shall see," the king said. He stood, indicating that the interview was over. "Thank you for coming, Your Grace. It is good to know where we stand."

"Indeed," Peter said. That was another threat. He'd bet his life on it. He wondered, suddenly, if he'd even be allowed to leave the palace. If the king was prepared to push matters . . . he might take the risk. But it would be absolutely insane. "I ask you, seriously, to rewrite the bill."

"I cannot," the king said. "We made commitments."

"*You* made the commitments," Peter said, tiredly. "Your father, Your Majesty, made sure to get Parliament to back the commitments. You did not. You stood up and made a whole series of promises you should have *known* you couldn't keep. And now you're looking to us to pull your chestnuts out of the fire. And we *can't* do it."

He bowed, then turned and walked out of the room. The equerry met him, her pretty face completely expressionless, and led him back to the aircar. Peter could hear the noise from the protest as he stepped onto the landing pad, despite the forcefield around the palace. They were shouting about unfair competition and demanding an immediate end to foreign work permits. Definitely the newly unemployed, then. It was going to get a lot worse before it got better.

The driver glanced back at Peter as he climbed into the car. "Where to, sir?"

"The mansion," Peter said absently. There was no point in going back to the Houses of Parliament. "I have work to do."

He keyed his terminal as the car rose into the air and headed over the city. "Yasmeena, clear my appointments for the rest of the day," he ordered. "Call Masterly and Masterly to my office; tell them I want them to look at a set of financial and economic projections. And then inform Israel Harrison that I need to talk with him as soon as possible."

"Yes, sir," Yasmeena said. She sounded reassuringly confident, as always. "Which projections are those?"

"The king will be sending them to us," Peter said. He hoped the king *would* send them. It wasn't as if he had anything to gain by keeping them a secret. Peter could understand why someone would cover up unfavorable facts, but why classify something that gave you an edge? Who knew? The projections might be so favorable that opposition to the budget would just melt away. "Assuming he does, I want them assessed as quickly as possible."

"Yes, sir."

Peter closed the connection, then forced himself to think. He'd underestimated the king; no, he'd underestimated his determination to push the budget forward despite a near-united opposition. Peter could see his logic, he could understand his reasoning . . . but the cold hard truth was that the kingdom simply couldn't afford the king's proposal. They couldn't fund the projects, they couldn't borrow money . . . no, it couldn't be done. And the king was stubbornly ignoring economic reality in favor of . . . of what?

He thinks he has a duty, Peter thought. The Commonwealth was worth preserving, if it could be preserved. But *could* it be preserved? The cost of building up and maintaining the prewar system had been bad enough. Now they were a great deal worse. *And yet, we have duties too.*

He stared out over the city. It looked peaceful, now that the protesters were behind him. But he couldn't help wondering how much trouble was simmering down below . . .

. . . and just how long it would be before the trouble exploded into the open.

CHAPTER TWENTY-FIVE

AHURA MAZDA

"No change, Admiral," Lieutenant Kitty Patterson said. "Deep Space Shipping is refusing to hire out its freighters unless they're guaranteed a heavy escort, guaranteed reimbursement for any expenses, and guaranteed profits."

"Which they're not going to get, because they're moving refugees," Kat said. She had yet to find a planet willing to pay for the privilege of taking refugees. "Can we not offer them time-and-a-half?"

"They found that unacceptable," Kitty told her regretfully. "And we can't go much higher without exceeding our discretionary funds."

This wasn't a problem during the war, Kat thought grimly. *But now, everyone is counting the pennies.*

She rubbed her forehead. She'd hoped that matters would improve during the voyage from Asher Dales to Ahura Mazda, but, if anything, they'd only gotten worse. The local population was panicking and demanding protection, protection she was in no position to provide, while independent shippers and interstellar corporations were steadily pulling out of the sector. Her staff hadn't been able to round up enough transports, even independent tramp freighters, to even *begin* to make a dent in Dorland's population. And the constant threats of having half of her fleet withdrawn back to Tyre were making it impossible to draw up any long-term plans.

"Send a message to Tyre requesting permission to exceed our funds," she ordered. There had been a time, hadn't there, when she'd just needed to sign some paperwork to release the money. But now . . . how was she expected to get anything done? "Are we still due to receive a replenishment convoy?"

"Yes, Admiral," Kitty said. "They . . . ah, it hasn't been canceled yet."

"We may have to hold the ships in the sector long enough to complete the evacuation," Kat said. It wasn't a good solution, but it would have to do. "And, if we can't find anywhere else for the refugees to go, we'll ship them back here. There are a few islands that would provide living space, for the moment."

Kitty looked doubtful. Kat understood, all too well. A semipermanent enclave of refugees on Ahura Mazda would require semipermanent protection, if they weren't armed to the teeth. But there weren't many other options. Dorland's farmers simply weren't suited to life on a space habitat, even though it would have been the easy place to put them. Putting them on an asteroid colony might well be nothing more than a death sentence.

They might have to learn, she thought. *Is there anyone in this wretched sector that isn't looking out for number one?*

She dismissed Kitty, then turned and strode over to the window. Smoke was rising in the distance, signifying yet another bombing. The local insurgents had been coming out of the woodwork over the last few weeks when they'd heard that there was a Theocratic fleet running around the sector. They seemed to believe that Ahura Mazda would be liberated at any moment. Kat's lips twitched. Perhaps she should encourage the rumors. Insurgents who came into the open generally ended up dead. And the marines were already using the bodies to trace their families and break open insurgent cell after insurgent cell.

We might even win this, if we could just keep them popping up, she thought. *At the very least, we'd get some breathing space.*

She turned back to the starchart, silently wondering which target would be hit next. So far, the Theocrats had managed to avoid systems with StarComs . . . frustrating, but unsurprising. A StarCom could be detected from light-years away. But that would have to change, sooner or later. The enemy fleet would run out of targets that would do nothing more than spread misery across the galaxy. And besides, she had a nasty feeling that the people back home were growing inured to the horrors emanating from the Theocratic Sector. The daily atrocities were a very long way away.

Of course not, she thought. *They're more interested in arguing about the Royal Wedding than considering something important.*

She'd done her best to follow the local news, although it was sometimes hard to understand what was going on. Everyone seemed to be hellishly partisan, pushing their own side's arguments while slandering the other side, while media talking heads seemed to swap sides with monotonous regularity. Perhaps they simply forgot which side they were supposed to be on. She wouldn't have been surprised. The media had always been slanted towards one side or the other, but now . . . now it seemed to have exploded. The narrative changed every day.

Her terminal bleeped. "Admiral, we have a priority-one StarCom call for you," Lieutenant Cloud said. "It's keyed to your personal code."

Kat felt a flicker of excitement as she sat down at her desk. The king? They'd talked fairly regularly before the crisis started. Or . . . she lifted her eyebrows as she read the details on the display. The call, which was *heavily* encrypted, was coming straight from Falcone Mansion. And that meant . . .

"Peter," she said, as her brother's face appeared in front of her. He looked to have aged twenty years since the last time she'd seen him. "What can I do for you?"

"You can start by assuring me that you're alone," Peter said. "Where are you?"

"My office," Kat said, puzzled and alarmed. Peter was normally polite—achingly polite. He affected an old-time formality that had annoyed her as a child and amused her as a grown woman. "And yes, I am alone."

Peter looked relieved. "And this call is secure?"

Kat frowned. "It's as secure as reasonably possible," she said. Peter was using a family encryption program as well as the StarCom Network's standard coding. It wouldn't be *completely* impossible to decipher, given the nature of the transmission, but even the most powerful computers would take years to unravel the transmission. "This room is alpha-blue secure too."

"That's good to hear," Peter said. "Kat . . . have you been following political developments on Tyre?"

"A little," Kat said. She'd spent most of her childhood trying to stay away from politics, at least partly because it was her elder siblings' meat and drink. "I understand that there are problems."

"You could say that," Peter said. He made an odd sound. It took Kat several seconds to realize it was meant to be a laugh. "I wish, I really wish, that you'd declined the chance to become a privy councilor. Or that you'd consulted with me first."

"It was my choice," Kat said. She hadn't been used to thinking of Peter as Duke Falcone. Even now, it wasn't easy to draw a line between the stuffy older brother and the duke. "Father was on the Privy Council."

"Yes, he was," Peter agreed. "But no one doubted where his loyalties lay. Where do *yours* lie?"

Kat felt a hot flash of irritation. "With the Kingdom and Commonwealth of Tyre," she said, allowing ice to creep into her voice. She was no longer the little sister who'd been bossed around by her adult brother. "Peter, I am a very busy person. I have work to do. Can I ask you to get to the point?"

Peter's lips quirked, although Kat didn't see the funny side. "There are things we need to discuss," he said. "Kat . . . the king and Parliament are deadlocked. They simply can't make any progress. And there's no chance of that changing."

". . . Crap," Kat said.

"The Opposition may just force a vote on withdrawing forces from the Theocratic Sector," Peter added. "The king's men have been stalling, but they're running out of procedural tricks to delay matters. We might be voting as soon as tomorrow."

Kat's blood ran cold. "Peter . . . I need those ships."

Peter looked pained. "Why?"

"I don't care about the Royal Wedding," Kat said. Privately, she was inclined to agree with the people who insisted that the ceremony should be simple and, more importantly, cheap. "I don't care if Parliament votes funding for the wedding or not. But Peter, having ships out here is important. I'm not sending those requests for reinforcements because I like filling out the paperwork!"

"They're not going to come," Peter said. "Right now, it's more likely that ships that get rotated out of the sector will not be replaced."

Kat gritted her teeth. The wear and tear on her ships, made worse by her throwing them all over the sector in a bid to catch the Theocrats, would eventually force her to send them back to the shipyards. And her crews would need shore leave too, preferably somewhere where the locals wouldn't be shooting at them. And . . . she reached for her terminal and tapped a note for her assistant. Her staff would have to look at what they could expect if large numbers of crewmen reached the end of their enlistments. She couldn't keep them if they wanted to leave.

And I might not be allowed to keep them in the first place, she thought numbly. *Too many crewmen were involuntarily dismissed anyway, after the war.*

"I need those ships," she said. "More importantly, Peter, I need the logistics base that supports them."

"There's someone already complaining about you transferring missiles to Asher Dales," Peter told her. "They're going through the reports to find *something* they can use to attack you, and, through you, the king."

Kat swallowed a curse. "I had every right to transfer those missiles," she said sharply. "And I can point to precedents if you wish."

Peter snorted. "Kat, this is *politics*," he said. "What makes you think that *right* matters when it can be used as yet another weapon against the king?" He shook his head. "Kat, over the last week . . . things have just exploded right out of hand. I don't think it was this bad during the Putney Debates. People are dragging up all sorts of accusations and counteraccusations and rumors and . . ."

"Now you know why I refused to pay any attention to politics," Kat said. "Look what it did to Ashley. Or Dolly."

"They're both fighting for the family," Peter said. "And . . ."

Kat held up a hand. "Peter, *listen* to me. The situation is dire. There is a rogue enemy fleet rampaging through this sector, attacking worlds and colonies . . . they're even taking out cloudscoops to put further pressure on the economy. So far, they haven't *deliberately* targeted any major population centers or attempted to render entire planets uninhabitable, but it's only a matter of time. Millions of people are already dead.

"There's no way I can guarantee catching the enemy fleet in the act. I've got some ideas that *might* lead to an ambush, but I can't be sure. I need more warships, enough to let me cover the remaining population centers, and I need more transports to evacuate people from targeted worlds before they die. God, Pete! What I wouldn't give for a mere *tenth* of the family's freighters!"

She met his eyes. "You can't imagine the devastation. The people here need help and protection, and we are failing on both counts. We need everything from medical supplies to prefabricated buildings, teaching modules to basic construction tools. There are shortages everywhere, to the point where we cannot fix *one* shortage because of *another* shortage. Do you realize we're even short of carpentry tools? I have a bunch of machine shops turning out saws, hammers, and nails because the locals need to cut down trees to turn them into homes or simply burn the wood for heat. We're short on power plants too.

"And . . ." She shook her head. "And nothing we can do, with what we have on hand, is going to be enough."

She met her brother's eyes. "Forget political games, Peter. *Please.* There are people here who are suffering now, people who will suffer *worse* if the Theocrats resume control. Do you have any idea how many people will be slaughtered, just because they accepted help from us? Even now, the bastards are killing children because their mothers dared take them to our clinics! This isn't about the king and Parliament. This is about the lives at risk throughout the entire sector!"

Peter recoiled, as if she'd somehow reached through the display and slapped him.

"Kat . . . we can't pay for it. Even the fleet deployment alone is expensive. And who is going to pick up the tab?"

Kat glared. There wasn't a single world in the occupied sector that could pay to house even a small naval squadron. Asher Dales had done amazingly well, aided by some careful investments during the prewar years, but they had practically risked everything to purchase the four destroyers. They could make no more contributions. Even the handful of other worlds that had managed to preserve some space-based industry couldn't afford to build a full-sized naval base. The cost would simply be too high.

And we're not just talking destroyers here, she thought. The Commonwealth could operate a fleet of destroyers on shoestring logistics, using freighters to store supplies and perhaps a single repair ship to do any work that happened to be needed, but not superdreadnoughts. She cursed the enemy under her breath, once again. *It would be a great deal easier to convince Parliament to pick up the tab if all we needed were destroyers and light cruisers.*

"Either we pay for it," she said finally, "or millions of people—millions *more* people—will die."

"And what happens," Peter asked, "if the stress of funding the naval deployment brings our economies crashing down?"

He held up a hand before she could say a word. "I understand your concerns, Kat," he said, firmly. "But I also have concerns of my own."

"*Dad* would have understood that some expenses have to be met," Kat said. "And you're penny-pinching while people die."

Peter's eyes flashed. "You have a duty to the family," he snapped. "And that duty includes *not* steering everything we have built over a cliff!"

Kat felt her temper start to crack. "I have a greater responsibility to the navy," she snapped back. She tapped the insignia above her breast. "I am an officer in the Royal Navy, sworn to protect the people! And right now your political games are making it impossible to do my duty! How many times am I going to be told that a superdreadnought squadron is going to be withdrawn in the morning only to have the redeployment canceled in the afternoon?"

"The king is . . . moving to secure more power for himself," Peter told her. "The balance of power that has kept the kingdom running for centuries is starting to crack."

"It was starting to crack *years* ago," Kat said. She took a long breath, forcing herself to calm down. Her oldest brother had always brought out the worst in her. "Peter, from my point of view, the king is the only person who seems to be concerned with the crisis. You and the rest of the political class are playing games while the whole edifice starts to fall apart. How many people do you want to die?"

Peter made a very visible effort to calm himself too. "Kat . . . do you think that the average man or woman in the streets, on Tyre, cares one jot about the endless series of atrocities from your sector? Look, I get what you mean. I know that each of those statistics represents a living breathing person, a person who was killed by the remnants of the enemy fleet or died in the aftermath. But the average man doesn't care. He is more interested in keeping his job and feeding his family."

"He's in no danger of losing his job," Kat said.

"Yes, he *is*," Peter said. "I'll send you the files, if you like."

Kat glanced at her datapad. "Half the stories on the datanet, the ones forwarded through the StarCom network, suggest that the king's proposals will lead to an economic boom," she said. "And the other half suggest that we could be on the verge of complete collapse."

"We are," Peter said. "Kat, where do your loyalties lie?"

"I told you," Kat said sharply. "With the Kingdom and Commonwealth of Tyre."

"And you're a privy councilor," Peter reminded her. "Did you not swear an oath to the king?"

"I swore an oath to the king when I entered Piker's Peak," Kat said. Officially, the navy served the monarchy; unofficially, Parliament had considerable influence. "Or have you forgotten that *all* naval cadets swear loyalty?"

"It was a more *personal* oath," Peter said, "wasn't it?"

Kat placed her hands on her lap to keep them from clenching. The oath had *meant* something to her, the day she'd stood up to make it. She'd believed that she was joining something much greater than herself. It had never occurred to her, not then, that she might not keep her oath. Even now, the thought of going against the navy, or the king, was thoroughly unpleasant. She loved the navy. And she liked and respected the king.

But what happens, she asked herself, *if the situation goes entirely to hell?*

"You play your political games," she said, icily. It was hard, so hard, to keep from snarling at him. She'd detested politics to the point she'd been prepared to surrender her family name if it meant she could join the navy. And she had never quite forgiven her father for meddling in her career. "And I will do my duty."

"You have a duty to the family," Peter snapped.

"I swore to forsake all other duties," Kat snapped back. Had he never looked up the text of the oath? But then, he probably didn't take it seriously. Too many officers, clients of powerful patrons, didn't take it seriously either. "Peter . . . people are dying out here."

"So you said." Peter glared at her. "Kat, the family . . ."

"Doesn't need me," Kat said. She made a show of looking at her wristcom. "I have duties to attend to. We'll talk later."

Peter nodded, stiffly. "Be careful out there," he said. "I'll see you soon."

CHAPTER TWENTY-SIX

UNCHARTED STAR SYSTEM

"You are sure of this?"

Simon Askew leaned back in his chair, smiling coldly. "Have I ever led you astray?"

"I wouldn't know," Admiral Zaskar said. He resisted, barely, the urge to start pacing his office. "Are you *sure* of this?"

"My superiors have their sources within the Commonwealth," Askew said. "And they have confirmed that the data is accurate. The Royal Navy *will* be running a major convoy through the Gap on this date, three weeks from now. And yes, they will stop here"—he jabbed a finger at the display—"long enough for you to intercept them."

"A gift from God," Moses said.

"It's suspicious," Admiral Zaskar said. "They're sending this convoy with *no* escort?"

"No superdreadnoughts," Askew corrected. "The largest ship in the escort squadron is a heavy cruiser."

"But they will be making a stop at Cadiz," Admiral Zaskar pointed out. "They could easily pick up a superdreadnought squadron there for transit through the Gap."

"Not according to my superiors," Askew told him. "They're relying on making a fast run through the Gap to . . . to your former homeworld. They aren't expecting trouble."

Admiral Zaskar eyed him doubtfully. The target seemed far too good to be true. Hitting defenseless or semidefenseless worlds wouldn't really harm the Commonwealth, not directly. Taking out a hundred freighters and their escorts, on the other hand, would be a poke in the eye the Commonwealth could *not* ignore. The more he looked at the convoy's details, the more he had to admit that it was a tempting target. His superdreadnoughts could make mincemeat of those freighters and then withdraw back into hyperspace before the escorts could stop them. Hell, he could take out the escorts *too*. It was a *very* tempting target.

But it was also suspicious. The Royal Navy could easily have arranged for the convoy to link up with a superdreadnought squadron, once they were well outside sensor range. The entire convoy might be nothing more than a trap. He'd need to bring his entire fleet to the engagement if he wanted to take out so many freighters before they could jump back into hyperspace and flee; he'd have to run the risk of encountering superior firepower if he wanted to *really* hurt the enemy. He couldn't replace any of his ships. The destroyer he'd lost at Asher Dales had represented a major fraction of his scouting element. She was literally irreplaceable.

And there's no way we can hope to obtain another superdreadnought, he reminded himself. *We have no shipyard. Even significant damage will be enough to put my heavy ships out of commission for good.*

He looked at Askew. "You *say* they're not expecting trouble," he said. "But how do you know it isn't a trap?"

"The plans for the convoy were put together long before you started your attacks," Askew pointed out. "And, as far as my superiors can tell, they haven't changed."

"But they could be wrong," Admiral Zaskar snapped. He jabbed a finger at the display. "I don't see how you can be *sure* this isn't a trap!"

"There is always an element of risk in war," Askew told him. "But this is a target you cannot ignore."

"No," Moses agreed. "This is a chance to *really* hurt them. And then, when they're reeling, we reclaim Ahura Mazda."

Admiral Zaskar shook his head curtly. The enemy would *not* leave Ahura Mazda defenseless. There was no way he could commit his fleet to an invasion, or even a siege, as long as the enemy kept a super-dreadnought squadron or two there. It was why the convoy was such a tempting target, he admitted sourly. The chance to hit the enemy hard, at relatively little risk, was one that could not be ignored. And yet, he had the nagging feeling it was too good to be true. Whoever had organized the convoy might have laid their plans before he'd revealed his existence, but surely they would have changed things. Unless they genuinely believed that a combination of cruiser escorts and an unpredictable flight path were enough to keep them safe . . .

The hell of it, he conceded silently, was that the enemy might be right. No, they *would* be right. Under normal circumstances, intercepting an interstellar convoy, either in hyperspace or at a waypoint, would be incredibly difficult. He certainly didn't have enough scouts to be sure of detecting the convoy in hyperspace, even in the relatively confined region near the Gap. And besides, the dangers of fighting an engagement in hyperspace were well understood by both sides. A handful of warheads detonating in hyperspace would be more than enough to start an energy storm.

Perhaps we should trigger storms in the Gap, he thought. The old minefields were long gone, but he was sure his people could improvise something. *They'd either have to go the long way around or simply give up completely.*

He dismissed the thought with a gesture of irritation. The intelligence they'd been given was too good. It was pretty much *perfect*. Too perfect. The convoy's path glowed on the display, set in stone . . . except it wasn't set in stone. There was nothing stopping the convoy's

CO from changing course as soon as the flotilla entered hyperspace. The Theocracy would have been furious if someone as insignificant as a convoy CO had dared to change course, or do anything that deviated in the slightest from his orders, but the Commonwealth had always given its people a high degree of discretion. Admiral Zaskar had envied their freedom, once upon a time. How many battles had been lost because the Theocracy's commanders hadn't been allowed to change their dispositions? How many ships had been destroyed because their captains hadn't been allowed to withdraw when the battle was clearly lost?

"Admiral, we need to do this," Moses said. "If we can make them *hurt*, just once . . ."

"It needs to be considered carefully," Admiral Zaskar said. He had the nasty feeling he'd been trapped. *Moses* thought it was a good idea, damn him. The cleric wasn't as . . . unthinkingly stubborn as some of his fellows, but his knowledge of military matters was almost nil, making his freedom to override a genuine commanding officer all the more irritating. "We might be throwing our entire fleet away on a fool's errand."

He glared at Askew, who merely looked back at him blandly. The intelligence was good—too good. Admiral Zaskar would have accepted a flight path, but not precise details on just where and when the enemy convoy would drop out of hyperspace. Even the Theocracy reluctantly accepted just how hard it could be to stick to a precise timetable while crossing the interstellar void. It felt like a trap. And yet, if he set an ambush, he would have plenty of time to back off if a fleet appeared to be waiting for him. He could get his ships to the waypoint long before any enemy forces could arrive.

Particularly with their ships running around trying to catch us, he thought. *We are keeping them hopping.*

"But God has given us a clear shot at them," Moses said eagerly. "It would be a *sin* to waste it."

Yeah, Admiral Zaskar thought. *And you'd raise the crews against me if I let it pass.*

He felt another flicker of envy for his enemy counterparts. He'd heard that the Royal Navy's commanding officers had absolute authority over their ships. *They* didn't have anyone contradicting them in public. *That is going to have to change*, he told himself firmly. *But not until we're well away from here.*

"We can certainly prepare an ambush," he temporized. "But I'd like a *clear* picture of where the intelligence actually came from."

"I was given to understand that my superiors had a spy somewhere on Tyre," Askew said, as if it were a very minor matter indeed. "But you'll understand I was not given the details."

Admiral Zaskar nodded, crossly. Of *course* Askew wouldn't have been given any details. A man with his training and implants would not talk easily, but . . . he might be made to talk anyway. His implants were presumably designed to kill Askew if they sensed he was being interrogated, yet . . . someone might just manage to get around them. Admiral Zaskar was too aware of the Commonwealth's technological skill to dismiss the possibility. Askew wouldn't have been told anything more than what he needed to know.

But, obviously, that made it hard to judge the value of what they'd been given.

"We'll discuss the matter," he said, gesturing to the door. "And we'll tell you our decision later."

"As you wish," Askew said, standing. If the sudden dismissal perturbed him, he didn't show it. "I will be in my quarters."

He walked out of the hatch, which hissed closed behind him. Admiral Zaskar watched him go, feeling conflicted. Askew had had ample opportunity to betray them over the last few months if he wished. There was no reason to think that Askew was being dishonest, *this* time. But he couldn't help thinking that the data in front of him, the data Askew had given them, was simply too good to be true. Askew or his superiors could have been tricked. And they, in perfect innocence, would hurl Admiral Zaskar and his fleet into the fire.

"This is too good an opportunity to miss," Moses said firmly. "Admiral, we *have* to take it."

Admiral Zaskar sighed. "And what if it's a trick? A trap?"

"God is with us," Moses said. "We will not be deceived as long as we put our faith in Him."

"God is with us," Admiral Zaskar echoed.

He resisted the urge to sigh again. He understood just how much the cleric *needed* to cling to his faith, but . . . he'd seen enough to wonder if God was truly on their side. They'd lost the war. Admiral Zaskar had no illusions about himself. He was not the perfect, god-fearing warrior of propaganda. Indeed, there were times when he'd even come to doubt the existence of God. It wasn't something he could share with his cleric, not even now. He had no doubt Moses would prescribe something nastier than a scourging.

And none of us can discuss our doubts with the clerics, or anyone, he reminded himself. *We all learn, as soon as we are old enough to talk, to be careful what we say when we go to confession.*

"We don't have many targets," he said slowly. "We can keep hitting undefended worlds, but . . . we're not really hurting the *real* enemy."

"That's why we should hit the convoy," Moses said. "That *would* hurt them!"

"Yes, if it isn't a trap," Admiral Zaskar said. "But we have women and supplies now. We could take the fleet and set off into unexplored space. It wouldn't be hard to find a planet and set up a new homeworld. Given time, we would wax powerful again."

And evolve, perhaps, he added silently. He knew just how little stood between his crews and total anarchy. His people were slowly coming to realize that the surveillance they'd taken for granted since birth was starting to develop holes. *Who knows what will happen when we're on a planetary surface?*

"But they would still be powerful," Moses pointed out. "What would happen when they stumbled across us, again?"

"We built a spacefaring society once before," Admiral Zaskar said. "We can do it again."

He kept his face expressionless, waiting to see what the cleric would say. Zaskar knew that the Theocracy's official story was full of holes—he'd known enough to pick out the lies and misrepresentations a long time before anyone had given him access to the sealed files—but did *Moses*? A group of religious exiles, dumped on a harsh world with nothing more than the clothes on their backs, could not have hoped to build a spacefaring civilization, certainly not in less than five hundred years. No, the Theocracy's emigration to Ahura Mazda had been a carefully planned endeavor, with a sizable technological base being established right from the start. Admiral Zaskar didn't know all the details—most of the files had remained resolutely sealed, even to him—but he was sure it had been an amazing feat. And one he knew his fleet couldn't hope to repeat.

We can raid worlds for farming and colonization supplies, he told himself, *but there's no way we can capture everything we need to set up a spacefaring civilization.*

"We have a duty to our brethren, groaning under oppression," Moses said. "What will happen to them if we abandon the war?"

"We wouldn't be abandoning it," Admiral Zaskar assured him. "We'd just be taking time out to regroup."

"And how much damage would be done in the meantime?" Moses stood and started to pace the cabin. "How many believers would be seduced from the path of righteousness?"

Admiral Zaskar kept his face under tight control, even though he knew he'd lost the argument. "How many believers would be seduced if we were destroyed?"

"We are already winning," Moses snapped. He turned around to face Admiral Zaskar. "You saw the reports. They are already on the verge of giving up!"

"Maybe," Admiral Zaskar said.

He wasn't so sure. The Commonwealth's free press was a constant puzzle to him. He simply didn't understand why their governments allowed the media to be so openly critical of their rulers. Nor, for that matter, why the media was allowed to slander and belittle public figures without challenge. One particularly amusing attack on Kat Falcone had been easily proven inaccurate by counting the years and noting that she wouldn't even have been a glint in her father's eye at the time. Kat Falcone was ingenious—Admiral Zaskar admitted that, in the privacy of his own head—but even *she* couldn't do something scandalous before she was born. Unless the Commonwealth had secretly invented a time machine . . .

Nonsense, he told himself firmly. *The media is lying about her. And they might be lying about everything else too.*

"One final push, and they will crumble like a house of cards," Moses said.

"And if they don't?" Admiral Zaskar asked. "What then?"

He met the cleric's eyes. "Are we going to keep hitting targets until our luck finally runs out? Or are we going to head away from settled space and set up a whole new colony of our own?"

"We have a duty to keep fighting the war," Moses said.

"And what happens," Admiral Zaskar asked, "when our mystery backers decide they no longer need us?"

He leaned back in his chair. "We don't know who they are," he said. "We don't know what they *really* want. We know *nothing* about them, save that they're rich and powerful enough to take the risk of doing something that could easily be construed as an act of war. Askew and his superiors have their own agenda, Your Holiness, and it may not coincide completely with ours. What happens to us when they decide we're a liability?

"We captured enough supplies to settle a whole new world. We can do that now and, many years from now, our descendants will resume the war. And then . . ."

"But it would mean abandoning the believers," Moses said.

He sat down with a *thump*. "Let us hit the convoy," he said. "Let that be enough to drive the unbelievers out of our sector. And, if it isn't enough, we can find a colony world and regroup there. Will that be acceptable?"

"As you wish," Admiral Zaskar said. He knew he wouldn't get a better offer. The cleric couldn't be pushed too far. "But we have to be careful. The enemy could be using the convoy as bait in a trap."

"They started planning the convoy months ago," Moses pointed out. "Back then, they didn't even know that we'd survived."

"So we were told, Your Holiness," Admiral Zaskar countered. "Even if that happens to be true, and we have no independent verification, there's no reason they couldn't have attached a superdreadnought squadron to the convoy as an afterthought. *And* it would be easy to have that squadron link up with the convoy in deep space, well away from prying eyes. I . . . I have to be careful. We cannot afford to lose any more ships."

"They may feel the same way too," Moses said. The confidence in his voice was striking. "The unbelievers fear to die."

Admiral Zaskar rather doubted it mattered. The Royal Navy had fought well, even when it had been caught by surprise. And they had won the war. But it wasn't something he could say to the cleric. The man's hatred for the enemy was without peer.

"They can afford to replace their losses," he said, instead. He didn't pretend to understand how the enemy's economy worked, but he couldn't deny its efficiency. "We can kill ten of their superdreadnoughts for every one of ours, and they will still come out ahead. Losing a single superdreadnought, Your Holiness, will cut our fighting power in half."

"Then we will put our faith in God," Moses said. "Start planning the attack."

Admiral Zaskar bowed his head. "Yes, Your Holiness."

CHAPTER TWENTY-SEVEN

ASHER DALES

The message was relatively clear but brought no relief.

William scanned it three times, looking for hidden meanings. Scott McElney had always been careful, even before he'd left Hebrides to become a smuggler. His brother had taken an unseemly delight in defying the social norms and conventions of their homeworld, constantly on the verge of being ostracized for challenging the authorities, and he'd learned plenty of ways to get messages across without flagrantly breaking the rules. But none of his tricks were visible here. The message appeared to be nothing more than what it seemed.

And that isn't good news, William thought. *If Scott is to be believed, the smugglers aren't supplying the Theocrats.*

He sat in his cabin and contemplated the message. Scott wouldn't have *lied* to him, not directly, and there were none of the tells that suggested he was being deliberately misleading even though nothing he'd said was a lie. Besides, he couldn't imagine Scott helping the Theocrats. Their mere existence was bad for business, even before they'd turned Hebrides into a radioactive hellhole. And yet . . . Scott wasn't the sole smuggler chief in the sector. He wasn't even the largest. Could one of the others be supplying the Theocrats? It would be an insane risk for any of them.

His wristcom chimed. "Captain, we're picking up two ships approaching the planet," Patti said. "They just dropped any pretense at sneaking in."

William stood. Pirates? Or Theocrats, intent on finding out what had happened to their missing destroyer. The hulk was currently orbiting the moon, waiting to be turned into a training ship. In hindsight, perhaps he could have rigged a false IFF and lured the enemy into a trap. No, too risky. They simply hadn't been able to recover enough intelligence from the captured datacores to make the masquerade work.

He walked through the hatch and onto the bridge. "Report," he said. "What do you have?"

"Two ships, both apparently light cruisers," the sensor officer said. "One of them appears to be an ex-UN design, the other is of unknown origin. The warbook doesn't have a record of her design."

Which means she's either a completely new model or someone refitted her to the point she's unrecognizable, William thought. *And that means she could be carrying all sorts of surprises.*

"Sound battlestations, then alert the planet," he ordered. "We are about to be attacked."

He sat down and checked the displays. The enemy ships were heading right towards *Dandelion* and *Petunia* without making any attempt to hide their approach. They clearly hadn't realized that *Lily* and *Primrose* were under cloak, unless they'd decided they could take all four destroyers without risking serious damage, let alone defeat. It all depended, he reminded himself, on just how long the new enemy had been watching the system. They might not even know that *Lily* and *Primrose* existed.

"All weapons and drives are at full readiness," Patti reported.

"Very good," William said. "Use the StarCom to send an alert to Ahura Mazda. Ask them for immediate reinforcement if they have ships on station."

"Aye, sir."

William leaned back in his chair and silently assessed the situation. The enemy ships *had* to be pirates, unless their ships had been captured and pressed into service by the Theocrats. That was both good and bad: good, because pirates would break off if they were given a bloody nose; bad, because pirates could be even more violent and destructive than the Theocrats. He was more than a little dismayed by the appearance of pirate ships, particularly given the political trouble on Tyre. If the Royal Navy was withdrawn, the system would collapse into anarchy sooner rather than later.

And someone with a handful of dated warships could set up his own kingdom, William thought. *Whoever is coming at us now might be trying to beat the rush.*

"*Lily* and *Primrose* are moving into backstop position," the communications officer reported, calmly. "And the planet-side defenses are requesting orders."

"Tell them to go dark," William said. "They're not to reveal themselves until the planet comes under attack."

He had to smile at how efficient his crews had become. The raw material had been there right from the start, of course, as many of his crewmen had fought during the war, but they hadn't gelled properly until they'd won their first victory. Soon they would start absorbing new recruits from Asher Dales, recruits who would learn from men and women who'd actually been on the front lines. And they'd absorb a tradition of victory . . . His lips twitched at the thought. They'd have to be careful not to become overconfident.

The enemy ships came closer, angling straight towards the planet. William wasn't too surprised. His ships could outrun the light cruisers if they reversed course and fled, ensuring that the enemy would never be able to bring them down. The enemy had countered by forcing him to either stand and fight in defense of Asher Dales or run away and surrender the high orbitals to a bunch of pirates. It was a fairly standard military tactic. He couldn't help wondering if some of the pirates had been in the Theocratic Navy before deserting.

And they might just have enough firepower to smother all four destroyers with missiles, he thought. Two light cruisers certainly carried enough missiles to give his ships a very hard time. Even if the missiles were as outdated as the ships that carried them, they would make his life difficult indeed. *Time to take a third option.*

"On my mark, order the squadron to execute maneuver alpha-three," he said. "The ships in stealth are to remain in stealth."

He smiled. They were lucky the enemy had given them plenty of room to maneuver. Perhaps they hadn't been able to decide if they'd wanted to force an engagement or . . . *encourage* . . . his ships to turn tail and run. Their attack vector could easily have been a compromise between the two objectives, a compromise that tried to be both and managed to be neither. Yet another piece of proof, he supposed, that he wasn't facing Theocrats. *They* would have sought to pin his ships against the planet and blow them away.

"The squadron has acknowledged," Patti said, checking her console. "*Lily* and *Primrose* are still in cloak."

"Tell them to remain under cloak until I give the order or they are specifically targeted," William ordered. Even if the pirates knew the cloaked ships were there, they probably didn't know their exact positions. His officers would have plenty of time to drop their cloaks and raise shields. "*Petunia* is to stick close to us."

"Aye, Captain."

"Then *mark*," William ordered.

He watched the display, wondering precisely what the enemy would make of his ships suddenly sliding back towards the planet. Would they see it as incompetence, the sort of maneuver that might be pulled by captains and crews who didn't know what they were doing and hadn't had the time to learn better? Or would they suspect a trap? They had to know that Asher Dales's defense force was so young they didn't even have ship prefixes or proper uniforms, let alone time to learn the ropes. But they might also know that the crews had been recruited from the Commonwealth . . .

They'll see what they want to see, William thought. *Us blundering ass-backwards into a killing zone. But will they believe what they see?*

The enemy ships slowly picked up speed, angling for an interception just short of the high orbitals. William grimaced as the missile spheres—the lines on the display showing presumed missile ranges for the enemy ships—moved closer to the defenders. There was no way to know *what* they might be carrying, let alone their effective range. William was fairly certain they wouldn't have any of the enhanced range missiles—they'd barely been rushed into production in time to take part in the Battle of Hebrides—but would they have modern missiles? Or would they have dug up pieces of crap from the UN era, missiles so old and cumbersome that the Theocracy would have sniffed at them? William wouldn't know until they opened fire.

"Establish a laser link to platforms alpha through gamma," William ordered as the missile spheres came closer. His ships were starting to run out of room to maneuver. "Order them to prepare to fire."

"Aye, Captain," Patti said. "They're bringing their active sensors online now."

"Understood," William said. There was a good chance that the enemy ships would spot the lurking platforms, but . . . they were already too close for their own good. They'd have to break off in the next few seconds if they wished to avoid disaster. "I . . ."

The display sparkled with red light. "Missile separation," Patti snapped. "They've opened fire!"

"Get me a tactical assessment," William said. God, he'd *kill* for a proper analysis deck. He hadn't realized how lucky he'd been until he'd lost it. "And prepare to activate the platforms!"

"The missiles are about thirty years out of date," Patti said. "They're not showing any signs of being revamped over the years."

William allowed himself a moment of relief. The enemy missiles would have been hot stuff when they'd first been produced, but now they were just targets. They lacked the speed and penetrative power of the Theocracy's missiles, let alone some of the advanced missiles the Commonwealth had developed towards the end of the war. They were still dangerous—he reminded himself, sharply, not to underestimate the enemy—but his ships could fight the cruisers on better terms. He'd feared far worse.

And they haven't seen the cloaked ships, he thought. *All their missiles are targeted on the visible vessels.*

"Point defense is to engage the enemy missiles as soon as they come into range," he ordered, crisply. The enemy missiles didn't stand a chance unless they'd been modified at some point. "And give me control of the platforms."

"Aye, sir," Patti said. "Transferring control to your console now."

William smiled, grimly, as the enemy cruiser slid into engagement range. They clearly *hadn't* seen the platforms, which was unusually careless of them. They weren't making any attempt to hide, so why weren't they watching for mines? Normally, mining space was a waste of time, but he'd deliberately lured the enemy onto the minefield. But would they see the mines in time to either evade or open fire . . .

"Firing . . . now," he said.

The platforms were, in many ways, strikingly primitive, nothing more than a handful of single-shot bomb-pumped lasers, each one stabbing a ravening burst of energy straight into the enemy shields. One ship lost its shields completely, exploding into a ball of superheated plasma seconds later; the other staggered out of formation, atmosphere leaking from a gash in the hull. William felt his smile grow wider. Pirates, in his experience, rarely bothered to wear shipsuits. There was a very real chance that the enemy crew was already dead.

Just like the Theocracy, he thought. *They're nothing more than pirates.*

He keyed his console. "Dispatch a boarding party," he ordered. Thankfully the crew had time to prepare a proper boarding party. The local militiamen were nowhere near as heavily trained as the Royal Marines, but they knew what they were doing. "Communications, try to raise them. If they surrender, we'll spare their lives."

Which they probably won't believe, he added, silently. The Royal Navy had standing orders to execute pirates upon capture. William had a little more leeway. The pirates could go to a work gang instead, if they wished. *They can help to build Asher Dales instead of destroying it.*

"Message sent," the communications officer said. "No response."

William wasn't too surprised. Pirates were no better than Theocrats at maintaining their ships; indeed, arguably, pirates were *worse*. Their commanders found it harder to maintain discipline, even when the lives of everyone on the ship depended on keeping the hull intact and life support functional. He'd once boarded a pirate ship that had stunk so badly, far worse than a cesspit, that he couldn't understand how the crew had survived.

"They may have lost their communications," he said. The enemy ship was apparently harmless, but it was well to be wary. Pirates didn't normally commit suicide, yet if they believed they'd be killed as soon as they were captured . . . they might just try to take the boarding party with them. "Order the boarding party to be extremely careful."

"Aye, sir."

William waited, feeling sweat trickling down his back, as the boarding party slowly entered the pirate ship. It felt . . . wrong, somehow, to be sitting on his bridge in perfect safety when his subordinates were putting their lives at risk, even though he knew that his bridge wouldn't be safe when—if—a larger enemy warship turned up. He wondered, grimly, if he'd ever get used to sending people into danger that he couldn't share with them.

"Captain Tomas is hailing us, sir," the communications officer said.

"Put him through," William ordered.

"We have secured the ship," Tomas said. The militiaman's voice was very composed. "We have also taken a dozen prisoners, including their captain. He wants to speak to you."

"Scan him for surprises, then bring him back here," William said. "And *then* shut down the entire ship."

"Yes, sir."

William looked at Patti. "When they return, have the enemy captain brought to my cabin," he said. "I'll be there to meet him."

Captain Tomas was very efficient, William decided. It took him no less than ten minutes to transfer the pirate to the destroyer and push him into William's cabin. The man was shaking with terror, sweating like a pig . . . William didn't bother to keep the disgust off his face. He'd known Theocrats who'd been convinced they were going to hell who'd shown less terror than the piece of human waste in front of him. But then the pirate knew there was no point in being defiant. His ship was a burned-out hulk, his crew was either dead or captured, and he thought the gallows were in his future. How could he not be scared?

"You have two choices," William said flatly. "You can cooperate with us, which means answering our questions as fully as possible, or you can refuse. In the case of the former, we'll spare your life; in the case of the latter, you will rapidly come to regret it. Do you understand me?"

The pirate nodded, rapidly. "Yes . . ."

"Very good," William said. "Where is your base?"

"They'll kill me," the pirate said. He blanched. "They'll fucking kill me . . ."

"You are mere *seconds* away from being moved into an interrogation chamber," William lied, smoothly. ONI and the other intelligence services did everything in their power to defeat secrecy implants or forced conditioning, but their success rate was low. The criminals often died on the operating table, taking their secrets to the grave. "But if you tell us the truth, you will live instead. You'll spend the rest of your life on a reasonably nice penal island instead of having the techs poking and prodding at you in hopes of extracting your secrets."

He eyed the pirate as the man stuttered and stammered. Did he have an implant? Had he been conditioned? The only way to find out was to test it . . . and that might easily kill him, if the implant thought he was being interrogated. William doubted the other pirates knew much of any real use, although they'd have to be questioned too. Pirate captains tended to try to keep their crews as ignorant as possible.

And they certainly don't need to know the location of any pirate bases, he thought. *Or even worlds that might be willing to buy stuff that fell off the back of a freighter.*

"You'll let me live?" The pirate looked torn between hope and fear. "And you'll make sure they don't get me?"

"Yes," William said. "But you have to tell us everything."

The pirate hesitated, then spilled his guts. William listened, silently making a mental note to have the conversation replayed time and time again, just to make sure he picked up the important details. The pirates did have a base, and the prisoner knew where it was . . . but it was quite some distance from Asher Dales. William had hoped he'd be able to dispatch a destroyer or two to deal with it. Instead, it was starting to look as though he'd have to whistle for help. The Royal Navy would be *very* interested in destroying a pirate base.

And the base is very close to Ahura Mazda, he thought. *How did it manage to escape detection?*

"We'll have to pass the information up the chain," he said, when he returned to his cabin after touring the ship. The pirate captain and his crew were already on their way to holding facilities on Asher Dales, while their ship was carefully dissected for evidence. "The Royal Navy will have to deal with them."

Tanya looked displeased. She'd been trapped on the planet during the brief engagement and had only just managed to return to the ship. "We can't deal with them?"

"No," William said. He silently composed the message to Kat Falcone. "We don't have the mobile firepower. Or the time. And besides, that base is *far* too close to Ahura Mazda. We might just have stumbled across a link to whoever is supplying the enemy ships."

Tanya had to smile. "Does that mean we can claim the credit?"

"Some of it, perhaps," William said. He grinned at her. "But credit isn't important. The real problem is wiping these bastards out. And if someone else does it . . . well, I'll raise a glass in their honor."

He sighed. "And now we have to replace the platforms," he added, "before someone *else* comes calling."

CHAPTER TWENTY-EIGHT

PIRATE BASE

"Admiral, Captain Davis's compliments and we'll be dropping out of hyperspace in twenty minutes," Midshipman Edgeworth said. He held himself so stiffly that it was clear he was terrified. "He wishes to know if you'll be watching from the bridge."

Kat concealed her amusement. The midshipman was so young that she couldn't help thinking that he should be wearing diapers. Had she ever been so young? She didn't really want to *think* about the number of mistakes she'd made as a young officer, mistakes that had embarrassed her more than she cared to admit. She'd been young and ignorant—and unaware of the depth of her own ignorance. And now she was the Old Woman.

No, she corrected herself. *I'm not the Old Woman. I'm just the tagalong.*

"Please inform the captain that I'll be watching from the CIC," Kat said. She could have stepped onto the bridge, but unwritten protocol suggested she should stay off the bridge during an engagement. The last thing the superdreadnought's crew needed was confusion over who was actually in command. "And dismissed."

The midshipman vanished so quickly that Kat was mildly surprised the hatch opened in time to allow him to escape. She didn't really blame him. She'd been a duke's daughter, back when she'd been a midship-woman, but a word from the wrong person would have been more than enough to ruin her career.

She sat back in her chair and watched the timer slowly tick down to zero. The pirates had been either very brave or very stupid to put their base so close to Ahura Mazda, although she rather suspected they'd had an agreement with the Theocrats. Her investigators had encountered countless Theocrats who'd secretly purchased everything from alcoholic beverages to porn, all smuggled in from the Commonwealth or the Jorlem Sector. The gap between pirates and smugglers was smaller than the latter would like, she suspected. A down on his luck smuggler might just decide to play pirate long enough to put himself back in the black. Who knew? William might just have pointed her at the Theocratic Navy's hidden base.

Unlikely, she told herself, before she could get too enthusiastic about the prospect of winning the war in a single blow. *Too many people know about this base.*

"Admiral," Lieutenant Graves said, "we will be dropping out of hyperspace in two minutes."

"Very good," Kat said calmly. She forced herself to sit back in her chair and relax. She'd issued her orders; she'd done everything she could to ensure victory . . . now, all she could do was wait. She had nothing to gain by micromanaging her officers. "Inform me the moment the situation changes."

Violence shuddered as she opened a vortex and slid back into real-space, followed by the rest of the squadron. Kat leaned forward, watching the display as powerful sensors started to sweep space for targets. It was easy to see why the pirate base had remained undetected for so long. A tiny cluster of asteroids, so far from their primary star that they were practically worthless; hell, the entire *system* was practically worth-less. The only item of interest, save for the asteroids, was a large comet that seemed to be on the verge of breaking free of the star's gravity and starting to wander through interstellar space. And . . .

She smiled, coldly, as her sensors picked up a handful of starships hastily cutting loose from the asteroids. There were no signs of any superdreadnoughts, nothing larger than a midsized cruiser, but they'd definitely stumbled across a pirate base. One way or another, they'd do some good. The enemy had been caught completely by surprise. If she was lucky, they'd have no time to power up their vortex generators before her fleet was on them.

"Transmit the signal," she ordered. The enemy was already activating a handful of ECM buoys, but they were pathetically out of date. "And then order the destroyers forward."

"Aye, Admiral."

Kat watched the display update, wondering how many, if any, of the pirates and smugglers would heed her call. She'd be in some trouble, back home, for unilaterally offering to guarantee the lives of anyone who surrendered, although she had a nasty feeling that most of the people who knew useful pieces of information would be implanted or conditioned never to reveal it. Her techs were already preparing to see if they could beat the implants, this time. It would be hard on the pirates, but she found it hard to care.

We can put pirates out of business by dropping them on a penal colony, she thought, as the squadron converged on its target. *They won't threaten anyone ever again.*

"Some of the ships are powering down their drives," Lieutenant Graves reported. "The remainder are still breaking for space."

"Repeat the signal, then order the destroyers to open fire," Kat ordered. Ideally, she wanted to take the pirate ships intact. Pirates had a habit of press-ganging captives into working for them, and if they could be rescued . . . "If possible, they are to cripple the pirate ships."

"Picking up targeting sensors," Lieutenant Graves added. "Their defenses are going online."

"Probably trying to buy time," Kat said. She doubted the enemy base could stand off anything larger than a destroyer, if that. "Order the destroyers to take out any active weapons or sensor platforms."

She watched, grimly, as her destroyers began to exchange fire with the pirate ships. The pirates were outmatched but fought back with a mixture of desperation and brutality. Kat wondered, not for the first time, how the pirates could even keep themselves supplied . . . although she knew, from bitter experience, that colonists along the edge of explored space were often careful not to ask too many questions about where their supplies had actually come from. They simply needed the supplies too much to risk angering their suppliers.

And most of their tech is ancient, she thought as a starship old enough to be her great-grandmother vanished from the display. *They're tough enough against civilians, but not against the military.*

"The pirate base is opening fire," Lieutenant Graves said. "They're throwing everything at us."

Kat nodded curtly. William's report had, if anything, understated the case. The missiles the pirates were deploying were so badly out of date that she doubted even one of them would get through her point defense. They hadn't been bad designs, a couple of decades ago, but now they were useless.

And that's something to raise with the Admiralty, she thought as the enemy missiles crawled towards her ships. *Our advantage in missile ranges and speeds may not last very long.*

She watched, coldly, as the missiles entered her point defense envelope and were rapidly scythed out of space. No interstellar power could allow itself to be at a disadvantage in missile range and speeds, not now. The Commonwealth-Theocracy War had been the first major interstellar conflict in history, certainly the first fought with modern technology, but some basic cynicism in her insisted that it would not be the last. Every interstellar power had sent observers to the front line, taking notes to prepare their navies for the future. The Commonwealth could not allow its lead to slip away . . .

Which will mean spending more money on R&D, she reminded herself, remembering her disagreement with her brother. *And there will be no enthusiasm for* that *back home.*

"The last of the missiles has been picked off," Lieutenant Graves said. "There wasn't a single wasted shot. They didn't even get through the outer defense envelope."

"Repeat the signal to the pirate base, then deploy the marines," Kat ordered. "And then order the destroyers, squadrons two and three, to sweep space around the base. If anyone is lying doggo out there, I want to know about it."

Lieutenant Graves blinked. "Admiral?"

Kat felt an odd flicker of disquiet. *William* would have understood. And he would have carried out his orders without questioning them. She understood the importance of understanding *why* as well as *what*, but being questioned was still annoying.

We allowed too many standards to slip, she thought crossly. She'd been in command. The fault was hers. But she'd been too depressed to care. *And now we have to practically start from scratch.*

"Do it," she ordered. No point in making excuses. "We don't want to give anyone a chance to sneak away." She relented, slightly, as Lieutenant Graves passed on the orders. "The smarter ones will know they don't have time to power up their vortex generators and flee before we either force them to stop or kill them. So they'll run silent instead, hoping to get far away enough to escape altogether. It won't be pleasant, particularly when the life support starts to die, but it should be enough to keep them alive and free."

"Um . . . yes, Admiral," Lieutenant Graves said. His console bleeped. "Admiral, the base is offering to surrender, but they want to discuss terms."

"I bet they do," Kat said. She smiled, thinly. "Inform them that they are to shut down all weapons and defenses, then open the airlocks and await the marines. Any resistance will be met with deadly force, but we won't execute anyone who surrenders peacefully. There will be no other terms."

"Yes, Admiral," Lieutenant Graves said.

Kat felt her smile widen. They were in occupied territory now, a place the Commonwealth ruled by right of conquest. There would be no messy questions over jurisdiction, not here. The Commonwealth had taken the Theocracy's place and no one had even *tried* to challenge it, save for the Theocratic die-hards. There would be no cozy arrangements with system governors or independent asteroids to save their lives, no suggestion that the Commonwealth didn't have the right to pass judgment on the captured pirates.

"The remaining ships are powering down their drives," Lieutenant Graves said. "And the asteroid is surrendering."

Kat nodded, although she didn't relax. Questions would be asked back home. She might be blamed for allowing murderers, rapists, and thieves to live, even though life on a penal world would be no bed of roses. Perhaps she should simply drop them into one of the roughest areas on Ahura Mazda and see how they got on. Who knew? Perhaps they'd improve the place.

"The marines are boarding the asteroid," Lieutenant Graves told her. "No resistance so far."

"Good," Kat said. She keyed her console, accessing the live feed from the marine combat suits. "Let's hope it stays that way."

She wondered, as she watched the marines make their way deeper into the asteroid, just who had originally built it. The designers hadn't attempt to spin the rock to generate gravity, something that would have been a dead giveaway if someone took a careful look at the asteroid; instead, they'd installed a fairly basic gravity generator. They'd probably assumed, and they hadn't been wrong, that the rock would hide the energy signature. The prisoners looked a fairly degenerate lot, clearly terrified. Their former captives were in a very bad state indeed.

"Get them to sickbay," she ordered, although she knew the marines were already doing the best they could. "And make sure you keep an eye on them."

"Four hundred captives," Lieutenant Graves reported, once the asteroid was swept from top to bottom. "And fourteen ships."

"The ships might come in handy for something," Kat said. She wondered, morbidly, if she could train enough locals to operate them before the Commonwealth finally gave up on the Theocratic Sector. Perhaps she should ship them directly to Asher Dales. *William* would be able to make use of them. "How many of the pirates claim to have been conscripts?"

"Seventy, so far," Lieutenant Graves said. "They've been separated from the others."

"Good," Kat said. "Perhaps they'll want to stay here instead of going back home."

She sighed, inwardly. Pirate conscripts could *not* expect a warm welcome when, if, they got back home. *That* was something that was going to have to change, particularly if the Royal Navy found itself running more and more antipiracy campaigns. A conscript who believed that the best he could expect, when he got home, was being flung into jail was one who might commit himself wholly to the pirate crew. She had no sympathy whatsoever for anyone who chose the pirate life, and it was terrifying to see how many sociopaths and monsters pirate captains managed to recruit, but an unwilling conscript was a different story.

As if we didn't have enough problems, she thought. *But where do we draw the line?*

◆ ◆ ◆

"The bad news," Colonel Dagestan said, two days later, "is that this base was *not* supplying the Theocratic Navy."

"I figured as much," Kat said tiredly. Two days of watching as pirates were interrogated and their ships and base dissected had taken their toll. "Did we locate any clues as to their real base?"

"No," Dagestan told her. "If any of them know anything useful, they've managed to keep it from us. We even offered to up the reward, and they still had nothing to say."

And they'd sell out their own mothers if the price was right, Kat thought. *And the prospect of dying on a penal world had to concentrate a few minds.*

She took a sip of her coffee. "So . . . what were they doing here?"

"Apparently, the Theocracy left the base alone in exchange for them harassing our shipping, back before the war," Dagestan said. "They largely abandoned the base for a few months, after we crushed the Theocracy, then came crawling back. We'll probably discover that the Theocracy's records relating to the base—and the smuggling—were destroyed during the occupation."

Kat looked up. "Smuggling?"

"The smugglers were shipping in technology, apparently," Dagestan said. "Much of it was civilian-grade, but still effective. The trade slowly shut down after the war began."

"As we clamped down on tech transfers," Kat guessed. The Admiralty had wanted to crack down on tech transfers for years, but no one had made any progress until war was formally declared. There had been too many people with a vested interest in continuing the transfers, despite the risk of material ending up on the far side of the Gap. "Did we capture anyone with links to the smugglers?"

"Not as far as we know," Dagestan said. "It will take *weeks* to interrogate everyone completely."

"And then ship the survivors to a penal colony," Kat finished. "What about the base itself?"

"It's in good state—surprisingly good state for a pirate base," Dagestan said. "I'd actually suggest keeping it, if there were any value in doing so. But it's really too large to move somewhere more effective."

Kat nodded, slowly. "We might be able to make use of it," she said. "Particularly if there is an attempt to set up an interstellar authority for the sector . . ."

She met his eyes. "Have the base swept one more time, then transfer everything that might be useful to the freighters. We can use their supplies to fill the hole in our inventory. Then shut down the fusion reactor and everything else. Power it down completely. Once it's dark and cold, we can rig up a warning system to keep everyone else away."

"Or we can just leave a ship on duty to intercept anyone who happens to return," Dagestan pointed out. "There will be pirates out there who won't know that we captured the base."

"I don't think we can spare the ships," Kat said. She'd taken a major risk pulling so many ships away from Ahura Mazda. There was no real danger of the planet being captured while she was gone, unless they'd significantly underestimated the enemy fleet's size, but there wouldn't be many ships to respond to a crisis anywhere else. "Maybe one ship . . . I'll think about that."

"Yes, Admiral," Dagestan said.

Kat felt an odd pang in her heart. He sounded *just* like Pat, when he was politely disagreeing with her. Perhaps she should have asked for someone different . . . No, she was being silly. She couldn't go through life rearranging her command structure because someone happened to sound like her dead lover. It was no way to behave.

"Let me know as soon as the supplies have been transferred," she said. "And tell your men I said *well done*."

"Thank you, Admiral," Dagestan said. He saluted, smartly. "I'll let you know."

He turned and strode out of the compartment. Kat took another sip of her coffee. Smashing a pirate base wasn't *much*, in the grand scheme of things, but it was a step forward. The pirates had clearly been trying to get a foothold in the sector. It would be a long time before anyone else started to set up their own base.

By then, we might even have local forces patrolling the spacelanes, she thought, allowing herself a genuine smile. *The bastards might never have a chance to turn into a real menace.*

Her smile grew wider. They'd won a victory. A small one, but a victory nonetheless. And that would play very well back home.

And maybe they'll stop trying to take my ships, she told herself. *I might even have a chance to finish the matter once and for all.*

CHAPTER TWENTY-NINE

MAXWELL'S HAVEN

"We'll be dropping out of hyperspace in ten minutes, Captain," Lieutenant Poitiers said as he turned to face her. "The convoy will follow us into realspace."

"One would hope so," Captain Jackie Fanning said, crossly. "Communications, I want contact made with the StarCom as soon as we exit hyperspace."

"Aye, Captain."

Jackie put a lid on her temper with an effort. Whoever had written her orders hadn't been able to make up their minds. What *should* have been a relatively simple mission—escort a hundred freighters to Ahura Mazda—had turned into a nightmare. Their orders had been revised so many times that she sometimes fretted that they weren't actually following the latest set. Commodore Kipling had made a joke of it, damn the man, but everyone knew it was only a matter of time before the old man was discharged. *She* wanted to stay in the navy.

Bloody RIF, she thought. She'd been offered a bonus if she accepted a discharge, quite a sizable bonus, but civilian life had never suited her. Her place was on HMS *Invincible*'s command deck. *And damn the idiot who wrote the orders.*

She pushed the thought aside as she checked her ship's status. There was no reason to expect trouble anywhere near Maxwell's Haven, but she knew better than to take chances. The bureaucrats were constantly looking for excuses to put officers on the shortlist for discharge, regardless of their war records. Jackie understood that the navy needed to slim down, now that the war had come to an end, but it was irritating. She wasn't a short-termer. She'd devoted her life to the military.

And everyone is being switched around, she reminded herself. There were times when she felt that the Admiralty was playing a demented game of chess with its personnel. She'd heard of decent officers being sidelined into dead-end posts, while others—without sterling war records—had been promoted over their heads. The increasingly worrying rumors coming out of Tyre didn't help. The politicians were deadlocked, and the bean counters were running amok. *Who knows where it all will end?*

"Captain," Lieutenant Poitiers said, "we will be leaving hyperspace in one minute."

"Very good," Jackie said, concealing her irritation. No doubt they'd pick up a whole *new* set of orders when they made contact with Maxwell's Haven. No one had managed to find a way to send signals to a starship in transit, although she was sure the techs were working on it. The bean counters would *love* to find a whole new way to micromanage their subordinates from a safe distance. "Take us out of hyperspace as planned."

"Aye, Captain."

Jackie leaned forward, despite herself, as the vortex blossomed to life in front of the starship, allowing them to slide back into realspace. The display flickered, then started to light up with green and blue icons. Maxwell's Haven had been a major enemy fleet base during the war, until it had been bypassed during the final campaign; now, it was slowly turning itself into a major shipping hub. There were fewer starships in the area than the reports had suggested, Jackie noted as the remainder of the fleet followed them into realspace, but she wasn't particularly surprised. The interstellar traders would be reluctant to send more ships into the sector while an enemy fleet was on the rampage. Even if they avoided encountering the enemy, they'd have no way to know if their destination would even be *there* when they arrived. It would be a long time before regular shipping routes were established into the sector . . .

Red icons blazed across the display. "Incoming missiles," Lieutenant Sanders snapped, as alarms began to howl. "Incoming missiles!"

Jackie kept her voice calm. "Bring up the point defense, then link us into the datanet," she ordered. Incoming missiles? Here? Maxwell's Haven was supposed to be *safe*. "And repower the vortex generator."

She gritted her teeth as her sensors picked out the enemy fleet, slowly emerging from cloak and closing the range with terrifying speed. Three superdreadnoughts and nearly forty support ships, firing wave after wave of missiles with a speed and efficiency that surprised and horrified her. The Theocracy had clearly been forced to improve its game. They didn't look to have had any problems with their external racks, not this time. They'd put hundreds of missiles in space.

"Captain, they're not targeting us," Lieutenant Sanders said. "They're aiming at the freighters!"

Jackie blinked in surprise, then cursed as the implications struck her. No one had ever used *superdreadnoughts* to ambush a convoy, but there was always a first time. The Theocrats weren't here to capture the freighters, they were here to *destroy* them. They'd taken a calculated risk in not attacking the escorts—they'd left the warships free to defend the freighters and return fire—but it might well have paid off for them. No freighter ever produced could stand up to such a barrage.

"Orders from the flag, Captain," Lieutenant Poitiers reported. "We're receiving fire directions now."

"Then fire as ordered," Jackie snapped. Commodore Kipling was combining his ships into groups, hoping to delay the enemy superdreadnoughts long enough for the freighters to escape, but she knew the plan was futile. The freighters couldn't repower their vortex generators fast enough to escape, nor could they run to the planet's fixed defenses before they were overwhelmed. "And target the incoming missiles!"

Invincible shuddered as she unleashed a barrage of missiles. They looked pathetic, compared to the wave of destruction raging down on the freighters, but they would have to do. If nothing else, the enemy CO might be a *little* alarmed by their fire. She wouldn't have cared to operate so many ships without a shipyard, not when even relatively minor damage could be impossible to repair. The enemy might take out the convoy—there was no doubt they'd do immense damage—but if the engagement cost them their superdreadnoughts, it might be worth it . . .

Should have randomized our exit point, she thought. They'd taken precautions everywhere else, but not here. Maxwell's Haven had been *safe*. Besides, there had been a very real chance of a friendly fire incident if they'd opened a vortex outside the designated emergence zones. *This would never have happened during the war.*

"Enemy missiles entering engagement range," Lieutenant Poitiers reported. "Point defense is engaging . . . now."

It won't be enough, Jackie thought grimly. *Invincible* was free to cover the freighters, but she didn't mount enough point defense to take out *all* the missiles. And the enemy superdreadnoughts were still closing. *It really won't be enough.*

◆ ◆ ◆

Admiral Zaskar had honestly not expected the plan to work. Maxwell's Haven was nowhere near as busy as it had been during the war, when warships and freighters had been mustered before passing though the Gap, but it was still busy enough for him to be seriously concerned about a wandering freighter picking up a sniff of his presence. The Commonwealth's freighters tended to have top-of-the-line sensor suites, particularly when they were entering disputed space. But Maxwell's Haven was also the only waypoint where they knew where the convoy would return to realspace.

This would never have happened during the war, Admiral Zaskar thought as his missiles slammed into the enemy flotilla. *They wouldn't have allowed themselves to follow a fixed flight path when they thought they might be intercepted.*

"The enemy missiles are entering engagement range," the tactical officer reported. "They're . . . they're very good."

"Order the point defense to engage," Admiral Zaskar said. The enemy couldn't match the sheer volume of missiles he'd thrown at them—he'd risked expending his external racks on the freighters—but their missiles were better. He didn't need to do more than glance at the display to know that his ships were about to take a beating. "And put the damage control teams on alert."

He allowed his smile to grow wider as his missiles started to strike home. The Commonwealth had designed the freighters to maximize the amount of goods they could carry, not for defense. Their shields were so weak that a handful of missiles were more than enough to blow them to atoms, while they maneuvered like pigs in muck. They had no hope of evading his missiles. There was no way they'd be able to reopen their vortexes and return to hyperspace before he ran them down. No, the only *smart* thing to do was scatter . . .

A low rumble ran through the superdreadnought, followed rapidly by two more. He glanced at the report, silently relieved that the enemy didn't seem to have improved their warheads or their seeker heads. He'd made some careful estimates of their fighting power, relative to his, but it was good to have hard data. The Royal Navy didn't seem to have concentrated on making bigger and better weapons since the end of the war. Unless, of course, the ships in front of him had been at the back of the line for improved missiles. The Commonwealth's industrial base was terrifyingly large, but they had to have some limits.

And they wouldn't need first-class missiles against pirates, he reminded himself, as another missile slipped through his defenses and expended itself against his shields. *They'd be quite capable of swatting pirates with prewar weapons.*

"Admiral, they're switching to rapid fire," the tactical officer said. "And they're closing the range."

"Order all ships to watch for suicide tactics," Admiral Zaskar said. The clerics might insist that the Commonwealth's officers weren't prepared to die, but he knew better. A light cruiser could take out one of his superdreadnoughts by ramming her. "And prepare to engage with energy weapons."

"Aye, Admiral."

◆ ◆ ◆

"Seventeen freighters have been destroyed, Captain," Lieutenant Poitiers reported. "Seven more are significantly damaged."

And they switched their targeting to any ship trying to open a vortex for the freighters, Jackie thought. Sweat was trickling down her back. The squadron was pinned in place, unable to either run or fight. *They're going to smash us like bugs.*

"Orders from the flag," Lieutenant Sanders called. "The freighters are to scatter!"

"Adjust our fire and ECM decoys to cover," Jackie ordered. *Some* of the freighters would get away. The Theocrats simply didn't have enough ships to chase them down before they powered up their vortex generators or made it to the planet. "And stand by energy weapons."

The enemy ships drew closer, their weapons blazing furiously. They were damaged; one of the superdreadnoughts was leaking atmosphere but still operational. Jackie knew it was only a matter of time until they entered energy range and then . . . no battlecruiser ever designed could stand and trade knife-range blows with a superdreadnought. Her shields wouldn't last long, certainly not long enough to let her inflict the sort of damage that might slow the enemy down. Unless . . .

Lieutenant Poitiers raised his voice. "Captain, *Crescent* has been destroyed!"

Jackie cursed under her breath. The commodore was dead. The datanet shivered, nearly coming apart before recovering. She mentally kicked herself for not demanding that they worked more on squadron operations. Losing the datanet, even for a few seconds, could be disastrous in the middle of a battle. And the enemy fleet was still closing.

"Contact the fleet, inform them that I am assuming command," she ordered. "All ships are to deploy their remaining ECM drones and decoys, then prepare for a high-speed pass."

"Aye, Captain."

Jackie forced herself to think as the remainder of the escort squadrons oriented themselves on *Invincible*. They needed to buy time, and they needed to give the freighters a chance to run and hide . . . They could simply cut their drives, once they were out of immediate danger, and go dark. It wasn't ideal, but Maxwell's Haven would have already sounded the alert. If there were any reinforcements nearby, they'd be on their way by now.

Her hand danced across her console. "All ships are to engage with energy weapons as soon as they enter range," she added. Once they opened fire, the enemy would *know* which ships were real and which were sensor ghosts, but that wouldn't matter. Their superdreadnoughts would have immense difficulty in reversing course once the battlecruisers had made their pass and vanished into deep space. "On my command . . ."

She braced herself. "Go!"

♦ ♦ ♦

"Admiral," the tactical officer said. "They're deploying ECM . . ."

"I can see that," Admiral Zaskar said with heavy sarcasm. The display was suddenly *full* of contacts, ranging from hundreds of warships to thousands of freighters. There were so many contacts and simple sensor disrupters that it was suddenly impossible to tell which freighters were real and which were fake. His lips thinned in disapproval. He'd done the same to the enemy, once upon a time. "Reset the tactical computers, then start tagging the ships that actually fire missiles."

He felt his expression darken as the display filled with static. Sensor disrupters were relatively rare, if only because it was normally easy to locate and destroy them. They bought time for whoever had deployed them, sure, but only a few minutes. Here, though . . . he had to admit they might serve a useful purpose. It was suddenly very hard to track the fleeing freighters, let alone destroy them. His ships might waste their time trying to hunt down and destroy a flotilla of sensor ghosts.

"Launch probes of our own," he ordered. "And redirect missiles to take out the sensor disrupters . . ."

"Admiral," the tactical officer interrupted, his voice filled with alarm. "They're charging us!"

"Prepare to intercept," Admiral Zaskar snapped. Nineteen warships were racing towards his position, firing as they came. The two fleets were converging with terrifying speed. He silently saluted his enemy's bravery, even though he knew that there was no way he could replenish his losses. "Fire at will."

He braced himself as the enemy ships came closer, two falling out of formation and vanishing from the display. They were expending their fire on his superdreadnoughts, rather than his smaller ships; he acknowledged their cunning, even as he cursed it. A civilian might count the number of ships destroyed, but losing even one of his superdreadnoughts would cut his effective firepower in half. The Commonwealth could sacrifice the entire flotilla for one of his superdreadnoughts and still come out ahead.

In hindsight, he honestly wondered why the Tabernacle had launched the war. Had they simply never realized the vast potential of the Commonwealth's industrial base?

"They're entering energy weapons range now," the tactical officer reported. "Firing . . . *now!*"

Admiral Zaskar gritted his teeth. The enemy ships were coming alarmingly close . . .

◆ ◆ ◆

"Direct hits, decks five through seven," Commander Hanford reported. "Damage control teams are on the way."

Jackie looked at the display and knew it was useless. *Invincible's* drive field was already starting to collapse. She'd lost too many drives in the last barrage to keep the field operational long enough to get out of the enemy's range. Most of the squadron would survive, she was sure, along with the remaining freighters, but not her. She didn't even have time to order her crew to abandon ship.

"Point us straight at the nearest superdreadnought," she ordered. They *should* have enough power left to do that. "And then reroute all remaining power into the shields."

"Aye, Captain."

At least I got to die on a command deck, Jackie thought. *We . . .*

◆ ◆ ◆

"Admiral," the tactical officer said. *"Faithful One . . ."*

Admiral Zaskar swore out loud as the enemy battlecruiser slammed into the superdreadnought, both ships vanishing in a colossal explosion. *Faithful One* had survived a dozen skirmishes with enemy superdreadnoughts, only to be destroyed by a battlecruiser . . . It was not to be borne. But it was too late. His fleet had taken a beating . . . No, it had been crippled. They'd need weeks, if not months, to do what few repairs they could.

And Askew and his backers might not be able to replace the missiles we expended, he thought grimly. *We burned up two-thirds of our remaining stock.*

He looked at the display, but he already knew that the enemy sacrifice had not been in vain. The remainder of the enemy warships were already out of range, while their freighters were going dark or running towards the planet. Half of them were probably sensor ghosts, he thought, making their presence a little too obvious. In hindsight, he should have fired one barrage and then retreated at high speed, thus saving his fleet from losing a third of its capital ships.

"Order the fleet to open vortexes and retreat to the first waypoint," he said. The cleric would complain, but there was nothing to be gained by prolonging the engagement. Enemy reinforcements would be on their way. "And then we'll go home."

He allowed himself a smile of smug satisfaction as the fleet broke off the engagement and returned to hyperspace. Losing the superdreadnought and its crew had *hurt,* he couldn't deny that, but he'd given the enemy a real bloody nose. And then . . . He felt his smile grow wider. If he increased the tempo of attacks, hitting worlds right across the sector, he might just manage to convince the Commonwealth that it was going to lose. Cold logic would suggest otherwise, but the Commonwealth didn't seem to be governed by logic. Their system was frankly incomprehensible to him. He was mildly surprised they hadn't turned Ahura Mazda into a radioactive desert by now.

They can't ignore us any longer, he thought. A dull quiver ran through the superdreadnought as she picked up speed. If any enemy ships had the presence of mind to try to track the retreating fleet, they'd find it a difficult task. *And as long as they can't find us, we can jab at them at will.*

CHAPTER THIRTY

TYRE

All this room needs, Peter thought as the guests were ushered into the conference room, *is dim lights and someone smoking in the background.*

He smiled at the thought, although what was happening wasn't funny. News of the convoy disaster—the convoy *slaughter*, the media were calling it—had hit Tyre two days ago. The recriminations had been immense, drowned out only by accusations of everything from carelessness to betrayal and outright treason. Parliament had been cleared, twice, when MPs had practically started fighting on the chamber floor, while protest marches on the streets outside had turned into riots. Peter was old enough to remember the Putney Debates, back when the Commonwealth had been founded, but *they* had never been so bad. His security officers had reported that the volume of threats against MPs, the aristocracy, and the king himself had quadrupled. Peter had responded by reinforcing the armed guards around the mansion, corporate offices, and orbiting facilities.

Either someone fucked up badly, he told himself, *or someone openly betrayed us.*

It wasn't a pleasant thought. In absolute terms, as Masterly and Masterly had made clear to him, the disaster wasn't particularly serious. Losing the freighters was more of a problem than losing their cargos.

But, from a political point of view, it was a nightmare. The average man on the streets didn't care much about the populations of worlds that he'd never seen and probably never would. But the loss of an entire convoy was a far more serious matter.

He took the chair the usher offered him and surveyed the room. It was bland, save for a state portrait of the king in his military uniform and a small drinks cabinet, but that was in many ways a sign of the room's true importance. The king and his government had no need to make a blatant show of wealth and power, not in his private hunting lodge. He couldn't help feeling a thrill of excitement as the king entered, followed by the prime minister and Grand Admiral Tobias Vaughn. Parliament might debate and pass laws, but here, *here* was where the real decisions were made. Peter looked at Israel Harrison, his face blank, and Duke Rudbek, looking grim. Being *here* was clear proof that a man had made it. No one would be invited to such a meeting without being extremely powerful in political or economic terms.

And the prime minister started from the bottom, Peter reminded himself. *No wonder he's so devoted to the king.*

The ushers moved around the table, distributing tea and biscuits, then retreated silently through the wooden doors. Peter glanced at his datapad, unsurprised to see that the link to the datanet, even the ultra-secure connection to the family datacores, had failed. The room was as secure as modern technology and human ingenuity could make it. Even a very basic recorder wouldn't operate within a privacy field.

"I believe we can skip the formalities," the king said. "Admiral?"

Tobias Vaughn cleared his throat. "We have recordings of the engagement from Maxwell's Haven, as well as the surviving warships," he said. "I can confirm that fifty-seven freighters and fourteen warships were either destroyed or heavily damaged during the brief encounter, although they took five enemy warships with them. The enemy fleet chose to retreat after losing one of their superdreadnoughts . . ."

"Which is lucky for us, I suppose," Harrison said sarcastically. "How did our ships wind up in *that* position again?"

Vaughn looked embarrassed. "We are still conducting an investigation," he said. "It may have been simple misjudgment . . ."

"A misjudgment that led to the loss of more than seventy ships," Harrison said. "What *happened*?"

"When the . . . emergency situation began, when the enemy ships revealed themselves, we designated emergence zones for worlds like Maxwell's Haven and Ahura Mazda," Vaughn said. "It was determined that any ships that returned to realspace *outside* the emergence zones would be considered hostile. You may recall that we took similar precautions during the war. In this case, the emergence zones ensured that the ships returned to realspace at a roughly predictable location. The enemy took advantage of it."

Harrison glared. "And how did they know to have their ships be there on time?"

"The convoy made a layover at Cadiz, before crossing the Gap," Vaughn reminded him, grimly. "It's quite possible that someone at Cadiz passed on a message to the enemy commanders. The Theocrats spent decades, literally, building up a network of spies and informers right across their territory. I don't believe that we have successfully rounded up or neutralized all of them."

"The timing doesn't work," Harrison said. "My staff ran the numbers too, Admiral. They believe that the enemy fleet must have been alerted much earlier."

I need to check with Kat, Peter thought as the Leader of the Opposition and the Grand Admiral locked eyes. *She might be able to shed more light on the situation.*

He scowled, inwardly. It might have been a mistake to let Kat run so free for so long. She'd devoted herself to the navy, not to the family. And that meant she couldn't be relied upon to put the family first.

"They do not have access to a StarCom," Harrison insisted. "If they did, *Admiral*, we would have tracked them down long ago."

"But we have been emplacing StarComs ourselves, in threatened systems," Vaughn countered. "They may have used our own system against us."

"Which should not have been allowed," Harrison said. "The investment alone . . ."

The king tapped the table, sharply. "The Inspectorate General will carry out a full investigation," he said. "If there was a leak, if information was somehow relayed to the enemy ahead of time, we will track down and expose the source."

"I insist on an *open* investigation, conducted by the TBI," Harrison said. "We will not tolerate any attempt to sweep the truth under the rug."

"Quite," the king agreed. "But the TBI has been excessively politicized in recent years."

"And the Inspectorate General has not?" Harrison met his eyes firmly. "This is not a matter that can be left in the navy's hands."

"A joint investigation, then," the king said. "Right now, Mr. Harrison, we have other problems."

"Quite," Harrison said. "Let us leave aside the accusations of incompetence or treachery and concentrate on the facts. And the facts are that the situation in the Theocratic Sector is out of control. Nor can it be gotten *back* under control."

"Admiral Falcone is doing the best she can with the forces under her command," Vaughn said, firmly. "However, she needs heavy reinforcements to secure the sector *and* track down the enemy fleet."

"Reinforcements that cannot be provided," Harrison counted. "The entire sector is a money sink."

The king looked displeased, but said nothing. Peter eyed him thoughtfully, wondering what he was thinking. His flagship program had run aground on simple bad luck, or treachery, and yet he was very calm. Perhaps, just perhaps, he'd realized that the whole crisis was an opportunity to back down without looking weak. Or he was simply keeping his cards close to his chest. There was nothing to be gained by arguing *here*.

And we're meant to set policy for an entire kingdom, Peter reminded himself. *Here, we can afford to forget politics and be blunt.*

"We believe that we can force a withdrawal vote now and win," Harrison added. "I assume you do not agree with us?"

"You may assume that," the king said evenly.

Peter said nothing. His analysts hadn't had time to conduct a proper assessment, but they'd been unsure if the convoy attack would fuel a demand for violent revenge, at the cost of sending more heavy ships to the occupied sector, or a wish for immediate withdrawal. There were simply too many factors to be considered for them to be certain about anything. And Harrison clearly had his doubts too. He would have pushed for the vote if he'd thought he had a better-than-even chance of winning.

Except that would have alienated the king permanently, Peter reminded himself. *Both sides would be happier thrashing out a compromise.*

"We wish to propose a compromise," Harrison said calmly. "We will make one final investment in the sector, with the intention of help-ing the occupied worlds to defend themselves, then withdraw. Perhaps, depending on the situation, we will continue to hold Maxwell's Haven, so we have naval bases at both sides of the Gap, but otherwise we will pull out completely. The locals can take care of their own defense."

"The locals *cannot* take care of their own defense," the king said. He didn't sound angry, merely . . . dispassionate. "Even now, with one of the Theocratic superdreadnoughts little more than dust and ashes, the ships can still cause havoc."

Peter eyed him. "We've been over this, again and again and again," he said. "We simply cannot *afford* to defend them."

"So you would leave them defenseless?" The king's voice didn't change. "Alone against their former masters?"

"We can station a superdreadnought squadron or two at Maxwell's Haven," Harrison pointed out. "If the Theocrats *do* show themselves, we can stomp on them."

"Until you manage to get that squadron withdrawn too," the king said. His eyes flickered around the room. "Can you even *get* consensus on this?"

Harrison smiled. "I believe that most of the Opposition will accept this compromise," he said, briskly. "It won't please anyone, including you and me, but . . . we will accept it."

And it will be a step towards stemming the money flow, Peter thought. They'd planned the compromise to ensure that government funds flowed into the corporations, but he was grimly aware that the move wasn't going to be enough. Like it or not, Tyre was in for some hard times. *We will have to find other solutions.*

"We must discuss the matter," the king said. "Please, make yourselves at home."

Peter watched him and the prime minister depart, then looked at Israel Harrison. The Leader of the Opposition seemed . . . distracted, as if he was being bothered by a far greater thought. It was hard to escape the impression that he'd failed in some way, even though he'd convinced his MPs to back the compromise. His position might be weakened because he hadn't managed to get everything the Opposition wanted from the government.

But the government didn't get everything it wanted either, Peter told himself. *And that's why the compromise will pass.*

He leaned back in his comfortable chair. The room was supposed to be secure—his datapad had picked up four different privacy fields—but he knew better than to take that for granted. His father had shown him just how easy it was to subvert a privacy field, if you happened to be the one who'd set it up. The king's security officers might be recording every word spoken. Peter wouldn't feel safe talking openly until he got back to his mansion.

And we're going to have to make some hard decisions soon, he thought. *The compromise will slow the bleeding, and it might win us time to put a more reasonable solution into place, but the underlying problem is not going to go away in a hurry.*

He sighed. The convoy disaster had merely ratcheted up a war of words that had been raging for the last two months. Accusations of everything from incompetence to treachery had been exchanged by both sides, with attitudes hardening as moderates were driven to one side or the other. It was worse on the streets, he knew; there had always been problems with immigration, but he'd thought they were under control. Now . . . now, there had been attacks on immigrants and refugees that had left helpless men and women bleeding and broken. Rumors of worse were spreading at terrifying speed. The situation was out of control.

It felt like hours before the king returned, his face an expressionless mask. The prime minister followed him, looking like a dog who'd just been kicked. Peter wondered, sourly, just what they'd said to each other, in the privacy of their own chambers. Had the king decided to run roughshod over his servant's advice? Or had he decided that the prime minister would make a suitable scapegoat for the king's failings? *Someone* would have to take the fall if the king's position was weakened . . .

"We will accept your compromise, based on the changing situation," the king said. His voice was completely atonal. "A single major investment, geared towards defending the liberated worlds, then a phased withdrawal to Maxwell's Haven. I trust *your* compromise meets with *your* approval."

Harrison's face flickered, just for a second. "It *was* our compromise, Your Majesty," he said. "I daresay that not *everyone* will accept it calmly, but . . . it will suffice."

The king frowned. "And will you *then* use the same argument to justify a withdrawal from the outermost worlds? And then the Commonwealth as a whole?"

Harrison didn't rise to the bait. "We also intend to put forward a formal inquiry into precisely what mistakes were made over the last few months," he added. "Even if treachery wasn't involved, Your Majesty, it is clear that we became complacent. A number of officers may need to be . . . reassigned."

"No doubt," the king agreed blandly. "I'm sure a parliamentary inquiry, conducted in the full glare of publicity, will be as open and honest as you could wish."

Ouch, Peter thought. His father had told him, once, that parliamentary inquiries existed to put a rubber stamp on the official version of events. He had no doubt that everyone involved would be fighting desperately for control of the inquiry, if only so they could either accept the official truth or find an alternate truth of their own. *This will not end well.*

"There are other matters to discuss," Duke Rudbek said. "But we believe they can wait."

And see who comes out ahead, Peter thought wryly. *Opening another front right now might be disastrous if things don't go our way.*

"I agree," the king said. "And I'm glad we could come to an agreement."

And if that wasn't the most insincere thing you've said, Peter thought as leaving formalities were exchanged, *I'll eat my hat.*

No words were spoken as Peter and his allies made their way back to the landing pad, where their aircars were waiting for them. Peter climbed into his, told the driver to head back to the mansion, and activated the security sensors. A handful of tiny nanotech devices had attached themselves to him, signaling back to . . . *someone*. Peter felt his blood run cold. The king's security staff were paranoid, with good reason, but they shouldn't have maintained their surveillance after he left the king's hunting lodge.

He reached for his datapad and skimmed through the latest set of reports as the aircar flew back towards the mansion. Thankfully, no one outside the very highest levels of society had realized that the meeting had taken place. There were no crowds of angry protesters and media figures besieging the king's gates. And yet . . . He read through the summaries and cursed under his breath. It seemed too much to hope that society would calm down in a hurry. Too many people were about to become unemployed.

And too many others are about to throw gas on the fire, he thought, sourly. One MP had introduced a bill to repatriate—deport, in other words—every foreign worker. But it had been so poorly drafted that the law would have demanded the immediate termination of people the corporations and the military *needed. If we don't get control soon, someone else will take control himself.*

The aircar landed. He walked through a security field, feeling a little better when the three nanobugs were unceremoniously removed. They'd made his skin crawl, even though he'd *known* the feeling was psychosomatic. The bugs were too tiny to see with the naked eye, smaller even than flecks of dust or dead skin, a reminder of just why there were so many laws surrounding privacy. A person's life could become public knowledge very quickly if they were targeted for surveillance. He didn't want to think about how they might be misused.

"They were mil-spec gear, sir," his security officer said. "I'd say they were top-of-the-line stuff."

"I know," Peter said. "Have you swept the mansion today?"

"Yes, and we have a continuous sensor watch," the security officer assured him. "If you'd taken the bugs indoors, sir, we would have detected them."

"Very good," Peter said. He was no stranger to industrial espionage, as the corporations often sharpened their claws on each other, but this was a dangerous escalation. "Sweep the aircar, just to be sure, then send me a full report. I want to be sure we can keep these bastards out of our secure rooms."

"Yes, sir," the officer said. "I should point out, though, that it can be very hard to detect one that isn't transmitting."

"Yes," Peter said. His skin itched. Was there a fourth bug? Listening quietly to everything he said, but waiting until he was back outside before it started to signal its master? The scanners would have picked it up, wouldn't they? "Send a warning to the other corporations and politicians. Let them know what we found."

He supposed that the nanobugs could have been left attached to him by accident. It was also possible that someone had been trying to please the king by acting without formal orders. But he didn't believe it.

And then we will have to start a more serious discussion, he thought. *And decide if we can formally vote to impeach the king.*

CHAPTER THIRTY-ONE

AHURA MAZDA

"The remainder of the convoy is safely under the planetary defenses," Lieutenant Kitty Patterson said. "But their escort has been badly battered and requires reinforcements."

Kat glared at the display. It didn't seem fair, somehow, that their victory over the pirate base and the capture or destruction of enough material to put the pirates out of business for a very long time had been overshadowed by a convoy disaster. What had the idiots been *thinking*? They knew they were jumping into a warzone . . . hadn't they? The latest update from the Admiralty had informed her that a full inquest had been ordered, but that could mean anything. The board might reach its conclusions only after everyone involved was safely dead.

"At least we killed one of their superdreadnoughts," Commander Bobby Wheeler pointed out. "That's a third of their capital ships gone."

"Unless they have more," Fran said. "If they had more ships . . ."

"Commodore, we would have seen them by now," Wheeler said. "They wouldn't be keeping anything in reserve. They'd be doing their level best to keep us hopping."

"They're succeeding," Kat said. Her voice cut through the tension like a knife. "Lieutenant, how many supplies have been offloaded at Maxwell's Haven?"

"Just the pallets assigned to the naval base," Kitty said. "But they've put in a request for replacements, Admiral. A couple of the destroyed freighters were meant for them."

She checked her datapad. "We could make up the losses by transferring supplies that were meant for us . . ."

"Perhaps," Kat said. She rubbed her forehead. The political briefing Peter had forwarded to her was only a few hours old but was probably already out of date. It was starting to look as though the politicians were giving up. She was mildly surprised they hadn't ordered the surviving freighters to return through the Gap immediately. "Fran, detail three superdreadnoughts to escort the remaining freighters here. See if you can stagger the details and make it look as though the escort hasn't been reinforced."

Fran smiled wolfishly, although it didn't quite touch her eyes. "Aye, Admiral."

"Wheeler, inform Maxwell's Haven that they have two days to determine what supplies they wish to claim from the remaining freighters," Kat added. "I'll make my final decision then."

"Yes, Admiral," Wheeler said. He paused, significantly. "I should point out that the naval base has first call on supplies . . ."

"I know," Kat said, cutting him off. "But they are already heavily defended."

She sat back in her chair, feeling bitter. What had they been *thinking*? Hadn't they thought to take a few basic precautions? God! The emergence zones had been far enough from the planet for the convoy to prove its identity *long* before the defenses could open fire. Some politicians were already talking about treachery and betrayal, but she suspected it was nothing more than incompetence. Standards had slipped since the war. A convoy CO who took security so lightly, during the war, would have been lucky not to be unceremoniously dismissed.

And my people had the same issue, she thought. *I just didn't realize that the naval deployments on the far side of the Gap would have it too.*

"We have a problem," she said. "What implications does this have for us?"

"The politicians are running scared," Wheeler said. "Admiral . . ."

Kat held up a hand. "Leave the political implications out of it," she said sharply. "This isn't a debating club."

She sighed, inwardly. Wheeler could get in *real* trouble if someone heard him talking so disrespectfully about their political lords and masters. She didn't think he was entirely wrong—Parliament had made so many cuts to the military that disaster had only been a matter of time—but there was nothing to be gained by allowing him to throw away his career.

Not that it will matter, she thought. She knew that rumors were already spreading, despite her best efforts. Someone, somehow, had tipped off the insurgents. They were celebrating a great victory that, they claimed, had consumed more than ten thousand superdreadnoughts, even though there weren't ten thousand superdreadnoughts in the entire *galaxy*! *People are already talking about what it means.*

Wheeler looked abashed. "Yes, Admiral."

"The good news is that we do have a major tactical advantage," Fran said. She tapped her console, adjusting the display. "Their missile warheads and penetrator aids have not advanced, unsurprisingly. And we scored more hits on their ships than we should have done, if their defenses had been up to our standards. My analysts believe that their superdreadnoughts are actually decaying rapidly, even if someone *is* supplying them with weapons, spare parts, and technical help."

"And they will have problems replacing so many missiles," Wheeler added. "Their fire discipline was appalling."

"They wanted to kill as many freighters as possible within a comparatively short space of time," Kat pointed out, gently. "But yes, you're right. They're not going to get those missiles replaced in a hurry."

"They could have set up an automated factory," Fran pointed out. "It isn't as if finding fissionable materials is *hard*."

"They'd have needed to use it to keep their war machine supplied, during the war," General Timothy Winters stated. "I don't believe they would have started making preparations to continue the war after their defeat, not until it was too late."

Kat nodded. The Theocracy had refused to see the writing on the wall until her fleet was laying siege to Ahura Mazda itself. They'd certainly been unwilling to make preparations for an underground conflict, if only because they would have seen that as defeatist. There was something oddly foul about relying on one's enemies to kill anyone who took a realistic view of the situation, but she had to admit the tactic had proved useful. She dreaded to think what Admiral Junayd would have done if he'd had a completely free hand. The war would have dragged on far longer.

"And the smugglers will be unable to replace their losses," she said. She remembered the report on the missiles they'd captured from the pirate base and smiled. If the Theocracy wanted to arm itself with out-dated missiles, *she* wasn't going to stop them. "Their backers will have to either retreat or find them something more . . . *traceable*."

"Yes, Admiral," Wheeler said. "This may be the high-water mark for them."

"Let us hope so," Kat said.

She studied the display for a long moment. The enemy was running out of targets. Perhaps she could try to lure them into a trap? William's idea of using decoys to fake superdreadnoughts might work, if the enemy was sensitive to losses. Or even using one *real* superdreadnought per system, with a handful of decoys. If the enemy had only three superdreadnoughts left, they wouldn't want to face even a *single* super-dreadnought. She was fairly sure that one of her superdreadnoughts could take two of theirs.

And even if we're wrong, they'll know they've been in a fight, she thought. *They might win the battle, but lose the war.*

Fran cleared her throat. "Admiral, I know you didn't want to discuss politics, but . . . what happens if we're ordered to withdraw?"

"We'll deal with that when it comes," Kat said. She could fudge a little, when her orders allowed her a little discretion, but a direct order to withdraw could not be disobeyed. The StarCom network she'd set up, with the best of intentions, would make it harder to delay matters. "Right now, we have too many other things to do."

She looked down at the table. "I won't deny that this . . . *incident* . . . has been a major blow," she added. "But as Wheeler says, it may be their last gasp. We can weaken them, we *will* weaken them . . . If nothing else, they have to be hitting some pretty hard limits now."

"I believe so," Fran said. "I don't believe that anyone, even us, could keep three superdreadnoughts running indefinitely without a proper shipyard."

Kat forced herself to remain calm. "We calculated that the ships would be defunct by now and their crews dead of atmospheric poisoning," she reminded her friend. "We need to be very careful about making assumptions."

She looked up. "General, stay behind," she added. "Everyone else, dismissed."

"The disaster did bring a lot of rats out of the woodpile," General Winters said. "We might even be getting a grip on the situation."

Kat met his eyes. "Enough?"

"It's hard to be sure," Winters said, bluntly. "The real masterminds rarely show themselves openly, let alone take part in attacks. They have cannon fodder for that, Admiral. Young men who have no jobs, no wives, no hopes . . . they go out and they get themselves blown away while the *real* bastards continue to plot and plan. But right now, we are making rapid progress on blowing their networks wide open. They may already have realized that coming out of the woodwork has been a mistake."

"Understood," Kat said. "Keep the pressure on."

"We will," Winters said. "But Admiral . . . all this talk of withdrawal is making people nervous. Every man who signed up with us, every woman who went into one of the refugee camps . . . they're all scared about what will happen if we withdraw. Will they be left behind to face their former friends? And believe me, Admiral, the enemy is using their fears as part of a propaganda exercise. We may see the stream of informers and volunteers begin to dry up if they're allowed to continue."

And so the politicians make life harder for us, Kat thought. *Can't they see beyond their noses?*

She remembered the words she'd exchanged with her brother and scowled. The dukes were supposed to look to the future, but Peter was more interested in the corporation than in Tyre itself, let alone the Commonwealth. And the MPs were more interested in winning reelection than in winning the war. They'd vote for immediate withdrawal if they thought the action would please their constituents. She had no doubt they'd come up with a way to justify their behavior to themselves.

"All we can do is keep going," Kat said. "And, if we are ordered to withdraw, to take our allies with us."

Winters met her eyes. "The logistics will be hell, Admiral. Where do we *put* them?"

Kat shook her head, wordlessly. None of the liberated worlds would want a few hundred thousand more refugees. Taking them to the far side of the Gap wouldn't be any better. She doubted that *anyone* would want them. There were too many horror stories about refugees who'd picked up bad habits.

"I'll think of something," she said. "General, I . . ."

Her wristcom bleeped. She keyed it. "Go ahead?"

"Admiral, you have a priority-one StarCom call," Kitty said. "I've transferred it to your office."

"I'll be there in a moment," Kat said. She felt cold. Normally, StarCom calls were planned ahead of time, but this one was a surprise.

Was she about to be ordered to withdraw? Or . . . She'd find out soon enough. "General, duty calls."

"I understand," Winters said. "Good luck."

Kat nodded and hurried down the corridor to her office. The marines standing guard outside saluted as she approached, although she was fairly sure they'd have preferred to be on the front lines instead. Pat had told her, more than once, that guard duty wasn't his favorite duty. She made a mental note to ask for her guards to be rotated. Their skills would start to atrophy if they spent all their time inside the compound.

She stepped through the door and closed it behind her, then turned to the terminal and blinked. The Royal Crest was clearly displayed, just waiting for her to press her finger against the sensor and confirm her identity. She took a moment to gather her thoughts, put a note on her wristcom that she would be busy until further notice, then sat down at the desk and tapped the terminal. The king's face appeared in front of her a second later.

"Kat," he said. "It's good to see you again."

"And you, Your Majesty," Kat said automatically. "I'm sorry for keeping you waiting."

"It is of no concern," the king said. "You're hundreds of light-years away."

"Thank you, Your Majesty," Kat said. She'd known officers and politicians who would take it as a personal affront if someone didn't answer their calls at once, even if they were on the other side of the planet. "I assume this isn't a simple courtesy call?"

The king looked pained. "I'm afraid not."

Kat studied him for a long moment. King Hadrian was only two years older than she was, and the recipient of enough genetic modification to ensure he'd have a lifespan of well over two centuries even *without* rejuvenation treatments, but he looked haggard, as if the constant battle to keep the political system from tearing itself apart was slowly grinding him down. He was as handsome as ever, yet . . . there was an edge to his expression she found worrying, as though he was reaching the end of his tether.

"There is a bid to start a phased withdrawal from the occupied sector," the king said. His voice was grim. "You may find yourself ordered to pull your ships back to Maxwell's Haven before too long."

". . . Shit," Kat said. "Your Majesty . . . we might be on the verge of *winning!*"

The king nodded. "That's my read on the situation too," he said. "We cannot let everyone who died die for nothing. And yet, Parliament is on the verge of surrendering to their fears."

"They can't," Kat protested. "I . . . I can try to convince them."

"They're not listening to anyone," the king said. "Some of them genuinely believe that our economy is on the verge of collapse, some of them believe that whatever happens in the occupied sector doesn't matter to us, some of them . . . some of them are more interested in battling for power than anything else. The political situation is a mess."

"I've heard rumors," Kat said. "And Peter talked to me . . . Is it really that bad?"

The king said nothing for a long moment. "Parliament has always been insular," he said, finally. "And they have been historically unwilling to risk expansion beyond our solar system. The Commonwealth was my father's brainchild, and you know how hard it was to get even the stage-three and stage-four colony worlds cleared for membership. It was almost impossible to get them to sit MPs from the Commonwealth worlds."

"And their votes are practically meaningless," Kat said. She'd done her best to ignore politics as much as possible, but serving with William had left her with a new appreciation of just how badly the system had failed the colonies. "And that isn't going to change in a hurry."

"No," the king agreed. "And, as long as they make it difficult to ennoble colonials, it isn't going to get any better."

William's a knight, Kat thought. *But he had a few unfair advantages over his fellows.*

She took a long breath. "I don't want to be rude, Your Majesty, but I do have a great deal of work to do."

The king smiled. "You're bored stiff behind a desk, Kat," he said. "*That's* why you went gallivanting off to hunt pirates."

"Yes," Kat said flatly.

"Your old friend Justin Deveron made a big song and dance about it last night," the king said. "He was quite insistent that things would have been different if you'd remained on Ahura Mazda. I'm surprised your brother didn't have his bosses sued for slander. He really did push the line."

"Peter has always been unconcerned about what people say about him," Kat said. It was admirable, she supposed. Justin Deveron was a gnat. No one who knew anything about naval realities would believe that Kat could have done something if she'd stayed on Ahura Mazda. The Theocrats had vanished back into hyperspace long before any reinforcements had arrived. "And I don't care what Deveron says."

"There are others who *do* care," the king said. "He did have quite a reputation, once upon a time."

He made a dismissive gesture. "Right now, I want you to carry on and not worry about withdrawal," he added. "Plan on the assumption that the Commonwealth will remain engaged for the foreseeable future. I'm doing everything in my power to stall the vote until I have enough backers to defeat it. And . . . we need a victory."

"I understand," Kat said. She wasn't sure what to make of what was happening on Tyre. "I wish I could guarantee a victory."

"I wish you could too," the king told her. "Do everything in your power to make one happen." He paused. "We knew there would be . . . problems . . . in the aftermath of the war," he added. "But these are the problems of victory! *They* are not having such a good time."

"Yes, Your Majesty," Kat said.

The king saluted, then closed the connection. Kat leaned back in her chair, feeling unsure of herself. Technically, she hadn't been given any orders to withdraw; practically, Parliament might expect her to see which way the political winds were blowing. And that might leave her trapped between King Hadrian, who appeared to be the only one actually trying to deal with the situation, and Parliament. And her family.

"Crap," she muttered.

She stood and walked over to the window. General Winters had been right. There were hundreds of thousands of people who had placed their lives in her hands. They could not be abandoned, whatever it took. It was a debt of honor. She had no intention of refusing to pay.

CHAPTER THIRTY-TWO

ASHER DALES

"They're doing better than I expected," William said as Tanya and he watched the trainees slowly making their way through the captured hulk. "But don't tell them that, please."

Tanya glanced at him, sharply. "Why not?"

William grinned at her, then returned his attention to the monitors. "They cannot be allowed to think that they'll be praised for every little thing," he said. "That leads to overconfidence, and overconfidence leads to disaster. I *really* don't want to lose a trainee so soon."

"I see, I think," Tanya said. "I was never told *that* when I was in law school."

"If you make a mistake as a lawyer, it can be fixed," William reminded her. "Here . . . if someone makes a mistake, the consequences can be fatal. And there's no way to remove the risk completely without ruining the training."

He shrugged expressively. There was no way they could duplicate the extensive facilities and concealed safety precautions of Piker's Peak. And even the Royal Navy's officer training center lost cadets from time to time. William had read some of the reports, during his bid to become a mustang. Some cadets had done stupid things, making the sort of mistakes that William found hard to believe; others, more tragically, had done everything right and *still* died during training. It was only a matter of time before Asher Dales lost its first trainee in an accident. He wondered, morbidly, just how the planetary government would cope when the recriminations began.

Probably very well, he thought. *They know that life isn't safe.*

He turned away from the display as the trainees completed their exercise and returned to their makeshift barracks. They were doing well, for young men who'd only been in space for the last two weeks; they had a long way to go, but the raw material was definitely there. It helped that they were colonials, he told himself firmly. Colonials understood that the universe was red in tooth and claw, something that civilians on more developed planets tended to forget. They also understood that accidents happened.

"I read the latest news from Tyre," Tanya said. "Is it true we're getting one final investment?"

William had his doubts. "I wouldn't take anything for granted," he said. "The investment will be intended to allow you to purchase supplies from Tyre, not . . . They won't want to just give you the money and let you do what you want with it."

"And then we'd have to get whatever we purchased here," Tanya said. "*That* won't be easy either."

"True," William agreed. He'd been doing his best to follow the developing political situation, but it was impossible to tell which way the Commonwealth would jump. He hadn't seen so much vitriol in media broadcasts and private blogs since . . . ever. The tensions that had been a part of the Commonwealth since its founding were coming into the open, while politicians were gleefully throwing gas on the fire. "We may have to wait and see what happens."

His wristcom bleeped. "Captain, long-range sensors are picking up two starships dropping out of hyperspace," Patti said. "Warbook calls them midsized cruisers. No IFF. They'll be in engagement range in ten minutes."

William felt his blood run cold. "Activate Plan Omega, then alert the planetary government," he ordered. The intruders were almost certainly unfriendly. Anyone who wanted to open peaceful discussions about trade or political alliances would be broadcasting an IFF code. It was basic good manners. "I'm on my way."

He glanced at Tanya. "Do you want to get back to the planet?"

Tanya shook her head. "There's no point in going back," she said. "I might not get down to the surface before they start throwing rocks at us."

William smiled. "Then come with me," he said. "And *don't* touch anything."

He led the way to the bridge, silently noting how well his crew moved to battlestations. The drills and engagements had definitely paid off. They could have passed for a Royal Navy crew from the war . . . hell, they *had* served in the Royal Navy during the war. He reminded himself, once again, to ensure that the trainees learned from the older hands. It was easy to slip into bad habits once one passed through basic training if one didn't have proper supervision.

Two red icons glowed on the display as he entered the bridge, both cruisers. It was impossible to be sure, but he'd bet half his salary they were Theocrats. Pirates were rarely so bold unless they were *entirely* sure their targets couldn't put up a fight. And besides, Kat Falcone had smashed the local pirate base to rubble. It would be a long time before the pirates managed to recover, if they ever did. The Commonwealth would be withdrawing—William was sure withdrawal was coming—but hopefully the sector would be able to put up a defense. Even a handful of destroyers on patrol would be able to keep a lid on piracy.

"Nonstandard ships, definitely," Patti said as William waved Tanya to an unoccupied console. He was careful to lock it out, just in case she touched a button by accident. "But they're built on Theocratic hulls."

"Theocrats, then," William noted. This time, they were in for a real fight. Two cruisers would *definitely* be able to wipe out his entire squadron. Their vectors showed they were spoiling for a fight too. "Establish a laser link to *Trojan One*."

"Aye, Captain," Patti said. "But the time delay . . ."

"We'll have to deal with it," William cut her off. It would be *neat* if the techs came up with a way to communicate in real time across interplanetary distances, but he wasn't going to hold his breath. Mobile StarComs were hideously expensive and, so far, no one had managed to slim one down enough to cram it into a superdreadnought. "Order the remainder of the fleet to form up on the flag."

"Aye, Captain."

William sat back in his chair, wondering just how much the Theocrats knew about what had happened to their missing ship, or for that matter, to the pirates. They'd given him very little room to maneuver, deliberately or otherwise; he rather suspected they were hoping for a clear shot at his ships before they turned and fled. They *certainly* weren't acting as though they suspected a trap. A lone superdreadnought would be more than enough to kick their ass.

Which would be nice, if we had a superdreadnought, William thought. He checked his console. An alert had gone out, of course, but it would be hours at best before reinforcements arrived. *We'll just have to make do without one.*

"Signal from the planet, sir," the communications officer said. "They're going dark."

"Good," William said. Asher Dales had dispersed a lot of its population and industrial base, but he was grimly aware that the Theocrats could render the entire planet uninhabitable fairly easily. Merely shoving asteroids towards the planet, after they'd smashed his squadron, would be more than enough. "Let us hope they restrict themselves to tactical bombardment."

He felt Tanya's eyes boring into the back of his head as the enemy ships converged on his position. She probably thought he could blow the Theocrats away with a snap of his fingers, but . . . the defenders were heavily outgunned. The missile ranges were closing rapidly too, although the enemy had yet to open fire. He wondered, wryly, if their reluctance to try to overwhelm his point defense owed something to the vast number of missiles they'd expended at Maxwell's Haven. He'd read the reports very carefully, followed by the analysis. It was impossible to be sure, of course, but it was hard to imagine the Theocrats replacing their lost missiles in a hurry. They might indeed have hit their high-water mark.

"Enemy ships are locking weapons on us," Patti said. Her voice was cool, professional. "They're preparing to fire."

"On my command, execute beta-one," William said. "Try to make it look like we're panicking."

His mind raced. Had the Theocrats seen the hulk? The captured ship wouldn't be *easy* to spot, not until they got closer. But they could easily have probed the system under cloak before mounting an overt attack. His sensor crews were good, but he had no illusions. There was no way they could spot a cloaked ship that kept its distance until it was too late. Asher Dales simply could not afford anything like the vast network of scansats that protected Tyre. The planet barely had complete coverage of the high orbitals.

He wondered, coldly, what his opponent was thinking. Was he facing a cool professional or a fanatic? William wouldn't have allowed the latter to take command of a starship, but the Theocracy had different ideas. And besides, he'd seen enough interrogation records to know that a cool professional was watched at all times. A captain who appeared to be insufficiently aggressive might end up being shot in the back by his own crew.

"Their missile sensors are going active," Patti added. "Sir?"

"Execute beta-one," William ordered. "Pull us back . . . now."

He smiled as the display sparkled with red icons. The enemy missiles wouldn't burn out before they reached his ships, but they were going to have a difficult time of it. They hadn't expended their external

racks either, he saw. The chances were good they didn't *have* external racks. Perhaps the enemy had redeployed ships after the attack on
Maxwell's Haven. They might not have had time to go back to their
base and replace their external racks.

*Or maybe they're just very cautious about expending their remaining
missiles,* William thought as his squadron kept pulling back. If they were
lucky—if they were *very* lucky—the enemy missiles wouldn't be able to
go into sprint mode for the last few seconds. It wouldn't make them *that*
much less dangerous, but it would buy his ships some extra time. *Let
us hope they don't decide to give up on us and start bombarding the planet.*

"Deploy drones," he ordered. "Lure as many of the enemy missiles
off-target as possible."

"Aye, sir."

"And stand by the missile pods," William added. "Prepare to fire
on my command."

He felt his expression darken as the engagement developed. The
enemy missiles were dumb—too dumb. They didn't seem to be falling
for the decoys. It looked as though the enemy ships had given them
their targeting data upon launch, instead of allowing the seeker heads
to constantly update themselves. It was wasteful, but William had to
admit it had paid off for them. They weren't going to expend their missiles on harmless drones.

"Point defense is engaging now," Patti said.

"Fire the missile pods, then run the deception program," William
ordered.

The display updated, again, as the missile pods went active and
opened fire. A stream of missiles appeared on the display, blazing towards
the enemy ships. The ECM went active seconds later, trying to convince
the enemy ships that there were more missile pods lurking behind the
real ones. An illusion, but one that would be very difficult to disprove.
If the Theocrats were being genuinely sensitive to losses, they wouldn't
want to risk going into engagement range.

Of course, they could just spit ballistic projectiles at the pods from beyond engagement range, William thought. It was a classic technique, one that predated hyperspace and interstellar settlement. *But they have to think that reinforcements are already on the way.*

Dandelion rocked, sharply. "Direct hit, nuclear warhead," Patti snapped. A second impact ran through the hull. "Shields failing!"

"Rotate us," William snapped. "Keep the strongest shield towards the enemy . . ."

"*Primrose* is gone," Patti said. "*Lily* has taken heavy damage."

Shit, William thought. Behind him, he heard Tanya gasp. Captain Descartes was dead and, judging from the display, hadn't had any time to order his crew to abandon ship. A quarter of William's mobile fire-power was now nothing more than free-floating atoms drifting in space. *They could still win this.*

He watched the enemy ships, noting sourly how their point defense systems had improved over the last year or so. Whoever was in command was no slouch. He'd drilled his crews relentlessly, probably pitting them against simulated missiles with twice the speed and hitting power of anything they were likely to encounter. The Royal Navy did the same, ensuring that real engagements were easier. They'd been lucky, he supposed, that the enemy commander hadn't held a higher post during the war.

"We damaged one of the ships," Patti said. "But I don't believe the damage was serious."

William nodded, slowly. The enemy ships hadn't lost their shields. They certainly weren't leaking atmosphere or superheated plasma. The only *good* news, as far as he could tell, was that they weren't showing an eagerness to press matters any further. They might well be reluctant to risk exposing themselves to the remaining missile pods. But the pods were nothing more than illusions . . .

"Order *Trojan One* to go active in five minutes," William ordered. "They're to advance towards the enemy at their best possible speed."

319

"Aye, sir," Patti said. Her console bleeped an alarm. "Sir! They're opening fire!"

"Return fire," William ordered. The enemy were trying to swat the destroyers before battling the planetary defenses. He considered, briefly, moving back to the high orbitals, before dismissing the concept. Encouraging the enemy to test the defenses was *not* a good idea. "A long-range duel works in our favor."

As long as one of their missiles doesn't get past us and hit the planet, he added silently. *That could be devastating.*

He wondered, idly, just what was going through his counterpart's head. The opportunity to smash the remaining destroyers could not be missed, but they were dangerously exposed. A single battlecruiser would be more than enough to take out both cruisers, and the enemy CO *had* to assume that reinforcements were on the way. William was surprised they'd made no attempt to take out the StarCom. The old interstellar agreements not to destroy StarComs or interfere with navigational systems presumably no longer bothered the Theocrats. They were little more than terrorists now, and they knew it.

"*Trojan One* is going active . . . now," Patti reported. A spike of energy appeared on the display, followed by two superdreadnoughts. "They're shaping an intercept course towards the enemy."

And let's hope they believe the superdreadnoughts are real too, William thought. *If they decide to exchange fire with drones . . . it might start them wondering what else could be an illusion.*

The enemy ships seemed to flinch, just for a second, before altering course to widen the range between the superdreadnoughts and themselves. William had no doubt that the cruisers *could* outrun the superdreadnoughts, if they wished to do so. Even the most advanced superdreadnought in the galaxy couldn't match a light cruiser's acceleration curve. But . . . but what *would* they do? Would they assume they'd run into a trap? Or had a simple dose of bad luck? Or . . . would they think they might have been tricked?

They couldn't hope to survive an engagement with real superdreadnoughts, he thought. *But they'd realize they were being tricked the moment the superdreadnoughts failed to open fire.*

"Captain!" Patti said. "They're powering up their vortex generators."

William glanced at the display, then took the plunge. "Pass tactical command to Captain Young," he ordered. "And prepare to take us into hyperspace."

"Aye, Captain," Patti said. On the display, the enemy ships were turning away, moving with a stately elegance that belied their speed. "They're opening vortexes now."

"Take us into hyperspace," William ordered. "Rig the ship for silent running."

Dandelion shuddered as she opened a vortex and slid into hyperspace. The enemy ships were clearly visible on the display, already heading away from Asher Dales as fast as they could. They didn't seem to have realized that they were being followed, although William knew they could merely be pretending to ignore him. They might well want to lure *Dandelion* into a trap.

And hyperspace makes it easy to ambush someone, William reminded himself. Experienced spacers knew better than to take anything for granted in the maelstrom. *Or even to make their lives miserable by triggering an energy storm.*

"Silent running engaged, sir," Patti said. "Your orders?"

"Hold us at extreme range, but maintain the sensor lock," William said. The enemy CO had clearly panicked. He'd had options when the fake superdreadnoughts had shown up, but he'd chosen to break off the engagement and run. There was a chance, a good chance, that he'd fly straight back to his base. "And prepare to follow them out of hyperspace if they try to throw us off."

"Aye, sir."

Tanya caught his attention. "How long are we going to be away from home?"

"I don't know," William admitted. She didn't sound pleased, but he'd given her the chance to take a shuttle back home, before the engagement broke out. "We could be away for days or weeks. But if we can shadow them back to their base, we can whistle up a fleet of *real* super-dreadnoughts. And then we can put an end to this once and for all."

He leaned back in his command chair, knowing it wouldn't be easy. The enemy *might* have realized that they were being followed. Even if they hadn't, they would be fools *not* to take some basic precautions as they approached their base. *William* had been taught to be very careful, even when heading to a location everyone knew. The enemy commander would presumably have been taught the same lesson.

And we would have caught them by now if they hadn't, William thought. The Royal Navy had certainly tried to shadow the enemy ships as they returned to their base. *This time, it's going to have to be different.*

CHAPTER THIRTY-THREE

TYRE

As parties went, Peter thought, it was singularly depressing.

He was, as a Duke, expected to host at least one social gathering every two months and attend a number of others. It wasn't a duty he enjoyed. On one hand, inviting the wrong person could cause all sorts of drama; on the other, failing to attend the right party or attending the *wrong* party could be seen as an insult. His sister Candy might enjoy selecting the guests, arranging entertainment, and all the other duties that came with being the host, but Peter hated it. He much preferred quiet backroom discussions to pretending to make pleasant, and meaningless, conversations with his guests.

But the parties do have their uses, he told himself. He swept through the chamber, exchanging brief formalities with the guests. *They give us a chance to gather everyone together without looking suspicious.*

He winced inwardly as he caught the eye of a society dame who was already well on the way to drinking herself silly. The dress she wore was designed to draw the eye to her cleavage without *quite* revealing everything she had. But then, she had nothing else. Her family had cut her allowance years ago, even before the financial crisis had hit. She made a living by seducing someone, letting him take care of her for a while, then moving on to her next victim. Peter would have felt sorry for her if she hadn't tried to seduce him in front of his father and wife.

And we probably shouldn't have invited her, he thought tiredly. Every family had someone who was too wellborn to cut out completely, but too useless to actually *do* anything for the family. *And yet we needed to make sure that the guest list was as wide as possible.*

He turned slowly, surveying the room. Hundreds of guests, wearing a mixture of suits, dresses, and fancy costumes, were crowding around the buffet tables, slowly dancing on the marble floor, or splashing around in the pool at the far end of the room. Men and women with power, flanked by their dates . . . the latter doing everything in their power to make themselves look important, because their patrons were important. They should have looked happy—Peter and his sister had gone to some trouble to make the affair sparkle—but there was an air of despondency that pervaded the entire gathering. The older guests, the ones with true power, looked bowed down by some immense weight, while the younger ones were desperately trying to cheer themselves up. He caught sight of a young man swimming naked in the pool, followed by a handful of young women, and winced at the sight. Everyone was trying to convince themselves that nothing was wrong . . .

The butler materialized beside him. "Sir, the select group has been guided to the meeting room," he said. "They're waiting for you now."

"Good," Peter said. He didn't bother to hide his relief. The party was starting to look and feel like a wake. "Make sure that none of the other guests go wandering."

He strode across the room, passing a handful of young men and women sitting by the pool. A couple of them were junior aristocrats, trying to shock their betters, but others were nothing more than group-ies, trying to carve out a place for themselves in the aristocratic world. They looked fresh and pretty and carefree—they were trying to pretend that they belonged—but the effect was ruined by their constant glances at their social betters for approval. Peter felt a stab of sympathy, knowing that most of them would not enjoy their time in High Society. They'd certainly never enjoy the security of someone born to the aristocracy.

The sound of people trying to be happy cut off abruptly as he passed through a secure door, which closed firmly behind him. Peter allowed himself a moment of relief—he'd never had time to just relax and enjoy himself at parties—and then kept walking until he reached the conference room. The king would have observers at the party, he was sure, but they'd have great difficulty in telling just who had and who hadn't been invited to the meeting. It wasn't uncommon for an aristocrat to find a bright young thing and take them to bed. Or for someone to just sneak off early.

He stepped into the conference room and looked around. The space was crammed with political and economic power. Ten of the fourteen dukes, along with a dozen other aristocrats who represented financial and corporate interests; the Leader of the Opposition and his closest allies; a pair of media moguls; and even a handful of military men. Peter's gaze swept the room, silently gauging their mood. United, Parliament could bring the king to heel; disunited, the king could play divide and conquer to his heart's content.

The door closed. "This room is secure," Peter said bluntly. The guests had insisted on checking the security arrangements for themselves. Given what was at stake, Peter didn't blame them. "We can talk freely."

"The king is no longer in his right mind," Duke Rudbek said. He wore a suit that had been out of fashion for longer than Peter had been alive, but his eyes were sharp and his voice was clear. "This latest attempt to spy on us is a step too far."

"To say nothing of his attempts to undermine the compromise," Duchess Zangaria said. "He promised much, but gave little."

"A trick made easier by your actions," Duke Tolliver pointed out. He looked young, but his eyes were old. "You did everything in your power to ensure that the money would be given to *your* corporation."

"So did you," Duchess Zangaria countered.

"I know," Duke Tolliver said evenly. "Let us be brutally honest. We all saw advantage in manipulating affairs to suit ourselves as individuals, rather than as a group. And we have paid a steep price."

Peter nodded, stiffly. There had been no intention of simply giving the money to the liberated worlds. That would have been a bad idea. Instead, the money had been earmarked to pay for goods and services from the corporations. It would benefit the liberated worlds, eventually, but it would also benefit the corporations, making it harder for them to oppose the king. He wondered, grimly, if it had been deliberate. The king might have counted on the corporations allowing the money to divide them.

Or he might just have had a contingency plan for both possibilities, he thought. The king didn't lack for either courage or cunning. *We cannot afford to overestimate him any more than we can afford to underestimate him.*

"We need to move, now," Peter said. "Can we introduce a Bill of Impeachment?"

Israel Harrison cleared his throat. "We could," he said. "But the problem would be getting it through the Houses of Parliament."

"If all of us dukes worked together, it wouldn't *matter* what the rest of the world thought," Duke Rudbek growled. He glared at Peter. "Why weren't the others invited?"

"Three of them have been playing their cards very close to their chests," Peter said. "And Cavendish is . . . Cavendish is hoping the king can provide a miracle."

"Which he can, if we give him free rein to spend money," Duchess Zangaria said. "Without it, Cavendish is doomed."

"That doesn't give them much incentive to support us," Duke Tolliver pointed out. He sounded more amused than anything else. "And if we happened to lose the vote, it could get very bad."

Peter made a face. Israel Harrison would have to resign if he staked everything on an impeachment vote and lost. Even if he tried to hang on, his former allies would demand his immediate removal. Burning up every scrap of political capital they'd gathered over the years for *nothing* would not go down well with them. And while the dukes were more secure, anyone who pushed for impeachment and lost might be forced to resign too. The family council would not be amused if their duke alienated the king.

"The king has been amassing power for the last four years," Peter said. Masterly and Masterly had run a comprehensive analysis. The king had gathered a lot of power to himself during the war, political and financial as well as military. No wonder he didn't want to give it up. "I submit to you that it could get far worse if he reaches a position of unchallengeable power."

"I understand your point," Duchess Turin said. "How do you intend to proceed? Present the king with an ultimatum? Or simply rush into impeachment?"

"The former might be enough to get the king to back down," Duke Tolliver said. "But it would also give him time to build a counter-coalition of his own."

"And split us," Duchess Zangaria added. "He has plenty of ways to convince struggling people to join him."

"But pushing for an immediate vote could lead to disaster, if we lose," Duke Tolliver said, coldly. "There is something to be said for giving him room to retreat."

"He's already had that chance," Peter reminded him. "We were able to use the convoy disaster to give him a chance to back down, without losing too much face, but he turned that back against us. Our choice is between tolerating him, knowing that he may be planning to remove us as soon as possible, or removing him. Now. While we still can."

Isabel Harley, MP for the North Dales, leaned forward. "Aren't we being a little paranoid? We have no evidence the king *intends* to turn on us."

"He's amassing power," Harrison reminded her. "And, sooner or later, he will need to make that power secure."

"The balance of power has been smashed," Peter added. "And we must either restore it or accept permanent subordination."

"Or death," Duke Rudbek muttered.

"Surely you can't think he'd go *that* far," Isabel protested.

"The king has vast resources," Rudbek snapped. "He controls a significant chunk of the military, directly and indirectly. Countless men and women owe their careers and positions to him. And a *lot* of money was steered into black programs during the war. Where did that money go?" He took a long breath. "And then there's the death of the former Duke Falcone," he added, nodding to Peter. "The assassins who killed him were never caught."

Peter sucked in his breath. "The official report concluded that they were Theocrats . . ."

"And yet, they were never caught," Rudbek repeated, tapping the table. "Why didn't they launch more attacks? Why didn't they sell their lives dearly? Every infiltration cell fought to the death when it was discovered, but this one seems to have gone completely underground and vanished. That's simply not possible in the long run."

Perhaps, Peter thought. *But Father and the king were working together.*

He forced himself to think. It wasn't possible to vanish on Tyre, not completely. Someone who lived deep in the countryside might be able to stay out of sight, but anyone who lived in one of the cities would leave an electronic trail for investigators to follow. The police and security services had gotten good at tracking people who might be enemy agents, simply by analyzing their progress through the system. And all the normal constitutional safeguards had been abolished during the war. The king could use the surveillance systems in ways their designers had never anticipated.

Rudbek was right, he conceded grimly. The assassins should *not* have been able to hide indefinitely. They'd have great difficulty even boarding a starship and fleeing the system before being caught. And even if they did have the skills to hide, Peter had to admit that it was atypical. The Theocrats had expected their infiltrators to do as much damage as possible before their inevitable deaths. There was no reason to expect them to remain in hiding now that the war was over.

"You can't accuse the *king* of assassinating a duke," Isabel protested. "Even if it was true, you'd need a *lot* of proof."

Peter met Rudbek's eyes. "Do you *have* any proof?"

"None," Rudbek admitted. "But who actually benefits? The Theocracy? It was too late for the death of a single man to save them. Or the king, who used your father to rationalize our industries and, just incidentally, put a lot of his people in positions of power. Your father might well have known a great many things the king didn't want to make public . . ."

"This is an absurd theory," Peter spluttered. He didn't want to think about the possibilities, even though he had no choice. "And we can't even make it public without proof. We'd be laughed out of court."

"I know," Rudbek said. "But it's a good example of why we need to act fast."

"If, of course, the king actually ordered Duke Falcone killed," Isabel pointed out. "We have nothing but a chain of inference. The onus would be on us to prove that the king gave the orders, and we couldn't. Could we?"

"No," Rudbek said. "We remove the king first, then we dissect everything. We work out where the money went, where it was spent, and what it bought; we open up the entire planetary security infrastructure and determine, if we can, if a black ops team was used to kill Duke Falcone. And then . . . we dismantle his infrastructure, return to the *status quo ante bellum* . . . and *then*, well, we find someone in line to the throne and give it to him or her."

Isabel coughed. "And if the king is innocent?"

"He's already abused his position," Duke Rudbek said firmly. "We'll pension him off, perhaps to a distant estate where he can spend the rest of his life."

"We are putting the cart before the horse," Peter said. "How *do* we build up a majority in Parliament?"

Duchess Zangaria snorted. "Cavendish is the sticking point," she said. "The others will fold if they know we're united."

"Then we have to buy them out," Peter said. Thankfully, Masterly and Masterly had worked out the figures for him. "We make them an immense long-term loan, funded by the remaining duchies. The deal will hurt us badly, but will keep them afloat."

"It will not be easy to balance that payment with the austerity regime," Duchess Zangaria said quietly. "My corporation is already laying off employees."

"They won't accept anything less," Duke Tolliver said. "Even offering to purchase their facilities will be seen as insulting. They don't want to end their careers as pensioners."

We should be so lucky, Peter thought. *If we all go bust, we'll be lucky if we spend the rest of our lives begging in the gutter.*

Harrison cleared his throat. "A united front, then?"

"If we can convince everyone to join us," Duchess Zangaria said.

"We should also make preparations for a violent response," Rudbek added glumly. "Does anyone believe we can keep our plans secret for a couple of months?"

"We must all hang together," Isabel quoted, "or we will all hang separately."

Peter couldn't disagree. The king had plenty of informers. *Everyone* who was anyone had a network of informers, ranging from the trustworthy to men and women who'd sell their own grandparents if the money was right. Even if everyone in the room kept their mouths firmly shut, *something* would leak out when they started widening the conspiracy. The king would have a window of opportunity to do something before time ran out.

And if we don't move fast, he'll be able to rally the navy to his command, Peter thought. *And who knows what will happen then?*

"We tighten both our security and grip on the planetary defenses," he said. "If we manage to impeach the king, we *should* be able to sever his ties to the navy."

"His people are loyalists," Duke Rudbek commented. "They'll have to be removed as quickly as possible."

"Which might be tricky," Duchess Zangaria countered. "They might not take it calmly."

Isabel blanched. "We're talking open civil war," she protested. "Your Grace . . ."

"That's why we have to act fast," Duke Rudbek said.

But we can't act fast, Peter thought. It would take weeks to build consensus, then make the loan to Cavendish. *We only get one shot at removing the king legally.*

His mind raced. If the king had assassinated Peter's father, why not assassinate the king? It might solve all their problems, except he couldn't see a way to do it. The king was heavily protected. Peter's guards wouldn't be able to get through the defenses, assuming they accepted the mission in the first place. The political struggles on Tyre had never turned violent. Perhaps that was why hardly anyone had suspected that the king might have had a hand in Lucas Falcone's death. Assassinating one's rivals was unprecedented.

And I don't want to believe it, he thought. *If the king killed my father, what else will he do?*

"Then we need to sort out the details now," he said. "I'm expected back at the party."

Rudbek smiled. "You poor thing."

Harrison nodded. "We'll start work at once," he said. "Ideally, we'll be ready to put forward the impeachment bill by the end of the month.

And then . . . we can take the king into custody before he can do something stupid."

"It might be too late for that," Duke Rudbek said. "The young fool is losing his mind."

"But not his cunning," Peter said warningly. The king had nerve. Even his worst enemies admitted it. "Remember, we only get one shot at this. If we fail, we will be *far* worse off."

"And if we succeed, our position will be a great deal stronger," Rudbek said. "Let's look on the bright side, shall we?"

CHAPTER THIRTY-FOUR

Uncharted Star System

William jerked awake, feeling sweat running down his back. He'd been dreaming of home, a home he'd never see again . . . a world that was now covered in radioactive dust. His parents had been there, as had his brother and cousins and . . . He shook his head, wiping the sweat from his brow. A dream. No, a nightmare. He'd known, even as he'd joined them for dinner, that it hadn't been real. Hebrides was gone. She'd never be made habitable in his lifetime. If anyone tried at all.

His console chimed. "Captain?"

"Go ahead," William ordered. He sat upright, wondering when his bed had suddenly become so hard. He'd spent *years* on starships. "I'm listening."

"The enemy ships appear to be preparing to open vortexes," Patti said. "We're quite close to a possible star."

But we can't be sure, because of hyperspace, William thought. It wasn't easy to navigate in hyperspace, not outside the charted regions. *The gravitational shadow might be caused by something else.*

He swung his legs over the side of the bed and stood, reaching for his jacket. "I'm on my way," he said as he checked the ship's status. The seven days they'd spent in hyperspace had been largely uneventful. They'd managed to keep shadowing the enemy ships despite a series of evasive maneuvers that had made life more than a little exciting; now, if they were lucky, they were going to see the enemy base. "If they open a vortex, take us out of hyperspace immediately."

"Aye, sir."

William splashed water on his face, glanced at his appearance in the mirror, and headed for the hatch. He looked a mess but found it hard to care. Some of his old commanding officers would have made sharp remarks about stubble, yet William had always believed that one had a choice between *looking* good and *being* good. Besides, he was the CO. No one would say anything to him if he came onto the bridge looking like he hadn't shaved for weeks.

He stepped through the hatch and onto the bridge, his eyes searching out the display automatically. The enemy ships were slowing, as if they intended to merely glide back into realspace. That made sense, he supposed. Their energy signature would be smaller, making it harder for them to be detected. Such a move also suggested they weren't concerned about being ambushed. Either they'd randomized their emergence point or, more likely, they believed there were no hostile ships for light-years around.

"They're opening a vortex," Patti said urgently.

"Then take us into realspace," William said. He sat down, bracing himself. This was the most dangerous part of the mission. Normally, if he'd wanted to sneak into a star system, he would have opened the vortex and emerged on the very edge of the system, well out of detection range. This time, though, they *had* to stay close to the enemy ships. "And stand by to run for it."

The ship shuddered as the vortex opened, casting them into realspace. William watched the display blank out, then hastily reboot itself as data flowed into the passive sensors. The star was right where his computers had placed it, a dull red sun of no interest to anyone. He checked the location and nodded to himself. The system would have been way down the list for a formal visit, let alone a survey, even if the war hadn't continued after the enemy homeworld had been captured.

"Engage the cloak," William ordered. "And alert me if they start sweeping with active sensors."

"Aye, sir."

"The enemy ships are heading towards a collection of asteroids," Patti reported. "Passive sensors are picking up a handful of other signatures."

Muffled signatures, William thought. *And if that isn't proof we've found a base, I'll eat my hat.*

He hesitated, suddenly unsure what to do. The safest course of action was to sneak out of the system and whistle up a superdreadnought squadron. They could be at the nearest StarCom in less than a day and summon help, or head all the way to Ahura Mazda if he didn't feel like trusting the communications network. Someone might have betrayed the convoy, after all. But he wanted, needed, to gather as much information as possible. Who knew what might be waiting for the Royal Navy when it arrived?

"Take us after them very slowly," he ordered. "And don't let them catch a sniff of us."

He frowned as the system continued to reveal its secrets. Two superdreadnoughts . . . no, *three*. But the third looked to be largely powered down. Judging from its energy signature, he doubted it could fly or fight. The Theocrats might simply be cannibalizing the hulk for spare parts. Beyond them, a handful of other ships . . . including a number of freighters. He shuddered, remembering the reports of missing ships. The Theocrats might have been engaged in piracy for fun and profit between hitting planets. Who knew how many ships they'd snatched and taken to their base?

"The base itself looks old," Patti commented. "They might not have built it."

William agreed. He'd seen hidden colonies that had been captured by pirates before. The original settlers hadn't been given a choice, assuming they'd survived either the colony itself or the invasion. The Theocrats had probably stumbled across the asteroids during their period of expansion, captured them, and then simply sliced their existence out of the records when the war ended. Or maybe their existence had never been recorded at all.

"Don't take us any closer," he ordered. "But see if you can get a headcount."

"Yes, sir," Patti said. "Will the Royal Navy be able to take the base out?"

"Easily," William said. "If they can kill those superdreadnoughts, the rest of the ships won't pose a problem."

And then they can withdraw from the sector with a clear conscience, he added silently. *I wonder what that will do for politics on Tyre?*

◆ ◆ ◆

"Asher Dales was defended by two superdreadnoughts?" Admiral Zaskar wasn't sure he believed the report. "And they drove you away?"

"Yes, sir," Captain Miles said. He looked as if he was expecting to be executed on the spot. "We thought it would be better to retreat."

"You were probably right," Admiral Zaskar said. "We need to preserve our ships."

He kept his real thoughts to himself as he watched the recording one final time. He had a suspicion that Miles and Captain Hammed had been tricked, but he had no solid proof. They certainly hadn't lingered long enough to see if those superdreadnoughts would actually open fire. The enemy could have been simply incompetent, or messed up the timing, but he doubted it. The Commonwealth had learned from its mistakes. Their ships were no longer sitting around in orbit for him to smash at will.

"Return to your ships and complete your repairs," he ordered finally. "You'll be going out again as soon as we obtain new missiles."

"Yes, sir."

"They could have pressed the offensive," Moses said once the two captains had been escorted out of the office. The cleric had been unusually quiet during the debriefing. "If they'd hit Asher Dales . . ."

"It wouldn't have been worth the cost," Admiral Zaskar said. Moses might believe that Asher Dales represented a long-term threat, but Zaskar suspected it didn't matter. They'd done all they could; now, they'd just have to wait and see if the enemy really *did* abandon the sector. "We couldn't replace the cruisers." He leaned back in his chair. "And we're having problems replacing the missiles too."

"Askew isn't able to find new missiles?" Moses looked worried. "None at all?"

"Not so far," Admiral Zaskar said. "I imagine he's having problems."

And he might want to keep us helpless, a voice whispered at the back of his mind. *If we've served our purpose, he might consider us expendable.*

"So . . . when can we resume the offensive?" Moses started to pace the compartment. "And when can we hit them again?"

"For the moment, we should wait and see what happens," Admiral Zaskar said. "Right now, we are in no state to meet even one of their superdreadnoughts. We need to replace our missiles, repair our ships, and *then* decide what we want to do next."

Moses stopped pacing and turned to face him. "And what if we don't get any more missiles?"

Admiral Zaskar didn't need to think about his answer. "Then the next enemy ship we encounter will smash us," he said. A slight exaggeration, but a pardonable one. "We will lose everything."

He rested his elbows on his chair. "Askew told us that the convoy's destruction would be enough to make them abandon the sector, allowing us to retake control," he said. He had his doubts about that too, but he couldn't say them out loud. "If he's wrong . . . we need to start considering other options."

"We have a duty," Moses insisted. For once, his words lacked conviction. "What if . . ."

Admiral Zaskar cut him off. "We have the tools we need to colonize a whole new world," he said. "Given time, we could return to the sector and liberate Ahura Mazda from the unbelievers."

"But . . ." Moses shook his head. "But . . . what if we leave our brothers under enemy rule? What will happen to them?"

"What will happen to them if we get smashed?" Admiral Zaskar tried to sound reassuring and failed. "If we lose our ships, the war is over. We have a duty to survive."

"And yet, we would be abandoning our brothers," Moses protested.

"We would have no choice," Admiral Zaskar said. "If we lose our ships, as I told you, the war is over."

Moses scowled. "What do you propose?"

"We transfer most of our captured goods into the freighters," Admiral Zaskar said, as if he hadn't spent weeks considering the possibilities. "We take everything we can, then destroy the rest. This base gets abandoned, as does *Sword of Righteousness*. She's in no state for anything but the scrapyard. The prisoners who refuse to go with us get left behind on the base."

He nodded towards the starchart. "And then we fly well away from explored space," he added coolly. "A few hundred light-years ought to be sufficient. We find a suitable world, set up a colony, and rebuild."

And I'm making it sound easy, he reflected. It was not going to be easy. The task of settling a habitable world would change them, for better or worse. Standards would slip, then be loosened . . . and it would be hard to tighten up again. *A very long time will pass before we're ready to return home, and by then we will no longer be the same.*

"And our brothers will be left behind," Moses said.

338

"Yes, but they will remain faithful," Admiral Zaskar lied. Some would, he was sure, but others would abandon the Theocracy without a second thought. "And we will return to save them."

"As you say," Moses said. He hesitated, as if he didn't believe his own words. "God is with us."

"I'll start the preparations at once," Admiral Zaskar said. "We'd need to transfer everything to the freighters anyway, if we were going back home, so we might as well do it now."

"Very good," Moses said. "But we will wait to see what happens before we abandon our homeworld for decades."

Centuries, more like, Admiral Zaskar thought. Human expansion had slowed in the past hundred years or so, after the UN had fallen and Earth had become a dead world, but he had no doubt the Commonwealth would begin expanding again soon. *They may stumble across us before we're ready to encounter them.*

He considered, briefly, heading farther away. It seemed a good idea, but he had no idea just how far his ships could go. Their drives had been pushed to the breaking point. A few hundred light-years might be the upper limit, particularly in uncharted space. He really didn't want to run afoul of a hyperspace storm or something worse.

"We can wait," he said with the private thought that he could probably rush everyone into leaving once the ships were ready. "But when the time comes, Your Holiness, we will have to leave. And we won't be able to look back."

"I understand," Moses said placidly. "God is with us. He will not let us down."

◆ ◆ ◆

"I think we've seen everything we can, at least at a distance," Patti said. She looked up from her console. "There's no way we can tighten our readings up."

"Not unless we go closer," William added. They'd pushed their luck as much as they dared. The enemy wasn't running active sensor sweeps, but he was fairly sure they'd seeded local space with passive sensor platforms. The slightest hint of his ship's presence might set off alarms right across the system. "I think it's time to call for help."

He studied the enemy superdreadnoughts for a long moment. The enemy crewmen were actually trying to repair the ships, even though they didn't have a shipyard or even a mobile repair vessel. He would have been impressed, he admitted freely, if he hadn't been so sure the ships and crewers needed to be destroyed. The Theocrats would return to Asher Dales one final time if Kat Falcone and the Royal Navy didn't get them first.

And there's no way to tell if they've replenished their missiles or not, he thought. The Theocrats could have been stocking the base for years, although he had to admit the possibility was unlikely. At first, their leadership had never considered that they might lose the war. *They might already have rearmed their ships.*

"We could put a couple of stealth probes next to their hulls," Patti suggested. "They'd never see them."

"Too great a risk," William said. He had every confidence in stealth technology, but he was also aware of its limitations. They didn't dare alert the enemy to their presence. "I . . ."

An alarm sounded. "Report!"

Patti checked her console. "A single ship, dropping out of hyperspace," she said. "Warbook calls it a Class-VI courier."

"She's well away from us," William mused.

Tanya coughed. "Do we know where she came from?"

"Class-VI couriers are used just about everywhere," William said, understanding the *real* question. "The Theocrats used them. They're about as anonymous as you can get. There's no way to know where she came from or who's inside without capturing her."

He looked at Patti. "Take us out of here, as sneakily as possible," he ordered. "We won't risk opening a vortex until we're on the other side of the star. And then we'll head straight for the nearest StarCom."

"Aye, sir."

William leaned back in his chair. In truth, he didn't know if the StarCom network could be trusted. In hindsight, he and Kat should have set up a code to deceive any unwanted listeners, but it was the only way to summon the fleet quickly. Flying straight to Ahura Mazda would add too much time to the journey. Who knew what mischief the enemy fleet would get up to if left alone for a couple of weeks?

Even if we don't catch them, we'll smash their base, he thought. *That might just buy us some time.*

◆ ◆ ◆

"Admiral," Askew said, once he was seated in the office. "I was able to obtain a number of missiles for you."

Admiral Zaskar glanced at the datapad. "This isn't enough."

"Merely getting these was not easy," Askew said shortly. The agent sat down without being invited. "I got a line on a collection of older missiles, but they wouldn't meet your standards. The ones en route are the last ones compatible with your systems."

"It depends on what we're fighting," Admiral Zaskar muttered. Older missiles would be useless against the Royal Navy, but they'd be quite effective against pirates, insurrectionists, and tin-pot navies. "When will they arrive?"

"In two weeks," Askew said. "Things are a little tighter now. The Commonwealth is throwing its weight around."

And you're making excuses, Admiral Zaskar thought. *Are you telling the truth, or are you setting us up for a fall?*

He looked at the chart. "There's no way I can risk an engagement as long as I don't have new missiles," he said, partly to see how Askew would react. "We can keep raiding their shipping, such as it is . . ."

"Insurance rates for this sector have gone through the roof," Askew said blandly. "It will be a long time before any of the midsized shipping firms clear their people for working here."

"And the bigger firms have other problems," Admiral Zaskar said. "What do you want us to do?"

"Keep the Commonwealth busy, keep convincing them that you're going to win," Askew told him. "And focus on recovering your home-world as soon as they withdraw." He rose. "I'll discuss the rest of the matter with you later, Admiral," he said. "Right now, I need to hit my bunk."

And we may no longer need you, Admiral Zaskar thought as the hatch closed behind Askew. *If you can't get us any more missiles, what good are you?*

He looked at his datapad. The plan for transferring supplies to the freighters was well underway. Askew might notice something, if he kept an eye on their work, but . . . but what would he do? What *could* he do? Try to sabotage the escape plan? Or simply let them go?

We know too much for his comfort, Admiral Zaskar thought. The risk of discovery was incalculable but ever-present. He had nothing to lose, if they were caught, yet Askew and his backers certainly *did.* The Commonwealth would see them as war criminals, at best, and their actions an act of war.

Askew may simply plan to dispose of us before too long. And if we're not ready to leave . . .

CHAPTER THIRTY-FIVE

UNCHARTED STAR SYSTEM

"Admiral," Lieutenant Kitty Patterson said over the intercom, "we will reach the RV point in thirty minutes."

Kat sat upright. "Are there any signs we've been detected?"

"The ship's sensors haven't picked up any contacts," Kitty said. "This entire section of space appears to be clear."

"Which proves nothing," Kat said as she climbed out of bed. "We just have to hope our approach hasn't been noticed."

She reached for a towel, then walked into the shower. She'd taken every precaution to keep the enemy from learning that she was coming, including sending fake messages and ECM drones to suggest that she was heading in the other direction, but she was grimly aware that all her preparations might be for naught. If someone really *was* leaking information to the Theocrats, someone who had remained undetected since the convoy's destruction, the enemy might already know she was coming. She'd seriously considered not informing the Admiralty of her deployment, just in case. But that would have ended with her facing a court-martial board . . .

They wouldn't care about why I'd done it, she thought as she turned on the water. She hadn't slept well. *The admirals would just be angry that I'd treated them as potential spies.*

She cursed under her breath. Ahura Mazda was, at least in theory, far away enough not to be affected by the political chaos on Tyre, but she had her doubts. Everyone had seen the news reports, everyone had their own take on the situation . . . Kat couldn't help feeling that the navy's unity was a thing of the past. She wondered, sourly, if she should have cracked down on political discussion right at the start. But who could have imagined that things would go so bad so quickly?

The tensions were with us all along, she reminded herself. *The war merely brought them into the open.*

She washed thoroughly, then turned off the water and dried herself before stepping back into the cabin. Lucy had laid out a clean uniform already, along with a pot of coffee and a tray of sandwiches. Kat dressed rapidly, keeping one eye on the display. The local region of hyperspace still looked clear, but she didn't like the look of the energy distortions in the distance. They might turn into full-fledged storms at any moment. The Theocrats might have relied on the distortions to help cover their path.

Her terminal bleeped, reporting that a new message had arrived. Kat glanced at the header and the string of reports waiting for her attention and ignored them. Catching up could wait until they were on their way back to Ahura Mazda, where she was certain there would be thousands *more* reports waiting for her. If there was one advantage to being on deployment, it was that they were out of touch with the StarCom network until they powered up the mobile unit. Anyone who wanted to waste her time would have to wait.

At least until we power up the communications ship, she reminded herself, glancing at the fleet display. The communications starship seemed out of place, like an oversized bulk freighter, but it represented the changing face of war. Kat knew, from grim experience, that she should be *delighted* with a mobile StarCom, yet it wasn't an unmixed blessing. *And then we'll know everything that happened while we were in transit.*

She ate her breakfast, then stepped through the hatch and into the CIC. The timer had started a steady countdown, ticking down the seconds until the fleet reached the RV point. Kat sat down at her chair, hoping and praying that the Theocrats hadn't moved. She'd pushed her ships to the limit, but it had still taken five days to reach the enemy base. The Theocrats had had ample time to pack up and leave if they'd detected *Dandelion*'s presence. She wouldn't have blamed them for moving regularly either. The longer they stayed anywhere, the greater the chance of being detected and destroyed.

"Admiral," Kitty said, "we'll be at the RV point in five minutes."

"Very good," Kat said.

"And Captain Rogers sends his compliments, Admiral, and wonders what you intend to do with *Dandelion*," Kitty added. "She isn't one of our ships any longer."

Kat made a mental note to have a word with Captain Rogers, in private. She'd never really understood just how badly the Royal Navy looked down on colonials until she'd become a commanding officer in her own right. William had told her, more than once, that it irritated the colonials while making life harder for the Royal Navy. Irritated people were not inclined to cooperate.

"Please inform Captain Rogers that I will ask Captain McElney to accompany us to the enemy base," Kat said. She had no idea if *Dandelion* could be slotted into the squadron's datanet, but it should be possible. The destroyer wasn't *that* old. "If not . . . if he wants to return home . . . his loyalty is unquestionable."

Kitty nodded. "Aye, Admiral."

Kat keyed her console, bringing up the latest set of readiness reports. The training sessions she'd ordered had boosted the squadron's stats back to their wartime level, although she was all too aware that there were still problems. They'd simply allowed too much to slide in the year between the fall of Ahura Mazda and the return of the Theocratic diehards. She promised herself, silently, that she'd make sure that changed, once the diehards were dead and gone. She'd declined the king's offer of an appointment to Piker's Peak, or anything else that might take her off a command deck once and for all, but she could still have a major influence. Any fleet under *her* command was going to drill as if they were expecting war to break out tomorrow.

If you want peace, prepare for war, Kat thought. The galaxy would eventually see another major conflict. *And if you look ready to fight, you don't have to fight.*

"Admiral," Kitty said, "long-range sensors are picking up *Dandelion.*"

"Send a standard greeting," Kat said, "and invite her to take a place in our formation." She allowed herself a cold smile as the icon appeared on the display. "And then set course for the enemy base. I want to come out of hyperspace as close as possible to our target."

"Aye, Admiral."

Kat's smile grew wider. Most tacticians would raise hell about a plan that involved splitting the fleet, but Kat had considered it carefully before deciding the idea was workable. Four superdreadnoughts and their escorts would return to realspace while five more would lurk in hyperspace. If the enemy managed to jump into hyperspace, rather than fighting to the last, they'd run into a trap. There was significant risk in fighting in hyperspace, as Kat knew all too well, but it was manageable. The Theocrats could not be allowed to escape.

And they won't, she promised herself. *This is the end of the line.*

◆ ◆ ◆

"I've transferred most of the prisoners to the freighters, sir," the supply officer said. "But the ship isn't designed for transporting so many people."

"Then expand the life support," Admiral Zaskar ordered tartly. Why couldn't anyone think for themselves? He cursed his former superiors under his breath. "Make sure they know to behave during transit."

"Aye, Admiral," the officer said. "We made it clear to them . . ."

The alarms started to howl. Admiral Zaskar froze in horror, then spun around to look at the near-space display. A string of vortexes had opened, disgorging a fleet of enemy warships. Only four superdreadnoughts, according to his sensors, but they might as well have been a hundred. His missile supplies were so badly depleted that he suspected he couldn't have put up an effective fight against even *one* superdreadnought. They'd been found.

He turned and ran for the hatch, slapping his communicator on the way. "Bring the fleet to battlestations," he snapped. "Prepare to engage the enemy!"

His mind raced as he ran down the corridor, passing dozens of crewmen as they hurried to their combat stations. They'd kept their vortex generators powered down to avoid unnecessary wear and tear on the fragile devices, but . . . in hindsight, that might have been a mistake. The enemy hadn't *quite* come out of hyperspace right on top of them—he rather thought the enemy CO could have his navigator shot for stupidity—but they were far too close for him to avoid engagement. And a quarter of his supplies were still in the asteroid base.

We're doomed, he thought. Even if he managed somehow to get his fleet into hyperspace, it would mean abandoning things he desperately needed. The odds of successfully establishing a colony, already low, would drop still further. *There's no way out.*

He forced himself to slow down as he stepped into the CIC, doing his best to project an air of calm competence. Moses was already there, standing next to Askew; Admiral Zaskar wondered, sourly, what the foreign agent was thinking. There was no expression on Askew's face, damn the man, but he had to be terrified. Who knew what would happen if he were taken alive?

Admiral Zaskar took his seat. "Status report?"

"The fleet datanet is coming online, Admiral," the tactical officer reported. He sounded frightened, although he was trying to hide it. "Our ships are linking in now."

Too slow, Zaskar thought. Keeping the datanet down was another mistake, although it hadn't been unjustified at the time. The risk of a stray emission being picked up by a prowling enemy scout ship was too great. *They have us dead in their sights.*

"Order the freighters to start moving away from the fleet," he said. He was kicking and screaming on the way to the gallows, and he knew it, but something in him refused to give up. "And bring *Sword of Righteousness* into the battle line."

The tactical officer glanced at him. "Admiral?"

"Do it," Admiral Zaskar snapped. The superdreadnought's skeleton crew would have to use her maneuvering jets to get her into position, but there was no choice. She might absorb a handful of missiles that would otherwise strike his battle-worthy ships. "And stand by to deploy our remaining ECM drones. *All* of them."

"God is with us, my son," Moses said. "We will prevail."

Zaskar didn't bother to look at him. There was no escape, unless Askew's mystery backers chose to step in. And he had no idea if they *could* step in. And even if they could, why *would* they? None of the Great Powers would risk war with the Commonwealth over the pitiful remnants of the Theocratic Navy. Better to let Admiral Zaskar and his fleet die in fire, taking the evidence of outside involvement with them, than start a war.

"Admiral," the communications officer said, "I'm picking up a wide-band transmission on an open channel. They're signaling us!"

"They're signaling everyone," Admiral Zaskar said. The entire system would hear the message. "Put it through."

A voice, a woman's voice, echoed through the air. "This is Admiral Katherine Falcone of the Royal Tyre Navy," she said. "You are outnumbered and outgunned."

Admiral Zaskar stared, torn between horror and a grim awareness that God had brought the Theocracy's most dangerous enemy within striking range. If he killed Admiral Falcone, if he . . . He shook his head tiredly. Killing Kat Falcone would not bring the Theocracy back to life, let alone reverse the outcome of the war. Besides, he had no idea which ship was her flagship. His sensor systems appeared to believe that the message was coming from *every* enemy ship.

"If you surrender now, and make no attempt to kill prisoners, destroy your datacores, or otherwise cripple your vessels, we will spare your lives," Kat Falcone continued. "You will be returned to Ahura Mazda, where you will spend the rest of your days. But if you refuse to surrender, there will be no second chance. You and your ships will be utterly destroyed."

"Silence that woman," Moses hissed. "She will lure our men into sin!"

For once, you might have a point, Admiral Zaskar thought. *Everyone* could hear the enemy message. The fanatics would fight to the last, of course, but the less-committed spacers might be glad of a chance to surrender and return home. *How many of our men will decide that surrender is the best option?*

He considered it, briefly, before dismissing the thought. His spacers might be allowed to return home, but he'd be lucky if he was merely dumped into a penal colony. He'd committed war crimes, at least by their standards. Kat Falcone might be willing to let bygones be bygones, but very few others would agree. *She* certainly wouldn't be deciding his destiny. Admiral Zaskar and his senior officers would be marched to the airlock and thrown into space. There was little to be gained from surrendering his ships.

But my people would live, he thought. *My crew would survive.*

"I will address her," Moses said. He strode forward. "Give me the microphone."

"And stand by point defense," Admiral Zaskar added. The enemy was already in missile range. "They'll open fire at any moment."

Moses shot him a sharp look, then took the mike. "We are the custodians of the True Faith . . ."

◆ ◆ ◆

Well, Kat thought, *at least we know we found the right people.*

"Prepare to fire," she ordered, ignoring the misogyny. Still, the enemy CO, or whoever was speaking, was unusually polite for a Theocrat. She'd heard a great deal worse on Ahura Mazda. "Bring up tactical sensors to full power. Let them *know* they're being targeted."

"Aye, Admiral," Kitty said.

Kat nodded, studying the live feed from the stealth drones. The enemy didn't seem to have spotted them, even though they were quite close to their hulls. They'd kept their drives and sensors powered down to minimize the odds of detection, something that had come back to bite them hard. Their sensors were powering up now, but her drones had already gone dark and silent. The Theocrats would have real trouble spotting them.

One of their superdreadnoughts is in a very bad state, she thought. *But is it for real?*

Her eyes narrowed. The enemy ship wasn't even *trying* to power up her drive. Was she nothing more than a shipyard queen, used only as a source of spare parts? Kat tapped a command into her console, ordering the tactical crews to regard the enemy ship as a potential threat anyway. There was no reason to assume she couldn't fire missiles, even if her drives were offline. A Royal Navy superdreadnought was designed to continue fighting till the very end, with so many redundancies built into her command systems that it would take one hell of a battering to put her out of commission. She was sure the Theocrats had followed the same philosophy.

She frowned as her eyes moved to the freighters and, beyond them, to the asteroid base. It clearly hadn't been built by the Theocrats, at least not as a naval base. The freighters were maneuvering like wallowing sows, suggesting that they were fully laden. Kat gritted her teeth, wondering precisely what the Theocrats had taken. Starship parts? Or prisoners? Or . . . she shook her head. The freighters would need to be taken intact. They *had* to know what the enemy had been doing over the last few months . . .

And who has been backing them, Kat reminded herself. *We need to know that too.*

Kitty coughed. "They're still babbling . . ."

Kat sighed. "Signal all ships," she said. "Firing pattern beta-nine. Prepare to engage."

"Aye, Admiral," Kitty said.

We have them, Kat thought. *And they have to know we have them.*

She shook her head. There was nothing to be gained by waiting any longer. She'd hoped they'd surrender, but she hadn't expected it. The Theocrats had no reason to believe that she would keep her word, even though she certainly *intended* to honor her promises. She would happily allow their crewmen to return to their homeworld in exchange for their datacores and clear proof of who'd supplied them with weapons and tech.

"Fire," she ordered quietly.

Violence rocked as she emptied her external racks. The other three superdreadnoughts followed suit, their missiles boring through space towards their targets. Kat could have fired a bigger barrage—she was wryly aware that there would be plenty of armchair admirals who'd criticize her for not emptying her missile tubes too—but she wanted to try to take some of the enemy ships intact. If she was lucky, the missiles would cripple the ships, allowing them to be boarded.

"The enemy ships are returning fire," Kitty reported as red icons flashed to life on the display. "Missile tubes only, Admiral. No external racks."

And that one superdreadnought hasn't fired at all, Kat thought. It was quite promising. The enemy CO clearly didn't have enough missiles left to put up a proper fight. She could force him to expend his remaining stockpile relatively quickly. *And then we can batter his fleet into submission at leisure.*

"Tighten up the datanet," she ordered. The enemy missiles didn't seem to have any improved seeker heads, let alone penetration aides, but there was no point in taking chances. "And stand by to fire a second salvo."

"Aye, Admiral." Kitty checked her display. "The freighters are pulling away from the base."

"Detail a squadron of destroyers to round them up," Kat ordered. "And remind their commanders that they are authorized to accept surrenders."

She turned her attention to the display. Her missiles were entering the enemy point defense envelope. One way or the other, the engagement would be over soon . . .

CHAPTER THIRTY-SIX

UNCHARTED STAR SYSTEM

"Admiral," the tactical officer said, "the enemy missiles are getting through our defenses!"

"I can see that, idiot," Admiral Zaskar snarled.

He gritted his teeth. The Royal Navy's missiles had always been good—far too good. And their missile technology had clearly advanced over the last year. He'd done everything in his power to improve his point defense systems, particularly when he'd started integrating new technology into his ships, but it hadn't been very successful. Too many enemy missiles were breaking through the screen and flying towards his hulls. His ships were about to take a battering.

They could have fired more missiles, he thought as his ship fired a barrage of her own. It made no sense. *They're holding back.*

His blood ran cold. The Royal Navy wanted to *capture* his ships. Of *course* they did! They'd even tried to convince him to surrender, despite the political firestorm it would unleash back home. No, they wanted to take his ships reasonably intact. They'd aimed to cripple his ships, not destroy them. And . . .

A series of rumbles ran through the hull. "Direct hits," someone snapped. Red lights washed across the status display. "Major damage, decks . . ."

Admiral Zaskar tuned him out. *Righteous Revenge* could still fight, he assumed, but she wouldn't be able to fight for long. The damage was mounting up rapidly. Captain Geris had already dispatched the damage control teams, according to the stream of updates scrolling up in front of him, but they wouldn't be able to do enough to save the ship. The fleet was doomed. He doubted he could get even a single ship out of the trap before it was too late.

And they probably wouldn't accept surrender, he thought. *Not now.*

He sucked in his breath. They couldn't win a missile duel. He barely had enough missiles left for one final salvo. No, he needed to close the range and try to punch through the enemy formation. It wasn't much of a plan, and the odds were against them managing to survive long enough to open a vortex, but at least it would give him a chance to hurt the enemy. Who knew? Maybe they'd kill Kat Falcone after all.

"Captain Geris, ramp up the drives as much as possible," he ordered. "Take us into energy range."

"Aye, Admiral."

Admiral Zaskar glanced at Askew. "Sorry you came?"

The foreigner looked unconcerned. "I knew the job was dangerous when I took it."

"No doubt," Admiral Zaskar agreed. There was no way Askew could get off the ship, let alone transfer himself to his courier boat. The Royal Navy wouldn't shoot at lifepods deliberately, but the pods could still be mistaken for a weapon and blown out of space in passing. "Thank you for trying, at least."

He glanced at Moses, who was still raving into the microphone. Admiral Zaskar had no idea who Moses thought was listening, but it hardly mattered. They were on a death ride now, hoping to survive just long enough to get into energy range and give the enemy as hard a time as possible before inevitable destruction. It was hard to believe that a last-minute miracle would save them. Oddly, the thought calmed him. If there was nothing he could do to avoid death, he might as well accept it.

"Energy range in seven minutes," the tactical officer said. Another series of impacts ran through the hull. "Captain Geris is devoting all power to weapons, shields, and drives."

"Good thinking," Admiral Zaskar said. Turning off the life support was always chancy, but it wasn't as if they were going to need the resource for much longer. "Order all weapons to go to rapid fire as soon as we enter range."

"Aye, Admiral."

◆ ◆ ◆

"They're picking up speed," Kitty reported. "Admiral, they're heading right towards us!"

Kat had expected as much. The Theocracy had no qualms about using suicide tactics when necessary, even though they knew as well as she did that this was their *last* fleet. But then, they had no hope of getting out of the trap anyway. Ramming her ships was their only hope of taking a few of them with her. None of their missiles had broken through the point defense network.

"Order missile tubes to go to sprint mode," she said. "They are *not* to be allowed to enter energy range."

"Aye, Admiral."

Kat leaned back in her chair, projecting an air of calm as the enemy ships advanced on her position. Normally, they'd be spitting missiles at a terrifying rate; this time, their fire was slacking off rapidly. They were either running out of missiles or trying to conserve them against some hypothetical future contingency. She shook her head. That was unlikely. Their only hope of hurting her ships involved firing so many missiles that her point defense couldn't swat them all out of space. But their tubes were falling silent.

They need to get into energy range, she thought. The damage was mounting up rapidly, but the enemy ships were still coming. She would have been impressed if the situation hadn't been so dangerous. *And I can't let them get into energy range.*

An icon—an enemy cruiser—vanished from the display, followed by a pair of destroyers and an armed freighter. Their superdreadnoughts kept advancing, even though their tubes had stopped firing. They really were determined to just come to grips with her. She watched, coldly, as one of the superdreadnoughts staggered, bleeding atmosphere and debris into the icy vacuum of space. It fell out of formation, then exploded into a ball of superheated plasma. Kat grinned, savagely. Of the four enemy superdreadnoughts confirmed to have survived the battle over Ahura Mazda, two had been destroyed and a third was a powerless hulk. The final superdreadnought wouldn't last long.

"Concentrate missile fire on the superdreadnought," she ordered. "The smaller ships are to be engaged once they enter energy range."

"Aye, Admiral."

◆ ◆ ◆

"Admiral . . ."

"I saw," Zaskar said stiffly. He had one superdreadnought left. Deep in his heart, he *knew* his ship was about to die too. "Keep us heading straight towards the enemy and . . ."

His ship shook, violently. The lights dimmed, just for a second, before the emergency power came online. He felt lightheaded as the gravity field weakened, suggesting that he might find himself floating at any moment. A number of consoles went dark and refused to boot up again, no matter how many times their operators kicked and swore at them.

Admiral Zaskar found his voice. "Report!"

"The drive section has been destroyed," the tactical officer said, after a moment. "Power is down throughout most of the ship. Shields are gone, weapons are offline . . . we're drifting out of formation!"

And doomed, Admiral Zaskar thought numbly. He could *feel* the ship dying. The constant thrumming of the drives was gone. *There's no hope any longer.*

"Get me a link to the rest of the fleet," he ordered. "Now!"

The communications officer paled. "Admiral . . . communications are down too."

"I see," Admiral Zaskar said. The unfortunate officer looked surprised that he hadn't been summarily shot. "What *do* we have?"

"Nothing, sir," the tactical officer said. "The internal datanet is barely functional, external sensors are offline, and . . ."

Admiral Zaskar held up a hand to cut off the list of failed or failing systems. The ship was definitely doomed. *That* much was true. And they no longer had even the faintest hope of taking an enemy ship with them. It was a minor miracle they'd survived the impact that had taken out the drives. A powerless ship was a sitting duck. Soon the enemy would either blow them to dust or land marines on the hull. And then . . . it would be the end.

My crew will survive if I surrender, Admiral Zaskar thought. *Or if they get into the lifepods in time . . .*

"Order the crew to head for the lifepods," he said. "This ship has to be abandoned."

The tactical officer's head exploded. Admiral Zaskar stared at the headless corpse in shock, then spun around. Askew was holding a gun in his hand, sweeping it around to target everyone in the CIC. Zaskar reached for the pistol at his belt, but it was already too late. Askew was pointing his gun directly at Admiral Zaskar's head.

"What . . . ?"

"It hasn't been a pleasure," Askew said. The foreign agent's face looked different. "And we don't want any of you taken alive."

"You'll die too," Admiral Zaskar managed. He'd expected that Askew would eventually find it convenient to betray them, but not like this. "You'll . . ."

A dull rumble ran through the ship. The gravity reversed itself a second later, sending them both flying upwards. Askew fired, but the sudden change in perspective caused him to miss before he crashed into the ceiling. Zaskar heard a dull thud as his head cracked open, the gravity reversing itself back again seconds later. He fell back to the floor, landing badly. His leg shattered under the force of the impact.

He's dead, Admiral Zaskar thought through the pain. His vision was already blurring. *He's dead and . . .*

Askew's body exploded.

◆ ◆ ◆

"The enemy superdreadnought has lost power completely," Kitty reported. "She's streaming atmosphere and lifepods."

"Order the marines to board," Kat snapped. It was risky—the enemy might be waiting for her marines to come within range before they triggered the self-destruct—but she needed whatever information could be drawn from the superdreadnought. They had to take the chance. "And mop up the remaining enemy ships!"

She gritted her teeth as the final starships plunged into her point defense like lemmings running over a cliff. They didn't have a hope of getting close enough to do any damage, let alone actually damaging her ships, but they kept coming anyway. She would have accepted a surrender, she told herself, time and time again. She *would* have let them live. But the enemy were too proud or too desperate to let themselves be taken alive. One by one, they died.

And the Theocracy is dying with them, Kat told herself. *This is the end.*

"Admiral, the majority of the freighters are offering to surrender," Kitty said. "But they want ironclad guarantees of their personal survival."

Kat frowned. *That* didn't sound like the Theocracy. Pirates? Smugglers? Or simply the unreliable officers the enemy CO would normally have had executed if he hadn't been so desperately short of manpower. ONI had concluded that the superdreadnoughts hadn't had full crews, and Kat was inclined to agree with the intelligence. The Theocracy had been running short of experienced officers and crew long before the end of the war.

"Agree," she said. If the enemy crews had conducted atrocities, they'd spend the rest of their lives on a penal colony. "But they are to *cooperate*."

She glanced down at her display. "And send marines to secure the asteroid base as well as the freighters," she added. "I want to know *everything* they've been doing."

"Aye, Admiral."

Kat allowed herself a thin smile. They'd won. There might be a handful of smaller ships out there, destroyers or frigates that had been hunting for targets while their base had been attacked, but they wouldn't pose a long-term threat. Asher Dales and the other liberated worlds would be safe enough with a couple of destroyers each. The compromise King Hadrian and the Opposition had worked out wouldn't please everyone, particularly the fire-eaters on either side, but the agreement would calm down the entire sector. Pirates, freebooters, and would-be empire-builders couldn't take root when the planets were defended and spacelanes were regularly patrolled.

And many of the liberated worlds will become our allies, in time, she told herself. *And new markets for our goods too.*

"Order the communications ship to power up the StarCom," she said. "I'll need to send a message home as soon as possible."

"Aye, Admiral."

"And invite Sir William to join me," Kat added. "We have a lot to discuss."

She returned her attention to the display. The marines were going through the ships now, steadily arresting their crews and powering the vessels down until they could be searched from top to bottom. A number of crewmen were claiming to have been kidnapped and forced into servitude, but they'd still be kept under arrest and separated from the other prisoners until the truth could be established. Hopefully, Kat told herself, they wouldn't have been forced to commit atrocities. They didn't need *that* sort of stain on their record.

She studied the display, her eyes tracking the damaged ships. The Theocratic Navy was dead now, dead and gone. There would be people on Ahura Mazda who'd refuse to believe it, of course, and do their best to make sure that others didn't believe it . . . It didn't matter now. A handful of destroyers would be more than enough to keep control of the high orbitals and back up the provisional government. Who knew? Perhaps this final crushing defeat would be enough to convince the bitter-enders to give up.

Sure, she told herself. *And pigs will fly.*

◆ ◆ ◆

Lieutenant Chas Potter tried hard not to feel nervous as he glided through the gash in the superdreadnought's hull and dropped down to the deck. His combat suit flashed up a series of warnings, reminding him that there was neither atmosphere nor gravity. He wondered, wryly, if whoever had programmed the suit's systems thought that marines were idiots. The gash in the hull was pretty clear proof, as far as he was concerned, that there was no atmosphere. The only real question was just how *much* of the ship had vented. There was a very good chance that there were compartments, deeper within the hull, that had remained pressurized.

He signaled for his squad to follow him, then headed down the corridor. The enemy ship was dark and creepy, illuminated only by his helmet's lights. Bodies drifted through the shadows, some mutilated so badly that there was little hope of identifying them. Not, he supposed, that it mattered. The bodies would probably be sent plunging into the nearest star after they'd been logged, unless they happened to have living relatives on Ahura Mazda. He couldn't help wondering just how many of those relatives would be keen to claim *any* connection to the dead men.

Probably none of them, since they were on the wrong side all along, he thought. He'd seen enough of enemy society to know that a connection to a defeated military unit wouldn't be taken lightly. *They'd be happier if they had a chance to claim the men died long before the end of the war.*

"The CIC should be through here," he said as the marines made their way deeper into the ship. The ship's internal systems had apparently failed completely. Hatches that should have slammed closed at the merest hint of a hull breach had remained open, allowing the entire vessel to vent. He suspected deliberate sabotage. A failure on such a scale was largely unprecedented on a warship. The only compartment that had remained sealed was the CIC. "We'll have to break through the hatch."

His squad set the charges, then took cover as they detonated. The hatch exploded inwards, revealing a blackened compartment. Chas frowned, wondering, for an insane moment, if the ship's consoles had actually exploded. *That* only happened in bad movies, where the scriptwriters thought that starship designers concealed explosive packs under consoles to make sure they exploded at the right moment. But the CIC had been completely destroyed.

"The blast went off inside the compartment," Sergeant Smyth said. He was the squad's explosives expert as well as Chas's second-in-command. "And it was largely contained by the bulkheads."

"Thus ensuring the complete destruction of everyone in the room," Chas finished. The briefing notes had claimed that a superdreadnought normally had around nine or ten people in the CIC. If they'd been there when the blast had gone off, they'd been vaporized. It didn't look as if any DNA or anything would be recovered. A suicide attempt? Or something much more dangerous? "Why didn't they just trigger the self-destruct?"

"Perhaps they'd lost all connection to the rest of the ship, sir," Smyth speculated. "Or something along those lines . . ."

"Then we continue to search the ship," Chas said. "Maybe someone survived."

"I doubt it, sir," Smyth said. "I'm starting to think that they *intended* to make sure that none of their crew survived."

"Yeah," Chas said. "I'm starting to think so too."

His radio bleeped. "Lieutenant, get your squad down to the weapons bay," Captain Loomis said. "I'm going to need your help to secure the section."

Chas blinked. "On our way, sir," he said. Had Loomis discovered a handful of survivors? Or . . . or what? He didn't know. "What have you found?"

"Bad news," Loomis said. The captain sounded shaken. "Get down here at once. I think . . . I think this is political."

"Understood, sir," Chas said. He'd heard all the rumors. None of them had been very reassuring. Anything that could shake Loomis, a man who'd been in combat since before the war, couldn't be good. He'd seen the elephant long before Chas had gone to boot camp, let alone passed through OCS. "We're on our way."

CHAPTER THIRTY-SEVEN

UNCHARTED STAR SYSTEM

It felt, William decided as he followed Kat into the secure conference room, a little like old times. They were both older and wiser now, and they'd grown apart over the last year, but at the same time, he couldn't help feeling a camaraderie with her that went well beyond anything he'd felt for any of his other commanding officers. She'd treated him better, he thought, than any of the others. And, in some ways, she'd acknowledged her weaknesses in a way that none of his previous COs had. It was a lot easier to respect someone who was honest than someone who tried to hide her insecurities behind a brash or bullish exterior.

But this wasn't old times, he reminded himself sharply. *Someone* could object to his presence, on the undeniable grounds that he was a foreign naval officer, which would put Kat in an awkward position. William silently promised himself that he'd go, if someone complained. Kat's enemies wouldn't hesitate to use him against her if they saw an opportunity to strike. They'd be able to create enough of a stink to make her life difficult indeed.

"Be seated," Kat ordered. "What do you have for us?"

William sat, his gaze sweeping the room. Captain Janice Wilson was seated at the table, flanked by two of her underlings; her face was pale, as if she was unsure of just how bad the situation had truly become.

General Winters stood behind her at parade rest, but William had no difficulty reading the tension in his body. They were so concerned about what they'd found, he realized numbly, that they'd barely noticed his presence. He had a nasty feeling it was very bad news.

"We searched the disabled superdreadnought *thoroughly*," Janice said. She sounded badly shaken. "We didn't find much until we inspected the weapons bay, where we recovered a missile that had been removed from its launch tube. Their weapons officers believed, apparently, that there was a defect in the drive that meant it couldn't be fired at an enemy target."

And they never thought of turning it into a mine, William considered. *Did they even know how to remove the warhead or reprogram the seeker head?*

Kat nodded, impatiently. "Were they trying to set off the warhead inside the ship?"

"No, Admiral," Janice said. She took a long breath. "We . . . we discovered that someone had removed the original seeker head and replaced it with . . . ah, with a somewhat improved version. They . . . they took a number of freely available components and rigged them together, following an emergency conversion plan. And . . . and we checked the missile itself."

She paused. "Admiral . . . the missile's ID . . . we checked it against our records. And it was captured when we overran the enemy naval base at Galahad."

William blinked. "I thought the Theocracy's record keeping was so bad they might well have two or more missiles with the same ID."

"No, sir," Janice said. "We logged the ID ourselves when the missiles were captured and secured, then shipped to the dump at Razwhana. Missile production was falling as we retooled for the switch to next-gen missiles, so there was a concern that we might need to modify the enemy missiles and turn them against their former masters. Ah . . . a handful of engineers had quite a few ideas for jury-rigged improvements."

Kat's voice was very hard. "And then *what*? What happened to the missile?"

Janice twisted her hands. "There was some discussion about fitting them to older ships as makeshift convoy escorts, then . . . well, once the war ended, they were eventually slated for destruction. Officially, they were launched into the nearest star. That's what the records claim, Admiral. But instead they ended up here."

". . . Shit," Kat said. "Do you have any idea what you're saying? Any idea at all?"

"Yes, Admiral," Janice said. She made a visible attempt to calm herself. "Someone in the Commonwealth gave them back to the Theocrats."

"Not someone in the Commonwealth," Kat said. "Someone embedded within the Royal Navy."

William felt his heart start to pound. "It might not be someone very high up," he pointed out carefully. "A supply clerk at a place like Razwhana might well be able to cook the books without cover from someone further up the chain. Did anyone bother to verify that the missiles were actually destroyed?"

"Except someone backed Admiral Morrison, and then killed him," Kat reminded him. "This is a little more serious than selling the missiles to pirates! How would a mere supply clerk even be able to *locate* the Theocrats? *We* only stumbled across them by sheer luck!"

"True," William conceded after a moment. He had no doubt that a clerk could have had the missiles shipped to a designated location, then screwed around with the paperwork to make it appear that the missiles had been destroyed instead. And yet, making contact with the Theocrats would have been damn near impossible. There had to be more than one person involved. "What else did they get?"

"The conversion plan came out of an emergency engineering study," Janice said after a moment. "The components involved are all off-the-shelf, dual-use civilian stuff, but . . . putting them together would require a *lot* of trained engineers. I don't think the Theocrats did it themselves."

"They had help," Kat said. "Who? And why?"

"I don't know," Janice said. "Razwhana Depot was shut down shortly after the war. The records state that the vast majority of captured supplies were either destroyed or reprocessed for scrap. We couldn't *give* the captured spare parts away. The crew were reassigned and . . . well, I don't know what happened to them. They'll have to be tracked down."

"There must be records," William protested.

"I'm sure there are," Janice agreed. "But I don't have access to them. We'll have to submit a formal request to Tyre, then get the CBI involved. Whoever did this is an outright traitor."

"It will get political," General Winters rumbled.

Kat looked around the table. "Who benefits from killing millions of people?"

"You can justify anything if you try hard enough," Janice said cynically. "A million lives? It's so unimaginably huge that it's just a statistic. No one can grasp the sheer *size* of a million lives. They're just . . . *numbers*."

"They have lives." William's voice was icy. "They were born, they grew up, they had lovers and children and ups and downs . . . and then they died. They're not just *numbers*."

"Yes," Janice said. "But how can we grasp a million individual lives?"

William felt sick. He knew, from growing up on a harsh world, that sometimes one *did* have to make hard decisions when a community's survival hung in the balance. Yes, there were times when someone had to be left to die because keeping them alive would cost the community dearly. The cold equations demanded it. But cold calculation didn't make such decisions any easier to bear. A plan that required the cool sacrifice of millions of lives was truly horrific. Whoever was behind it was a monster.

"We can't," Kat said quietly. "Janice . . . what other evidence have you found?"

"Very little, so far," Janice said. "But there's a piece of circumstantial evidence that may, in its own way, be more alarming. The enemy CIC was destroyed, utterly. My experts say the blast was roughly comparable to an implant's self-destruct."

William frowned. "What . . . ?"

"A handful of Special Forces troopers are heavily enhanced to allow them to perform otherwise impossible missions," General Winters said. "Their implants are designed to self-destruct if the trooper is captured. The blast is powerful enough to literally vaporize the trooper's entire body, to the point where even DNA samples cannot be recovered. Anyone standing within ten meters would almost certainly be killed by the blast."

"I didn't know that," William said.

"It is not commonly advertised," Janice said. "But the experts believe that such a device, or something comparable, detonated inside that superdreadnought."

"So the Theocrats had help," Kat said. "Someone from the Commonwealth." She took a long breath. "Continue to gather information," she ordered. "Interrogate the prisoners, find out if any of them know anything useful; search the asteroids and the remaining ships from top to bottom, looking for clues. And do not, and I mean *do not*, share this any further. I'm going to have to take it to the king personally."

William frowned. "Just the king?"

"And the Grand Admiral," Kat said. "And"—she ran her hand through her hair—"I don't know, William. My father believed that someone very high up betrayed us, back when the war began. Right now, I don't know who we can trust. Any investigation into this affair is going to have to be conducted very quietly."

And quiet is one word that cannot be applied to the king, William thought grimly. *What happens if he starts shouting the news from the rooftops?*

"I believe this is something I have a duty to report to my superiors," Janice said carefully. "Admiral, I . . ."

"You will *not* discuss it with anyone until I've spoken directly to the king," Kat said. "That is an order, *Captain*, which you may have in writing if you wish."

She might need it in writing, William thought, concealing his wince. *Janice will wind up in real trouble if her superiors accuse her of withholding vital information.*

"Yes, Admiral," Janice said.

Kat stood. "I'll make contact now," she said. "Until we have clear orders, continue the investigation. If there are any more clues here, waiting to be found, I want them found."

"Yes, Admiral," Winters said. He cleared his throat. "Ah . . . what about Commodore McElney?"

William met his eyes, evenly. "I *do* know how to keep secrets, General."

"He does," Kat said. She smiled, just for a second. It made her look young again. "But William, you'll have to stay here for the moment. We could probably send *Dandelion* home now, if you wish."

"I probably should," William said. Neither Tanya nor her father were going to be happy, particularly if William couldn't return to Asher Dales. "And if the king wants me to stay here, that is what I will do."

◆ ◆ ◆

Kat felt her insides churning uncomfortably as she made the walk from the conference room to her cabin, the sensation reminding her of the times when she'd been summoned to her father's study as a young girl to explain the sort of misbehavior that couldn't be handled by her nannies or the governess. She'd never been quite sure what to expect when she knocked on Duke Falcone's door: a kind and caring father who'd understood his youngest daughter more than she'd realized at the time, or a stern patriarch who was irritated at having to take time away from important matters to deal with a little brat. Now . . . now she wasn't sure what to expect either. Who knew *how* the king would react?

He won't be pleased to hear this, she thought. She doubted the political problems on Tyre had gotten any better in the time she'd spent in transit. *But he has to hear it anyway.*

She walked into her cabin, keyed her terminal for a direct link to the StarCom, and through the StarCom to Tyre, and sat down. Her father had believed that someone had been Admiral Morrison's patron, and that someone had taken steps to make sure they were never identified, but he'd never quite figured out why. Had they been trying to cover up their mistake in pushing Admiral Morrison into a post that had proved disastrous? Or had they genuinely intended to sell out the Commonwealth to the Theocracy? Kat had seen enough of the Theocracy to know that they wouldn't hesitate to liquidate the former ruling class if they'd won the war, but someone back on Tyre might not have believed it. Or . . . She shook her head. Who had backed Morrison and why was a question that someone else would have to answer.

Someone would need to have a motive to start a war, she thought. *But that would be utterly insane.*

The king's face appeared on the display. "Good morning, Kat," he said. He sounded vaguely irritated. "I trust you have a good reason for summoning the Grand Admiral and myself from an important conference?"

"Yes, Your Majesty," Kat said. She glanced at the stream of details under the display. It was morning on Tyre, wasn't it? She'd been on Ahura Mazda time for months. "The good news is that we found and destroyed the Theocratic fleet."

The king's eyes darkened. "And the bad news?"

"We've discovered evidence that they were backed by someone in the Commonwealth," Kat said. "And that person would have to be *very* high up."

Her mind raced. How many people had that sort of power? Any of the dukes could have done it, with a little care; they could have funded the entire enemy fleet out of pocket change and used their facilities to produce spare parts.

But they'd get nothing out of it, she thought as she outlined the remainder of the story. Were they being blackmailed? Had Admiral Morrison genuinely been a Theocratic spy? Or . . . She gritted her teeth. Nothing about the affair made sense, which meant she was missing something. *I might not be able to see how any traitor might benefit, but the king or the Grand Admiral might have some ideas.*

"I see," the king said slowly. His face was very composed. "Do you have any solid proof?"

"We have proof that missiles we captured were returned to the Theocracy and used against us," Kat said, firmly. The records would have to be checked carefully, but she knew in her heart that Janice was right. "And that means that we were betrayed."

"Again," the king said. "There are certainly quite a few people who would go to extreme lengths to force us to withdraw from the sector."

Kat didn't doubt it. A year of battling to retain enough ships to provide the liberated worlds with at least some degree of protection had soured her on Parliament. She couldn't understand why her brother, as stiff-necked as he'd been when she was a child, didn't see that the sector needed protection. Hopefully, now that the Theocratic Navy had been destroyed for good, things would start to calm down. There would be no need to deploy superdreadnoughts. Perhaps they could work out a compromise that kept smaller vessels rotating through the sector.

Peter wouldn't sentence millions of people to death, she thought. She was fairly sure of *that*, no matter how irritating her brother could be. *But there are dukes and duchesses who would do whatever it took to improve their bottom line.*

"Thank you for bringing this to me," the king said. "How long do you think you'll need to complete your investigation of the asteroid base?"

"The preliminary investigation should be completed in a day or two," Kat said after a moment's thought. She'd seen asteroids searched before, and this one didn't look particularly unusual. "A more *thorough* search will take months."

The king nodded. "Very good," he said. "Once that preliminary investigation is over, you are to bring your fleet back to Tyre. Do *not* return to Ahura Mazda. Just head straight for the Gap and return home. Maintain strict communications silence. I also . . ."

Kat blinked. "Your Majesty?"

"It's impossible to tell who to trust these days," the king said. "I have a feeling that whoever is behind this, whoever it is, will do something stupidly violent. There are already mutterings in the hallways of power about something truly important being planned. I'd like to have people I can trust on hand in case the shit hits the fan."

Kat swallowed, hard. It wasn't obvious, certainly not to an outside observer, but a high-ranking nobleman had considerable resources. A ducal family owned everything from actual warships to clients in high places. Someone who decided to cause trouble could cause a *hell* of a lot of trouble, particularly if their actions came out of nowhere. And whoever was behind the scheme to keep the sector unstable, whatever they thought they stood to gain, had nothing to lose.

Particularly if they think they can seize enough of the levers of power to overawe any potential opposition, she thought. Someone who captured Tyre's high orbitals and the orbiting battlestations would be in a position to dictate terms to the planet. *And it might just be doable.*

"I can't believe we're discussing . . . *this*," she said. Her father would never have let it happen. "Your Majesty . . ."

"Things have changed while you've been away," the king said. "Politics have gotten nastier, Kat. There's a subtle war underway for control of the planetary defenses . . . as well as everything else. Clients are being swapped out at a moment's notice. We might need a fighting force we can trust."

"I understand, Your Majesty," she said. Her throat was suddenly treacherously dry. "I won't let you down."

CHAPTER THIRTY-EIGHT

TYRE

"That's another black-ops facility, Your Grace," Alexander Masterly said. "We were only able to obtain the project's codename: Hyperion."

Peter frowned. He'd ordered Masterly and Masterly and a few other agents to work on tracing the missing funds. It hadn't been an easy task. Some of the money seemed to have been diverted to pork projects—spaceports on isolated worlds, long-term industrial development programs—while the rest had either been blurred into the general military fund or earmarked for classified programs. It was hard to tell what had *really* been going on during the war.

Father must have known where the money was going, Peter told himself. *But why didn't he keep better records?*

"I see," he said. The king had to have kept proper records. If nothing else, he'd need to know where the money was going. Peter's father had often remarked that lying was bad enough, but not keeping track of your own lies was worse. "Make a note of it for later attention."

"Yes, sir," Alexander said.

Peter keyed his datapad, studying the latest developments. The bill to impeach the king hadn't been made public, yet, but everyone who was anyone knew that *something* was in the works. There were few true secrets in High Society. It was hard—almost impossible—to say which way *everyone* would jump. The Opposition wasn't sure of enough votes, yet, to press for impeachment, while the king presumably didn't have enough votes to make a show of strength. Peter found that reassuring and worrying at the same time. On one hand, if the king could defeat the bill before it was even read, he'd have done it by now; on the other, if the king felt insecure, he might do something drastic.

And the situation on the streets is getting worse, Peter thought. *Who knows where it will all end?*

He shook his head. The combination of the convoy's destruction and wave after wave of unemployment had proved disastrous. Violent crime, including attacks on immigrants and tourists, was on the rise, while his security staff were logging thousands of threats against him each day. Most of them would be nothing more than loudmouths relieving their feelings by sending threatening messages, but they all had to be investigated. Peter had doubled the security around the mansion and everywhere else of importance, as had everyone else, including the king. But there were limits to how much they could do.

"Keep me informed on progress," he said. He studied Masterly and Masterly's report for a long moment. Most of the money appeared to have been wasted, rather than put aside for selfish or malicious purposes, but it was hard to be sure. Just because he couldn't see any long-term value in the pork projects didn't mean that someone else couldn't either. "Are there any other issues of concern?"

"Just one," Alexander said. He sounded oddly hesitant. "As you know, Your Grace, we have been monitoring the long-term health of the corporation and its subsections."

"I should know that," Peter said, irritated. "I receive briefings every two days."

Alexander nodded. "It's not easy to monitor employee morale," he said. "No one believes, for example, that anonymous surveys are truly anonymous. A person who is dissatisfied may well decline to put that to paper, for fear that it will be held against him at his next performance review. It may be illegal to fire someone for expressing an opinion, particularly an opinion they were asked to express, but there are plenty of ways to get rid of someone without *technically* breaking any laws."

"I know," Peter said. His father had told him, time and time again, that people would tell him what they thought he wanted to hear. Worse, they would conceal problems until they turned into disasters if they feared he would shoot the messenger. Bad news could not be allowed to fester, yet how could he deal with it if he didn't know it existed? "And what's happening?"

"Morale is going downhill sharply," Alexander said. "There have been rumors of layoffs for months, Your Grace, but now they've actually started to materialize. People are worried that they're going to be next, and that is having an obvious impact on their work. Productivity is falling too."

"And there's nothing we can do about it," Peter said. "Or is there?"

He looked at his hands, helplessly. The hell of it was that there was no way to speed up the process and get it over with. He'd seriously considered making sweeping cuts, in the hopes it would be enough to allow him to preserve what was left, but the council had refused to even consider the option. They wanted to keep as much as they could. Peter understood the impulse, but he had a feeling it was making things worse. No employee could feel safe these days.

And we have too many other problems right now, he thought. *What do we do?*

"I don't believe so," Alexander said. "We do have some fairly precise estimates of how many cuts we'll need to make . . ."

"Which isn't politically feasible at the moment," Peter said. He wondered, again, how his father had managed to balance running a corporation with his political work. Lucas Falcone had had a good staff, which Peter had inherited, but there were still too many things that demanded his personal input. "But I'll take it back to the council . . ."

His terminal bleeped. "Your Grace," Yasmeena said. "You have a secure call from Duke Rudbek."

"Put him through," Peter said, dismissing Alexander and Clive Masterly with a wave of his hand. "And then inform my next appointment that I may be delayed."

Duke Rudbek's image appeared on the terminal. "Peter, my boy," he said in a jovial tone that had alarm bells ringing in Peter's head. "Perhaps you'd do me the honor of joining me and a few guests for dinner? My chef has prepared a delicious repast of traditional food from Eulalie."

Peter's blood ran cold. Eulalie. They'd agreed that *Eulalie* would be the codeword for any urgent developments related to the king and the bill to impeach him. Duke Rudbek would not have used it unless the situation was truly urgent. And his attempt to be coy about saying the word, doing his best to work it into casual conversation, was worrying. He might have reason to believe the secure line was not secure.

And any listening ears will probably have no doubt that something significant has been said, Peter thought. *It would be an insult to their intelligence to think otherwise.*

"I'd be happy to attend," he said for the benefit of any eavesdroppers. "Should I bring my wife and children?"

"It's more of a casual dinner," Duke Rudbek said. "We don't want to be in *all* the society pages."

"Merely the most important ones," Peter said dryly. Taking his wife and children would suggest that the affair had actually been a highly exclusive party rather than a networking dinner. People would talk, particularly the people who felt insulted that they hadn't been invited. "I'll see you tonight, then."

"Five o'clock, please," Duke Rudbek said. "And thank you."

His image vanished. Peter stared at the display, feeling a chill creeping into his heart. Something had happened, clearly. Something had happened that had forced Duke Rudbek, a man who was in no way a coward, to skulk around like a common criminal.

Kat is lucky, he thought ruefully. *She's allowed to have friends.*

He pushed the thought aside as he called Yasmeena, told her about the dinner appointment, and went back to work. The question of precisely what had happened nagged at his mind as he read report after report, chaired two committee meetings that went nowhere, and attended a session on training materials for the next generation of workers. He couldn't help thinking that that was a little optimistic. Masterly and Masterly had been right. The corporation was bleeding to death from a thousand cuts.

The situation will settle, eventually, he told himself firmly. The peacetime economy would stabilize sooner or later. *But we cannot hide from the fact that it will get worse before it gets better.*

He was almost relieved to board his aircar at the end of the day and take flight, soaring over the city towards Rudbek Mansion. He knew he had no shortage of reports to read and paperwork to sign, but he just relaxed into the seat instead and closed his eyes. Perhaps it was time to add another layer of senior managers, people who could make decisions without consulting the CEO. But that would just make it harder for him to truly understand what was going on. And someone could easily pull the wool over his eyes if they had bad intentions.

Rudbek Mansion came into view, a futuristic building resting in the middle of a forest. It looked, Peter had often thought, like an unrealistic starship on the verge of taking flight. His father had told him that the original Rudbek had disdained the fashion for mansion designs that dated all the way back to the prespace era on Old Earth. He'd wanted something that symbolized his corporation's determination to keep expanding until it reached the farthest star. Peter had to admit that the old man had succeeded.

And half the society dames say it lacks dignity, he thought. There was a message of defiance too, for anyone who cared to look. *But a duke doesn't have to care about dignity.*

The aircar landed neatly on a pad. A young woman wearing a formal uniform greeted Peter and led him through a maze of corridors. Peter couldn't help admiring the interior design, a strange combination of luxury starship and hotel. Walls were covered in screens rather than paintings; servants wore simple uniforms rather than the elaborate designs favored by the rest of High Society. It was, Peter conceded, rather refreshing.

"Peter," Duke Rudbek said, as Peter was shown into the small dining room. "Thank you for coming."

Peter nodded, looking around the compartment. Duchess Zangaria, Duke Tolliver, Israel Harrison . . . it was practically a working dinner. A chill ran down his spine as he realized the implications. They'd agreed not to meet regularly for fear of tipping off the king. Duke Rudbek wouldn't have called them if the situation wasn't urgent. The meeting alone would be far too revealing.

"I suppose you're wondering why I called you here," Duke Rudbek said once Peter had taken a seat at the table. A server delivered a mug of coffee and then departed as silently as she'd come. "Matters have . . . taken an alarmingly dangerous turn."

He paused. "Two weeks ago, the remnants of the Theocratic Navy were destroyed."

Duchess Zangaria blinked. "I think your definition of *bad news* requires some work."

"*That's* good news," Duke Rudbek said. "But this was two *weeks* ago."

Peter stared at him. "And we haven't heard a peep about this?"

"No," Duke Rudbek told him. "Most of my sources in the navy are entirely unaware there even was an engagement. I only heard about this through a source in the palace itself. There is a total information blackout. I'm not even sure that the garrison on Ahura Mazda knows that the threat is over."

"You'd think the navy would be telling everyone," Duchess Zangaria said. "Every crown we spent on the deployment to the occupied sector has just been justified."

"You'd think," Duke Rudbek agreed. He took a long breath. "It gets worse. The post-battle investigation, according to my source, uncovered proof that someone was supporting the Theocrats. Someone from within the Commonwealth itself. Someone . . . fairly high up the chain."

Peter felt as if the ground had just shifted under his feet. It was bad enough to think that one of the other interstellar powers might have quietly backed the Theocracy. He could see the logic behind keeping the Royal Navy distracted, but it was madness. The prospect of a full-fledged interstellar war against someone more advanced than the Theocrats was terrifying. But . . . if someone in the Commonwealth was behind the insurgency . . .

A nasty thought ran through his mind. He didn't want to face it.

Duchess Zangaria drew a long breath. "Who?"

"Well, any of us could have done it," Duke Rudbek said. He ignored Harrison's soft cough of disdain. "And so could a number of . . . let us say *lesser* aristocrats. But I think we know there is only one prime suspect."

"The king," Peter said. The thought was so shocking he could barely contemplate it. "Are you suggesting that the *king* deliberately *helped* the enemy?"

"It does make a certain kind of sense," Duke Rudbek pointed out. "Who benefits from a resurgent threat? The king, because it allows him to prolong the state of emergency and keep raking in taxes. How many of his powers will end with the state of emergency? And it isn't as if four enemy superdreadnoughts, or eight, or sixteen, would pose any *real* threat. They might be able to cause havoc in the occupied sector, but over here? They'd be smashed if they tried to hit a first-rank world. Maybe we should ask questions about why the bastards never tried to cross the Gap."

"I was under the impression that there was a greater chance of being detected if they tried," Peter said stiffly. Could the allegations be true? He didn't believe it . . . he didn't *want* to believe it. And yet, if one assumed the king might have set out to prolong his emergency powers . . . might he have provoked the war to *obtain* his emergency powers? Had it been the *king* behind Admiral Morrison? "I . . . if this is true . . ."

"If this is true," Duchess Zangaria repeated. "How do we know it *is* true? This . . . rumor could be designed to push us into an untenable position. Accusing the king of High Treason . . . if we were wrong, or right without a great deal of proof, we'd be in real trouble."

"My source was quite specific," Duke Rudbek said firmly. "And I have had no reason to doubt her before."

"That's how they lure you in," Duchess Zangaria said. "They feed you snippets of genuine information so that when they lie, you'll believe it. This could be nothing more than a cunning plot to destroy our credibility once and for all."

"Or a warning that the situation is an order of magnitude worse than we thought," Duke Rudbek said. "We will, of course, attempt to verify the information. However, assuming it is true . . . what do we do?"

"We move ahead with the impeachment bill," Peter said. "And brace ourselves for a violent response."

"And we move to secure the planetary defenses," Duke Rudbek added. "I'm trying to ensure that my clients are aware of the possible danger."

"And mine," Peter said. "But . . . you do realize this could end very badly?"

"It's already bad," Duke Rudbek said. "Israel?"

"Right now, there's no way we could guarantee a victory," Harrison said. "The impeachment bill rests on shaky foundations. We would have to prove that the king is either unsuitable for his position or engaged in criminal behavior. And, so far, we have no actual proof of either."

"I believe we can impeach him for whatever the hell we like," Duchess Zangaria observed archly.

"Yes, Your Grace," Harrison said. "We could impeach him for wearing flowered underpants, if we could convince a majority of Parliament to support us. And yes, it would be perfectly legal. But we would have to convince Parliament that wearing flowered underpants is something so . . . so unsuitable that it justifies impeachment. And the MPs, in particular, would have to justify their vote to their constituencies. I think it would be easier to impeach him for wearing the wrong underwear than high treason."

Peter resisted the urge to snort, rudely. "So we focus on something we *can* prove," he said. "Misuse of taxpayers' money—that should look good in the newscasts—and interfering with the withdrawal from the occupied sector. We can even press to impeach him on the grounds that he's done everything in his power to prolong the state of emergency. That's true, even if we *don't* have proof he supplied the Theocrats."

"And we keep making preparations to defang him as soon as the vote is passed," Duke Rudbek warned. "We *cannot* risk giving him a chance to hit back."

"We could move first," Duchess Zangaria pointed out. "Defang him, *then* impeach him."

"It would bring the political system crashing down," Harrison said. "Once the precedent for acting outside the law is set, we'd never be able to get away from it."

"Yes," Duke Rudbek said. He looked at Peter. "There's one other thing you need to know."

Peter looked back at him evenly. "And that is?"

"Your sister was in command of the force that smashed the Theocratic base," Duke Rudbek said. "And she contacted the king directly, as a member of his Privy Council. What does that tell you about where her loyalties lie?"

"I don't know," Peter said. "But if this . . . *situation* . . . really does get out of hand, a great many people are going to have to decide which side they're on."

"And hope it isn't the one that *loses*," Harrison muttered.

CHAPTER THIRTY-NINE

IN TRANSIT

Kat looked up and smiled as William stepped into her suite and nodded politely to her. He looked vaguely out of place in the drab shipsuit that passed for a uniform on Asher Dales, but he'd declined all offers of replacement uniforms or civilian clothes. She rather suspected the choice of attire was a statement of independence, aimed more at the king than her. She'd effectively kidnapped him when the squadron had departed the enemy base and set course for the Gap.

She rose to greet him. "Tanya isn't coming?"

"She's fiddling with the budget," William told her. "She thinks we can purchase a couple of additional destroyers when we reach Tyre."

"That might be a good idea," Kat said. "The Theocrats may be gone, but there will be other threats." She motioned for him to sit down at the table. "Lucy told me she's been cooking all day," she said. Her steward had been excited when she'd heard that Kat had invited William to a private dinner, even though it wasn't particularly formal. "I'm sure it's something good."

"I remember her cooking," William said. "It was almost enough to convince me to stay in the navy."

Kat met his eyes. "I could get your commission reactivated," she said gently. "You'd be welcome."

"Not everywhere," William said. "Colonials have been having a *very* hard time of it."

"You could set a good example," Kat pointed out, trying not to wince. "And if you rose higher . . ."

William shook his head. "Besides, I accepted a responsibility to Asher Dales," he added. "I can't just abandon them, not until they have a formal naval establishment of their own."

"They'll probably hire others," Kat said. She sighed, knowing that William wouldn't give in so quickly. He was an honorable man. "If you change your mind, please let me know."

"I will," William said. He looked down at the table. "I don't like the way things have been going on Tyre. This . . . someone backing the Theocrats . . . this is the very last straw."

Lucy entered before Kat could say a word, carrying a tray of food. "This is my very best turkey bake," she said, putting it down on the table. "Can I get you a drink? Either of you?"

"Water for me, please," William said when Kat glanced at him. "I'll have something stronger later."

"Water for me too," Kat said. She'd never been a heavy drinker, even when she'd been a midshipwoman. One hangover had been quite enough for her. "The food looks good."

"Thank you, Admiral," Lucy said. She took a jug of water from the drinks cabinet and poured them each a glass, then bobbed a curtsy and withdrew. "Ring if you need me."

Kat reached for the spoon and ladled a midsized helping onto William's plate. The food smelled good too, a mixture of turkey, pasta, cheese, and something she didn't quite recognize. She served herself afterwards, then sat back in her chair. Her stomach was rumbling hungrily, reminding her that it had been too long since she'd eaten. She'd been busy preparing her ship for war.

William cocked his head. "Who do you think did it?"

"Good question," Kat said, trying to disguise her irritation. Her family might enjoy discussing galactic politics over the dinner table, but *she* didn't. She'd expected better from William. But then, it was the first chance they'd had in the last three weeks to actually talk privately. Tanya had monopolized most of his time. "And I don't have an answer."

She took a bite of her food and chewed it slowly, enjoying the taste. "Father wouldn't have backed a fool like Admiral Morrison," she said. "And even if he had, he would have told me that Morrison was one of our clients. He would have been a great deal more deferential to me too."

William lifted his eyebrows. "I thought he spent half his time kissing your ass."

Kat had to smile, even though the mental image his words brought was revolting. "He would have been more willing to listen to me, perhaps even to do what I said, if he was one of our clients. Even if I hadn't known, William, *he* would have known. And he wouldn't have known that I didn't know."

"I'm sure that makes sense on *some* level," William said.

Kat snorted. "That's High Society for you," she said. "Now you know why I wanted to leave it. The navy . . . the navy is more *honest* than High Society."

"That's a matter of opinion," William said.

"But there's more at stake on a starship than back home," Kat countered. "And the environment will kill an idiot who doesn't know to maintain the life support."

She put her fork on the plate and looked up. "The problem is that *anyone* could have backed Admiral Morrison," she said. "Well, it would have to be someone fairly high up. But . . . even if they hadn't ordered Admiral Morrison to refrain from making any preparations for war, they'd be in real trouble when the truth came out. They'd have every reason in the world to cover it up. And they might succeed."

Her lips formed a faint smile. "They *did* succeed."

"But now we see something far darker than a desperate attempt to cover up a mistake," William pointed out. "Someone, perhaps the *same* someone, has also been backing the Theocracy. Who?"

"It would have to be someone wealthy enough to do so without causing more than a blip in the financial records," Kat said. "Someone arrogant enough to believe that they wouldn't get caught, or that they wouldn't suffer badly if they *were* caught. Or someone desperate . . . Cavendish is desperate. But I don't believe they had significant problems *before* the war."

"And if the Theocracy won," William mused, "they'd be executed."

Kat nodded. She'd seen enough horrors over the last five years to know, without a shadow of a doubt, that Theocratic occupation was an utter nightmare. The worlds the Theocracy had managed to occupy during the war were traumatized—Hebrides had been turned into a radioactive ruin—and the worlds they'd ruled for decades were even worse. Asher Dales had been quite lucky. There were liberated worlds that had been on the verge of civil war for the last year or so. No one in their right mind would *want* a Theocratic victory.

And Admiral Morrison's backers could have done much more to sabotage the war effort, if they'd wanted us to lose, Kat thought. Anyone with the sort of power and influence necessary to put Morrison in high office and then cover it up when he proved himself a cowardly incompetent could have done a great deal more damage. *Why didn't they?*

She put the thought aside for later contemplation and took another mouthful. "Duke Rudbek has a reputation for being ruthless," she mused. For once, she wished she'd paid more attention to Candy's endless gossipmongering. "Duke Tolliver isn't much better. He's skirted quite close to the legal lines in the past, if rumor is to be believed. Duchess Zangaria never liked me, but I don't think she'd use that as an excuse for treason."

William laughed. "Why didn't she like you?"

"I don't know." Kat shrugged. "I don't recall any time she liked me, even when I was a little girl. It isn't as if I went out of my way to give offense as a child."

She sipped her water, thoughtfully. "Point is, any of them could have done it."

William met her eyes. "What about the king?"

"The king?" Kat blinked in surprise. "Him?"

"He has the resources, does he not?" William didn't look away. "It would be easier for him to promote Admiral Morrison *without* making waves. And then he could arrange for the admiral's death after we rescued him. He has so much influence within the navy that he could probably also arrange for the captured supplies to go missing. Remember, everyone who joins the navy swears personal loyalty to the king."

"And everyone who joins Planetary Defense swears loyalty to Parliament," Kat said. "It doesn't mean that they'll carry out illegal orders . . ."

"The king told you to bring your fleet home," William pointed out. "And you obeyed."

Kat flushed. "He *is* the commander-in-chief."

"Yes," William said. "But only in wartime."

"That . . ." Kat took a breath, forcing herself to calm down. The suggestion was absurd—completely absurd. The *king* wouldn't commit treason. The king wouldn't sentence millions of people to death. The king had been the one pushing for more ships and resources to be diverted to the occupied sectors. The idea that Hadrian would deliberately throw entire planets into the fire was madness. "Why? Why would he do it?"

"Power," William said simply. "In peacetime, his powers are strictly limited. He's the nominal commander-in-chief, but in practice the navy is run by the oversight committee and his influence is informal. In wartime, by contrast, he *is* the commander-in-chief in all ways that matter. He outranks even the Grand Admiral. And that will remain true as long as the state of emergency remains in existence."

Kat shook her head in disbelief. "Even in peacetime, he's still incredibly powerful," she said, flatly. "The Royal Corporation is an immense power base if used properly. You're suggesting he would take the risk of throwing everything he has away, for what? For a few scraps of power?"

Her voice rose. "And if you're suggesting he deliberately *started* the war . . . why?"

"To get a state of emergency," William said, flatly. "And to start a war that could be contained. One he believed that the Commonwealth literally could *not* lose."

"Madness," Kat said.

"Is it?" William leaned back in his chair. "Think about it. Admiral Morrison kept his fleet at no more than peacetime levels of readiness, even as tensions heated up along the border and our shipping was being hit by pirates and privateers. Cadiz was a sitting duck. But, at the same time, the Admiralty dispatches Admiral Christian to reinforce the borders . . . secretly. Even if First Cadiz had been a total disaster, Admiral Christian would have been able to buy time to bring the rest of the navy into the war."

He paused. "And it worked out even better than anyone could have expected," he added, "because we were there. We saved much of the fleet. We even managed to retake the high orbitals long enough to pull our people off Cadiz before the Theocrats rallied and kicked us back out again. The odds of us losing the war, already low, go down still further."

Kat shook her head. "William . . . do you know how many things would have to go *right* for such a plan to succeed?"

"Fewer than you might think," William said. "Cadiz *has* to be attacked. The fleet *has* to be neutralized, or it will be sitting in a perfect position to block the enemy supply lines. And the Theocrats *have* to tie up much of their striking power in a blow aimed at a world most planners considered worthless."

"I was told as a cadet, time and time again, not to try to be *clever*," Kat said, remembering all the cunning battle plans she'd developed that would never have worked in the real world. Her instructors had been quite scathing about some of them, pointing out that they depended on everything going exactly right or, perhaps more dangerously, made no provision for what to do if something went wrong. "This plan is . . . madness. Utter madness."

"Yes," William said. "It's the sort of plan that might be devised by someone who had absolutely no *real* experience at all."

The king has no real military experience, a treacherous voice whispered at the back of Kat's mind. *He didn't even have to compete for his post.*

"The king is already on top," Kat said, telling that voice to shut up. "That's like . . . me assassinating Admiral Falcone on the assumption I'd succeed to her post. But it's the post I already have."

William shrugged. "But the king *did* benefit, hugely, from the state of emergency. And prolonging it does make sense."

"If your theory is correct," Kat said sharply.

"Even if it isn't, the king does benefit from keeping the state of emergency going," William reminded her. "He has an excellent motive." He frowned. "And he's made other missteps too," he added. "Pushing for major investments in the liberated sectors . . . even demanding more investments in the colonies. *That* was a political misjudgment, particularly as he made no attempt to get support from Parliament first. Instead, he backed himself into a corner where there's no way he can retreat without making himself look like an idiot."

"I would have thought you'd support him," Kat said flatly. "Those investments would have helped your people, as well as the liberated worlds."

"Yes," William said. "But he demanded too much and walked away with nothing. If he'd come to Parliament with a more reasonable set of requests, he might have done a great deal of good. Instead, nothing. The only thing he can reasonably be said to have accomplished in the last year is uniting Parliament against him."

Kat looked down at her hands, suddenly aware, very aware, that similar discussions might be taking place all over the Commonwealth. Very few people knew what they'd found at the Theocratic base, unless the news had leaked on Tyre, but it hardly mattered. The king and Parliament had been heading towards a clash for nearly a year, as both sides struggled to press their agenda. The conflict could easily turn violent. She knew, all too well, that some aristocrats would do *anything* to boost their personal power.

"I don't believe it," she said. "The king would have to be absolutely insane to take such a chance."

Kat held up a hand before he could say a word. "It was the king and his father who founded and nurtured the Commonwealth. It was the king who pressed for greater military preparation before the war, even though Parliament was reluctant to spend money on our defenses; it was the king who insisted that the colonies be defended too, even if it probably prolonged the war. It was the king who stated that we should help the occupied worlds rebuild, after the war; it was the king who fought to keep warships in the liberated sector, despite Parliament's constant attempts to withdraw the fleet. It was the king . . ."

She felt an odd pang of . . . *something*. "It was the king who also saved my career, after Justin Deveron tried to ruin it. And he put me on the Privy Council, after my father died . . ."

"A move that might have separated you from your family," William pointed out.

"My father was on the Privy Council until his death," Kat reminded him. "And he was never separated from the family." She took a breath. "And I know Hadrian. I've known him since we were both children. And I believe he means well."

"A person can do a great deal of harm in the belief they're doing the right thing," William said quietly. "Kat . . . the king may mean well. But he's created a disaster."

"If you're right," Kat said. "William, what if you're wrong?"

William leaned back in his chair. "We'll see what happens when we reach Tyre," he said. "But am I the only one to wonder why he ordered you to bring the fleet home?"

"He doesn't know who to trust," Kat said. "And he's not wrong. You can't trust *anyone* in High Society."

William lifted his eyebrows, again. "Even you? Or the king?"

Kat snorted. "We were both odd ducks," she said. "He was going to be the king and everyone *knew* he was going to be the king, while I was the tenth child and everyone knew I would never be anything important. That's why I ran away to the navy."

William frowned. "How close *were* you?"

"Not that close," Kat assured him. "We weren't best friends, if that's what you're asking."

"You make High Society sound *wonderful*," William said, dryly.

"My father once said that if you wanted a friend in High Society, get a dog. Or a pony." Kat laughed, although she knew it wasn't really funny. There was too much truth in it for anyone's peace of mind. "There are few true friends in High Society. Everyone knows that everyone else will betray them if they see advantage in doing so. A person who is shunned for a social crime like addressing a haughty dowager by the wrong title wouldn't commit a harmless little prank like murder, you know. If you grow up there, you develop a warped view of the world."

"You seem normal," William teased.

Kat snorted, loudly. "Do you realize how many mistakes I made in my first year at Piker's Peak? Not the classic mistakes, but social mistakes? A lot of things I'd taken for granted simply weren't so. My supervisor gave me a very hard time. And I never quite realized . . ."

She shook her head. "The point is, I like the king," she said. "And I find it hard to believe that he would commit treason on such a vast scale."

"Yeah," William said. He didn't sound convinced. "But how many people will agree with you?"

CHAPTER FORTY

TYRE

William didn't see Kat for several days after their dinner. He might have wondered, if she had been someone else, if she was avoiding him, but he knew that was unlikely. And yet . . . He knew their discussion had been difficult. He replayed the conversation time and time again in his head, wondering what, if anything, he should have said differently. But he knew obsessing was futile.

He understood her belief that the king was innocent, better perhaps than she realized. But he also had far more experience in dealing with younger officers than *she* did. He'd seen more than one junior officer struggle desperately to avoid admitting that they'd made a mistake, or they'd come up with a perfectly reasonable explanation that no longer sounded *quite* so reasonable. The king had always struck him as a junior officer who was in way over his head and, to some extent, on the verge of drowning. And junior officers were the ones who would come up with the most unbelievable plans that would fall apart immediately when they encountered the real world.

In truth, the whole concept of monarchy frightened him. The aristocracy was bad enough, although the aristocrats had to battle for supremacy; the monarchy allowed its heir to inherit without proving his worth, let alone his competence. That much power in the hands of an untested man? It was like giving a battlecruiser to a midshipman fresh out of the academy, the sort of thing that might be amusing if you weren't charged with cleaning up the mess afterwards. He'd worried about Kat's competence, and she'd been in the navy more than long enough to pick up the basics.

He was still mulling over the problem when *Violence* and her consorts returned to realspace, near Tyre. The thought of returning to the Commonwealth's homeworld didn't excite him—he had a feeling he'd be answering questions for months to come, even though he hadn't been directly involved with collecting evidence—but Tanya was delighted. William didn't have the heart to tell her that they'd most likely not be allowed down to the surface. They'd probably remain sequestered on the ship until someone in power figured out what to do with them.

Including making all the evidence go away, he thought. If he'd still had his navy access codes, he might have linked into the datanet and tried to look for clues, but they'd been canceled when he resigned. *It might be interesting to see who issued the orders to dispose of the captured supplies . . .*

His wristcom bleeped. "William, can you and Tanya meet me in my quarters?" Kat sounded tired. "It's important."

"We're on our way," William said.

He knocked on Tanya's door, passed on the message, and headed for the hatch. Tanya followed him, looking every inch the professional lawyer. She'd been downloading brochures from all over the system as soon as *Violence* slid out of hyperspace, trying to see who might have ships they could buy. William was more than a little disturbed to notice that prices had quadrupled in the last few months. Clearly *someone* was investing in a great deal of military hardware.

Maybe it's the Jorlem Sector, he thought as they picked their way through the superdreadnought's corridors. *The worlds there are richer, and they have every reason to want to buy ships . . .*

The hatch opened as they approached, allowing them to step into Kat's quarters. William had seen them before, of course, but Tanya looked a little disdainful at the bare bulkheads and bland surroundings. An experienced officer would have recognized it as a sign of another experienced officer, one who knew better than to allow herself to get surrounded by junk. It was good, he supposed, that a couple of years as a flag officer hadn't blunted Kat's edge. Admiral Morrison had been an indolent man long before he'd found himself on the front lines.

"William," Kat said. She looked tired too. "And Tanya. Thank you for coming."

"You are more than welcome," Tanya said. "However, I have requested permission to leave this vessel . . ."

"That's what we need to discuss," Kat said. She nodded towards the sofa. William sat down, gently pulling Tanya with him. "Martial law has been declared on Tyre."

William cursed. "That's not a good sign."

"No," Kat agreed. "The news channels are full of hysterical raving. I've requested a formal sitrep from both the Admiralty and my family's intelligence staff, but so far neither of them has arrived. The only thing that *has* arrived is a strict warning that neither of you are to go down to the planet."

"This is outrageous," Tanya snapped. She made to stand up. "I'm a citizen of Tyre, and *he's* a respected naval officer . . ."

"Right now, all normal civil liberties have been suspended," Kat said. "If you arrive at the orbital tower, you will probably be arrested."

"I'll file a complaint," Tanya said. "I . . ."

"*Sit down,*" Kat snapped. "This isn't anything personal. Everyone on this ship, everyone in the squadron, has been denied the same permission. Fortunately, for better or worse, you *do* have permission to visit the scrapyards. I was able to swing it as a favor for an allied world, as you'll be purchasing ships here. That said"—she met William's eyes—"you are to stay away from the media and return to the ship when you're done."

"They can't do *that*," Tanya said.

"It's martial law," Kat told her. "As I said, all civil liberties have been suspended."

"Which will *really* do wonders for the economy," William muttered. Martial law had also been declared when the war broke out, making life much harder for the average citizen. Something as simple as getting to work became a great deal more difficult when aircars were grounded and public transport shut down. "Kat . . . how long is this going to last?"

"I don't know," she admitted. "And the news reports are so vague as to be unreadable."

Tanya huffed rudely. "We'll leave immediately, if you don't mind," she said. "And we'll find a hotel . . ."

"We'll return to the ship," William said. He ignored the betrayed look she sent him, as if she'd expected him to back her up. She'd been on Tyre during the war. She should know not to play games during martial law. They were lucky they were even being allowed off the ship. "Thank you for your assistance, Kat."

She gave him a wan smile. "You're welcome, William," she said. "Your shuttle is already waiting for you. Good luck."

Tanya spluttered in outrage as they left Kat's quarters and headed down to the airlock. William ignored her, taking his datapad from his belt and checking for updates. There was no outgoing channel—it seemed that no one on the ship was permitted to talk to anyone—but a whole collection of messages from various news services crashed into his datapad as soon as he identified himself. The news was wholly bad. Mass unemployment, riots on the streets, rumors of everything from treason to alien invasions . . . He shook his head in disbelief. Had the whole world gone crazy?

He undocked from *Violence*, set the autopilot to take them to the nearest shipyard, and started to read the reports more carefully. Almost nothing seemed to be *confirmed*, not even the destruction of the Theocratic Navy, but so many contradictory rumors abounded that it was impossible to tell what was true. Was the king going to be impeached? Or were his political supporters going to push back hard? Or . . . It was madness. Protest marches right across the Commonwealth, for and against the king; rioters on the streets of Tyre, despite the best efforts of the planetary police. Some in Parliament were even calling to send in the army.

This is not going to end well, he thought. He had the uneasy feeling about the whole crisis. *And where will it end?*

◆ ◆ ◆

Kat paced the CIC, torn between relief and irritation that no one had tried to get in touch with her. *Violence* and her crew, and the entire squadron, seemed to be hanging in limbo, neither part of the planetary defense network nor completely detached from it. The communications lockdown was in full effect. No one, save for Kat herself, could send a message off the ship . . . and even *she* couldn't send a message very far. She couldn't talk to anyone . . .

. . . and none of the reports she'd read were very reassuring. There *had* been riots, there *had* been protests, there *had* been threats to everyone from the lowest MP to the king himself . . . and so many rumors had leaked out that the truth was overshadowed by the lies. Too many problems were bursting into the open for anyone, even the king, to handle them; too many tensions that had been buried for decades were exploding under their feet. The planet seemed doomed to go through a long period of civil unrest.

She turned her attention to the display. Home Fleet was concentrated, although God alone knew what it was concentrated *against*; it floated in orbit around the moon, ready to respond to any crisis. Tyre itself was ringed with Planetary Defense's battlestations, gunboats flittering to and fro as if they expected trouble at any moment. Kat felt her heart sink as she assessed the battlestations. They were Parliament's, not the king's. Whoever was behind the whole affair might already be planning to seize them and take control of the high orbitals.

And taking them back would be damn near impossible, she thought. Tyre was the most heavily defended world in explored space. *Even Home Fleet would have problems punching through the defenses.*

She turned as Kitty's console bleeped. "Admiral, the Admiralty is calling you on a secure channel," Kitty said. "The header insists you have to take the call in private."

"Route it into my office," Kat ordered.

She stepped through the hatch, silently relieved that *something* was finally happening. The hatch hissed closed behind her, plunging the compartment into silence. Kat walked across to her desk, pressing her finger against the scanner as she sat down. A moment later, Grand Admiral Tobias Vaughn's face appeared in front of her. He looked older than she remembered, old and fatigued and worn out. He'd been in the navy longer than she'd been alive.

And he was the previous king's client too, Kat reminded herself. *And he rose high because of the king's patronage.*

"Admiral Falcone," Vaughn said. His voice was weary. "It's good to see you again."

"Thank you, sir," Kat said. She reminded herself that it was late evening on Tyre. Starship lag was working in her favor. "It's good to see you too."

"Your report has set off shockwaves, despite our best efforts," Vaughn said. "Enough of it leaked out to make life difficult for all concerned."

Kat kept her face blank. That wasn't her fault. She'd upheld the communications embargo as soon as it had been ordered. As far as she knew, no one back in the liberated sector knew that the enemy fleet had been destroyed. Only a handful of people on her ship knew what else had been found at the enemy base. And they certainly couldn't have sent any message while the fleet had been in hyperspace. No, it hadn't been her fault. Someone in the palace had blabbed.

Which is no surprise, she thought. *Everyone who is anyone has their own little network of spies.*

"I understand that, sir," she said calmly. "How may I be of service?"

"It is not clear if we will have time to start a reasoned and reasonable investigation into the matter," Vaughn said. "Preliminary investigations have made it clear that almost everyone who served at Razwhana Depot has been reported dead. They may well *be* dead."

Kat stared. "What? All of them?"

"The depot only had a skeleton crew," Vaughn pointed out. "At its height, we only ever assigned thirty crewmen, all reservists deemed too unfit for service on more . . . *active* . . . bases. There were fifteen men and women assigned to the depot when the supplies were destroyed, then the depot itself shut down. All of them have been reported dead."

"But if someone can fiddle the records," Kat said, "they may have simply assumed other identities."

"Quite," Vaughn said. "Or they *were* killed, but not at their reported *places* of death. Their bodies were certainly never found." He rubbed his forehead. "But that isn't a problem right now, Admiral," he said. "We need you to do something for us, quietly."

Kat frowned. William's words rang in her ears. "What do you want?"

If Vaughn noticed her tone, he gave no sign. "There have been a number of threats against Princess Drusilla," he said. "We'd like to send her to your ship for safekeeping. Keep her safe until the situation stabilizes."

"Is it that bad?"

"Right now?" Vaughn looked her in the eye. "It's worse than anything I've ever seen."

"Very well," Kat said. She'd never really *liked* Princess Drusilla, but she could put up with her company. "I'll have quarters prepared for her."

"She'll be with you in a couple of hours," Vaughn said. "And . . . thank you." He let out a long breath. "Tomorrow, they're going to vote on impeaching the king," he added. "And then . . . we will see."

Kat swallowed, hard. "I understand."

"I'd be surprised if you did," Vaughn said. "We're in uncharted waters, Katherine. And who knows what will happen next?"

◆ ◆ ◆

Peter stood at the window, staring out over the shadowed city. The streetlights had been turned off, as had the lights illuminating the palace and the other magnificent buildings in the center of town. Martial law had been declared, and everyone had been warned to keep their shutters down, plunging the city further into darkness. The troops on the streets wouldn't hesitate to enforce the rules with as much force as necessary. It was a return to the darkest days of the war.

And we're fighting ourselves, he thought numbly. *There's no external enemy any longer.*

It was a bitter thought. If anything, the last week had been worse than he'd expected. The torrent of layoffs had well and truly begun, throwing hundreds of thousands of people out of work. They'd responded badly, taking to the streets and smashing things . . . His security staff had even had to clamp down on workplace violence. Workplace violence! It had been largely unknown, a week ago. The combination of a booming economy and a meritocracy had kept the vast majority of his workers happy. But now . . . now, *nothing* could keep them happy. They all suspected their jobs were on the line.

And many of them are right, he told himself curtly. The workers earmarked for layoff were not, by and large, low-performers. Nor were they the type of people who simply refused to fit in. No, they were merely unlucky enough to be in the wrong place at the wrong time. *We fire so many in hopes of keeping the rest.*

But that simple truth didn't make it any easier for the newly unemployed to take . . .

A light darted over the city, heading north. He eyed it for a long moment, wondering what it was. A police skimmer? An aircar with special permission to fly in the restricted airspace surrounding the city? A shuttle? Or something else? He felt a flicker of envy for the pilot, flying away from his troubles. Peter couldn't leave, not unless he wanted to abandon his family for good.

There was a knock on the door. Peter didn't bother to turn around. "Enter!"

He saw Yasmeena's reflection in the window as she approached. "Your Grace, I have continued to try to get a message to HMS *Violence*," she said. "However there's a block on all personal messages. I believe our messages remain languishing in the buffer."

Peter nodded. He'd been surprised when *Violence* and his sister returned to the system. They must have pushed their drives to the limit to get back so quickly if they'd been on the far side of the occupied sector when they destroyed the Theocratic fleet. But they had . . . and he couldn't help finding that ominous. The king presumably had some reason for calling them back home.

Kat won't side with him, he told himself firmly. But, in truth, he was no longer sure that was true. He and Kat had never really been friends. Perhaps, if they'd been closer, he could have ensured that she was more aware of the political realities behind her appointment to the Privy Council. Or . . . He sighed to himself. Everything he'd done had seemed logical at the time but had led to crisis. *She won't turn against the family.*

He sighed, again. Kat *had* turned against the family. Maybe not directly, maybe not to the point of working against the family's interests, but she had committed herself to the navy and would put the navy first. She'd made that clear when they'd talked. And he understood all too well. Kat had been born to wealth and privilege, but she'd never had a chance at real power. He supposed he should be relieved she'd made something of her life. So many others did not.

"It's late," Yasmeena said. "Your Grace, you should be in bed."

Peter glanced at his wristcom. "Very well," he said. "But I won't sleep well until tomorrow."

His thoughts were bleak. *And then we'll see if we have enough power, in votes and force, to impeach a king.*

CHAPTER FORTY-ONE

TYRE

Peter could feel the tension in the air as his aircar landed neatly on top of the Houses of Parliament. Armed guards were clearly visible on the streets, while police skimmers and military helicopters patrolled the air. The protesters had been dispersed; some forced to flee into the suburbs, some arrested and transported to detention camps. It would take months, if not years, to sort the guilty from the innocent. A line had been crossed. Tyre had never had to repress its own citizens before.

We had a nice planet once, he thought sourly. The *next* wave of layoffs was lurking at the back of his mind, mocking him. He'd have to give the order to terminate the next group soon, perhaps by the end of the day. *What happened to us?*

He stepped out of the aircar and nodded politely to the two guards. Parliamentary Security was on the alert, its officers wearing body armor and carrying heavy weapons. His own guards accompanied him as he walked through the door and down the long corridor towards the parliamentary chamber. It felt *wrong*, somehow, to be shadowed by armed guards in Parliament. Parliament was supposed to be *safe*.

The chamber was oddly quiet when he entered, MPs and lords talking in hushed voices. He could *feel* their tension, hanging in the air like a shroud. Too much had leaked out over the past couple of weeks for him to feel confident they could ram the impeachment bill through before the king could rally his supporters and counterattack. Whispers already circulated that someone in a very high place had committed treason. It might not be the king.

Duke Rudbek caught Peter's eye as he sat down. "There's been no word from the king," he muttered as if the privacy fields wouldn't keep their words to themselves. "But I've heard rumors that the government has been meeting in emergency session."

Peter leaned over slightly. "What about our people? Are they in place?"

"Mostly," Duke Rudbek said. "But you know how chancy it will become if all hell breaks loose."

"We've never had to do this before," Peter reminded him. "God alone knows what is about to happen."

He settled back in his chair and surveyed the room. By law, certain votes could not be cast by proxy, not even over a secure telecommunications network. They had to be in the Houses of Parliament if they were voting to impeach anyone, from the lowest MP to the king himself. Peter had no idea what his great-great-grandfather had been thinking when he'd passed that law, but it had clearly been a mistake. Parliament could no longer be reckoned safe. Too many angry people were milling through the city despite the military and police presence. Some might start heading back towards Parliament too.

At least that gives us a slight edge, he thought. A number of neutral or opposition MPs had chosen to send proxies. They'd effectively given up their vote. *But will it be enough to impeach the king?*

His heart started to race. They were committed now, committed in a way they hadn't been a month ago. If they tried and failed to impeach Hadrian, their positions would be weakened beyond repair. Peter had no doubt that the family council would remove him as soon as possible. They'd have no choice, not if they wanted to mend fences with the monarch. A king who *survived* an attempt to impeach him would, perversely, be in a far stronger position, if only because his enemies would be in disarray. And if the affair turned violent . . .

He studied the MPs as they took their seats, their faces grim. There had been no official announcement of what was about to happen, but he was sure they knew what was coming. A number would vote to impeach, a number would vote against impeachment . . . How many of them would vote in his favor? He and the others had called in every favor they could to stack the odds against the king, but it was hard to be sure. The MPs were all too aware that the king was popular, outside the chamber. Their rivals wouldn't hesitate to accuse them of treason if that was required to unseat the sitting MPs and take their place. The bastards might even get away with it.

Particularly if we lose, Peter reflected. He glanced towards the king's empty chair. By custom, the king had not been invited to the session. His prime minister, currently taking his seat, would speak for him. *An MP who loses the king's favor so openly will be lucky if he isn't recalled within the week.*

The speaker stood, slowly. He looked pale. Peter wondered, wryly, what the poor man was thinking. The speaker was meant to be neutral, but surely he had thoughts and opinions of his own. Did he support the king? Or did he support the opposition? Or . . . was he terrified that he'd lose his post, either way? The losers would seek to extract some recompense for their defeat, particularly if they blamed the speaker. A cunning man in the speaker's chair could slant the debate in a particular direction, if he was careful. But it would be hard for such a deed to remain unnoticed. Every word the speaker said was thoroughly scrutinized by every political analyst on the planet.

"A bill has been put before us," the speaker said. His voice was hushed. Thankfully, the chamber was designed to project his words to the audience. "The bill . . ."

Arthur Hampshire stood. "On a point of order, Mr. Speaker!"

A low rumble ran through the chamber. Peter tensed, wondering what the prime minister thought he was doing. A point of order could delay matters for quite some time, particularly if made at the right time, but this one wouldn't last for more than a few minutes. Had Hampshire blundered? Perhaps. Yet . . . he was too old a political hand to make such an overt mistake. What was he *doing*?

"I speak on behalf of the king," Hampshire said. "And I claim the Royal Prerogative!"

Peter tensed. The Royal Prerogative? Was the king insistent on pushing them right to the brink? He did have considerable authority, but using it without Parliament's approval was . . . not exactly illegal, merely frowned upon. Sure, the king's representative did have the right to speak first, yet two centuries of precedent stood against it. And interrupting the bill being read . . .

"His Majesty's investigators have discovered proof of treason," Hampshire said. "Treason at the very heart of our government. Treason committed by men and women who wish to return to an era when Tyre was alone in the universe! We have solid proof that individuals within this room gave aid and comfort to the enemy, sacrificing millions of lives, in order to advance their agenda!"

Duke Rudbek elbowed Peter. "He's trying to blame us, some of us, for his crimes."

"Crimes we can't prove," Peter muttered back. A week of careful investigation had turned up nothing more than circumstantial evidence. It would be quite easy for the king's defenders to point out that the people responsible could quite easily have been working for one of the senior aristocrats instead of the king. "He's trying to derail the bill."

Hampshire spoke over a growing rumble of unrest. "This bill—yes, we know what it is—is nothing more than an attempt to escape justice! The people behind it want to distract the king, to distract everyone, from the canker in their midst. This is not opposition! This is outright treason! And it will not stand!"

The rumble grew louder. MPs were on their feet, shouting backwards and forwards. Peter gritted his teeth, forcing himself to think. The king had outmaneuvered them, it seemed. By accusing his opponents of treason, presumably with just enough faked evidence to make the charges reasonably compelling, the king had made it much harder for his opponents to impeach him. And yet, the accusation wouldn't last. Any halfway competent investigation would prove their innocence.

There isn't going to be an investigation, he thought, feeling ice trickling down his spine. *The king is gambling everything on one final throw of the dice.*

"Send the signal," he said urgently. "Tell our people to move in, now!"

Duke Rudbek nodded. "Done," he said, tapping his datapad. "If we can secure the planetary defenses . . ."

"By order of His Majesty, under the provisions of Martial Law, everyone in this chamber is under arrest until a full investigation can be carried out," Hampshire thundered. It was lucky his voice was amplified. No one would have heard a word otherwise. MPs were practically *throwing* things at each other. "You will sit down and wait quietly . . ."

Peter's datapad bleeped loudly, warning him that a jamming field had just snapped into existence. All datalinks had been cut, even the secure link to his mansion. He stood. Parliament was heavily defended, but . . . A roar broke out in the lower levels as a bunch of MPs rushed the prime minister. Some government MPs moved to shield him, but others looked uncertain or turned and fled. Alarms howled a moment later, alerting the MPs to move to shelters. Peter hadn't heard those alarms outside emergency drills. Parliament had never been attacked, not even during the opening hours of the war.

A war just started, he thought. *And all hell is about to break loose.*

A dull explosion rocked the chamber. Peter swallowed, hard. "What was that?"

"Someone trying to break in," Duke Rudbek said. "I daresay Parliamentary Security is under attack."

Peter's bodyguard hurried into the chamber. "Your Grace, armed troops arrived at the main entrance and opened fire!"

Duke Rudbek looked up, sharply. "Who fired first?"

"I don't know," the bodyguard said. "But there's a battle going on outside!"

Peter stood. "Where do we go?"

"You have to get to the shelters," the bodyguard told him. Peter wished, suddenly, that he knew the man's name. "This way, please."

"We have to evacuate the building," Duke Rudbek said. "Or take one of the tunnels."

Peter shot a questioning look at the bodyguard. "We can't guarantee your safety," the bodyguard said. "The building is surrounded, so going into the streets is a seriously bad idea; I don't dare take the risk. And the local airspace isn't safe. There are reports of gunmen with portable HVMs in the area."

"Then we go down," Peter said. Other bodyguards were flowing into the chamber, some grabbing their principals and half carrying them out without waiting for debate. "I . . ."

He stopped as he saw the scene in front of him. Hampshire was lying on the ground . . . bruised, battered, bloody, and apparently dead. Other wounded or dead MPs and lords lay next to him, looking as if they'd been trampled by a herd of wild animals. The speaker was sitting on his chair, staring blankly at the carnage. Blood stained the floor, mocking everything they'd hoped to achieve. They'd hoped for a peaceful resolution, but civil war had broken out.

Shooting echoed in the distance, followed by another explosion. Peter's bodyguard grabbed his arm and yanked him through the door, hurrying towards the drop-shafts. The alarms were growing louder, a howling dirge for democracy and civilization. Peter felt sick as they dived into the drop-shaft, wondering, a second too late, if the power would fail. But it held up long enough for them to land at the bottom safely. Duke Rudbek and his bodyguards followed a moment later.

The king wanted to capture us, Peter thought. The army was riddled with the aristocracy's spies, which meant the men attacking the Houses of Parliament had to be the king's household guards, loyal to him personally. *And that means . . .*

He forced himself to think as he was pushed into a secure chamber. The king's household guard was normally limited to a couple of thousand men but had expanded, of course, during the war. It had been one of the issues Parliament had meant to address, before the growing crisis drowned it out. The horse had definitely bolted on *that* one. And yet, it wasn't entirely bad news. The king probably didn't have the manpower to secure *all* his potential targets. He'd have problems if he wanted to seize the mansions, or the industrial nodes, or the ground-based Planetary Defense Centers.

But if he takes command of the high orbitals, he can force everyone else to surrender, Peter thought. The ground-based defenses would need time to react and, by the time they realized how serious things had become, they could be smashed flat. *And then what? Does he think he can rule the Commonwealth?*

The bodyguard slammed the armored door shut, then sat down at a terminal and started to tap commands into the system. A series of images popped up in front of him: a live feed from the security sensors, a handful of news broadcasts, even a couple of emergency services and military channels. Peter glanced at his datapad, but it was still dead. The datalinks that should have been permanently open were closed.

"This terminal is linked into the city's physical infrastructure," the bodyguard said by way of explanation. "The jamming field doesn't affect it."

Duke Rudbek coughed. "So . . . what's going on outside?"

"A great deal of shouting and screaming," the bodyguard said. "Everyone seems to have something to say."

Peter leaned forward. "Are we in any immediate danger?"

"Not as far as I can tell," the bodyguard said. "But unless we get reinforcements, this building will fall very quickly."

And then we die, Peter thought. The king had definitely staked everything on one final throw of the dice. *We die and get condemned as traitors, while Hadrian continues with his plan.*

"Get me a link to the nearest garrison," Duke Rudbek ordered. "I need to speak to the CO."

The hour ticked by slowly. Peter linked his datapad to the terminal, alternately sending messages to his clients and trying to get a grip on what was happening. The news reports appeared to have been written in advance—they all claimed that traitorous elements in Parliament were resisting arrest—but the independent reporters were pointing out that matters were nowhere near so cut-and-dried. It was a nightmare. There were reports of an attempt to assassinate the king, gunfights on the planetary defense battlestations and even Home Fleet . . . reports that constantly contradicted themselves. He couldn't tell who was winning, if *anyone* was winning.

"Troops are on the way to lift the siege," Duke Rudbek said finally. "Parliament will be saved."

Unless the king decides to blow it up, Peter thought. The shelter was heavily protected but couldn't stand up to a kinetic strike. Or a penetrator warhead. Was the king desperate enough to deploy one? And what would happen if he did? Peter wondered, bitterly, what had happened to the other aristocrats. Their bodyguards would have gotten them to the other shelters, wouldn't they? *They might be dead already.*

"There are also reports of the king's troops digging in at the palace," Duke Rudbek stated grimly. "I've requested that my clients prepare to take the building, but they're hesitating."

"I'm not surprised," Peter said. There was so much confusion on the datanet that *everyone* had to be a little unsure of themselves. Which actions were legal and which were outright treason? His lips trembled at the thought, even though it wasn't really funny. Whoever lost would be the traitors, of course. "Do we have any updates from the orbital fortresses?"

"Five of them appear to be firmly under Admiral Fisher's control," Duke Rudbek said, after a moment. "I'm not so sure about the others. One of them appears to have dropped out of the datanet entirely."

Peter nodded. Admiral Fisher had been one of his father's clients, although ties had weakened somewhat in the year since his father's death. He was a good, and more importantly *reliable*, man—a man who understood the importance of keeping Planetary Defense separate from the Royal Navy. And he knew what the opposition had been trying to achieve.

Another hour went past, slowly. The king's household troops fought bravely, once the reinforcements arrived, but they were badly outnumbered. A handful surrendered, but the remainder fought to the death. Peter couldn't help wondering what the king had done to deserve such loyalty, although it hardly mattered. Perhaps the troops were colonials, or perhaps they expected to be executed if they were captured. He found it hard to care.

"Parliament is secure," Duke Rudbek said. Peter's datapad bleeped, confirming that the jamming field was gone. "And troops are on their way to the palace."

Peter scanned the reports that had started to flow into his datapad. Shootings, bombings, entire installations going off the air . . . Some of the most alarming reports had been updated before he saw them, suggesting that they'd been based on false data. But even the handful of confirmed reports were terrifying. The entire planet appeared to be at war with itself.

He scowled. Two of the orbital battlestations had dropped out of the datanet, while the datanet itself was starting to have problems. Someone had loaded chaos software into the datacores. Peter was no computer expert, but even he knew how dangerous chaos software could be. It mutated so rapidly that it could turn on its programmer before he had a chance to realize that something had gone wrong. The king had to be desperate.

"We have to find the king," he said as a string of new reports scrolled across his screen. "If we can capture him, we can put an end to this madness."

"Yes," Duke Rudbek said. "But where *is* he?"

CHAPTER FORTY-TWO

TYRE

"Admiral," Kitty snapped, "we just picked up a FLASH alert from the planetary defenses."

Kat looked up. "Sound red alert," she ordered. Alarms howled through the ship. A FLASH alert meant that the system was about to come under attack. It had never been used in drills. "Bring the fleet to battlestations!"

She stood as the display rapidly updated, alerts popping up all over the high orbitals. She'd expected to see vortexes opening and enemy starships pouring out, but instead all hell seemed to have broken loose in orbit. A number of orbital battlestations had dropped out of the datanet, and the datanet itself was flickering, as if it was on the verge of failing completely. She couldn't believe it. The datanet had so many redundancies built into it that nothing short of complete destruction of the entire network would silence it.

"Battlestation Thirteen reported armed men in the CIC, then went silent," Kitty said as she and her crew struggled to make sense of the torrent of information pouring into the sensors. "Battlestation Nineteen made a similar report, but insisted that all the men were killed before they could do serious damage."

She looked up, her face pale. "Home Fleet . . . Admiral, Home Fleet *also* reported men attempting to take control of the ships."

Kat felt her blood run cold. "Order our squadron put into lockdown," she ordered. "Full internal security protocols. And get me a direct link to the planet!"

"All links to the planet are down," Kitty reported. "I can't get a secure link to *anyone*." An image popped up in front of her. "A state of emergency, another one, has been declared over the whole planet," she added. "Global News is reporting that the king ordered the arrest of a number of aristocrats for high treason, but his men were met with armed resistance."

Kat sucked in her breath. Had the king discovered Admiral Morrison's backer? Or . . . had something gone spectacularly wrong? The tension had been so high that pundits had been openly predicting civil war. There were quite a few factions, now, that would have an excellent motive to try to capture both the orbital defenses and Home Fleet. Someone was clearly trying to seize unfettered control of the military.

And the hell of it is that I don't know who's doing what, she thought as more reports flowed into the network. A third of them contradicted another third, while the remainder were clearly untrue. Tyre City had not been nuked. Her sensors would have detected the blast even from their distance. *What is going on?*

"Two of the battlestations are bringing up their weapons, Admiral," Kitty reported. "They're sweeping space for targets."

"Order the fleet to prepare to move out of range," Kat said. They were outside conventional missile range, but she was sure the orbital battlestations would have extended-range missiles. "And try to figure out what's happening to Home Fleet."

She sucked in her breath as she studied the display. Home Fleet's formation was starting to look ragged. Some ships were remaining in the datanet, sharing information with the rest of the fleet, but others had dropped out completely. She wondered, morbidly, just who was trying to mount a coup and who was trying to mount the counter-coup. Someone could easily have seen a cough as a signal to start something violent. God knew *that* had happened before. How much time would pass before Home Fleet's ships started shooting at each other?

"Admiral, I'm picking up a wide-band message from the planet," Kitty said. "Everyone can hear it."

"Put it on," Kat ordered.

The king's image appeared on the display. He wore his military uniform, every inch the commander-in-chief. His face was grim, but resolute. Kat hadn't seen anything like it since the day the king had addressed the Commonwealth after the war had begun. He'd told his people that there would be many hard days ahead, but they would eventually prevail. And he'd kept the political coalition together long enough to win.

"My people," the king said. "It is with a heavy heart that I must inform you that our world, our star system, our sector, has been plunged into the gravest crisis since the collapse of the United Nations and the threat of interstellar anarchy. I have discovered that elements within our planet's aristocracy were plotting against our government, with the ultimate intention of seizing power for themselves. To this extent, they armed and supported the remnants of the Theocracy and used them to trigger a crisis that would allow them to seize power."

Kitty gasped. Kat barely noticed.

"It was my duty to move against them. As the monarch charged with maintaining and upholding the system our ancestors devised, I had no choice but to move against them immediately. They were already conspiring with innocent parties within the Houses of Parliament, plotting to remove their rivals from power, including me, and take control for themselves. The state of emergency they fostered, by deliberately pushing for mass unemployment and civil unrest, would have given them the power to ram through their agenda and make their dominion unchallengeable. I had to move immediately."

411

"Unfortunately, I failed. I was unable to deploy enough loyal troops to seize their persons before they escaped and rallied support. My prime minister and many of my supporters were killed by the traitors and their backers. Others have been taken prisoner. Their forces are already battling to take control of the orbital defenses and the navy. To my eternal shame, I have failed in my duty. Tyre is now ruled by men and women who have no loyalty to anything but themselves. And I have been forced to flee."

"Where's he going?" Kitty asked. "Admiral . . ."

"Quiet," Kat snarled.

"I swear to you that I *will* return," the king said. "Their tyranny will not last. Those of you who join them willingly, knowing what you know now, will meet a final end on the gallows. But those of you who remain loyal, who do everything in your power to prepare for my return, or even to stand aside and refuse to help the traitors, will be rewarded. I *will* return."

The image flickered, then the message started to play again from the beginning. Kat hit the console, pausing the message. It was . . . it was unbelievable. And yet, she had no doubt that there were elements in Parliament who would do whatever it took to tear down the king and gain power for themselves. Had the king discovered any real evidence? Or . . . or what?

Kitty looked up at her. "Admiral?"

"Order the fleet to hold position," Kat said. She had a feeling she knew where the king was going. Clearly, he'd anticipated *something* when he'd sent Princess Drusilla to her ship. "And remind all commanding officers that the fleet is to stay in lockdown."

"Aye, Admiral."

Kat's thoughts were churning. Peter . . . lead a coup? She doubted it. Her eldest brother didn't have anything resembling an imagination. He probably couldn't conceive of making a bid for supreme power, let alone risking everything on one throw of the dice. Falcone was powerful indeed, but not powerful enough to stand up to the king. And yet . . . there were others among the aristocracy who *were* ruthless bastards. They could easily have duped Peter into opposing the king.

The evidence we found could easily be twisted to frame the king, she thought. *Or they might even believe the king is to blame.*

"Admiral, the *Royal Tyre* is breaking orbit," Kitty added. "The king's ship is deploying chaff and ECM drones."

Her voice rose. "And all the fortresses are going active!"

Kat gritted her teeth. The fortress crews had to be incredibly confused. They were under Parliament's command, but Parliament itself might have been scattered. Or, worse, under the control of a single faction. They might try to hold their fire until the situation clarified itself, but if they came under attack . . . they'd fire back. And then all hell would break loose.

As if it hasn't already, she thought.

She looked at Kitty as the younger woman turned back to her console. "Is the king on his ship?"

"Unknown," Kitty said. "But he's well within engagement range. If the fortresses open fire."

And a lot of other ships are breaking orbit too, Kat thought. *The king might be on one of them instead.*

◆ ◆ ◆

"William," Tanya said, "what the hell is going on?"

"Someone is mounting a coup," William said. He kept his certainty that it was the king to himself. "And we have to go dark."

He cursed the timing under his breath as he brought the shuttle to a halt relative to the primary star. They'd been in transit when the shit hit the fan; too far from *Violence* to return to her, too close to the scrapyard for his peace of mind. Someone might easily assume, in the wake of the reports of firefights on a dozen starships and fortresses, that they were

413

infiltrators bent on wreaking havoc. He powered down as much as he dared, hoping that the situation soon calmed down. The shuttle wouldn't stand up to a plasma blast if someone assumed they were a threat and opened fire.

Tanya shook her head. "Why? Why are they doing this?"

"It doesn't matter at the moment," William said. The king's speech had sounded impressive—he'd give the young officer wannabe that much—but had lacked substance. He certainly hadn't named any names. "All we can do is wait to see who comes out on top."

The radio bleeped, announcing an emergency bulletin. "This is Israel Harrison, former Leader of the Opposition and currently prime minister pro tem," a voice said. It was so different to the voice William remembered that he honestly wondered if it really *was* Israel Harrison. But then, a computer-generated fake would be perfect, fooling all but the most thorough analysis. "Three hours ago, the Houses of Parliament met in concert to debate a bill to impeach the king."

There was a pause, as if the speaker was unsure how to proceed. "The bill was never debated," Harrison continued. "Instead, the Houses of Parliament were attacked by armed troops. Many members of both houses were killed, along with their defenders. The king, knowing that there was a good chance he'd be impeached, chose to mount a coup. His supporters made a desperate, and ultimately futile, attempt to take control of the orbital and groundside defenses. However, the king himself escaped."

Harrison took a long breath. "We are aware that many people feel a personal loyalty to the king. We do not fault them for feeling that they should honor their oaths. But Parliament has the ultimate right to judge the king and, if necessary, remove him from his post. His actions have put him beyond the pale. It is our belief that he was responsible for provoking the war and, perhaps worse, assisting the Theocrats in an attempt to justify keeping the wartime state of emergency in existence.

"The king will be given a fair trial. We swear this on our honor. The trial will be open to the public. There will be no attempt to hide anything. The entire galaxy will see the debate and judge his guilt or innocence for itself. But he cannot be allowed to roam free. If he comes to you, take him into custody. Not for us, not for yourself, but for the good of the entire planet. The future of Tyre itself rests on you."

"Shit," William muttered.

Tanya looked pale. "What do we do?"

"Nothing," William said. Thankfully both sides would probably regard Tanya as a neutral party. God alone knew what they'd make of him. "We're out of it. All we can do is wait and see who comes out on top."

◆ ◆ ◆

Peter had never visited Planetary Defense's HQ, although he, like most of the other senior aristocrats and MPs, had a standing invitation. The Royal Navy might be the king's, but Planetary Defense was *theirs*. Now, it was one of the few safe places on Tyre. The king's household troops might have been scattered, at least for the moment, but the chaos on the streets was growing worse. Too many people had heard the king's broadcast and listened. They believed him . . .

Because they want to believe him, Peter thought. They could have coped with one crisis, but not several *different* crises at the same time. *They want to believe that they lost their jobs because we're all evildoers who delight in tormenting anyone below us, not because we had no choice.*

"*Royal Tyre* is breaking orbit," Admiral Fisher reported. His face hung in the center of the display, looking faintly out of place beside the image of the high orbitals and a dizzying series of icons that Peter couldn't even begin to comprehend. "She's heading straight for *Violence*."

"For Kat," Peter said.

"Yes, Your Grace," Admiral Fisher said. "She'll be out of engagement range in seven minutes."

Duke Rudbek leaned forward. "Is the king on *Royal Tyre?*"

"I don't know," Admiral Fisher said. "The records show a number of shuttles traveled between the palace and the ship, but we don't know who was actually on them. He could easily be somewhere else."

Particularly if he assumed the defenses would fire on the ship, Peter thought. *Royal Tyre* was heavily defended—she'd cost twice as much as a superdreadnought—but she was far too close to the orbital battlestations for comfort. *He must have assumed the worst.*

"If he gets away, this has all been for nothing," Harrison said. "We have to stop him."

"Agreed," Duke Rudbek said. "Admiral, you are authorized to attempt to disable his ship so she can be boarded."

"Disabling her will be very difficult," Admiral Fisher warned. "She's designed to take a battering."

"Do your best," Duke Rudbek said. "Fire!"

Admiral Fisher frowned. "As you wish, Your Grace."

◆ ◆ ◆

"Admiral, the fortresses are targeting the *Royal Tyre!*"

Kat gritted her teeth. The *Royal Tyre* was far too close to the fortresses for comfort. One of them was even close enough to risk firing missiles on sprint mode. The odds of scoring a hit would be poor, but they could fire more than enough missiles to ensure that some would succeed.

"Prepare to launch ECM drones," she ordered. There wasn't anything else she could do, unless she wanted to take her fleet a great deal closer. Dueling with heavy battlestations at knife-range was not a good idea. She could hit them, in theory, if she opened fire now, but their point defense would have ample time to take countermeasures. "And . . ."

The display updated, again. "Admiral, two of the battlestations just opened fire on the others," Kitty reported. "They're engaging everyone within range!"

Not enough, Kat thought. The royal yacht was coming under fire. Her defenses were cutting edge, but there were so many missiles that some of them were *bound* to get through. The damage mounted rapidly as *Royal Tyre*'s shield started to fail. *There's nothing we can do, unless . . .*

Royal Tyre exploded. Kat felt a stab of pain in her heart as she watched the expanding ball of plasma.

She'd *liked* the king. And yet . . . Her eyes narrowed. Trying to escape like that had been stupid. Very stupid. The king wasn't stupid . . .

"Admiral, a shuttle is heading right towards us," Kitty said. "We're being hailed."

Kat knew who she was going to see, even before Hadrian's face appeared in front of her. "Kat," he said. "Permission to come aboard?"

"Granted," Kat said. She had to smile in relief, even though she knew that matters had just become a great deal more complicated. Parliament's promise of a fair trial . . . could that be trusted? Or would they take the time to frame the king properly? "And I suggest you hurry."

"I will," the king said. "Once I've docked, set course for Caledonia."

Kat frowned. She still hadn't decided what to do. And yet, the king had the right to issue orders . . . Caledonia wasn't a bad choice either. A well-developed world that could support the fleet, at least for a few months. If they had to fight a war, they'd need bases as well as ships.

"Admiral," Kitty said, "the planetary defenses are targeting us!"

They must have had someone watching us from under cloak, Kat thought. *Someone close enough to see we picked up a shuttle, someone smart enough to realize that there was only one person who could be* on *the shuttle*.

She made up her mind. "General signal to the fleet," she ordered. "All ships are to open vortexes, then proceed directly to Caledonia."

"Aye, Admiral."

The orbital battlestations opened fire. But it was far too late.

◆ ◆ ◆

"Shit," Duke Rudbek snapped.

Peter was inclined to agree. Kat's fleet had left but wasn't alone. Dozens of Home Fleet ships had followed her into hyperspace, and while he would have liked to believe that they were chasing her, he knew better. The Royal Navy had always been loyal to the monarchy rather than Parliament. Indeed, it was more of a surprise that so many ships had *remained* at Tyre.

And the king is still alive, Peter told himself. *He wasn't on his ship.*

He took a breath. "What now?"

"Now?" Harrison laughed, humorlessly. "We're at war. A civil war. And it will tear the kingdom in half."

"It's already torn in half," Duke Rudbek said. He'd never taken his eyes off the display, even after the last starship had vanished into hyperspace. "And, no matter what we do, nothing will ever be the same."

"Our world is burning down," Peter agreed. "But, from the ashes, we will build something new."

EPILOGUE

In Transit

King Hadrian lay on his bunk, staring up at the unmarked ceiling, silently cursing his luck.

The plan had been perfect, more or less, and had worked better than he'd dared to dream. Simple yet audacious, the kind of plan—he admitted to himself if no one else—that very few people would consider. And yet he'd seen no choice. He wanted, *needed*, the kind of power his father and grandfather had been denied. It was the only way to accomplish his goals.

But sheer chance had made a mockery of his careful planning. He'd known, of course, that the Theocrats would eventually be destroyed. Askew had had very clear orders to steer them into a trap once they'd outlived their usefulness. King Hadrian had no qualms about stealing the credit for their destruction either, as he *had* been pushing for more active deployments to the liberated sector. But who would have imagined that the idiots would have allowed themselves to be followed home? Or that they would have left evidence for the investigators to find? Bad luck had nearly doomed everything; nothing but sheer good luck had saved him from total disaster. If Parliament had obtained solid proof of his activities, they would have impeached him at once. He'd barely been able to get his forces into place for one final, desperate gamble.

At least the evidence against me isn't conclusive, he thought. He'd taken care to bury his tracks. Many of the men who could have given his enemies more pieces of the puzzle were now dead. Others were a long way away. *There isn't enough to make my people turn on me.*

It was a bitter thought. He'd grown up in a world where he was both powerful and insignificant, important and unimportant . . . a figurehead and a figure of fun. His kingship was the core of his life, yet he'd never been allowed to prove himself. He was a bird in a golden cage, bound by laws and customs designed by people who had never allowed themselves to believe the universe could change. And yet, the universe *had* changed. The kingdom needed to change with it.

And I will make it change, he promised himself. He'd meant every word of the oath he'd sworn, back when he'd been crowned. He *would* do what was right for his people, and if that meant upsetting the entire apple cart . . . well, the apple cart had been unsteady for decades. *I will do whatever I need to do to make it change.*

He smiled, although he knew the task ahead of him would be hard. He'd always known this path would be difficult, perhaps even impossible. It would have been easy to resign himself to mindless hedonism, like so many younger aristocrats. But the memory of the sneers aimed at his father's back, when he wasn't looking, haunted him. *He* would be powerful, he would make them respect and fear him, and *no one* would ever treat him as a joke again.

Closing his eyes, he allowed the superdreadnought's background hum to lull him to sleep. He felt oddly relaxed, even though he knew that worse was to come. But the die was cast now. There would be war. And he would win . . .

. . . and nothing, absolutely nothing, would be the same again.